"The Doppelgänger" ... ge of my seat from first page to last.
—Kathy Boswell's Faves and Raves.

"Jane Ann Tun has turned out an exceptional story of the eerie legend of the doppelgänger. The story flows well with a fast pace and prime narrative. It is certain to please paranormal and suspense fans alike."
—Tracy Farnsworth

―――――――

…and for her first book, *Time Lapse*

"Readers are in for a treat with *Time Lapse*..a first-rate mystery that combines spine-tingling suspense with a time travel twist and a delicious romance. Enjoy!"
—Barbara Dawson Smith, author of
Romancing a Rogue

"I enjoyed *Time Lapse* enormously. The plot keeps the reader in suspense until the final page. This well-crafted, innovative romance is a keeper."
—Elizabeth Symes

"*Time Lapse* held my attention from the beginning to the end. The twists and turns definitely held me in suspense."
—Brenda Weeaks

"*Time Lapse* will have you losing track of time as you get carried off and away on a reading journey that you will not soon forget."
—Leann "Buzzy" Arndt

"*Time Lapse* is a treasure store of suspense, deceit, danger and heartwarming romance. Definitely a book for your keeper shelf."
—Scribbler's eBookShoppe

"Congratulations Jane, on a fabulous read!"
–Sue Waldeck, Road to Romance

"I found *Time Lapse* to have intelligent writing, sexual intensity, and a plot I couldn't predict. Among the surprises for me were characters I won't soon forget."
–Robert L. Iles , author of *Dead Wrong*

"Jane Ann Tun writes an interesting time travel romance that readers will relish."
–Harriet Klausner, Midwest Book Reviews

"Here's a book you won't want to put down. Jane Tun weaves a good mystery/suspense, successfully melding past and present. Her characters are strong."
–Theresa Gallup: *Midnight Scribe,* 5 stars

The Doppelgänger Connection

Jane Ann Tun

Avid Press, LLC Brighton Michigan USA

Published by
Avid Press, LLC
5470 Red Fox Drive
Brighton MI 48114-9079 USA
http://www.avidpress.com
1-888-AVIDBKS

ISBN 1-929613-86-5
© 2001 by Jane Ann Tun

Cover illustration by Trace Edward Zaber

My thanks for their invaluable help are due Barb, Elizabeth, Liz, Madona, Marianne and Robin - fellow writers all.

This story is for Tony. Always for Tony.

CHAPTER ONE

Dean stepped up his pace, eager to reach his destination before the sun surfaced from below the horizon. Dressing and shaving had been awkward and taken more time than usual. He had forgotten to allow for his sprained wrist. At least he no longer needed the sling. Now he hurried along the familiar path through the tightly-treed acres surrounding the house and yard, the path he had first taken as a small boy with his grandfather many years before.

A sense of anticipation gripped him, even as he smiled at his self-indulgence. The sight of the newborn sun seemed to energize him. As a boy he had somehow conceived the notion that a day begun by greeting the rising sun would be a good day, a day when nothing could go wrong. As if observing the small ritual somehow generated a protective force. Sheer nonsense, of course, but the harmless custom was the only superstition his rational mind would allow.

The freshening breeze made him pause at the edge of the tree line. He wished he had donned a parka instead of the light-weight jacket. Then he shrugged. It was too late to go back for heavier clothing. He stepped away from the protection of the trees, crossed the twenty feet of rocky tract, and carefully picked his way along the edge of the cliff to the highest spot on Sheffield property. The large flat boulder jutting out over the chasm afforded the view he cherished.

Before him, on the far side of the narrow gorge, gently sloping hills reminded him of plush green pillows heaped by careless hands. The absence of all signs of civilization created the illusion of being the only human on an empty planet. Tranquil solitude afforded him a measure of contentment sadly absent for the last few weeks.

Dean felt his mind stretch and sharpen as the breeze blew away the last of the effects of the midnight painkiller. Then the first rounded edge of morning sun peered over the eastern horizon. He breathed a welcome and allowed his gaze to roam over the land he loved.

Twenty minutes later the sun cleared the horizon, and Dean finally felt free of the minuscule, inner spasms that had disturbed him with their unwelcome reminder of his vulnerability, of his mortality. The accident had been a close thing. He had been very lucky. His bandaged left wrist was the only remaining sign of the near-fatal mishap.

A feminine voice called his name. Surprised, he pivoted and searched for the owner of the voice. The clearing was empty and no figure stood at the tree line.

"Who's there?"

No answer.

"Who's there?" Louder this time.

He stood a moment, waiting, then shrugged. About to turn for a final glance at the scene, he felt a subtle shifting beneath his feet. He froze and looked down. The rock quivered, the slightest of tremors. A sudden, loud crack startled him. He felt as much as saw the slab of rock drop an inch.

Instinctively he flung himself forward. One foot came down on the grassy ground just as the ledge dropped away and tumbled into the ravine. His hip shouted in protest as he hit the ground hard, his head just missing a fist-sized stone. Blackness swirled in his head as he drew his legs away from the newly-formed edge. Fighting nausea, he lay gasping for breath.

Minutes later, he pulled himself to a sitting position and took stock of his injuries. Although his wrist had sustained no further damage, his left shoulder and hip throbbed, promising colorful bruises he would have been proud of as a boy. A thorough examination of his head convinced him the pounding ache was as much stress-related as physical.

Finally he forced himself to peer over the cliff.

"Good God!"

Twenty feet below, in three sharp-edged pieces, lay the giant stone that had balanced on the crest of the cliff since before he was born. Like the famous leaning tower, it had seemed immune to the pull of gravity. No more. Nature had finally prevailed.

Dean couldn't prevent a shudder as his imagination pictured his body plunging over the edge with the rock. Lord, that was close! This day certainly hadn't started as expected. His expression was almost accusing as he looked up into the morning sky.

Somehow it didn't surprise him to see a bank of black, menacing clouds overtaking the sun. The breeze had picked up and carried with it the smell of rain, a reminder of spring's fickle nature.

Shivering, he pulled himself painfully to his feet. For a moment he swayed, then he straightened his bruised body and headed back to the house, thoughts of a hot tub filling his mind.

Concealed among the trees on the far side of the clearing, a scowling figure watched him leave.

* * *

Carrie threaded her way around the perimeter of the room to the buffet table, her face aching from the effort of maintaining a pleasant smile. A surreptitious glance at her watch told her the party was still in its early stages, despite her inner feelings to the contrary. She should never have agreed to accompany Melinda to her cousin's open house. Better to have stayed home and caught up on sleep.

"My kingdom for a bed," she muttered to herself.

School had closed earlier that day for the holidays. Much as she enjoyed the children's excitement, their high spirits were exhausting. As always.

Not that sleep would come easily. The formless anxiety plaguing her for the last week seemed much stronger this evening. Her nerves quivered with a kind of anticipation, and mice feet scurried lightly over her back. She shivered and scanned the room again. None of Sandra's guests triggered the slightest sense of foreboding. Why did she feel so edgy? Or was it merely her usual self-consciousness heightened by fatigue?

She turned her back on the lively guests and filled her plate from the lavish assortment of finger-foods. Perhaps her churning nerves were merely the result of insufficient nourishment. Her meals lately had consisted of soup and sandwiches, the energy and the will to cook missing.

The only available seat was at the end of a comfortable-looking paisley sofa. Carrie sat down, relieved when the other two occupants greeted her courteously then resumed their animated conversation. She ate slowly, both to discourage another invitation to dance and to pass the time until she could make a reasonable exit.

The food seemed to help. Her body began to relax and the threatened headache dissolved before it could take hold. How often had Greta scolded her for her careless eating habits? She should know by now to take better care of herself. Maybe she would get a decent night's sleep tonight after all.

Suddenly the thought of her quiet apartment held enormous appeal. Carrie glanced at her watch again and decided to make a graceful exit. A genuine smile lit her face as she found her hostess and thanked her. Her attention firmly centered on the man by her side, Sandra's protests at her departure were no more than politeness demanded.

Carrie found Melinda in the kitchen, comfortably enthroned on her fiancé's lap.

"I'm off, Melinda."

"Alone?"

At Carrie's nod, Melinda sighed.

"Darn. I thought you might hit it off with that guy from Sandra's office. He certainly looked interested in you. I saw him corner you in the dining room."

"You mean the one whose inventory of conversational topics consisted of one, himself, two, himself, and three, himself?"

Melinda laughed and promised to be quiet when she came home. Privately, Carrie doubted her friend would return before morning, since her airline-hostess roommate had two days' leave until her next flight. She would spend every possible moment with her fiancé of three weeks.

Carrie stifled a wistful sigh. Delighted as she was for the friend who had stuck by her since childhood, Melinda's happiness contrasted sharply with her own barren emotional life. If only…. No. None of that. A good night's sleep would restore her perspective.

When she found her new spring coat under the pile of garments on the bed and pulled it on, Carrie paused for a moment in front of the dresser mirror. Melinda was right. The cherry-red color did flatter her, much more than the utilitarian beige she had intended to buy. With the Italian cream silk scarf and matching kid gloves her friend had given her for her birthday, she looked younger than her 24 years. The coat brought a rosy blush to her high cheekbones and seemed to diminish the dark smudges under her wide brown eyes.

Finally, eager to get away, she slipped unobtrusively out of the apartment and a few moments later drove out of the visitors' parking lot.

* * *

An hour later, Carrie felt halfway human again. Thank goodness for holidays. Ten whole days of freedom. Much as she loved her small students, Carrie had been glad to wish them a happy holiday that afternoon. Never had she needed the spring break more. She took a sip of hot chocolate, set it on the small table beside her favorite chair, closed her eyes and began to rock. The deliciously quiet apartment soothed her tired bones and added to the lassitude that had fallen over her after a long soak in the tub. Yes, she would sleep tonight, maybe even sleep for the entire holiday. She smiled at the foolish thought and settled deeper in the chair.

Mentally, she began to tick off the errands she meant to accomplish the next day. Pick up her dry cleaning, shop for groceries, return books to the library, take in her old Chevy sedan for an oil change and, most important, pick up more magazines and the liqueur-filled chocolates that were Greta's weakness.

Thinking of Saturday's visit with her grandmother brought a small frown to Carrie's face. If only she could afford to place Greta in a private nursing home. The employees at the state home seemed competent enough, but recent cutbacks in staff left them little time for socializing with the patients. The grim old building with its institutional green paint and small, uniform rooms made a depressing environment in which to recover from a broken leg. Though Greta insisted she was content, Carrie knew she missed her home and friendly neighbors.

Her brow creased in determination, Carrie reflected that one good thing would result from Greta's accident. Melinda's wedding and subsequent move from the apartment she shared with Carrie would coincide with the date Greta's doctor expected the older woman to be dismissed from the nursing home. Carrie was resolved Greta would live with her. The sale of Greta's house would enable her grandmother to share expenses with sufficient funds left to invest for her old age.

Greta had raised her since she was five. Now it was Carrie's turn to be the caregiver. She was looking forward to living with her beloved grandmother again. The two women had only each other. The day would come all too soon when Carrie would have no one at all.

Refusing to dwell on that last sad thought, Carrie opened her eyes. The street outside was quiet for a Friday night. She stood up. It was long past her usual bedtime. She drank the rest of the chocolate and turned to take the empty cup to the kitchen. Her gaze fell on the figure of a tall, massive man standing in the entrance to the kitchen. She inhaled sharply.

Oh no! Not again! Not here!

An arctic chill enveloped her and goosebumps broke out over her body. The cup fell from her nerveless fingers and bounced unnoticed on the carpet. He stood ten feet from her, silent and unseeing. Like before, his open eyes were vacant. No, not vacant exactly, but staring as if into a great distance. He didn't speak and seemed unaware of his surroundings or of her presence. Unlike the last time she'd seen him, his left wrist was no longer in a sling. His clothing, too, was different.

A sob caught in her throat. Carrie wanted to scream at him, to demand an explanation, but she had no breath. How had he gotten into the apartment? Why had she heard nothing? Who was he and what did he want?

A part of her waited for him to disappear as he had twice before. But on a deeper level, something about him called to her. She found she wanted him to stay, to talk to her, to speak with a human voice, to assure her he was more than a delusion fabricated by her own mind. She closed her eyes and sent up a brief prayer that she would awaken to find herself in bed, the victim of a fiercely vivid dream.

Air pushed against her face. Her eyes snapped open to see him walking toward her, his face still remote and unknowing. A tiny part of her mind noted he seemed to be favoring his left hip.

"*Please. Leave me alone.*"

His stride continued, unchecked by her whispered plea. When he was almost upon her, she threw up her hands in defense and braced herself to push him away. He showed no reaction, no awareness of her presence. She drew in a great breath but before she could call out he stopped a few inches in front of her. A puzzled look crossed his face, the first expression he had shown.

"Now look here, whoever you are, you have no right to—"

The defiant, shaky words stuck in Carrie's throat as her eyes widened at the sight of her hands buried deep in his chest. With a convulsive movement she snatched them back and wrapped her arms around herself. He didn't move. His eyes swiveled from side to side as if looking for something. Then he again stared over her head, his towering frame as motionless as a piece of furniture.

Carrie recognized the look now and knew he wasn't seeing her. Slowly, reluctantly, she lifted her trembling hands, palms outward, and forced them toward his chest. Her eyes saw the blue cable knit of his sweater but her skin registered nothing. She pushed her hands forward and saw them disappear into his chest. He didn't move. Except for his lack of solidity, her visitor fulfilled none of the other known attributes of the usual ghost. Apparitions were said to haunt the place where they died, yet she had seen him in a men's clothing store, at the door of her classroom, and tonight, in her apartment—each time wearing different clothing. Did ghosts change their apparel for each haunting?

Not daring to breathe, she slowly withdrew her tingling hands. A glance at his face revealed the same bewildered frown as before but no awareness of his surroundings. An inch at a time, Carrie edged to the side, until she could step past without touching him. Her heart pumping madly, she darted to the other side of the room. When she turned to confront him, he was gone. Like before—without a sound, without a step—he was gone.

Her relief felt a little like disappointment.

* * *

Carrie tiptoed into her grandmother's room and peered down at the soft, lined face on the pillow. Encouraged by the touch of color in the old woman's cheeks, she smiled at the sleeping woman. Silently, she pulled the visitor's chair to the side of the bed and sat down to wait for Greta to awaken.

Her head fell back against the headrest and her eyes fluttered closed as she sank deeper into the chair. The night before, sleep had eluded her for hours. Every time she closed her eyes, the image of her insubstantial visitor appeared on the screen of her eyelids. Dawn had been near when she finally fell into a restless slumber. Habit and the discomfort of tangled sheets woke her at the usual time. Knowing she wouldn't sleep again, Carrie rose and spent the morning in a frenzy of housecleaning, deliberately refusing to dwell on her ghostly visitor.

Now she was too tired to fight off the memory. Her mind dredged up everything she had ever heard or read about ghosts. Although she had never seen one before, and didn't know anyone who had, her own experiences prevented her from rejecting the idea outright. Who could prove, really prove, such beings didn't exist?

The problem bothering her the most was not the ghost itself. It had seemed totally unaware of her presence and hadn't shown the slightest inclination to hurt her. She felt certain, without understanding why, that her ghost intended no harm. *Her* ghost? She smiled slightly at the possessive trend of her thoughts. As if their three meetings had forged a bond between them.

Where were the moans and rattling chains? Her ghost said nothing, seemed to see nothing, though something like sadness moved in the back of his blue eyes. Did his own death grieve him? Carrie felt a twinge of pity mixed with regret that she had not known her visitor while he still lived. He was—had been— a giant of a man and extraordinarily good-looking. She felt a sense of connection, of attraction—even a sense of loss, all the more inexplicable since they had never met in life. A soft sigh escaped her.

"*Liebchen*, is something wrong?"

Greta's soft voice brought Carrie upright. She reached for her grandmother's hand and leaned forward to kiss her cheek. She smiled into the brown eyes so like her own.

"Hello, darling. The apples have returned to your cheeks. You are feeling better, aren't you?"

"*Ja*. But I will feel even better when you tell me what has happened to disturb you. You look worn out. The *Polizei*, they have needed you again?"

Carrie shook her head. She knew her grandmother worried whenever the police asked for her help.

"No, no. I am only tired. The children were excited about the holidays. Every teacher in the country needs sleep right now." She laughed lightly, but seeing the skeptical look in Greta's shrewd eyes, she added, "Melinda talked me into going to a party last night. Tonight I'll catch up on sleep, I promise."

She patted the thin wrinkled hand, then picked up the violet plant from the bedside table, pretending to examine it carefully. She had no wish to upset Greta with an account of her ghostly visitor. Her grandmother had enough to endure. The medication couldn't eradicate all of the pain, and Carrie knew the loss of mobility was even harder for her grandmother to accept.

"I think you are more than tired. Something has upset you."

Carrie shook her head and didn't answer.

"*Ach*, mule-stubborn you are," Greta scolded her beloved granddaughter, her tone laced with affection. She paused. "Well, I expect you will tell me all about it when you're ready, won't you?"

"Yes, of course," Carrie answered, then snapped her mouth shut as she realized her mistake. She shot an exasperated look at Greta, then smiled sheepishly when she saw the sly glint in the old woman's eyes. "You're impossible!"

They both laughed and the conversation turned to other things. Carrie listened with amusement to her grandmother's tales of the eccentricities of some of the staff and patients in the nursing home. In turn, she described the humorous behavior of her small pupils.

Too soon, visiting hours were over. After promising to return a few days later, Carrie left the room, determined to follow Greta's loving instructions to take care of herself.

She crossed the front lobby heading for the corridor that led to the parking lot. A figure wearing a soft blue coat over a white uniform and standing just within the front door caught her eye. Carrie recognized the pretty nurse who worked on Greta's floor and always had a cheerful smile for the patients. She swerved and approached the woman.

"Excuse me. Nurse Sheffield, isn't it? I'm Carrie Richards,

Greta Sonnheim's granddaughter. I'd like to thank you for look-ing after Greta so well. She likes you very much. And it's good of you to water the violet plant for her."

The two women shook hands. Alanna Sheffield, a few years older than Carrie, seemed pleased by the attention. Her pale blue eyes brightened as she assured Carrie her grandmother was recovering very well for a woman her age. They talked for a few minutes, and Carrie offered the nurse a lift.

"Thank you, but my cousin is coming for me and—oh, here he is now." Her face lit up as she looked over Carrie's shoulder to the figure pushing through the glass door.

"Are you ready, Alanna? If I'm interrupting something I can wait in the car."

Carrie felt the hairs on her neck stiffen. The unfamiliar, vel-vet-smooth voice touched something deep inside her. Her chest constricted and a bolt of panic shot through her. She stepped to the side and would have left without looking back, but the nurse stopped her with a hand on her wrist.

"I'm coming now. Dean, this is Carrie Richards. Carrie's grandmother is one of my patients. Carrie, this is my cousin, Dean Sheffield."

Trapped, Carrie sucked in a deep breath and turned. A very large hand, the back covered with curly black hairs, was extend-ed toward her. As their hands met she raised her head.

Her purse fell from her suddenly nerveless fingers and the color drained from her face as she gaped in disbelief into the sky-blue eyes that had stared through and past her the previous evening. An icy chill enveloped her body as her heart began to race. Blackness pressed against the edges of her vision. Then she became conscious of the warmth of his hand enclosing hers and the darkness receded.

"No!"

She snatched her hand away and stumbled back a step. A

gasp of surprise reminded her of Alanna's presence, but she could not tear her gaze from the astonished face of her ghost, whose eyes most definitely were focused on her.

"What the devil—?"

He stepped closer and instinctively Carrie thrust out her hands. This time his chest was a solid barrier. Beneath her palms she felt the smooth texture of his knit sport shirt and the play of well-developed muscles. She wrenched her gaze down and stared at her hands pressed against his immense chest. His heartbeat was steady—and real. His warmth seemed to expand to encompass her body. When her hands began to tremble against him, she felt his indrawn breath.

"You're alive," she whispered in a barely audible voice. Her eyes flew back to his bemused face. "Aren't you?"

Her mind tumbled in confusion but deep inside her a frantic hope took root and grew. This man was no ghost.

Two large hands clasped her shoulders. She started but didn't move away.

"I believe so. No one's told me any different." His mouth twitched at the corners, though his voice held a mix of concern and curiosity. "We've never met, have we? I couldn't have forgotten."

"No. Yes. Not exactly. I mean … I … really must be going now." Carrie slipped out from under his hands and backed away. She turned to the nurse. "It was nice meeting you, Alanna. I'll probably see you when I visit Greta again. I…. Good-bye."

Forgetting her purse, Carrie turned and strode quickly down the hall to the exit, her hand automatically digging the ring of keys from her coat pocket. Behind her, a voice called out for her to wait, but she pushed through the door and ran across the lot to her car. A moment later the nursing home receded in the rearview window.

Only when she stepped out of the elevator did Carrie realize she had no memory of the drive across town from the nursing home. It took several tries before she managed to insert the key into the lock. The moment the door closed behind her she slumped against it and leaned her head back. Her quivering legs refused to support her any longer. Slowly she slid down to the floor and drew up her legs to wrap her arms around them. Her head slumped to her knees as she gave in to the tremors shaking her body.

When the paroxysm finally passed, she felt drained. She pulled herself to her feet and walked unsteadily down the hall to her bedroom, grateful to find her mind idling in neutral. Later. She would think about it all later.

By nine o'clock she was curled up on the sofa, a cup of coffee on the table beside her. A long shower, as hot as she could stand, had relaxed her tight nerves and thawed the icy lump in her chest. In an effort to delay the inevitable, she had cooked and eaten a full meal, then cleaned up the kitchen. Now she pulled the comfortable old terry robe tighter around her and allowed her mind to replay the incident that had rocked her so severely.

What exactly had happened? The obvious answer—she had met the man whose ghost had appeared to her three times in the past week. But how could such a thing be? Shouldn't the order be reversed? *First* there's a living person, *then* there's a ghost. If such things actually existed.

Or did she imagine the whole thing? She remembered feeling forlorn, almost cheated, when she thought Dean Sheffield had died before she had a chance to meet him. Could she have been so attracted to an apparition her subconscious conjured up a flesh and blood man? Could a wish be so powerful? Impossible.

"If wishes were horses, beggars would ride." The old saying echoed around the quiet room. No help there.

So, Dean Sheffield was a real, live man. A linebacker of a man, well over six feet tall, with the widest shoulders and broadest chest she had ever seen. His blue-black hair looked professionally styled and just reached his collar. It curled thickly around his ears. Was it as soft as it appeared? High, sharp cheekbones framed deep-set eyes that seemed to see more than most. His nose was straight, patrician and his lips full and firm. Enticing. Just thinking about the man sent shivers of awareness down her spine. Carrie shook her head in a vain attempt to will his image away.

Although she had abilities others did not, she'd never experienced anything remotely like this. If the man today was real, how could she explain seeing his ghost? Or were the three appearances merely a product of her fatigue? Was it mere coincidence the ghost looked exactly like Alanna Sheffield's cousin? It hardly seemed likely. She'd been tired countless times before without being sought out by some apparition.

Sought out? Why would such an expression come to mind? It was obvious the living man didn't know her. There was no reason why his ghost should seek her out. Did he even know he had a ghost roaming at will? She almost giggled at the thought of his reaction, should she ask him about his insubstantial double.

Maybe it was all a vivid dream. Or maybe she'd been in some accident and was hallucinating the whole thing. Or … or maybe she was merely going crazy. Her work with the police was usually pretty traumatic. Maybe she had reached emotional overload and simply didn't know it. But deep inside she knew that wasn't the case. So what was really happening here? What was going on?

"Who are you? What are you?" She mused aloud. "And why me?"

The brisk staccato knock on the door drove her heart into

her mouth. Who in the world…? Then her lips turned up in a shaky smile and her heart retreated into her chest. It must be Melinda. Carrie jumped to her feet and started down the hall to the door, surprised her roommate hadn't stayed the night with her fiancé as she usually did.

"Don't tell me, you forgot your key ag—"

The words died in her throat as she flung the door wide. Only her grip on the knob kept her from falling. She flinched as a massive fist stopped inches from her face, then dropped out of sight.

"Oh!"

"Sorry."

She looked up and felt her heart begin pumping madly. Him again! A bubble of hysteria caught in her throat as she wondered if this was ghostly appearance number four or reality check number two. Whichever, her skin began to prickle with excitement.

Unable to speak, Carrie stared at the man in her doorway. Dean's gaze dropped to her parted lips. He leaned forward. When Carrie gasped he straightened and swallowed hard. The movement broke the spell surrounding them.

"You knocked this time." The words were out before Carrie could stop them. She colored at the bewilderment in his eyes. "I mean…." She drew a deep breath. "Would you like to come in?" Just in time she bit off the word 'again.' "I … was just about to have a glass of wine." It was a lie, but suddenly she didn't want him to disappear again.

"Yes, thanks, I'd love to."

Carrie stepped back. When he closed the door and turned around, she was astonished at how small the hallway seemed. Dean Sheffield towered a good foot over her and his shoulders almost brushed the opposing walls. Her throat suddenly dry, she gestured at the entrance to the living room, then hurried to the kitchen.

As she searched the cupboards for the seldom-used goblets, she could hear him moving around and knew he was examining her bookcases. Well, he hadn't seemed to notice them, or anything else, during his visit the night before. She swallowed a giggle and decided that if her imagination had created this beautiful man, well, hurrah for it. And speaking of her imagination, did he really almost kiss her? Would she have felt it if he had? His fist had sounded solid enough against the door. She closed her eyes, tilted back her head and envisioned his lips on hers.

They were warm and tender and sweet. She purred and brushed her mouth back and forth over his. A scent of man and spice teased her nostrils and trickled into her brain. Warm breath caressed her face and—

Carrie's eyes snapped open. A few inches away, dazed eyes stared intently into her face. Then a ripple of surprise spread over his features and Dean backed away.

"I'm sorry. I shouldn't have done that. But you looked so…." He stopped, an embarrassed expression on his face. "I don't know what came over me."

Carrie could only gaze at him.

He shrugged and lifted a hand to rub at the back of his neck. Suddenly one dark eyebrow arched and a wide grin transformed his face. Carrie's heart leaped in her chest. It was a smile to fuel any woman's daydreams.

"I think you must have magical powers. Are you a witch, Carrie? Have you put a spell on me?" His voice was soft and teasing, totally unlike the crisp tone with which he had greeted his cousin.

The questions brought Carrie back to earth. She had been called *witch* in the past and didn't like the feeling it invoked. She turned to the counter, grabbed the bottle of wine and thrust it into his hands. Snatching up two goblets, she threw a feeble smile at a point near his chin and led the way into the living room.

Wondering at the strange look that had curtained her eyes in response to his teasing, Dean followed her. Most of the women he knew would have answered his banter with a coy look and an equally flirtatious reply.

He'd spoken the truth this time—he didn't understand what had come over him. Had she known he was in the room he would have taken her pose and the expression on her face as an invitation. But she thought she was alone. She had looked … what? Flushed, soft, a little fey. And desirable. So desirable. He hadn't been able to resist. At least she didn't seem to be angry that he'd kissed her. He smiled inside at the thought.

When they had settled and were sipping wine, Carrie cast about for something to say. A part of her was astonished he was actually here, in the flesh. The feel of his mouth on hers prevented any doubt about that. She wondered if she should be frightened. Maybe if she wasn't so confused she would be.

"You, uh, you…. Is there some reason why you wanted to see me?"

Dean looked blank, then nodded.

"I'm returning your purse."

"My purse?"

"You dropped it at the nursing home. I called after you but I guess you didn't hear me. You seemed to be in a terrible hurry. Did you run away because of something I said?"

Only then did Carrie notice her purse sitting on the coffee table between them.

"Oh, yes, of course. Thank you. I assumed Alanna would take it to the manager's office and I meant to pick it up tomorrow. But, how did you know where I live?" She tensed, waiting for his answer. Had his ghost told him where to find her?

Dean's eyes narrowed. Why did recovering her purse upset

her? She hadn't denied she'd run away, nor had she answered his question. Her strange behavior intrigued him. He leaned back in his chair.

"I must confess I searched your purse for your address. I thought if you didn't remember where you'd left it, you might worry about credit cards and such."

Shrugging, Dean searched for another topic, any topic, that would serve as an excuse to linger. "Alanna told me how frequently you visit your grandmother. I'd like to hear your impressions of the nursing home. I, or rather my father, is thinking of opening a similar residence, mostly for Alzheimer's victims and others suffering from mental deterioration. What do you think of the facilities at the nursing home?"

Carrie exhaled in relief. He didn't want to talk about her or her unguarded reaction on meeting him. She pulled her scattered wits together and began to describe the changes she would make at the nursing home if she were able.

"The physical environment first. All those identical little rooms, like tiny boxes. The sameness has to be upsetting. I'm not a psychologist, but it seems to me if the senses were stimulated with pretty colors, maybe interesting paintings on the wall, with room for some of their personal belongings, the rooms wouldn't seem quite so much like cells. Each room should be different than the others, more like a home. A hospital setting must surely add to a patient's depression."

Dean nodded. He had been thinking along the same lines. "I picture gardens available whenever the weather is fine. Maybe some comfortable benches, even a play area with slides and swings, for those unfortunates who have reverted to childhood. And also to encourage visitors to bring their children."

Carrie's face brightened.

"That's a wonderful idea. Vegetable gardens too. Working with plants and earth in the fresh air is known to be relaxing and healthy." She leaned forward. "But I think the most important thing is the staff. Their numbers as well as their medical training. I'm sure your cousin has told you how busy the staff is. Greta is well looked-after medically, but no one has much time to just sit and chat. I should think dementia patients have an even greater need for company, especially during lucid periods. But of course, staff salaries are the single biggest expense for institutions. It's a terrible problem."

"What do you think of this idea?" Dean said. "I'm not concerned with those patients whose families are wealthy. There are private, luxury facilities for them. I'm thinking of the heartbreak for families who must institutionalize a member of the family because they can't afford to pay a companion and can't afford for one of the family to forego a salary in order to stay home with the patient. In addition to medical personnel, I was thinking of the possibility of hiring family members to be sort of paid volunteers, or rather paid visitors, thereby fulfilling both the needs of the patients and the need to bring in an income. Those persons would be available as company for other patients as well as their own relatives. Does that sound feasible to you?"

Carrie beamed at him.

"What a marvelous idea! How did you happen to think of it?"

"I have to give the credit to my cousin. Alanna often bemoans the fact she has so little time to treat her patients as people, especially those who will never be able to take care of themselves again. I'm sure you know how dedicated a nurse she is."

"Yes, my grandmother speaks very highly of her. But is there some reason you target Alzheimer's victims in particular?"

Dean hesitated then decided there was no reason for secrecy.

"My Uncle Dick has the disease. Well, actually he's not a blood relation. Richard Harrington is my father's best friend, has been since boyhood. Dick never married and now he has no family left alive. He's been living in my father's home for the last five years. Until now there's been enough of our family around, but his disease is progressing and soon he'll need someone whose only duty is to keep an eye on him. He's wandered away twice now. My father won't hear of institutionalizing him. The idea of paid visitors grew from this situation at home."

Carrie nodded in understanding. Although she had never known an Alzheimer's victim personally, she had once been instrumental in locating a woman afflicted with the disease who also had wandered from home. The woman's condition and her family's anguish had been heartbreaking.

A little later Dean rose to leave. Carrie found she didn't want him to go. They would probably never meet again, and the thought brought a wave of loneliness deeper than she'd ever felt before.

At the door, she searched for some excuse to delay his departure. When she noticed his awkward maneuvering to don his jacket, she spoke without thinking.

"Your wrist is still bothering you? I notice you're not using the sling anymore."

"My wrist?" Dean went very still.

"Last Thursday you were wearing a black—" Carrie gasped and bit her tongue. After a lifetime of caution how could she have forgotten to guard her speech? If he knew about her he would give her *that look*. She couldn't bear the thought of this man recoiling from her. Suddenly tears welled up behind her lids. She turned away to hide them.

Dean put a finger under her chin and turned her back to face him.

"How did you know I hurt my wrist?"

Carrie tried to laugh lightly but she could hear the quaver in her voice.

"Body language, I guess. I must have noticed subconsciously that you were favoring your left hand. Your movements seem a little stiff. You've hurt your hip and shoulder, too, haven't you?" She really had noted the hesitation in his step when he first arrived. *Please, please let him put it down to simple observation!*

"Well, yes, I did. But how did you know my wrist was in a sling on Thursday?"

"Just a lucky guess. People often use a sling to ease the strain on a sore wrist." All at once she couldn't wait for him to go. "Thank you again for returning my purse. And be careful, Dean."

Why had she said that? Even as she asked herself the question she knew the answer. An aura of danger, of dark menace suddenly enveloped him, like an invisible mist that touched her as tangibly as a splash of cold water.

"Be very careful," she repeated.

She wrenched her eyes away, frantic to escape the gaze that seemed to see deep into her mind. Trembling, she waited for him to do something, to say something, to demand an explanation. But after a long silence he reached for the doorknob. She exhaled in relief.

"Thanks for the wine. And for the company. Could we do it again, Carrie?"

"What?"

"I'd like to see you again. May I take you to lunch tomorrow? The Hotel St. Denis puts on a delicious Sunday brunch."

Surprise stole Carrie's tongue. Dean seemed to take her silence as reluctance. His voice lowered to a persuasive purr, setting the nerves under her skin tingling.

"I'd like to discuss the nursing home with you again. Please say you'll come."

When she nodded in agreement, he gave her a brilliant smile

and left. Carrie closed the door behind him, stunned at the feelings swirling inside her. Exhilaration that he wanted to see her
again. Fear of the unknown danger she sensed threatening him.
Admiration for his generosity. Confusion. Reluctance.
Eagerness.

Finally abandoning the futile attempt to think rationally, she
turned out the lights and fled to the oblivion of sleep.

Chapter Two

As he left the house to keep his lunch date with Carrie Richards, Dean's mind lingered over the morning's conversation with his father. Though John Sheffield had not alluded to the devastating news he had shared with his son two weeks earlier, the knowledge had hovered like an invisible presence in the room. Both men had assumed a gruff, business-like voice to ward off a display of sentiment.

Dean shook off his incipient depression and forced himself to concentrate on the plans they were formulating for the transformation of the mansion into a home for victims of dementia. His father had listened attentively and with obvious approval to Carrie's suggestions. His first comment, however, had surprised Dean.

"Sounds like quite a woman, son. You going to see her again?"

Dean cocked an eyebrow at his father. He had mentioned only briefly the circumstances of their meeting. Nothing in his account should have caused the speculative, slightly sly expression on John's face.

"We're meeting for lunch today." When satisfaction flowed over his father's face, Dean added hastily, "She's a very bright lady. I asked her to think some more about our project. That's all, Dad, so forget whatever's running through your head. Carrie's a bit too … offbeat for me."

"Hmmm. Bright, different, works with children, cares about people in distress—she sounds perfect. Bring her to the house sometime soon. I'd like to meet her. By the way, what does she look like?"

Dean visualized the large, coffee-brown eyes in the heart-shaped face, the unruly mop of toast-brown curls, the straight neat nose and the generous fullness of the lips that had brushed so delicately against his. The bulky terrycloth robe had not been able to disguise her slim, nicely rounded shape.

The amused expression on his father's face interrupted his contemplation of Carrie's charms. He hastened to answer.

"She's pretty, I guess."

He tried to shrug his indifference but when the eyes of the two men met, they both grinned. Father and son had been close friends all of Dean's life. Neither man could keep anything important concealed from the other. John waved him away with a deep chuckle.

As Dean pulled out of the driveway and started down the winding road to the highway that led to the city limits, he thought about his father. Dean's mother had died when he was twenty-one. Both men had loved her deeply, but at least they had had each other to get them through the tragedy. They shared their sorrow and their memories, grew even closer than before and became best friends. There would be no one there for Dean this time.

He knew his father's sister, Bev, and brother, David, and David's children would be saddened at his father's passing. Although they all lived in the mansion, they didn't see very much of each other. Unfortunately, they had no bond like the remarkable one he and his father shared. None of them were aware of John's heart condition. Only Dean understood the shadow in John's eyes and was privy to the doctor's diagnosis.

Secret too, was John's wish to honor and provide for his

friend Dick, and establish the mansion as a final refuge for those suffering a like illness. The settlement of a trust to finance the home meant a radical change in the disposition of John's wealth. In total agreement with his father's wishes, Dean had promised to carry the project forward if John's time ran out before he could accomplish his goal.

The fact that his inheritance would be vastly reduced bothered him not at all. He wasn't certain how the rest of the family would greet the news, although each was generously remembered in the new will John was composing. Generously, but not as lavishly as under the old will. Dean brushed away the thought. None would have reason to complain.

When Carrie's apartment building came into view, all thoughts of family fled. His heart began to thump in anticipation. Though he had not admitted it aloud to his father, he had been intrigued by Carrie and her inexplicable reaction to him. Fear, confusion, disbelief, panic and—most baffling of all— recognition had sped across her face. Dean smiled. The face imprinted on his eyelids, keeping him awake until dawn, was much more than pretty.

Carrie Richards was altogether lovely. Although not as beautiful as some of the women he had dated in the past, she exuded an air of mystery and reserve that piqued his interest in a way he had never experienced before. An interest beyond the riddle of her words and her strange behavior when they first met.

He remembered the brief kiss in the kitchen and his groin tightened. Her lips were warm and soft and sweet. The blush that pinked her silky skin hinted she'd enjoyed the kiss as much as he did. It delighted him and suddenly he realized his father must have sensed something of his feelings in spite of his disclaimer.

As he pulled into a visitor's parking space, Dean decided to invite her to the mansion that very afternoon. It pleased him to think how much his father, who considered truly ordinary people boring, would enjoy meeting the off-beat Carrie.

* * *

Carrie put down her fork with a contented sigh. The Caesar salad had been superb and the cherry cheesecake the best she'd ever eaten. The Hotel St. Denis dining room deserved its reputation.

The conversation had been casual, low-key and wide-ranging. Gradually her taut nerves relaxed when it became clear Dean wasn't going to quiz her on her inadvertent remarks the day before. He probably hadn't really been listening. After all, Alanna had forced the introduction on them and Dean had been in a hurry to leave the nursing home. Her usual vigilance wasn't necessary.

As the attentive waiter refilled their coffee cups, she smiled at the massive man across the table. His big-boned face seemed more attractive each time she saw him. It was far from Hollywood-handsome, but something in it spoke of strength and passion, especially when he spoke of his father's plans. He really cared about people. The thought warmed her and without her knowledge, her face softened as she gazed at him.

"Penny for them."

She heard the smile in the low rumble of his voice and knew he'd noticed her lapse into reverie. Her cheeks colored as she searched for something to say. Then she remembered the reason for the lunch meeting.

"I've been thinking about your project. We need to learn more about the symptoms people experience as they go through the various stages of the disease, but I seem to recall hearing or reading the lucid periods for some patients occur most frequently during the small hours of the night. So it would be important to have as many paid visitors as possible to take the night shifts. That might be an order more difficult to fill."

"Good point. But we'll do it somehow. Maybe a higher pay scale for those willing to work nights." Dean frowned. "It never occurred to me Dick might lie awake in the dark, in a silent house, aware of what's happening to him. How frightened and hopeless he must feel. God, it's a horrible disease!"

He closed his eyes as a shudder ran through his body. Instinctively, Carrie reached out and covered his hand with hers. She was astounded at the depth of her longing to comfort him. Surprise was followed by dismay. How had he crept under her skin so quickly? Intuitively she knew this man had the power to hurt her. A normal relationship with a man wasn't in the cards for her; she'd discovered that the hard way.

Before she could snatch back her hand, he turned his over and twined his fingers with hers.

"Carrie, you're on holiday just now, aren't you? If you have no plans for the afternoon, would you come back to the house with me? My father would like to meet you." At her doubtful look, he added hastily, "I told him about your ideas and he'd like to discuss his scheme in more detail with you. Please say you'll come."

The momentary flash of pleasure at the thought that Dean had spoken of her faded as Carrie realized his invitation was business-related, nothing personal. Still, playing a small part in his father's altruistic plans would help to dispel the helpless feeling brought on by the miserable plight of so many people who suffered through no fault of their own. Philanthropic gestures required money and time. She had no money but there was no reason why she shouldn't contribute some of her holiday time. And she really didn't want to say good-bye to Dean just yet.

"Yes, I'd be glad to come. But let's stop at the library on the way. The more knowledge we have about the disease, the better we can plan."

Dean signaled for the check and tried to ignore the buoyant feeling in his chest. The intimate sound of the word 'we' in her soft musical voice echoed through his body.

As they made their way to the exit Carrie couldn't help but notice the admiring looks many of the women threw at Dean. He seemed oblivious to them all. Carrie felt a surge of pride that he was with her. She ignored the warning voice at the back of her mind. She had only to remember his interest was limited to her contributions to his father's plans. No law said she couldn't enjoy his company during the interim. Or enjoy the firm touch of his large hand on the small of her back as he guided her from the room.

* * *

Although she had been expecting something special, Carrie's mouth dropped open when Dean's low-slung sports car cleared the long, tree-lined lane and the Sheffield mansion came into view. The central building was three stories high, made of snowy white brick, with multi-paned windows the length of the building. Broad steps led the eye to the centered black door that matched the shutters framing each window. Water gushed from the white marble nude gazing into a majestic, tiered fountain in the perfectly-groomed lawn. Low shrub roses, just beginning to green, bordered the circular drive.

With two extensions angling back at the sides, the house gave the appearance of a huge white bird with outspread wings poised to drink from the fountain. Despite its vast size, Dean's home appeared light and airy, welcoming rather than over-whelming.

Carrie scrambled out of the car the moment it drew to a stop at the foot of the wide marble steps. Enchanted by the fairy tale loveliness, she gazed around in wonder. When Dean circled the car to join her, he was staggered by the shining delight in her face.

"You like it?"

"It's beautiful, Dean. I can't imagine what it must be like to live in this house. How can you bear to leave it for work every day?"

Dean laughed, inordinately pleased by her approval.

"As a kid, I didn't know it was different from most homes. I just knew there were a thousand hiding places and unlikely corners that could become anything I chose. I had toys enough for ten children but what I loved most were empty packing cartons. I kept at least one box in most of the unused rooms. Some were boats, some forts, some cars, whatever my imagination required at any given time. I have to admit I had a wonderful childhood."

Carrie smiled up into his face.

"I loved empty cartons, too. Especially empty beer cases." At his surprised look, she grinned. "A beer case on its side makes a lovely doll house. I would remove the cardboard dividers and decorate them as walls for rooms, cut out doors and windows, then put them back in the box. My mother taught me how to make people from pipe cleaners and furniture from pieces of popsicle sticks. We glued bits of fabric for curtains and clothes. I still think empty boxes rank up there with sliced bread!"

They laughed together, then Dean's expression sobered.

"Many people don't remember their early years. I'm glad you have that memory of your mother. How old were you when your parents died?"

He regretted his question when pain flashed across her face and her eyes became shuttered and distant.

"Seven."

Her answer was so abrupt and anguished he knew he should let it drop. But he sensed something more than a tragic occurrence. Her grief seemed too raw for a loss that had happened twenty years before. He stepped close and laid a gentle hand on the side of her face.

"Would you like to talk about it?"

Carrie inhaled deeply and looked up. Silver flecks speckled the blue of his eyes, and in them she read sympathy and a promise of comfort. She had never spoken of the vision she later discovered had accurately portrayed the manner and moment of her parents' deaths. Maybe if she related what happened, the recurrent dream that still plagued her, though less and less frequently as the years passed, would be exorcised for good.

Before she was fully aware of having made a decision, Carrie heard herself describe the narrow mountain road, the runaway truck, the sensation of flying and then falling.

"When they reached the site of the crash the car was in pieces but my parents were still clinging together, though their bodies were broken and smashed."

As she said this last, the deep well of tears she had never shed overflowed and streamed down her face. His own eyes moist, Dean wrapped his arms around her and held her tightly to his chest. What a terrible experience for a seven year old child to undergo.

When her tears gradually ceased, he loosened his hold and wiped her face with one gentle thumb.

"I'm so sorry, Carrie. But I'm grateful you weren't badly hurt, too. It's a miracle you survived. Were you thrown clear?"

Surprised, Carrie spoke without thinking.

"But I wasn't there. They left me with Greta while they were on holiday in Switzerland."

Dean stiffened in sudden anger.

"Who would tell a child such terrible details? No wonder you haven't been able to put it behind you."

"No one told me. I saw—" Blood drained from Carrie's face

as she realized what she was saying. "I … I mean, that's how I always picture the accident. Probably it was nothing like that." She stepped back out of his arms.

"Thank you for listening." She summoned a wobbly smile. "Could you show me to a washroom before I meet your father? He'll wonder what sort of stray cat you've dragged home if he sees me like this."

Dean smiled, impressed at the way she had pulled herself together.

"Of course. And don't worry, my dad likes cats."

Carrie relaxed and allowed him to take her hand as they entered the house. He seemed to accept her explanation for the details she'd described. And why not? A child's imagination was the only logical rationale possible.

And she did feel better, as if some long-frozen portion of her heart had finally begun to thaw. Maybe the dreadful details of her beloved parents' final moments would haunt her sleep no longer. Her heartbeat quickened and for the first time she found herself looking forward to the future with anticipation.

* * *

"So you are Carrie Richards. Welcome, my dear. Take the seat across from me so I can look at you. Dean, my boy," John Sheffield threw a mocking smile at his son, "your description of Carrie certainly didn't do her justice."

As he held her chair, Dean grimaced at his father over Carrie's head. He knew he could expect more teasing from John about his lukewarm description of Carrie's appearance. He grinned sheepishly and excused himself to find Aggie and ask her to make a pot of coffee and bring it to the sunroom. He was pleased to note John was drinking fruit juice. The doctor forbade any drink containing caffeine.

"You have a very beautiful home, Mr. Sheffield. My grandmother would love this room, so bright and sunny. The view is magnificent." Carrie's eyes admired the long sweep of lawn, broken by random groupings of rose bushes, not yet in bloom.

"Thank you. I may call you Carrie?" At her nod he continued. "You must call me John. I'm not old enough yet to want a beautiful lady to call me Mr. Sheffield."

Carrie sat back in the stuffed, chintz-covered chair and prepared to enjoy herself. John Sheffield, whose wealth outstripped her imagination, was charming, down-to-earth and harbored none of the snobbery usually associated with the very rich. Except for the color of his eyes, Dean closely resembled his father. It pleased her to see this preview of the man Dean would be in years to come.

"Before you leave, have Dean give you a tour of the house. The size is ridiculous, of course, but my father, Peter, was so in love with my mother that he claimed his wife was a beautiful jewel and it was only fitting he give her a beautiful setting. I know she would have preferred something smaller but she never let on to father. They both came from modest middle-class families and I think she regarded the extra rooms as no more than dust-catchers."

"Maybe your father had a premonition of the use to which you would one day put the rooms. Your mother certainly sounds like a woman who would approve of your plans for the house."

"Indeed she would, my dear. I'm sorry you never knew her. Everyone loved her. She mothered my brother David's two children when their own mother left. Alanna was only ten and Justin eleven. David moved back here, to an apartment in the west wing, but the children spent most of their free time with my mother. They were only fifteen and sixteen when my Lucy died of cancer. For them, it was like losing a second mother.

Dean and I at least had each other, but David had … problems at the time and wasn't up to comforting them.

"Ah well, it was all a long time ago. Forgive me, I didn't mean to get morbid."

Carrie shook her head. "There's nothing to forgive. I understand about memories popping up when you least expect them. It feels good to talk about people you loved."

Their eyes met and held. Suddenly Carrie understood the sadness she'd seen in the back of Dean's eyes. Before she could censor her tongue, she whispered to the middle-aged man sitting so calmly before her, "I'm so sorry. You are very ill, aren't you?"

Dean's father looked startled, then he smiled. "I knew you were special even before we met, Carrie Richards." He leaned across the small table and took her hands in his. "Promise me something. Promise me you'll take care of Dean and help him through this when it happens. I've been worrying about him being alone. It will be easier for him to cope if you're beside him."

Carrie squeezed the sick man's hands.

"Of course. I'll help him all I can. But you must realize, Dean and I have only just met. His interest in me is based on your plans for the mansion and on … curiosity. We may not even meet again after today."

Shaking his head, John released her hands and sat back. His mouth widened in a complacent smile. "You're wrong about that, my dear. I know my son. I just wish I were going to be here to see my grandchildren."

Carrie blushed, but before she could come up with a rejoinder Dean slipped into the chair beside her. He looked at his father and his eyes narrowed.

"Why do I have the feeling something's going on behind my back? You look like you've just arranged to open another branch of Sheffield Men's Wear."

John smirked. "Something like that."

He winked at Carrie. She couldn't prevent a grin from covering her face. Dean's head swung from one to the other. He looked mystified.

The questions hovering on his tongue went unasked when a tall, remarkably thin woman appeared in the doorway, holding a tray. Dean rose and took it from her.

"Thanks, Aggie. You're a doll. Come in for a minute. Aggie, I'd like you to meet Carrie Richards, a friend of mine. That is, if Dad doesn't steal her away from me. Carrie, this is Agatha Scully. She's been feeding the Sheffields since I was in diapers. And believe me, even though she's not exactly a walking advertisement for her food, she's the best cook in the country."

Aggie snorted but colored in pleasure at Dean's teasing. Carrie stood and shook hands with the woman, who greeted her very pleasantly, at the same time giving her a swift, thorough perusal. Then she flicked a glance at Dean. When she looked back at Carrie she was grinning broadly.

"You try one of those lemon tarts, miss. They're still warm from the oven." With a knowing look at her employer, she left.

* * *

Ten minutes later John excused himself, saying he needed to rest before dinner. Impulsively, Carrie rose to hug him. He returned the gesture with warmth and a delighted smile. Over her shoulder he grinned at his son.

"Fair warning, Dean. I may just decide to snatch this woman right out from under your nose." With that, he patted Carrie on the shoulder and left the room, humming under his breath.

Carrie kept her gaze averted from Dean as she sat down again, for fear he would spot the tears threatening to fall.

Deliberately she gave a loud sniff and bent her head to dig in her purse for a tissue, saying, "Goodness, I hope I'm not coming down with a spring cold. They're the worst kind, don't you think?"

When she had blinked away the tears and looked up again, she met Dean's thoughtful gaze. He ignored her comment and regarded her steadily for a moment.

"You know about Dad, don't you? Curious. He said he didn't want anyone to know. I suspect he only told me because he wanted my assurance I would see his project through if he couldn't. You've made quite an impression on him."

"Do you mind very much?" Concerned he might be hurt that his father had confided in a stranger, she hastened to reassure him. "Actually, he didn't tell me. I just guessed and he didn't deny it. Of course I won't mention his illness to anyone. I'm so very sorry, Dean. The knowing must be terribly difficult for you."

"Yes, it is. But it helps that we're working together on his plans for the mansion. I'm spending more time with him than usual and leaving as much of the work as I can to Uncle David. He manages the west end branch of the store. The frustrating thing is, I can't delegate overall policy implementation and that necessitates some traveling. When I was away last week all I could think about was the distance between us."

"You were out of town last week?" Carrie asked faintly. "Was that where you hurt your wrist?"

Dean's eyes narrowed but Carrie looked away just then, missing his speculative glance.

"Yes. I flew out early Monday morning and came back Wednesday afternoon. I had an accident in the street on Tuesday and twisted my wrist." He shook his head and added wryly, "I seem to have become accident-prone lately."

Carrie's head snapped up. "Accident-prone? What else has

happened?"

Dean began to describe his narrow escape on the cliff. He stopped speaking abruptly when the color fled from Carrie's face and her lips began to tremble.

"No need to be frightened now. I'm all right. That boulder has been defying gravity for decades, maybe centuries. It was bound to give way eventually. I was lucky, but it's all over now. The danger is past."

But Carrie could no longer maintain the fiction that imagination accounted for her experiences the week before. Her memory dredged up an ancient legend she had once happened upon in an old, out-of-print book of German myths. Fear shuddered through her. Her mouth was dry as she forced her unwilling tongue to move.

"That's when you hurt your left shoulder and hip. Tell me, was it Friday you almost went over the cliff?" She held her breath as she waited for his answer.

"How did you know? I haven't spoken of it to anyone."

She shook away his question and forced herself to continue. "And your wrist. That accident was nearly fatal too, wasn't it? Tell me what happened."

"Carrie—"

"Tell me!"

Anxious to alleviate the desperation on her face, Dean quickly described how, together with a group of others, he had been waiting to cross a busy street when some impatient jostling behind him had toppled him into the path of an oncoming bus. A quick-thinking woman in the group had grasped his wrist and pulled him back to safety with barely a second to spare. He emerged from the incident suffering only a mildly sprained wrist.

During this recital Carrie's face turned ashen. Her eyes grew huge with fear. Dean leaped up and rushed from the room. A moment later he returned with a snifter of brandy and held it to Carrie's mouth, ignoring her feeble protest.

The fiery brew scorched its way down her throat and brought tears to her eyes. Heat radiated from her stomach to her limbs and gradually her shaking nerves subsided. When her normal color returned, Dean drew her to her feet and placed his hands on her shoulders.

"All right, Carrie, now it's your turn for explanations. I want to know why you were so afraid when we met. Tell me how you know about the accidents. Tell me why you seemed to think I'd been at your apartment before. Tell me everything. Start from the beginning and don't leave out a thing."

Despair engulfed her. If she did as he demanded, he would stare at her in disbelief and edge away, putting a distance between them that would solidify into an unscalable wall. Or worse, he would laugh. Her heart cringed at the thought of being an object of ridicule to him. Her mind scurried frantically for some innocuous explanation to satisfy him.

Then her shoulders slumped as she accepted the inevitable. Only the truth would do, though it meant the end of the relationship that had been growing in importance since the first time she saw him. She had tried so hard to reject the probable meaning of the apparitions. Dean's near-fatal accidents were evidence she couldn't ignore. His safety was far more important than any blow to her ego.

She straightened.

"All right, Dean, I'll tell you everything. I can only beg you to listen with an open mind because *you are in grave danger*."

CHAPTER THREE

Carrie nodded and gestured to their chairs. They sat down, Dean pulling his chair close to hers, his expression skeptical, almost amused. She must convince him, if not of the truth, at least of the need to be careful. After a silent moment of reflection, she decided to start at the beginning. The weight of her background might add credence to her revelations about his own situation.

She began to talk. Twenty uninterrupted minutes later she finished, having touched on everything except what concerned him personally. During her recital her eyes never left his, but his expression was studiously noncommittal, displaying neither belief nor disbelief. She waited for him to speak.

"Did Greta sense your parents' deaths?" His low voice signaled sympathetic concern.

"She didn't *see* the accident as I did. But she knew in the same instant. The reports we received later confirmed the accident happened, in every detail, exactly as my vision portrayed."

"That's incredible. And a terrible thing to happen to a child. How in the world did you cope?"

"I had Greta. I don't believe I would have made it without her. We kept each other sane. Everyone, even a child, has to learn to accept loss."

Carrie felt a bubble of hope expand in her chest. Dean had neither laughed nor given her the look that meant he was questioning her grip on reality. Maybe, just maybe, things didn't have to change between them after all.

A second later she squashed that hope. He had only to witness one incident and their friendship would die a swift death. The memory of Gary's look of horror and revulsion told her she'd be foolish to expect anything different from Dean. She mustn't allow herself to be hurt again.

"I don't recall seeing anything in the newspapers about a psychic helping the local police. How do you manage to stay out of the news?"

Carrie smiled. "I threatened to hold a press conference and make the whole force look ridiculous if my name ever appears in the news in connection with one of their cases. They believed me, so I'm referred to as 'an anonymous source.' The few people who know are sworn to secrecy. My privacy would be non-existent if it came out."

"I understand and I'll keep your secret, Carrie. Thank you for confiding in me." He fell silent for a moment. "What you sensed about Dad, is that what's called precognition?"

"Yes. Sometimes I get a … feeling about someone. I don't always know what's wrong, just that something is. But sometimes I sense a thing only as it's happening, rather than before it happens. Only rarely do I actually *see* something."

"Do you have any control over your ability?"

Carrie shook her head. "No. I can't will it. Sometimes months pass between occurrences."

"Hmmm." Dean's mouth lifted at the corners. "So you can't make a living with a crystal ball, eh?"

Carrie tensed but instantly realized Dean wasn't laughing at her, only inviting her to laugh with him. A sense of enormous relief lifted the oppressive weight of dread from her shoulders. She grinned, then giggled and a moment later they were roaring with laughter.

Gasping for breath she realized that, however incongruously, she was happy. Not once had Dean given the slightest indication he regarded her as emotionally or mentally unstable. Instead, her story, and their laughter, had drawn them closer. She felt her spirit take wing. Together they could beat anything.

The thought brought instant sobriety. Could they change the future the sightings forecast? Nothing in the old writings indicated the final outcome had ever been changed by the living. Was it possible to change fate?

She had yet to give an account of the apparitions and her fear for his life. Dean would find the obscure legend harder to accept than the comparatively widely-known theories of psychic abilities. She found it difficult herself to accept the evidence of her own eyes. If there was any chance at all to save Dean's life, it was crucial he believe in his immediate personal danger.

* * *

A large figure stepped into the doorway.

"Dean, what's the meaning of all the racket I heard a minute ago? You're almost shaking the rafters. Is it really necessary to—? Oh! Who's this?"

Carrie saw a flash of irritation on Dean's face that disappeared so quickly she thought she must be mistaken. He rose to his feet and drew the speaker into the room.

"Come in, Bev. I'd like you to meet Carrie Richards. Carrie, my father's sister, Beverley Sheffield."

Carrie let her outstretched arm drop to her side when it became clear the woman had no intention of shaking hands. Taken aback by the unexpected rudeness, she stared at the overweight, middle-aged woman. Superficially she resembled Dean's father. The large brown eyes and the overall shape of the face were identical. But the lines in her face, unlike John's, turned down. Resentment and unhappiness disfigured the face of a woman who might have been attractive in her youth. And still might, if she would discard the thick gray braid for a softer, shorter cut and replace the belligerent frown with a smile.

The uncomfortable silence was broken by the sudden appearance in the doorway of a well-dressed couple. Carrie's relief was short-lived when a quick glance at Dean caught the momentary tightening of his lips. Then he smiled and introduced his cousin, Justin, and Justin's wife, Natalie.

Justin's greeting contrasted sharply with that of his glowering aunt. When their hands met he drew her close, a speculative gleam in his eyes. Carrie stiffened when he casually and openly swept his glance over her figure, in total unconcern for his wife's presence. His admittedly handsome face split into the predatory smile of a wolf.

Embarrassed, Carrie returned his fulsome greeting with a mumbled hello and pulled her hand free. She turned to Natalie, praying the woman hadn't noticed her husband's insulting behavior. The cynical gleam in the cool blue eyes making their own leisurely perusal of Carrie clearly indicated her familiarity with her husband's conduct. The two women touched fingertips. Natalie threw her a dismissive smile then turned to Dean and threaded her arm through his, pressing her breast against his arm.

"Dean, darling, I need a favor. Justin promised to go with me to my sorority's fund-raising dinner Thursday night and now he can't make it. Please say you'll be my escort. Those cats will tear me to shreds later if I go alone. You wouldn't leave me in that position, would you?"

To Carrie's ears, the sultry, seductive voice seemed to imply some hidden meaning in the last statement. She caught a flash of pain in Justin's face before he turned away. Natalie's wanton behavior with her husband's cousin was a cruel payback for

Justin's rude response to another woman's charms. Natalie and Justin were a beautiful but obviously unhappy couple.

"Sorry, Natalie, but I already have plans for Thursday. Plans I can't possibly break." Deliberately, Dean freed his arm and stepped away.

"With her, I suppose." She continued to smile, but the side-long glance she threw at Carrie was spiteful.

With a shock, Carrie realized the woman was jealous. Though she was his cousin's wife, her demeanor suggested she and Dean shared a history. Past or present history? Suddenly Carrie wanted desperately to know the answer.

"Suppose what you will, Natalie. The fact remains you'll have to find someone else. Though why you would even want to spend the evening with women you call 'cats,' I don't know."

Natalie's beautiful face flushed unbecomingly at Dean's rebuff. She glared at Carrie then tossed her head and left the room, calling brusquely over her shoulder for Justin to accompany her. He did so, with a shrug of apology to Carrie.

Beverley Sheffield, who had received only brief nods from the couple in way of greeting, chuckled sardonically and followed them. She had not spoken one word to Carrie.

"Carrie," Dean said, his voice full of regret, "I apologize for my family. Their behavior toward you was inexcusable." His face showed his distress as he took both her hands in his. "Please don't take it to heart."

Although shaken by the unpleasant encounters, Carrie tried to lessen Dean's discomfort. She shook her head and smiled. "No apology required. We don't get to choose our relatives, after all. Forget it, Dean. My ego's still intact."

Impulsively she stood on her tiptoes and kissed him lightly on the cheek. He looked startled then grinned down at her upturned, blushing face.

"You're quite a lady, lady. But let's get out of here before someone else interrupts. Let's go outdoors while it's still warm. That way, we'll see anyone coming."

They shrugged into their jackets. Dean took her hand and led her through to the back verandah and down to the edge of the cultivated lawn to a white, elaborately carved wooden gazebo, half-hidden in a grove of weeping willow trees. They settled on the cushioned bench, Dean's arm on the backrest behind her. Carrie resisted the urge to rest her head against his shoulder.

"Before we finish the conversation that was so rudely interrupted, I want to tell you about my family. Some explanation is definitely in order."

"It's not necessary, Dean. After all, I'm a stranger, there's no need."

"You're not a stranger and there is a need. For me, at any rate. Indulge me."

Carrie nodded and hoped the pleasure she felt at his insistence that she was no stranger didn't show. She wasn't sure she was capable of refusing him anything.

"Aunt Bev, well, she never married, although Dad says she was very attractive as a young woman. She was always aloof, but never unkind to me and my cousins when we were children. When I was a child I thought she was sad. She's always lived here, in her own apartment, with first her father and then mine taking care of all her expenses."

"But over the years she's become a bit … eccentric. Moody. Periodic food binges account for her weight. Bev can be very gracious at times and at other times, well, as you saw her today. The strange thing is, this last year or so, she seems to harbor some kind of grudge against Justin and Alanna and me—but not against her brothers. Maybe she's beginning to resent our youth as she gets older."

"That's a shame, Dean. If she would diet, and cut and style her hair, she would look ten years younger and, I think, quite attractive. She seems intelligent. I wonder why she treats herself so badly."

Dean sighed. "According to the prevailing psychological wisdom, people who overeat and deliberately cultivate an unattractive appearance have low self-esteem. But that can't apply to Aunt Bev. She's intelligent, educated, admired in her circle of friends."

He shifted on the bench and looked intently into Carrie's heart-shaped face. "Am I boring you?"

"Not at all. Other people's families interest me. I never had cousins or aunts and uncles, only my grandmother. I've always wondered what it would be like to live in a house full of people, all related to you in some way."

Dean laughed. "There are advantages and disadvantages, but on the whole, it's good to have that sense of belonging." He seemed unaware when his fingers began to twine idly in her springy curls.

"You'll like Uncle David. He had a bad break and fell into the bottle for awhile. His wife left him when Alanna and Justin were young. Because of the drinking, he lost his pharmaceutical license and his business. But he pulled himself up, joined A.A. and hasn't had a drop of liquor for years. He lives in the mansion—we all do—and manages the head branch of Sheffield Men's Wear.

"After their mother left, Alanna and Justin spent most of their free time in my parents' apartment, partly because of David's drinking but mostly because my mother took them under her wing. They were almost as devastated as I was when my mother died of cancer."

Carrie grimaced. "Money doesn't make a lot of difference, does it? I mean, tragedy and unhappiness take no notice of people's financial circumstances. No one is exempt from life's heartaches."

Dean's arm dropped to her shoulders and gently pulled her against his side. She told herself to move away from him, but instead found herself snuggling closer. It felt so right. What could be the harm?

"You're right. Money can certainly hold some of life's problems at bay, but it can't buy health or happiness. Or loyalty."

This last was said with so much resignation Carrie lifted her head in surprise.

"Loyalty?"

Dean's mouth pinched in distaste. Then he relaxed and chuckled.

"That brings us to Justin and Natalie. No, no, I want you to know this." He stopped Carrie's effort to protest with a quick kiss on the tip of her nose. Startled, she gave in, but resisted his attempt to tuck her head back into his shoulder. If she must hear about Natalie she wanted to see his face when he spoke of her.

"Natalie is the daughter of Lawrence Chambers, my father's lawyer. Four years ago she was bright, witty and beautiful. I fell in love with her—or thought I did. I was enormously flattered and so physically attracted I asked her to marry me. She agreed. I was on top of the world."

He paused. Carrie searched his face. Did he still love her? Her heart rose to her throat at the thought.

"Then one day I went to Justin's apartment to see him about something and I found the two of them in bed."

Carrie gasped in dismay. Her heart contracted at the thought of the pain he must have suffered. Dean traced his fingertips around her mouth, his eyes serious.

"I suppose I'm an old-fashioned man, at least in some respects. You see, my parents were madly in love and neither ever looked at anyone else. I know a love like theirs is not very common but it's what I wanted and expected. If Natalie had decided she didn't love me after all and had broken the engagement, well, that would have been one thing. But she went to Justin's bed still wearing my ring, still intending to marry me." He paused. A cynical expression crossed his face. "I was then, and will probably always be, a much better financial catch."

"Oh, Dean." Carrie's breath caught in her throat. Overwhelmed with a desire to comfort him, she laid a soft hand on his cheek. "How horrible for you."

"I was pretty upset for a few weeks, but I finally realized what I was feeling was anger and outrage. Not heartbreak. She betrayed my … sense of honor, I suppose you could say. When I understood my heart wasn't really broken, I knew I had never been in love with her, just dazzled by her beauty. She was equally dazzled by my money and eventual inheritance."

"I don't understand how she or Justin could do that to you." Under her honest concern, Carrie was guiltily aware of the secret spurt of joy circling in her veins. He didn't love Natalie.

Dean sighed. "Justin's part in it did hurt me, but I came to see he was genuinely in love with her. He still is. Believe it or not, I don't think he cheats on her. In retaliation for her treatment of her, he plays at coming on to women. But I've never known him to carry through." He shook his head. "I think she loves him too, but she can't seem to forget I was the better 'catch.' It's ridiculous, really, because every Sheffield has shares in the business. Justin is well off. Natalie has everything she could wish for."

He fell silent. Carrie opened her mouth to speak then closed it again. As an outsider, her opinion of Natalie Sheffield's behavior was one she had no right to express. Nor was she certain Dean was correct when he said the woman loved her husband. Surely women in love didn't treat their husbands so cruelly, especially not in public. Her sexy display with Dean seemed calculated to remind Justin he was her second choice.

Still, what did she know about relationships? With elementary classrooms staffed predominantly with females, she met few men who weren't husbands and fathers. The single males she did meet soon lost interest when it dawned on them that a few dates wouldn't gain them entry to her bed.

But then, she'd never met a man she wanted in her bed. The overwhelming feelings described by the romance novels simply hadn't happened to her. Remaining a virgin had never been a conscious decision. She didn't consider marriage to be a necessary prelude to sex, but a certain degree of caring was essential. At least for her. Whatever the evening out cost the man, he had not purchased the use of his date's body.

And like Dean, she held the old-fashioned view that marriage should be exclusive. If a marriage became intolerable for whatever reason, then divorce was an acceptable option. But cheating had no place in any relationship. Somehow she knew Dean would never betray his wife. And certainly that lucky woman would never have any reason to stray.

Carrie slanted a glance at Dean and blushed when she found his gaze on her face. His eyes darkened at her reaction. As if mesmerized, he slowly lowered his head until only a breath separated their mouths. He stilled then, offering her the chance to draw back.

Even as she told herself it would be a mistake, Carrie leaned forward to close the gap. Their lips met and held and clung, fitting together as if by design. Pleasure ignited and flared into heat that rushed like liquid fire through her veins. Her hands crept up his chest and circled his neck.

At her touch, Dean groaned and deepened the kiss, his tongue laving her lips before gently demanding entry. When her lips parted, his growl of pleasure sent shivers of excitement scampering over her skin and generated a hot, hungry ache deep inside her.

His arms wrapped around her and lifted her to his lap.

Carrie's head fell back when his mouth left her lips and began to rain small moist kisses over her jaw and down to the wildly beating pulse in her throat. She dug her fingers into his shoulders and pressed her aching breasts against his hard chest, moaning with needs she'd never experienced before.

Dean drew back. When the cool air between them registered in her consciousness, Carrie opened dazed eyes to see raw hunger in Dean's gaze and a wholly male smile of satisfaction on his face. She groaned in an agony of embarrassment and leaped to her feet. She couldn't believe…. How could she have….

Dean stood and put his arms around her waist from behind. His warm breath stirred her hair and set her whole scalp tingling. As she struggled to regain some modicum of dignity she became aware that his arms and shoulders were shaking. Was he *laughing* at her?

She stiffened, reluctant to further humiliate herself by struggling to escape his hold.

"Carrie, sweetheart, I've wanted to kiss you since we first met and you asked me if I was real. Do you mean to tell me you didn't see it coming?"

Carrie heard the amusement and the sensual tone in his voice and began to relax. He had done nothing she hadn't wanted him to do. She was smiling when she turned around in his arms.

"Maybe I *should* invest in a crystal ball. Although," she gave him a shy smile, "it's rather nice to be surprised now and again."

He grinned. "I'll keep that in mind, my lady."

He hooked her arm over his and led her back into the yard. His smile fell away to be replaced by a serious expression.

"Let's walk. We still have some talking to do."

His words reminded Carrie that what she had to tell him could very easily ensure he never surprised her with a kiss again. Would he think she was crazy, or at the very least, too flaky to get involved with? Ruthlessly she pushed away the sadness welling up inside her. The only thing that counted here was Dean's safety.

Still, she wasn't quite ready to say the words that would brand her a crackpot in his eyes. In an attempt to delay the inevitable, she asked to see the spot where the boulder had given way beneath him. His eyebrows rose but he said nothing, merely steered her toward the path through the woods.

When they broke through to the clearing he pointed to the spot. The gesture was unnecessary. The raw edge, not yet softened by time and weather, stood out clearly from the rounded, grass-smoothed areas on either side. Even that physical testimony was superfluous. Carrie didn't need the use of her eyes to locate the spot where Dean so nearly lost his life.

The closer they approached, the stronger became a sense of wrongness. Carrie felt her heartbeat accelerate and every nerve in her body leap to attention. The accident was in the past but the dark smell of danger still lingered. The sun slid behind a cloud at that moment as if to validate the apprehension gripping her throat. She knew, without knowing how she knew, that something more than gravity had been at work here.

"What is it, Carrie?"

The sharp edge of concern in Dean's voice broke through the fog in her mind. Belatedly, she realized her trembling hand had tightened compulsively in his and her nails were digging painfully into his palm. Her chest was tight with the need to breathe. Inhaling deeply, she turned to search his face for some sign he shared her perceptions.

Nothing showed in his expression except concern for her. For Dean, the incident was over. A close call but now a thing of the past. At the moment his only thought was for the white-faced woman staring at him with horrified dismay.

"What is it, Carrie?" he asked again, this time more urgently.

"I…. Can we get down there?" She pointed over the edge of the cliff.

"Yes." He pointed to the left. "Further along that way the land slopes lower. It's possible to scramble down into the gorge fairly easily and pick your way back to this spot. But why would you want to—"

"I'll explain later. Come on, Dean, please. I have to … see something." She tugged him in the direction he'd indicated.

Bewildered but willing to do anything to relieve her agitation and allay her seemingly irrational fears, Dean did as she asked. Ten minutes later they stood almost directly below the scene of the accident.

With a sense of real loss, Dean stared at the smashed chunks of the immense stone platform that had been a part of his life for so long. Regretfully, he thought of his dream that he would some day bring his own son to wait on the majestic boulder to welcome the sunrise. Disappointment tasted gray in his mouth.

Carrie's gasp interrupted his bleak contemplation of the broken boulder. He looked up quickly to see her eyes fixed on the upper area of the embankment. His gaze followed hers. The tough grasses and stubby bushes clinging stubbornly to the vertical wall of earth and rocks ended abruptly three feet from the top. Above them the earth was bare of vegetation and scarred by deep gouges in an irregular pattern.

For a long moment the significance of the markings eluded him. Then he inhaled sharply. The earthen wall just below the stone platform had been dug out with a shovel.

With the realization came the identification of the pair of rounded depressions on both sides of the area. Someone had positioned a ladder in order to reach the upper area of the earthen wall. What gravity had been unable to accomplish for decades, perhaps centuries, a human had managed with a few hours' work. Anger shuddered through Dean's massive frame.

With a little cry of fear, Carrie threw herself into his arms. Their findings didn't surprise her but she was appalled by their proof of violence. Nevertheless, a small corner of her mind rejoiced that rain and wind hadn't erased the marks left by the shovel. The physical evidence would surely make Dean more receptive to her warnings that his life was in danger.

She knew now with every fiber of her being that not only had his death been forecast but his death by murder, not by accident. Someone intended to kill him. Kill him in a way that wouldn't be questioned or cause anyone to be suspicious. People died by accident every day. Someone meant to turn Dean Sheffield into a statistic.

CHAPTER FOUR

When Carrie awoke the next morning her head ached with a dull, monotonous throbbing. After staring for hours at the textured shadows on the ceiling, her eyes felt scratchy and swollen. When sleep finally claimed her, murky dreams of death and sorrow kept her twisting restlessly on the bed. She sat up and clasped her arms around her legs.

She had never felt so helpless in her life. Although her attempts to help the police locate lost or abducted victims occasionally failed, none of the casualties had been known to her personally. The anguish she had felt on those occasions wouldn't compare to the pain she would feel if Dean became one of them.

Frustration swept through her as she remembered Dean's refusal to believe his life was in danger. Neither had spoken on the return trek to the house after the frightening discovery at the cliff. The drive back to her apartment had been accomplished with a minimum of conversation. She had been afraid to introduce the topic of attempted murder while he was behind the wheel.

When he agreed to join her for coffee Carrie was grateful for the opportunity to reveal the experiences that made her afraid for his safety. Her gratitude was short-lived. To her dismay, he had already concocted a theory to account for the shovel work that had led to the collapse of the boulder. Her suggestion that the accident was, in fact, a planned murder attempt was brushed away with a short laugh.

"It's obvious," he rationalized. "Someone, most likely the groundskeeper, decided the overhanging rock was a hazard, so he attempted to bring it down to prevent an accident. He couldn't manage it at one go and undoubtedly intended to return to finish the job. Naturally, he couldn't have anticipated that I would happen along before he got back to it."

"Don't you think it's strange he didn't warn the family of the danger?" Carrie argued. "If you had fallen and been killed he'd be criminally responsible."

"Responsible, maybe, but not intentionally so. Carrie, I'm the only member of the family who ever goes over there. I agree that Bill, if it was him, should have mentioned what he was doing. My hip and shoulder certainly wish he had. It was careless of him not to do so. But negligence is a far cry from willful murder."

He stood and walked round the table to lift Carrie to her feet. His explanation had done nothing to erase the fearful pleading in her eyes. Large, warm hands cupped her face. His voice was earnest as he tried to demolish her fears.

"Carrie, listen to me. Bill Hummell has no reason to kill me. He has nothing to gain from my death. And I've never done anything to him that would cause him to hate me. The man has only worked for the family for a few months. Mrs. Hummell, our housekeeper, is his mother. She's been with us for over a year. When her husband died, she asked us to hire Bill. There's absolutely no reason for him to want to hurt me."

Carrie was silent for a moment, wanting to believe him and to forget everything but the sensual comfort of his hands. But she couldn't.

"Someone else, then. Someone who paid Bill Hummell to do it or hired a person you don't know. Dean, believe me, *please,* your life is in danger."

He smiled fondly and noticed for the first time the golden flecks shimmering in her wide eyes. She was beautiful and best of all, she was genuinely concerned for him. But of course she was mistaken. By her own telling, not for the first time.

"You're wrong, sweetheart. But I'm flattered you care." He removed his hands from her face and glanced up at the kitchen clock. "Whoops! My plane leaves in an hour. I've got to run. I have a business meeting in Chicago tomorrow morning. If all goes well, I'll be back tomorrow evening. Please, stop worrying. I don't plan on shuffling off this mortal coil any time soon."

Carrie clutched at his sleeve.

"But I haven't told you…. Dean, I haven't told you how I know about your injuries. It's important. You have to know—"

"No time, love." He swept her into his arms and hugged her hard. Then abruptly, he let her go and was out the door before she could say anything more.

* * *

Now she sighed deeply and rested her head on her knees. There was nothing she could do until he returned. And nothing then, if he chose to disregard her account of the apparitions. Her head swung up as it occurred to her he might want nothing more to do with her at all. His father's condition had to be foremost in his thoughts. Why should he waste time with a woman he'd known only a few days, a crazy woman who claimed someone was trying to kill him, when he could be with his father? He hadn't said he'd call her when he returned.

Tears trickled down her face. The thought of never seeing Dean again hurt more than Gary's desertion. She drew her legs closer and rocked on the bed.

When her tears dried shame crept into her tired mind. She

shivered in self-disgust. What kind of person was she, blubbering over the loss of a man who was never hers, when Dean was in danger of losing his life? How much more terrible for John, if the dying man was condemned to suffer the loss of his only child during the last days of his own life.

She pictured Dean's father who, in spite of his imminent demise, was more concerned for his friend Dick and others like him. She hadn't known such bravery and selflessness existed. For his sake if not for her own, she had to find a way to save Dean. Not for nothing did Greta call her mule-stubborn.

Greta. Her grandmother was more versed in the old legends than she. Her knowledge and advice might be the key to Dean's survival.

Energized by the thought, Carrie scrambled off the bed. She showered quickly, applied the usual light makeup and, after a quick glance at the outdoor thermometer, pulled on matching jeans and jacket over a lightweight yellow turtleneck. Blessing her hairdresser for the recent cut that allowed her to manage her curls with a few swipes of a brush, she grabbed her purse and headed for the elevator to the underground garage.

Twenty minutes later she peered around the door of Greta's room. The older woman was propped in a sitting position, lazily turning the pages of a woman's magazine. The look of boredom on her wrinkled face dissolved into an eager smile when she spied her granddaughter.

"Carrie, I didn't expect you this early. Are you bored with the holidays so soon?"

A glance at her watch told Carrie she had arrived just before lunchtime. As she shook her head and kissed her grandmother's soft cheek, the lunch cart rumbled to a stop at the door. She straightened and stepped back from the bed to make way for the nurse and tray.

"Hello, Carrie. It's nice to see you again." Alanna's cheerful voice held a hint of curiosity. "Did my cousin get your purse back to you?" At Carrie's nod her smile grew wider. "You really knocked him off his feet, you know. I don't think I've ever seen him so disconcerted before."

With the efficiency of experience, she pulled up the table attached to the side of the bed and swung it over Greta's lap. When she had deposited the tray on the table she glanced at Carrie, her face intent and expectant.

Carrie blushed, suddenly realizing how strange her behavior must have seemed to the pretty nurse. Frantically searching for some logical explanation, she noticed the rather needless fluttering of Alanna's left hand. Flashing points of light offered her an out.

"Alanna!" Carrie exclaimed. "What a beautiful ring! I didn't realize you were engaged."

Immediately distracted, Alanna forgot that Carrie hadn't explained her reaction to her cousin. Her face pinked as she lifted her hand to show off the diamond ring.

"Tim gave it to me last night. I haven't told any of the family yet. Except for Aggie. No one else was up when I left the house." She grinned broadly at Carrie and Greta. "I hope you get a chance to meet him. He's a terrific artist. We met at the community theater. I was acting in a local production of Isben's *A Doll's House* at the time. Not that I've much talent, I haven't, but it's lots of fun. Tim was hired to paint the backdrops. He does whatever work comes along until he can make a name for himself with his paintings. He's wonderfully talented. Any day now the art world will realize it."

Alanna burbled on for a few more minutes, her face glowing happily. A message booming over the loud speaker seemed to bring her back to earth. She rolled her eyes and excused herself to return to her duties, promising to bring an extra cup of coffee for Carrie at the first opportunity. The moment she disappeared through the doorway Greta swung the hinged table out of the way and eyed her granddaughter.

"Sit down, Carrie, and tell me what's going on. Something is wrong and it involves Alanna's cousin. I don't need any special power to know that. Talk, *liebchen*."

Gratefully, Carrie obeyed. The story poured out in an eager torrent. With Greta there was no need to choose ambiguous phrases or hold back any detail for fear of sounding like a lunatic. Her grandmother was the one person in the world who took her words at face value and accepted their truth without question.

Finished, Carrie sat back and waited. Her expression turned inward, Greta folded her arms and gazed unseeing at the wall opposite her bed. Then she heaved a deep sigh and turned a somber face to Carrie.

"You saw the man's doppelgänger. I wasn't sure there was any truth to that old legend but I can't think of another explanation. Few books even mention it today. And I've never heard of anyone in modern times who has experienced a sighting."

Carrie shivered. "But I thought the person's ghostly double appeared only to that person, as a forewarning, a harbinger of his approaching death. Dean hasn't seen his apparition. Why would his double appear to me? I hadn't even met him at the time."

Greta frowned and reached for Carrie's hand.

"It doesn't seem to make much sense, does it? Still, there has to be a reason why his doppelgänger appeared to you, a stranger, and not to him or someone he knows."

The two women fell silent when Alanna returned bearing a cup of coffee for Carrie. She scolded Greta for not eating but luckily was too busy to stay for another chat. When Alanna was out of hearing, Greta startled Carrie with an unexpected question.

"Do you like this Dean Sheffield, *liebchen*?"

"I.… Yes, yes, very much." The corners of her mouth twitched but the smile never materialized. The man she'd barely met was destined to die in the near future. Her spirits plummeted but she struggled to remain calm. Hysterics wouldn't help.

"But what's that got to do with—?" The smile on Greta's face stopped her.

"You will save him, Carrie."

"But—"

"Listen to me. I think you have saved him twice already. Two attempts on his life have failed." Greta nodded decisively. "I feel sure of it."

"How did I save him? I didn't even know him then."

Greta shook her gray head.

"Doesn't matter. The appearance of a doppelgänger has to do with fate. I feel it here," she placed her hand over her heart, "you were meant to meet. Only you can save him. Maybe the doppelgänger connected the two of you until your meeting, to warn you of the danger and at the same time, to inform you that his survival rests in your hands."

Appalled, Carrie stared at her grandmother. Whether Dean lived or died was *her* responsibility? Fear moved sluggishly through her veins and pooled in a hard knot in her stomach. Unless she could discover who wanted Dean dead, and why, how could she hope to prevent his death? Especially since Dean didn't believe his life was in danger and would take no special precautions to ensure his safety. Greta's encouraging smile merely emphasized the apprehension and sympathy in her soft eyes.

* * *

Dean fumbled with the seatbelt until the stewardess noticed

his futile efforts and leaned over him to snap the clasp closed. He smiled his thanks and eased back in the chair, clasping his hands together on his stomach to hide their trembling.

"Are you all right, sir?"

"Yes, I'm fine." His voice was hoarse. He cleared his throat and added, "I'd appreciate a brandy as soon as we get airborne though."

The blue-eyed attendant smiled sympathetically and leaned closer to whisper. "No one has purchased the seats near you. If you promise not to tattle, I'll bring you a drink right now." Her eyes twinkled at the attractive but white-faced man who sat alone in the first class section.

"Ah, you're an angel of mercy."

She giggled and disappeared to return a moment later with a snifter of brandy. When he offered his fervent thanks, she smiled and remarked that her husband also had a phobia about flying. He didn't tell her a fear of flying had nothing to do with his present agitation.

He downed the liquor and felt his insides huddle gratefully around the trail of heat. Eyes closed, he waited for his quivering nerves to calm. Thinking was impossible; the phrase "Three strikes and you're out" looped endlessly through his mind, like the unwanted repetition of a commercial jingle. Only he wasn't "out." And that astonished him.

His business had been successfully completed in spite of the difficulty he experienced in maintaining his usual focused attention. Recurring thoughts of Carrie Richards had been a major distraction. After the meeting he had changed his suit for more comfortable clothing, then checked out of the hotel, intent on catching the next flight home. When his taxi stalled behind a bus disgorging passengers and luggage, he tossed some money into the front seat, grabbed his single piece of luggage and set out on foot to cover the last hundred yards to the entrance of the airport terminal. The only thing on his mind was Carrie and the hope she would be at home when he arrived. He cursed himself for neglecting to make a definite date with her.

When he registered the frantic shouts and looked up, only yards separated him from the careening car. He leaped aside but misjudged the direction and found the vehicle swerving straight for him. He should be dead or at the very least, badly injured. At the last possible second, the car jerked aside and missed him, crashing instead into a parked van. The driver leaped from the machine and raced away. The only description he could give the airport security was of a man of average height, wearing a maroon windbreaker. He hadn't seen the driver's face at all, though he had the impression of a man past his youth.

When the owner of the car was located in the airport restaurant, where he had been eating with another businessman, the police dismissed the incident as an attempted car theft.

Were the police right in their assumption that the thief lost control of the unfamiliar car? It was possible. Of course it was possible. Then why didn't he believe it?

But he knew why. As the plane left the ground and his body began to relax, he forced himself to picture again what he'd seen the second before the car swerved away. A hand had grabbed the steering wheel and jerked it savagely, forcing the car to change direction. It was crazy, because there had been no one else in the car. But he knew what he had seen.

The second reason he couldn't swallow the police theory was the events of the past week. He was a careful man. He didn't take risks. Yet three times in little more than a week he had come within a whisker of dying. Dying by accident. Or by design? How could he know?

Whichever the case, it seemed he had a guardian angel watching over him. He thought of the woman—he felt certain it had been a woman—who had yanked him out of the path of the bus the week before. She had disappeared before he had time to gather his wits and thank her. None of the other people waiting with him for the light to change could describe his savior. Where had she gone so quickly?

And whose voice had cried his name at the cliff top, a split-second before the boulder gave way beneath his feet? He had swung around at the call and that had given him the few extra seconds he needed to leap to safety. When he realized no one else was present he put the cry down to his imagination and forgot it.

Now he wondered. Accidents or murder attempts, someone had saved him each time. He didn't believe in guardian angels, but still….

His thoughts returned to Carrie, as they had a hundred times that day. He knew he could have her story checked, at least her claims of assisting the police to locate missing people. But she had to know that, so there would be no point in lying. That part of her story must be true.

That she hadn't wanted to tell him about herself had been obvious. She had kept her eyes firmly fixed on her lap as she spoke, her glance flying to his face only when she stopped. He sensed she was expecting he would laugh and call her imaginative and fanciful. He hadn't. But only because he believed that *she* believed every word of her incredible story.

Did he believe a seven-year-old child saw a vision of her parents' deaths? As they died, many miles away? He didn't know. He just didn't know.

Accidents happened every day. His had happened in three widely separated locations. If fate meant to end his life, why was he still breathing? And how had she known about the bruises he sustained hurling himself away from the falling rock? Body language, she'd said, but her answer had been tentative. Had she been lying? For what purpose?

Even more mysterious was her strange reaction when they met. He'd seen recognition in her eyes, and shock, as if she'd seen a ghost. And later in her apartment a remark quickly bitten back implied she'd seen him there before. Before they'd met. That made no sense at all.

For the hundredth time, he determined not to think about her story. The whole idea confounded him. It went against his practical nature. It lacked logic. It mocked what was real and tangible. It was driving him nuts.

Instead, he thought about Carrie's lips, the way she'd responded to his kiss, the feel of her in his arms. Suddenly, he wanted desperately to see her again.

He shifted in his chair, willing the plane to greater speed. Remembering how she had called after him to wait—that she had something important to tell him—he decided to use that as an excuse to go directly from the airport to her apartment. He would simply apologize for not calling first. He needed to see her.

And he needed to know her reasons for believing his life was in danger. And most especially, why she claimed murder rather than accident would accomplish his death. Woman's intuition or a simple hunch couldn't account for her certainty.

With a groan, he realized his thoughts had circled once again to her story. A grimace swept over his face as he found himself wondering if she could possibly be right. Yet it didn't make sense. He had no enemies. Who would want to kill him? And why? Goosebumps trailed down his spine. He shivered, remembering the old adage of "someone walking on my grave."

* * *

Carrie shoved the door closed behind her with her elbow and walked down the hallway into the kitchen to deposit the bags of groceries on the counter. She filled the kettle and plugged it in to boil while she stored the perishables in the refrigerator. When all of the purchases had been stored away, she filled a cup with instant coffee and sat down heavily at the kitchen table, too tired to change her clothing.

She almost wished the holidays were over. With no work to occupy her mind and knowing Dean was out of town and would not be calling, she needed a distraction from her worry. She'd spent the afternoon visiting Greta and some of the other patients in the nursing home. Many were pathetically grateful for the attention, especially those confined to their beds or wheelchairs. When she finally left, with their thanks ringing in her ears, she felt good.

Exhaustion overtook her as she waited in line at the supermarket. After her sleepless night, the last thing she wanted was food, but Melinda would be arriving home in the early evening from her overseas flight. With her roommate away for much of the time, Carrie enjoyed an unequal use of the apartment. In the interest of fairness they had worked out a routine where Carrie did all the food shopping and prepared a hot meal to greet the tired stewardess after a long flight. The arrangement suited them both perfectly.

Willing her body to move, Carrie began to clean vegetables and peel potatoes. She basted Melinda's favorite ribs with barbecue sauce and placed the pan in the oven, then set the table for two. In twenty minutes everything was ready. The actual cooking would wait until her roommate arrived.

With nothing left to do, Carrie refilled her mug and settled in the small living room. Her eyes were too tired to focus on the small print in the newspaper. She abandoned the effort and flipped on the television, turning the dial until she found a newscast. She stared unseeing at the screen, unaware she had neglected to turn up the volume.

A jolt of sheer panic cut through her fatigue when her eyes focused on the slow motion replay of a plane spiraling to the earth. Her heart swelled in her throat as she leaped to her feet and fumbled with the remote control to raise the volume. The announcer's voice held an edge of horror as he described the deadly descent, but Carrie wanted to scream at him to repeat the location of the accident. Only when an enormous ball of fire rose from the point of impact did he repeat that the accident had taken place in northern Ontario.

Like a puppet whose strings were cut, she collapsed to her knees on the rug, horror and relief warring in her mind. Horror that so many had died. Relief that the plane could not have been Dean's.

Her defenses down, she was no longer able to hide from the fear simmering at the back of her mind. Dean had almost died, twice. But his doppelgänger, his double, had manifested itself to her three times. Had there been another 'accident'? Was he dead?

Carrie wrapped her arms tightly around her middle and doubled over with the pain of imagined loss. If it had happened … if he was dead … she swore to herself that she would uncover his murderer if it took the rest of her life.

Minutes passed before she regained control and pulled herself back onto the couch. He couldn't be dead. She would know. Wouldn't she?

She assured herself she was overreacting to the news report. The first two accidents happened within twenty-four hours after the apparition's visits. Two days had passed since Dean's double appeared in her apartment. Something must have happened to break the pattern of events. But what?

She caught her breath with sudden realization. They had met less than twelve hours after the third appearance of the doppelgänger. Had their meeting already changed fate in some way?

Was Greta right when she said Dean's survival depended on Carrie? Had her concern saved him from the two attempts on his life? Could their connection continue to hold off the dark angel? A bud of hope unfolded in her heart and flowered into a steely resolve to prove Greta right. She couldn't lose him now.

Dean himself was the biggest problem. She needed his cooperation. Deeply engrossed in the puzzle of how to convince him of the seriousness of his situation she almost missed the knock at the door.

"Just a minute, I'm coming." Melinda must have forgotten her key.

Carrie pasted a smile on her face and got up to open the door, hoping her roommate would be too tired to notice anything amiss. Melinda was her dearest friend, but Carrie preferred to keep the present problem to herself. Later she would tell Melinda everything.

She flung the door open and immediately forgot her fatigue at the sight of Dean's broad shoulders and muscular chest. Without thinking, she threw her arms around him and squeezed with all her strength. The soft wool of his sweater was heaven against her cheek.

"Oh, I'm so glad you're all right! I was so afraid. A plane crashed today and I didn't know where and I thought—but it wasn't yours and you're not hurt and nothing's happened to you and you're alive and—"

She stopped abruptly, suddenly aware she was pressed against him from chest to thighs. Her face flaming, she loosened her hold and tried to draw back. Prevented from retreating by his hands at her waist, she stilled and slowly raised her head. Instead of the consternation she expected to see, his face held a mixture of satisfaction and male pride. Hot sparks glittered in his eyes and his wide mouth turned up in an infectious smile.

"Can we do that again? I'll go back out into the hall and

knock, and you open the door and repeat the best welcome I've ever received." The husky amusement in his deep voice was an invitation to laugh with him.

Carrie did. Her humiliation vanished as if it had never been. "Greedy man!"

Laughing, she took his arm and led him to the leather recliner in the living room, the only chair big enough to hold his massive frame easily.

"Ahhh." He sank into the comfortable chair and lifted his feet to the footrest. Though he'd only been in the apartment once before it felt like coming home.

Belatedly Carrie noticed the jacket slung over his arm. She reached for it, intending to hang it up. Dean's gaze followed her movement. Suddenly he inhaled sharply. His hand shot out to grip her arm. Carrie froze, almost thrown off balance by his unexpected action.

"What's wrong?" Bewildered, she followed his gaze to her arm. The denim sleeve had pulled back to reveal the cuff of the yellow sweater. No stain or tear was visible to account for his incredulous stare.

"It was you," he whispered.

"What was me?" Carrie felt the hairs on the back of her neck begin to prickle.

Dean lifted his head to stare at her, his eyes full of wonder and something else she couldn't identify. Slowly, he levered his feet to the floor and stood, his gaze never leaving her face. His hand slid down her arm to thread his fingers with hers. Scarcely an inch separated their bodies. Carrie could feel his breath on her cheeks and smell the earthy masculine odor that was uniquely Dean.

"What?" Her lungs seemed unable to capture the air they needed.

"You don't even know what you did, do you?" Dean's voice

was filled with awe.

Mystified, Carrie shook her head. When he continued to stare at her without speaking, she reached up with her free hand and shook his shoulder.

"Dean Sheffield, if you don't tell me what you're talking about, right now, I'll … I'll put salt in your coffee!"

The silly threat broke the spell. Dean threw back his head and laughed, then growled something that sounded like 'beautiful angel' and hugged her hard against his solid chest.

"Dean," she gasped, "tell me!"

"Okay, okay. But I think you'd better sit down for this."

Before she could take a step he scooped her up in his arms and sat down on the couch, settling her comfortably on his lap. His smile faded as he looked intently into her eyes.

"I believe you saved my life today. And not for the first time. I don't understand how, but I think that, if not for you, I would be dead three times over."

Carrie's mouth dropped in astonishment. Of all the things he might have said, she had never anticipated this. She searched his face for signs of teasing but his expression was all sincerity. Then the implication of his words hit her like a blow on the head.

"Another accident!" Her eyes widened in horror. "But … but what do you mean, I saved you? I was here. I thought you were in Chicago. How could—?"

"I don't know how. And yes, I was in Chicago. But it was you. I know it sounds fantastic, but just listen."

Carrie listened without interrupting, her attention oscillating between his story and the hard strength of his thighs beneath her bottom. She listened while Dean told her of the car hurtling toward him and the arm—the yellow-cuffed denim-clad arm—that had caused the car to swerve away at the last possible moment; he told her of the unseen woman whose call had saved him when the rocky ledge disappeared beneath his feet; he told her of the woman in Toronto who had pulled him from the path of the bus, the woman no one saw.

The apartment was silent for long minutes when he finished speaking. Carrie thought of Greta's conviction that her grand-daughter was to be instrumental in saving Dean's life. Had she been right after all?

"Do you truly believe what you've just said?"

"Yes, sweetheart, I do. I know it flies in the face of common sense. But I believe you've saved my life three times. Not under-standing how doesn't change anything."

A slow smile spread over Carrie's face.

"I'm glad," she said simply. "So few people will accept things that can't be explained by science. They refuse to believe that some impossible things *are* possible. And," she drew a deep breath, "the fat lady hasn't sung yet."

"More impossibilities?" Avid curiosity filled Dean's intelli-gent eyes.

Carrie grinned, almost lightheaded with the certainty that he would take her story seriously.

"Let's say, an old legend reborn as recently as last week. But I'll make fresh coffee for us first. It's a rather long story."

As she measured the grounds into the filter, Carrie thought about Dean's story. Was it possible she had saved him, when she was miles away at the time and unaware of what was happening to him? Nothing like that had ever happened before. But then, she had been able to pinpoint Mary McGrath's exact location when the little girl was lost, miles from her family's camping grounds, in an area where Carrie herself had never been. And she had known the make and license number of the car used to transport a kidnapped new-born baby.

It seemed fate could be changed. Was it by accident or by design that she, Caroline Richards, was somehow an instrument, a conduit of information? Carrie didn't know. It wasn't important. It only mattered that she could help.

She was a quiet, private person, by nature as well as by necessity. She had learned to censor her tongue and to keep a distance from others, because a single unguarded remark would expose her at best to ridicule, at worst to persecution. If at times she envied Melinda her carefree, happy-go-lucky approach to life, the feeling was shallow and short-lived. Inner satisfaction was ample reward for her abilities.

The moment Dean stepped into the kitchen Carrie knew he was there. She glanced over her shoulder to find him staring at the table, a curiously closed expression on his face. The cords in his strong neck stood out rigidly as he turned his head to look at her with hooded eyes.

"Perhaps I'd better go."

Startled by the angry note in his voice, Carrie gaped at him, unable to understand the abrupt change in his manner. It was the first sign of temper she had seen in him. Tongue-tied, wondering what she had said or done, she heard the scratching of a key in the lock. At the sound Dean stiffened. Suddenly every line of his taut body appeared outraged and furious. Carrie stepped back. Where was the man who, for all his size, had seemed more civilized and gentle than any other man she'd met?

"Hi, Carrie. It's just me." Melinda's high-pitched voice sliced through the tension in the kitchen.

Dean blinked and raised his eyebrows questioningly.

"That's Melinda. We share the apartment."

Dean's gaze swung to the table and back to Carrie.

"Melinda's a stewardess. I always have a meal ready for her when she gets back from an overseas flight." Carrie eyed him carefully and wondered at the sheepish look slowly spreading over his face. All the tension left his body.

"Sorry," he muttered. Avoiding her eyes, he turned and left

the kitchen, leaving Carrie staring after him.

She moved forward and stopped in mid-step, realization flooding through her. It hadn't occurred to her that Dean might see the table set for two and assume she was expecting company. Presumably male company, or why would he be upset? A pleased smile lifted the corners of her mouth as she left the room to welcome Melinda home.

* * *

Dean set the last gnawed bone on the plate, wiped his fingers on his napkin and leaned back in his chair with a deep sigh of satisfaction. He couldn't remember when he'd enjoyed a meal more. He made a mental note to find a way to repay Melinda Cornwall for her generosity.

The pretty blonde woman, after a start of surprise at seeing him, had offered a cheery greeting when Carrie made introductions. For someone who measured no more than five feet on her tallest day, she proved to possess a reservoir of tact. Offering a few witty remarks about the need for a doctorate in psychology for those who had to deal with passengers in a storm-tossed airplane thousands of miles above an ocean, she declared herself too exhausted to eat a meal. Leaving her luggage where she had dropped it just inside the door, the tiny woman grabbed an apple and excused herself for the night.

Dean glanced at Carrie, wondering if she had noticed the speculative gleam in Melinda's cornflower blue eyes. Her slyly innocent suggestion that Dean share Carrie's meal was blatantly suggestive. He knew Carrie missed the mischievous wink her roommate had thrown over her shoulder at him as she headed for her room, her short, blunt cut hair swinging in time with her bouncing steps. Her alleged exhaustion certainly didn't show.

Now Dean watched, with masculine appreciation, Carrie's

neat, round bottom as she bent to retrieve coffee cream from the fridge. He still couldn't quite believe the bolt of jealousy that had stabbed him in the chest when he'd thought some other man was not only welcome at her table but had a key to her apartment. Not even finding his cousin in bed with his fiancé had elicited that emotion. Of course, he hadn't really loved Natalie at all. In fact, Justin had done him a favor. The thought of being married to the admitted beauty made him cringe.

So why had the green-eyed monster raised its unlovely nose tonight? No, it couldn't be. Four days' acquaintance was hardly time enough for love. As for the kiss in the gazebo.... Well, he was a man, after all, and Carrie was a very attractive woman. It meant no more than that. No, what he felt for Carrie Richards was curiosity and, of course, gratitude. His feelings of happiness and contentment were only to be expected in a man who had escaped death three times.

Reality returned with a painful jolt. The idea of one's own death had a way of clutching at a man's innards and squeezing with a steely fist. Although both were final, somehow death by murder seemed more terrible than death by accident. Surely Carrie's instinct went amiss upon occasion. He had no enemies.

But then, an enemy, a reasonably intelligent enemy, wouldn't be so foolish as to reveal his feelings. Not if he hoped to go unpunished for his crime. And murder disguised as accident would ensure his killer's safety from the law. Anger with the thought that his killer might go free to enjoy his life swept away the panic creeping into his gut.

Doing nothing would merely invite another attack, with no guarantee he would survive. The only way to prevent the killer from eventually succeeding was to discover who and why. Indulging his emotions would be counter-productive. With the single-minded obstinacy that had permitted him to successfully expand his grandfather and father's business empire, Dean ruthlessly tamped down his anger. Success in anything depended on a cool head and a clear plan. But first, he must hear what Carrie considered so important. She'd insisted the conversation wait until they'd eaten.

He helped her clear the table and do the dishes. Working together at the homey task seemed natural and comfortable. Dean enjoyed Carrie's amusing tales of the misadventures of her students, and reciprocated with similar stories of his and his cousins' mischief-making escapades as children loose in the large house and grounds.

"You must have driven your parents bonkers," Carrie teased, wishing she had known him then. It was hard to picture the mountain of a man who dwarfed her kitchen as a small boy.

"I expect so." Dean grinned complacently. "We got away with a lot of nonsense, thanks to Aggie's covering up for us. Not that she didn't give us what-for herself.

"I remember driving the riding mower over a grouping of newly-planted rose bushes. She made me pull up dandelions for a week. And Alanna once had to eat her supper cold for five days because she put spiders in Aggie's kettle of soup. She never told that Justin put her up to it."

"Did she pay Justin back for letting her take the rap alone?"

"You bet. She made him give her all his desserts the following week in return for her silence. I think Aggie suspected the truth though. The desserts that week were all Justin's favorites."

They were still laughing when they returned to the living room. Carrie curled her legs up under her on the sofa and watched from beneath her lashes as Dean eased his large frame into the recliner. He stretched out his long legs, making the material of his trousers pull tightly across his muscular thighs and flat stomach. When she realized she was staring, she looked away quickly and pretended to fluff the toss pillows her mother had embroidered so many years before.

Lord, he was beautiful. He had the physique of a natural athlete but not the ugly, over-inflated muscles of a body-worshiper. Every move he made rippled the muscles of his arms and chest and shouted of sensual power. She longed to tear the lightweight blue knit shirt over his head and press her palms to his massive chest. Her fingers itched to discover if the dark hairs curling over the neck of his shirt matted on his chest as thickly as she imagined.

His shirt! The breath caught in her throat as she realized she had seen him wearing it before. Before … in this very room….

Her chest tightened. It was time. Shivering with her life-long fear of exposure, she sent a silent entreaty to whomever might be listening. Please, please make him accept the truth, however implausible it sounded.

She clasped her hands tightly in her lap. Inhaling deeply, she fixed her gaze on his face. "Dean, I'm sure you're familiar with the concept of ghosts and spirits and apparitions. Have you ever heard of the legend of the doppelgänger?"

CHAPTER FIVE

"The dop— The *what*?"

"The doppelgänger. It's an old German word meaning double walker. It's a kind of apparition." She looked anxiously into his face but his expression showed only puzzled interest.

"You mean like a ghost?"

"Not exactly. A ghost is supposedly the spirit of someone dead. A doppelgänger is the spiritual duplicate of a person still living. Its appearance presages the imminent death of that person, a kind of warning or forecast of his or her approaching demise."

"Okay. What about this apparition?"

Dean's curious but detached expression told Carrie that he hadn't associated her explanation with his near-fatal accidents. She shrugged helplessly, dreading his reaction but knowing she had to spell it out.

"Dean, I…. Last week, before we met, I … saw your doppelgänger. Three times."

Dean heard the words, but for a moment they held no meaning for him. Then understanding dawned. Carrie saw his ghost? Only the pleading look in her eyes stopped the bellow of laughter that threatened to erupt. Intuition was one thing but this—this was crazy! It took a whole minute to bring himself under control.

He knew Carrie had sensed his reaction when her lips tightened and her face froze into an expressionless mask. His amusement disappeared. Hell, he hadn't meant to hurt her feelings!

"I'm sorry. I just—"

"It's all right, Dean." Carrie tried to smile. "I understand. Now you know why I insist that the police never identify me. But please, hear me out."

At his apologetic nod she drew a deep breath and described the three appearances of the doppelgänger. Dean listened without interrupting, his face somber but dubious. At the end of her recital, knowing he didn't believe her, she stared at him in despair. She had to convince him.

Then she remembered the last arrow in her quiver. She leaned forward, her eyes wide and desperate, and held up three fingers.

"Three appearances, three accidents. For the first, last Tuesday, in Chicago, you were wearing a charcoal suit, pale green shirt and a gray and green-striped tie. Earlier today, in Montreal, you were wearing a navy suit with a pale yellow shirt and a deeper yellow tie with some sort of pattern in navy. Thursday morning, at the cliff, you were wearing the shirt you're wearing now."

She sat back, her insides quaking with tension, and waited. Dean's unfocused gaze told her he was searching his memory. She watched as doubt turned to consternation and finally to something she couldn't name. For an instant he looked shaken. When he at last met her gaze his face was shuttered, civil, and distant.

"I owe you an apology. You are correct in every detail." A small smile pulled at the corners of his mouth but didn't make it to his eyes. "I hope you'll warn me if my … apparition makes another appearance. Who knows how long this run of accidents will go on. Forewarned is forearmed, as they say."

He drained the last of his coffee, set the mug carefully on the side table and started to rise from the chair, his movements stiff. Every line of his body screamed his desire to escape her presence.

"If I may use your phone to call a taxi? I want to see Dad before he settles for the night. Thanks again for dinner."

Carrie stared up at him. Couldn't he see that her description of the clothing he'd been wearing when the accidents happened proved the existence of his doppelgänger? How else could she have known?

She didn't know whether to laugh or cry. Dean believed she'd saved his life when they hadn't even met, yet he denied the far more logical conclusion that his near-fatal accidents were not accidents at all. Most rational, extremely wealthy people would have denied the former and accepted the latter—or at least chosen to keep an open mind about the possibility that real danger existed.

She wanted to scream her frustration. Her shoulders slumped with the painful realization that his rejection included the messenger as well as the message.

His defection mirrored the treatment she had received in high school when she begged Linda Ferguson not to use the vaulting horse in gym that day. Linda, the best vaulter in the class, merely laughed. But a moment later she lay crumpled on the floor. Her foot slipped on the springboard, flinging her headfirst into one of the uprights of the vaulting horse. The sight in her left eye never returned.

The story of Carrie's prediction soon spread. Only her friendship with Melinda survived. No one was cruel but all avoided her. The fact that she understood their discomfort in her presence didn't make their attitude any easier to bear. She'd been afraid of public scrutiny since that day. Let others seek their fifteen minutes of fame. Carrie preferred anonymity.

Dean's censure was a thousand times more devastating than that of the teenagers. In his eyes, she was a freak, a misfit, and no one he wanted to know. Carrie felt her heart splinter into jagged shards of ice.

The sound of his voice on the phone penetrated the desolation in her heart. She drew a harsh breath, suddenly impatient with herself. She had known from the beginning that he wouldn't be interested in a woman like her. But the danger was real and out there waiting for him. When the taxi arrived she would lose her last chance to convince him. She sprang up from the sofa and grabbed his arm as he hung up the receiver.

"Dean, you've got to listen to me! Someone is trying to kill you. I don't know who or why, but I swear to you that's the truth."

Dean looked into her desperate face and knew she believed what she was saying. But he just couldn't get his mind around the idea. It simply couldn't be true.

"How can you be sure that the death forecast by the appearance of the apparition isn't death by accident? Or even by some disease? Nothing indicates murder."

"I can't prove it, if that's what you mean, but I'm sure. Dean, your only protection is to figure out who's causing the accidents. Just because you don't know of a motive doesn't mean there isn't one."

Dean put his hands on her shoulders and shook his head. Her distress made him feel like a monster but he simply couldn't believe that someone hated him enough to want his death.

"I'd better get down to the entrance, the taxi should be here any minute." He pulled on his jacket and reached for the door to the hallway.

Carrie threw herself in front of the door and made one last attempt to break through his dangerously stubborn attitude. Denial could mean his death.

"Listen to me, Dean! Who would benefit by your death? Think about it. What is there to be gained if you're gone? And

John, too? Someone may have guessed how sick he is. I know he looks well but I'll bet his daily routine has changed. Someone may have noticed more than either of you think. Someone may have discovered he's making a new will. And what about your will, Dean? Think! You're both wealthy men. If you both die, who would gain?"

She held Dean's gaze for a moment but couldn't read his expression. Her shoulders drooped. Moving away from the door, she walked into the living room without looking back. A moment later she heard the door open, then close again. He was gone.

She walked to the glass doors and stepped out onto the small balcony. Hands curled tightly around the railing, she looked down at the roof of the taxi. A moment later a tall figure exited the building and climbed into the back of the cab. He didn't look up. She watched until the taxi pulled into the traffic and was lost to sight.

She was chilled to the bone by the cold night breeze when she finally re-entered the apartment. She had tried. And she had failed.

* * *

Carrie awoke to the smell of bacon and toast and the sound of off-key humming coming from the kitchen. She smiled. Unlike herself, Melinda always woke up in the best of spirits, a pint-sized bundle of energy eager to attack a new day. Not a morning person, Carrie needed at least a half-hour to gather herself for the coming day.

About to snuggle down in the covers again, the memory of the night before swept though her mind and flushed away all trace of drowsiness. She rolled to her back and stared at the ceiling. Despite her best efforts, Dean refused to believe in the danger. He had turned his back and walked away from her. Loneliness swelled inside her and warred with her fear for his safety.

Then anger blossomed. For an educated, intelligent man, knowledgeable in the ways of the world, his refusal to consider himself a possible victim was downright stupid. Even arrogant. Any wealthy man had to know there were those who envied him, those who wanted what he had. A sensible person took precautions to protect himself and his possessions.

Then her anger faded. She was being unfair. Under the circumstances, Dean's blindness was understandable. His thoughts were on his dying father. And the three attempts on his life did appear to be accidents. Especially since two of them occurred in other cities. Such accidental deaths happened every day.

Could she be wrong? She had been mistaken a few times before but never when the knowing was as strong and certain. Still, maybe—

No. The conviction lay solid and heavy in her mind. Someone was trying to kill Dean. And would try again. She was as certain of that as she was that sunlight, not moonlight, streamed through her windows.

She sat up and wrapped her arms around her knees. Warning him, sharing her deepest secret with him, had failed to convince him. There was nothing more she could do. Unless—maybe Greta, wonderfully wise Greta, could suggest a course of action.

Perceiving a candle in the darkness, Carrie scrambled out of bed. She quickly showered, brushed her teeth, and pulled on her comfortable old gown before she joined Melinda in the kitchen.

"Morning, sunshine. It's about time you got up. I've been going crazy waiting to hear all about that gorgeous hunk you were with last night. It's not nice to keep a secret like him from your roomy."

Melinda slapped a mug of coffee on the table in front of

Carrie and dropped into the opposite chair. At her place was a plate piled high with eggs and bacon and toast. Normally neither of them were much interested in breakfast. Then Carrie remembered that her friend had skipped dinner the night before to allow her roommate privacy. No wonder she was hungry.

The happy curiosity on Melinda's face faded when Carrie didn't respond to her teasing. After a careful scrutiny of Carrie's downcast expression Melinda sighed. The sight of the impressive man in their apartment had made her hope that her friend had finally found someone special. She was well aware of the emptiness of Carrie's personal life.

"Oh no, it didn't go well. Do you want to talk about it?" Disappointment and sympathy edged her gentle voice.

Carrie sipped at her coffee and thought about Melinda's offer to listen. She didn't feel up to relating all the details, but maybe it would make her feel better to confide in her friend. Melinda wouldn't doubt anything Carrie said.

"Someone is trying to kill Dean and he won't believe me. There have been three attempts on his life but he insists they were accidents. And of course, he thinks I'm some off-the-wall kook. I don't know what to do." She lifted her head and gazed beseechingly at her friend. "He's going to die, Melinda, unless I can find some way to convince him he's in real danger. How can I make him take me seriously?" Carrie's lower lip began to tremble as her voice cracked with pain.

Melinda gazed silently at her friend, not doubting for an instant that what she said was true. "You care for him a lot, don't you?" she asked softly.

"Yes. Yes, I do." Carrie shook her head in resignation. "But that doesn't matter. Even if his life wasn't in danger he wouldn't be interested in me. He's too pragmatic, too logical, too seeing-is-believing to want any kind of relationship with a … a schoolteacher who does psychic tricks on the side." Her tone was bitter. "He's too rich, too. I'm sure his wealth must have something to do with the murder attempts. No one could hate him for himself."

"You may be wrong about his feelings towards you. He looked pretty interested to me."

Carrie shook her head. "It's only curiosity. I'm probably the first psychic he's ever met. He's intrigued by that but he'll soon find something else—or some*one* else—to attract his attention."

Melinda didn't look convinced but she dropped the topic. She nibbled at her lower lip, then cast a wary eye at Carrie.

"You realize you as good as told him that a member of his family must be behind it all? That couldn't have gone over easily."

Carrie looked startled.

"Oh no. You're right. I asked him who would benefit from his death but I didn't think it through. He must have thought I was accusing some member of his family. I guess I was. No wonder he looked so angry. He'll never speak to me again."

The two women sat silently staring at their mugs. Melinda wracked her brain for a way to help her friend. She shivered at the mental picture of the large, virile man she'd met so briefly, lying cold and still on a table in the morgue. But she was more concerned for Carrie.

Her friend was a loner and lonely. Although everyone who met her liked her, Carrie kept herself at a distance. Her aloofness prevented most people from getting to know her. Carrie's psychic abilities had fashioned her into a quiet person, too serious for the fun-loving preferences of their contemporaries. Her retiring nature—and the secret of her unusual talent—kept her apart from others her age. Melinda often worried about her roommate's lonely life.

Now, for the first time, Carrie had met a man who seemed to be perfect for her. Melinda had noted with interest the way

Dean's gaze had followed her friend with a possessiveness that reminded her of her fiancé's attitude. A strong believer in love-conquers-all, Melinda concluded that keeping Dean Sheffield alive was definitely in her friend's best interest.

"Sheffield? Dean Sheffield? Of the Sheffield Men's Store chain?" she blurted suddenly. At Carrie's nod she drew a deep breath. "Wow! Wealthy is right! That family must have millions. The newspapers have mentioned that the chain is expanding into the States." She drummed her fingers on the table and did some furious thinking.

"There was an article on the family in Maclean's magazine last year. The chain actually belongs to John Sheffield, although Dean is responsible for much of the expansion in recent years. I suppose Dean will inherit most of it some day."

"The article said that John has a brother and a sister who share in the profits of the clothing chain and will presumably be left a tidy sum in John's will, even if Dean gets most of it. But Carrie, there's something wrong with that scenario. Say one of them badly needs money. Wouldn't it make more sense," she shuddered at her choice of words, "to murder the father rather than the son? They would inherit more if Dean was dead, but of course they would have to wait for the father to die. Still, killing John instead of Dean would give them money now, if not as much." She paused thoughtfully. "I wonder just what John's will says."

Carrie threw Melinda a look of respect and admiration. Her dissection of the situation was remarkably acute. "Hey, who said Melinda Cornwall is just a pretty face?"

"You mean, I'm on target?" Melinda's pleased smile stretched across her face.

"Almost. There are circumstances I'm not free to discuss but I can tell you that the relatives will inherit a great deal more if both father and son die in the near future. Millions of dollars more. Especially if Dean dies first. But I don't know what I can do to prevent it. Oh Melinda, I wish … I wish…." Carrie's face crumpled and tears stung behind her eyelids.

"No, you know you don't wish that, Carrie." Melinda, correctly guessing what Carrie was thinking, covered the distraught woman's hand with hers. "Your gift, power—I still never know what to call it—helps too many people to wish it gone. God knows it's a burden and I don't envy you, but remember the times your gift has prevented tragedies and saved lives. You're special exactly the way you are and I wouldn't change you for the world."

Carrie shook away the accolade and slumped in her chair.

"But Dean refuses to do anything to save himself. I've really failed this time."

Melinda straightened in her chair as her eyes began to sparkle.

"Pardon me for being crude, but it's too soon for graveside eulogies, right? Dean isn't dead yet. Don't look so appalled, sweetie. There's still one thing you can do."

"What's that?" Carrie felt her spirits lift as she noted Melinda's infectious grin.

"Elementary, my dear Ms. Holmes. If Dean won't save himself, why then, you'll just have to do it for him!"

A feeble smile twisted Carrie's lips. "And, my dear Ms. Watson, how would you suggest I go about doing that?"

"Simple." Melinda snapped her fingers with a flourish. "Investigate the family! Find out who needs money badly and can't wait. When you know the who and the why, Dean will have to listen. Someone in that family has trouble and you can bet the others don't know anything about it. So…. Carrie's the name and sleuthing's the game!"

The iron lump of fear in Carrie's chest softened as she chuckled at Melinda's dramatics. She gave herself a mental shake. Greta had once described her as persistent as a mosquito, as stubborn as a child and as relentless as the ocean tides. When she knew herself to be in the right she never gave in. Or gave up. Melinda was right. As long as Dean lived she had to try to save him. And if she failed, she vowed silently, she would uncover his murderer and make him pay.

Energy and determination straightened her spine. Color returned to her cheeks and her eyes began to sparkle. Melinda watched her with relief and satisfaction and felt a short-lived twinge of pity for the would-be murderer.

The two women put their heads together and began to lay out a course of action.

* * *

"I'll take care of this customer myself, Ron." Justin waved aside his disappointed employee and took Carrie's hand in his, flashing her his most charming smile.

"How wonderful to see you again, Carrie. Please tell me you're here to see me, and not to buy a gift for another man." He donned a tragic expression and placed one hand on his heart. "You wouldn't be so cruel."

Carrie laughed into the handsome face that was too close to hers and hoped he didn't guess at her satisfaction that he had dismissed the clerk to wait on her himself. Step one achieved.

"Actually, Justin, I need a birthday gift for a special man."

She smiled at the exaggerated chagrin on his face.

"At least, my friend says he's special. Since she's agreed to marry him, I guess he must be."

He gazed at her reproachfully and heaved an elaborate sigh of relief. He tucked her arm in his and together they examined the high quality merchandise. Carrie prolonged the search for a suitable gift as long as she could, then finally settled on a madras plaid sport shirt. To her relief, and to the salesclerk's obvious annoyance, Justin didn't leave her side. He brushed aside her half-hearted suggestions that he must have other work to do.

While she waited for the shirt to be boxed and wrapped, she made a show of glancing at her watch and deciding aloud that she would interrupt her shopping for a bite of lunch. With as innocent a tone as she could manage, she asked Justin if he could recommend a restaurant in the neighborhood.

To her delight, he claimed it was time for his lunch break and suggested he join her. She hesitated for what she hoped was an appropriate amount of time, then nodded a shy agreement. A few minutes later they left the store together. Step two achieved.

* * *

Unaware of the furious blue eyes watching her departure, Carrie waved good-bye to Justin and pulled away from the curb. She gloated to herself; her first foray into the world of detection had unearthed several possible motives for the attempts on Dean's life. Hints only, but substantial enough to suggest directions in which to search. And, best of all, she felt certain that Justin had no inkling of the information she'd gathered nor that her appearance in the store had been a deliberate attempt to seek him out.

He flirted shamelessly at first but gradually his manner changed as he realized that her friendliness extended to no more than that. Or maybe, as Dean would have said, he dropped the innuendoes since Natalie wasn't present to observe his lecher act. Whatever the reason, he stopped pushing and seemed to relax. A few subtle comments and questions on her part and he was soon talking about his family.

Carrie flattered him with her attention. In her experience,

few people really listened to others, their minds more occupied with the comments they wanted to make next. Not a chatterer, Carrie had learned to hear what people said. To hear and remember. Justin had told her more than he realized. Nothing concrete, but Carrie was adept at reading between the lines. Or rather, listening behind the words.

As she drove toward the nursing home, her thoughts switched to her grandmother. She knew Greta was bored and restless with her confinement, although she hadn't complained. She subscribed to a simple outlook on life; a person changed what she could and endured what she couldn't change. There was no room for whiners.

She knew Greta would sense she was up to something but that wasn't a problem. Carrie intended to tell her the plan she and Melinda had devised and ask for help, though she suspected asking wouldn't be necessary. Quick-witted as well as intuitive, Greta would realize that she was in the best position to garner information from Alanna. The pretty nurse visited with Greta as often as she could and, knowing Carrie had piqued her cousin's interest, would be curious herself. Greta was quite capable of controlling the conversation, gaining information even as she gave it.

Carrie could suggest lines of inquiry, thanks to Justin. For a moment she contemplated the image of Dean's handsome cousin. When he dropped his chauvinistic pose he seemed to be genuinely friendly. Or was his sincerity the act? If it weren't for the possibility that he might be contemplating murder, she could almost like him.

Shame washed over her as she thought of how she'd used him. She had never attempted anything so underhanded before and was embarrassed at the ease with which she exploited the man. But it was necessary, she reminded herself. Dean's life was at stake. She was prepared to do much more than manipulate a conversation to save him.

A few minutes later she parked the car in the lot beside the nursing home, locked it and headed briskly for the side entrance. Under her arm she clutched a copy of a recent romance novel and a box of German chocolates.

She slipped through the corridors, stopping briefly several times to chat with familiar faces, some harried with the press of work and others pale and dull with the tedium of inactivity forced on them by illness. The contrast between the sterile sameness everywhere in the nursing home and the diverse and lovely appointments of the Sheffield mansion emphasized the generosity of the mansion's owner. Determination that John's magnanimous intentions would be realized banished the lingering sense of meddling from Carrie's conscience.

A wry smile curved her lips as she thought of the phrase, I-did-it-for-your-own-good, a phrase so often resented by those on the receiving end. Well, Dean could resent from here to Australia. His disapproval at her snooping into his family's affairs was no match for her obstinacy. Greta could vouch for that!

Buoyed by her thoughts, Carrie gave a brief tap on Greta's door and entered, smiling, at her grandmother's invitation. She had no idea that her eyes were glistening with the light of battle and her posture was soldier-straight.

She kissed Greta's soft cheek and wasn't surprised at the invalid's first words.

"Start at the beginning, *liebchen*, and tell me what scheme you're cooking up." Greta pulled herself up higher against the pillows and grinned at Carrie's mock frown.

"I never could fool you, could I? Well, as it happens, I've become a temporary private eye and I want to deputize you as my assistant."

Greta's eyebrows rose, a sure sign of her interest.

As requested, Carrie launched into a detailed account of the situation. The small voice in her mind that protested the disclosure of the details of John Sheffield's will went unheeded. She knew Greta never gossiped. Whatever happened, Dean would never know she had betrayed his trust. Besides, it was necessary.

"That's it then. Dean refuses to believe he's in danger. So I have to prove it to him—at least show him that motives do exist and force him to take some elementary precautions." Carrie inhaled deeply and grimaced with frustration. "Men! They think they know it all. Are their egos so big they can't envision anyone wishing them harm?"

Greta patted Carrie's hand, her expression serious, though she smiled inwardly at Carrie's impatient complaint, a lament women had been voicing for centuries.

"Don't be too hard on him, *liebchen*. Think how disturbing it must be for him, to be told that a member of his own family is trying to kill him. And we both know how difficult it is for people to accept talents like yours. Give him time."

"Time is the problem." Carrie sighed, her face bleak. "There have been three attempts in one week. If the motive is about money, and I feel strongly that it is, then the murderer may be getting desperate. He could decide to risk a more direct means, rather than try to engineer another accident. He has to figure that Dean's too intelligent not to become suspicious sooner or later. And," she shivered convulsively, "it's not that difficult to obtain a gun these days."

"He's not dead yet, *liebchen*." Greta spoke briskly, unknowingly echoing Melinda. "What leads have you found so far?"

Rescued from her slide into despondency, as Greta intended, Carrie straightened her drooping shoulders and recounted the conversation with Justin over the lunch table. Holding out one hand, palm up, she ticked off her fingers as she summarized the possibilities.

"Justin may be living beyond his means, trying to keep Natalie happy. It seems she spends a fortune on clothes and is forever dashing off on little vacations. Without her husband.

"Natalie herself is the quintessential scorned woman. Maybe she hates Dean, even though *she* betrayed *him*. If Dean died, Justin would inherit a lot of money. She may think Dean owes her the rich living she would have had as Dean's wife. Or maybe she wants revenge because he discarded her. At any rate, she makes a logical suspect.

"Then there's Alanna." At Greta's gesture of protest, Carrie hurried to speak. "I know, I can't see it either. She seems to be a truly good, caring person. But she does have a possible motive. Remember what she told us about her fiancé? A penniless artist who has to take menial jobs to support himself. An inheritance could buy him showings of his art and pave his way into the society of wealthy people with money to spend on paintings.

"Then again," Carrie continued, "Tim could be acting on his own. Maybe his talent isn't as great as Alanna believes. If he knows that himself, he may see Alanna as the way out of poverty into the good life. And the more money Alanna has the better the life. A man who would use a woman like that might not balk at murder to get what he wants."

Greta nodded unhappily, loath to agree with Carrie's rationale, but she'd lived long enough to know that anything was possible—human nature being what it was.

The rattle of the tea cart put a halt to the conversation. They were discussing the movie Greta had watched the evening before when Alanna entered the room. Carrie noted that while her white uniform matched those of the other nurses in style, it was far superior in quality and obviously tailored to a perfect, and flattering, fit. Still, she couldn't fault the slender blonde for wanting to look her best.

"Hi, ladies. Fresh banana bread today. It's good, too. I

sneaked a piece when the head nurse wasn't watching." Alanna rolled the bed tray into place with the economical movements of long practice, and set two cups and two dessert plates on the tray. With a cheerful wink at Greta, she turned to Carrie with a teasing smile.

"One day when I have more time, Carrie, you must tell me your secret."

"My secret?" Carrie frowned in surprise.

"The secret of how you wound the men in my family around your little finger. Since you were out at the house the other day, all I've heard is 'Carrie this' and 'Carrie that.' My brother thinks you're beautiful, Uncle John keeps saying you'd make a lovely daughter-in-law and Dean glowers at them both. I think he wants to keep you to himself. Even Aggie says you're a—and I quote—a 'right fine lady.'"

Two bright spots of pink glowed on Carrie's face. "Well, ahhhh…."

Alanna laughed in delight. "Now I've embarrassed you." She threw a mischievous wink at Greta then grinned at the tongue-tied Carrie. "Too bad, I won't apologize. But I've got to finish serving the tea. See you later, Greta."

Carrie and Greta exchanged long, speculative glances when the pretty nurse had left the room. Then both shook their heads.

"I just can't picture—"

"Alanna wouldn't—"

"But how can we be sure?"

Nothing more was said until they had polished off the banana bread and tea. Greta sighed and leaned heavily into the pillows. "Alanna's curious about you. I'm certain she'll make time to visit with me. I'll try to get her talking about her family. I don't like it, but," she admitted, "I agree it's necessary."

Her eyes flashed fire for a moment. "When this is all over," she growled, "I'm going to tell that young man of yours a thing or two! He'll be groveling on his knees, begging you to forgive him for doubting you."

Dean groveling? Carrie couldn't imagine it.

"He's not my young man," she murmured. Then, noting the fatigue lining the older woman's face, she lowered the bed and pulled the shades down. After urging the willing woman to nap and promising to return the next day, Carrie whispered an affectionate good-bye and slipped out of the room.

Feeling drained but hopeful, Carrie pulled out of the parking lot and headed for home. To avoid thinking about Greta's description of Dean as her young man, she turned her thoughts to Melinda and her fiancé. Her friend had promised to ask Andy to use his resources as a rookie policeman to try to discover the sort of information about the Sheffield family that wasn't available in business magazines and the "Who's Who" type of publications. With vast databases and "unnamed sources" at his disposal, he might find an important clue.

Luckily, Andy was one of the few who knew of Carrie's periodic collaboration with the police force. The engaging young man didn't pretend to understand what happened in Carrie's head but he admired his fiancé's friend. As he once declared to Melinda, "I can't explain how electricity works either, but I believe in it anyway. Carrie will always have a fan in me."

Pushing her worries aside, Carrie told herself to be optimistic. Dean would be all right. All she needed was a little time.

* * *

Dean threw aside the reports he'd been attempting to study. It was no use, he couldn't keep his mind on them.

"Coincidences. Just coincidences." He jumped from his chair and began to pace back and forth in front of his desk. Coincidences happened every day in real life. Surely his accidents could be nothing else.

The woman was thirty cents short of a dollar, that's all. This psychic power she claimed to have must have rattled her brains. Her grandmother should have had more sense than to fill her mind with old legends. Now Carrie saw weird ghosts where none existed.

But how did she know what he was wearing the days of the accidents? She'd been in Ottawa in her classroom that week. Who could have told her? And why? None of it made any sense. Especially not the little voice in his head that insisted she had told the truth about her ghostly visitor.

He had to admit the ghost story answered those questions.

All right. Suppose he accepted the existence of the doppelgänger. That still left her outrageous claim that a member of his family was trying to kill him. Her words were offensive, slanderous. Anger choked him.

Who stood to gain by his death? she'd asked. He couldn't get the insulting question out of his mind. Sure, money was a frequent motive for murder. But no Sheffield lacked money. There was plenty to go around. And if, by some outside chance, some one member needed more, he or she had only to ask. Resorting to murder just didn't make sense.

He dropped into his chair and pounded a fist on the desk. The worst thing, the very worst thing, was the sense of disloyalty he felt towards his family. Why was he still even thinking about her allegations? But he knew why.

It wasn't so much what Carrie had said that stuck in his mind, but Carrie herself. His mind replayed the kiss in her kitchen. Her warm lips had felt like home. He wanted more, many more. Never had a woman's kiss shaken him so strongly. Never had sexual need erupted so swiftly. He wanted Carrie Richards in his arms, in his bed.

It wouldn't happen. He couldn't spend time with a woman

who believed his family included a would-be murderer. Not that she'd want to spend time with a man who doubted her words. No, he'd never make love to Carrie Richards.

"Damn!"

CHAPTER SIX

"I don't like it. There's something weird about the whole thing. I dunno … like somebody grabbed the wheel at the last sec—"

"Oh, shut up. You botched it, that's all. Though how, I don't know. You probably couldn't hit the side of a barn with a tank."

"I tell ya, I did everything right. He should be dead three times over. I still don't understand how—"

"Forget it. It's water under the bridge now. You messed up so maybe we ought to change the plan. Take a more direct approach."

Startled eyes lifted to meet a stone-cold face.

"What? You mean—? No. We can't do that. We agreed an accident was the best way. I ain't goin' back to prison. We just hafta try again. He can't be that lucky forever."

"He must be getting suspicious by now. He'll be watching his step."

"If we wait a couple weeks, he'll settle down 'n' get careless. Then we arrange another accident. We've waited a long time, another few weeks won't matter."

"Yeah, and what if the old man dies first? We'd have to kill Sonny soon after that or all that money will be in trust and untouchable. Two deaths in a month would be sure to bring in the police, even if the second one looked like an accident. No, we got to get Sonny first. Likely the old man will die from shock, a natural death. Nobody will think twice about the son's death."

The other hesitated. "The old man ain't gonna die anytime soon. Ya know I'm right. We give him a couple of weeks to relax-like, then we try again. No mistakes this time."

Silence. Finally, a nod of agreement. "Five days. That's all. We wait five days."

"Okay. Five days then. I better get outta here. I'll head out and keep watchin' him."

"Do you think he suspects he's being followed?"

"Hell, no. I've changed rentals three times. He's never even looked over his shoulder. Keep your ears open so you can warn me when he's gonna leave town again."

"I'll come by the motel if I hear anything new. Now, get going. Make sure no one's around before you leave. I'll wait here for another five minutes."

Nods were exchanged, then footsteps crossed to the door and hesitated briefly. A few minutes later the faint sound of a motor dwindled into the distance.

Behind, a voice muttered softly, "Five days. Then he's dead." Laughter filled the room. "And I'll have money to burn."

* * *

Carrie stepped into the floor-length, chocolate velvet skirt, then raised her arms to shimmy into the beige and burnt orange paisley silk over-blouse. She pulled on the matching, thigh-length velvet vest and quickly straightened the richly draped neck of the blouse. A wide, gleaming copper bracelet and matching earrings completed the outfit.

An alarmed glance at the clock told her there was no time to check her hair and make-up. Hissing in annoyance, she grabbed her coat and purse, checked to be sure she had her ticket and rushed from the apartment. If the traffic lights were kind she could just make it to the concert hall on time. It was the last concert of the season and the one she most wanted to attend.

Carrie hated to be late for anything. A part of her eagerly anticipated the Vivaldi and Chopin program but she couldn't fully rid herself of the anxiety that had her repeatedly changing her mind about attending. Her indecision accounted for her late departure. She told herself it was too soon for Andy to have gathered any news, and she would hear the next day anything Greta might have discovered after Carrie had left her a few hours earlier. She assured herself that if she stayed home by the phone she would miss the concert for nothing.

Luck and the traffic lights were with her. She slipped into her reserved seat in the first row of the lower mezzanine just minutes before the orchestra finished tuning up. The lights went down and soon the captivating music of Vivaldi's *Four Seasons* washed over her. Carrie gave herself up to enchantment.

Bemused by the music dancing in her head, Carrie blinked in surprise when the lights went up for intermission. She decided not to join the stream of people headed for the lobby. Instead, she stood to stretch her muscles then sat down again to watch the people milling about below. Contented and sated by the music, she began to indulge in one of her favorite activities, people-watching.

In restaurants, bus or train stations, wherever people congregated, she liked to amuse herself wondering what this one did for a living; what hobbies interested that one; what sort of home this one lived in; if that one could sing. It never occurred to her that loneliness prompted her musings.

Suddenly she gasped, her contentment shattered. She grasped the rail in front of her and stood, all her attention focused on the wide shoulders and inky black hair of a man slowly making his way up the crowded aisle. Was it Dean?

Carrie squinted and felt her heart beating heavily against her ribs. She leaned over the railing, unaware of the alarmed looks exchanged by the elderly couple beside her. Even from her fore-shortened angle of view, the man below stood head and shoulders above the others. When he lifted his head to gaze up at the balconies she recognized Dean's strong face. He looked puzzled, as if he sensed her scrutiny.

Carrie thrust herself back from the railing and sank into her seat, praying he hadn't seen her gawking at him like a schoolgirl. Flushed with the heat of emotion, she waved the program book-let in front of her face and jumped when a thin, wrinkled hand touched her arm.

"Are you all right, my dear?"

Carrie smiled weakly and assured the concerned woman beside her that she was fine. "I just saw someone I didn't expect to see." She inhaled deeply and gathered her poise around her like a protective shell. "Are you enjoying the concert?"

The elderly couple looked relieved and launched into a knowledgeable and enthusiastic discussion of the music. Carrie smiled and nodded and noticed, with a touch of envy, their clasped hands. What would it be like to spend your life with someone you loved?

Against her will, she found herself watching for Dean to reclaim his seat. There was no sign of him. When the lights flickered to warn of the resumption of the program she leaned back in her chair, wondering why he hadn't returned. Maybe he didn't care for Chopin. Maybe he'd met a friend in the lobby and decided to forego the remainder of the concert. Maybe the friend was a woman. Maybe—

Her gloomy conjectures scattered on the wind when a large hand settled on her shoulder. She squeaked in surprise and looked up. Squeezed between the back of her seat and the jean-clad knees of the young man seated behind her, Dean's linebacker frame bent over her. The pleasant smile on his face belied the angry glints in his dark eyes.

"Carrie, darling, what a surprise. Come and have a drink with me. I must hear what you've been doing with yourself lately." His deep voice purred with apparent pleasure but Carrie heard the steel beneath.

Gulping with sudden nervousness she noted the approving smiles of the elderly couple and the impatient movements of the people whose view Dean was blocking. Her refusal to join him would create an embarrassing scene. His tight-lipped smile told her he knew and didn't care. Because her private nature abhorred such attention, Carrie nodded and gathered her coat and purse to follow him.

The empty, dimly-lit lobby seemed like a huge, oppressive cavern. Carrie shivered, and stole a glance at Dean who kept a firm grip on her elbow.

"Where are we going?"

"Coffee," he answered grimly.

Neither spoke as he steered her into the lunch bar on the ground floor and led her to a table in the far corner. When the waitress brought two heavy white mugs of coffee and retreated, Dean's pleasant smile vanished. He clasped his hands around the mug and leaned across the table. His aggressive pose and granite face bewildered Carrie.

Frantically she tried to think why he should be so angry. It was true she had intimated that a member of his family wanted him dead. She could understand his outrage but a day had passed, time enough for his emotions to cool. Dean didn't strike her as the sort of man who nursed a grudge. As a hardheaded, seeing-is-believing personality, by now he should have either shrugged off her warning as nonsense or preferably, given her story serious thought. His present anger seemed excessive and out of character.

"Well, explain yourself. Why are you following me around?" Fury vibrated in his low voice.

"What?" Carrie's mouth dropped open in sheer astonishment.

"You were draped all over that railing watching me. If you've been following me that would explain how you know what clothing I'm wearing on any given day. Who put you up to this apparition business? And why?"

Carrie's face flamed as she realized he had seen her gaping at him in the concert hall. She barely heard his accusation.

"But … but I haven't been following you," she stammered.

"Then how did you know I'd be at the concert?" Dean's voice had softened, as if he suddenly perceived the absurdity of his charge or recognized her genuine confusion.

"I didn't know. How could I?" Carrie didn't know whether to be mortified or incensed.

"Then why were you there?"

"To hear the concert, of course. I have a season ticket." Carrie lifted her head in defiance. "Isn't that why you were there?"

A shamefaced look traveled slowly over Dean's face and his hunched shoulders relaxed.

"I've never seen you there before," he mumbled gruffly.

"Nor I you." Carrie knew she should be insulted but he looked so like a small boy caught in some juvenile foolishness that she had to swallow the bubble of laughter that rose to her throat. Her attempt to halt the upward curve of her lips wasn't so successful.

They stared at each other across the table. Then Dean rolled his eyes upward and clapped a hand over his mouth. They broke into laughter at the same moment, Dean shaking his head as if he couldn't believe what he'd said. He reached out and took her hand, turning it over to press a kiss into her palm.

"Lord, I'm sorry, Carrie. That wasn't what I meant to say to you. I didn't mean any of it. I don't even know where it came from. Will you forgive me?"

Carrie nodded, more aware of the burning sensation in her palm than of his words. She drew back her hand and picked up her mug, glancing at him through her lowered eyelids.

"But you owe me a Chopin concert," she teased, delighted to discover that he could laugh at himself.

"Absolutely."

"How about a small down payment right now? I'm starved. Do you think I could have a grilled cheese sandwich?"

Dean immediately signaled the waitress. Carrie noticed the alacrity with which the woman answered the summons. She smiled seductively at Dean as she took their orders. He didn't seem to notice.

They munched on the sandwiches, discussed Vivaldi's music, and debated the merits of various great composers. When their plates were removed and their cups refilled, silence fell between them.

Carrie stole a glance at Dean. His original anger had disappeared but his pleasant expression had faded also. She watched his face harden. What was bothering him now? She inhaled deeply.

"Dean, what did you mean to say to me?"

He stared at her, a curious light in his eyes. Then his lips tightened in decision.

"Natalie came crying on my shoulder this afternoon." He paused but Carrie's expression didn't change. "She claims you're trying to break up her marriage."

"What?" Carrie's eyes widened and her mouth dropped. "Why in the world—"

"She said you met Justin for lunch today. She wants to know how long the affair has been going on. She also told me to tell you that you wouldn't get away with it."

Dean watched her closely although he already knew from her obvious shock that Natalie's fears were groundless. Still, the woman had been vehement in claiming to have seen the two leave the restaurant together. Maybe Carrie's shock was due only to being discovered.

"We did have lunch together. But it was nothing like Natalie thinks." Carrie prayed desperately that Dean would believe her. "I was shopping for a gift for Andy." At his sudden frown she added quickly, "Andy Spencer, Melinda's fiancé. His birthday is next week."

The frown smoothed away.

"Anyway, I was ready to leave the store and Justin suggested he join me for lunch. I didn't see anything wrong with it. We weren't sneaking around. Dean, he's your cousin. I met him for the first time when you introduced us two days ago. I don't know why Natalie would think—"

Dean interrupted. "It's a … fragile marriage. Natalie…. For some reason she seems bent on driving Justin away, but at the same time, I think she's afraid she'll succeed in doing just that. It's a mess, I know. They seem to take every opportunity to make each other suffer. I don't understand either one of them."

Carrie thought that mutual guilt might be part of the reason but she caught back the words. It wasn't any of her business. Something else mattered a great deal more to her.

"Natalie needn't suffer on my account. Justin isn't interested in me and I'm not interested in him. Do you believe me, Dean?"

When Dean nodded she exhaled in relief, only then realizing she had been holding her breath. She couldn't bear it if Dean thought she was the kind of woman who would knowingly date a married man.

Neither spoke for a few minutes. It was a comfortable silence, the only sound the murmur of conversations at other tables and the crisp footsteps of the busy waitress. Carrie debated with herself. She was loath to spoil the relaxed mood but wanted desperately to know if Dean had given any consideration to her warnings about his safety. His continued obstinacy could well cost him his life, and she wasn't at all sure she herself could survive if he died.

Finally deciding that his life was more important than her pain if he again rejected her, she opened her mouth to speak. And froze.

More sudden than an unexpected blow to the head, a heavy cloud of darkness dropped over her, obscuring her vision and compressing her lungs into stone. She felt her eyes bulge as she gasped for air that wasn't there. Her surroundings disappeared, sight and sound vanished as if they had never existed. A part of her recognized the phenomenon, but fear coiled through her body at the unusual weight and density of the black cloud. She fought down the panic and waited for meaning to emerge.

* * *

"Carrie! Carrie! My God, what's wrong? Speak to me! Carrie!"

A jolt of pure panic rattled through Dean's body at the sight of her suddenly ashen face and white-knuckled fists. He ignored the toppled mug and spreading puddle of coffee. His chair hit the tiled floor with a crash as he leaped up and circled the table to grab her shoulders and shake them roughly. She seemed unaware of her head bobbing loosely from the force of his assault. Her blank eyes and slack mouth drove a dagger into his heart. Chaotic thoughts of heart attacks, strokes, epileptic seizures filled him with a sense of dread and loss that Dean had experienced only twice before—when his mother died and when his father informed him of his rapidly deteriorating heart.

Dean was about to holler for someone to call an ambulance when Carrie blinked rapidly and the color returned to her face. She looked up wonderingly into fear-filled eyes and felt her heart leap. Then the crowd of avidly curious faces surrounding the table brought her to awareness of her surroundings. For just a moment, she recoiled in mortification. How she hated making a public spectacle of herself.

Impatiently, she thrust away her embarrassment and clutched Dean's lapels.

"Dean, we have to go. Right away." She struggled to stand but Dean's grip on her shoulders didn't ease.

"Do you need a doctor, Carrie?"

"No! I'm fine. Please, let's go!"

He didn't budge. His worried eyes stared into hers. His concern outweighed his desire to demand she explain what happened.

"Dean, please! We—You have to go home, right now!" Desperation quavered in her voice. "It's your father. He needs you. *Now*, Dean," she sobbed in frustration. "You fool! I tell you your father is … is…."

Her feverish eyes and pleading expression finally registered. This foolishness was no act. Carrie really believed something was happening to his father. Dean released her shoulders, dropped some bills on the table and helped her to her feet. Gripping her elbow he rushed her to the door, stopping only momentarily to snatch their coats from the rack. "Where's your car?"

"In the basement, the first level."

"We'll take yours then. It's closer than mine."

Carrie nodded and dug in her purse for her keys as he hurried her into the building's elevator. When they reached her floor she ran ahead to unlock the car. Seconds later, Dean at the wheel, they careened down the ramp and headed for his home.

Carrie closed her eyes and sank against her seat, finally surrendering to the debilitating exhaustion that always followed such episodes. *Oh, let him be in time. Please let him be in time.*

CHAPTER SEVEN

Carrie stood in the study doorway, tears pouring down her cheeks. Forever etched in her memory would be the sight of Dean sitting on the floor, his father cradled in his arms, his body shaking with silent sobs. The circle of light from the desk lamp haloed the two men on the carpet.

John's tortured breathing and halting, strangled words told her his end was near. Then his eyes fluttered closed. A final, croaked "...love ... you" and a long exhalation marked his passing. Dean moaned aloud and buried his face in John's neck. His arms tightened around his father's body as he began to rock with the agony of loss.

Carrie knew she should leave and grant them privacy, but her feet wouldn't obey. She moved to Dean's side with unsteady steps. She fell to her knees behind him and leaned against his back, wrapping her arms tightly around him, trying to comfort him with her warmth. Long minutes passed, the silence broken only by their soft sobs.

A high-pitched shriek followed by the clatter of a heavy tray and the crash of shattering china startled them. She turned her head toward the door and saw a shaken Aggie, hands covering her mouth and her eyes wide with shock. Carrie tightened her arms around Dean for a moment, then rose awkwardly to her feet and approached the trembling woman.

"Come, Aggie. We have to call the doctor. I need your help." She grasped the woman's shoulder and turned her away from the door. "Do you know his name and number?"

Aggie drew a deep breath, then nodded and hurried away, the task helping her to control her emotions. Carrie knew the sound of breaking dishes would bring other members of the household. Wanting to leave Dean undisturbed for as long as possible, she shoved the mess of crockery away with her foot and started to close the door.

She paused at the sight of three broken cups among the debris. Why three? Dismissing the question, she glanced back at Dean. She found him staring after her with grief-stricken eyes.

"I'll try to keep everyone out until the doctor arrives," she whispered softly.

At his nod, she impulsively slipped back to his side and pressed a kiss on his cheek. Then she left and took up a defensive stance in front of the closed door.

* * *

By the time she reached home—shortly after midnight— and crawled into bed, Carrie's body was shaking with exhaustion and the weight of her compassion for Dean. She expected to fall asleep immediately but her mind seethed with questions. At half past three she finally abandoned her bed.

A giant mug of hot chocolate in hand, she curled up on the sofa, the living room illuminated by the soft flood of moonlight through the balcony doors. Step by step, keeping in mind her belief that a would-be murderer numbered among them, she reviewed the Sheffields' reactions to the tragedy.

Natalie, with Justin trailing at her heels, had descended the wide stairway, exasperation pinching her face. Justin almost tripped over her when she reached the bottom step and stopped short at the sight of Carrie standing guard at the door. Natalie stiffened. Catching sight of Carrie, Justin winced, shook his head and raised his eyes to the ceiling. Clearly he had already suffered his wife's wrath for taking Carrie to lunch.

Natalie strode toward Carrie, who wished for a suit of armor. Luckily, Aggie returned at that moment. Her tearful announcement that the doctor was on the way defused the situation. Justin shouldered his wife aside and demanded to know what had happened.

Aggie's wail, "It's Mr. John," shocked them both into immobility. Then Justin reached for the door. Carrie stepped in front of him.

"No. Dean is with him. Let him say good-bye to his father in private."

It took a moment for her meaning to reach him. His shoulders slumped and he backed away. He stared at the door then took his wife's arm and led her into another room. Natalie seemed equally stunned but as they walked away, Carrie saw her arm go around her husband's waist.

John's brother David didn't appear. According to Aggie he was working late. Alanna was out with her new fiancé and Aggie had no idea how to reach her. Carrie held the sobbing cook in her arms as they waited in the hall for the doctor.

Moments after the physician arrived and rushed into the study, a tall, wasted-looking man wearing a plaid robe over mismatched pajamas shuffled into the hall. Rumpled gray hair stuck out around his fine patrician face. His expression brightened when he caught sight of Aggie.

"Hello, uh, do you know where John is? I can't find him anywhere."

Before Aggie could answer he turned his back to her and seemed to forget her presence. He looked at Carrie, an uncertain smile on his face.

"Ah, hello. How … how are your children today?"

The man had to be John's friend, Richard Harrington. Carrie realized he had forgotten Aggie's name and wasn't sure if he should know Carrie. She pulled the study door closed and smiled brightly at the middle-aged man.

"My children are fine, Richard. Thank you for asking."

Relief flooded his face. His brilliant smile captured for a moment the good looks he once enjoyed. Aggie rubbed her sleeve across her wet cheeks and took Richard's arm.

"I'll help you look for him, Mr. Richard. Maybe he's in the kitchen. I think there's some apple pie left over from dinner. Would you like another piece?"

He turned eagerly to accompany the cook. Aggie threw a grateful glance over her shoulder. Carrie realized the woman had put aside her own sorrow to save Richard the sight of John's body. When the pair disappeared around a corner, Carrie wondered what she should do.

She longed to stay to comfort Dean but his family was here and he didn't need her. She didn't belong here. Hoping Dean had left the keys to her car in the ignition, she headed for the front door. It opened in her face and Beverley Sheffield sailed through, a determined look on her face. She stopped abruptly.

"You again! Is that your car blocking the drive? Move it immediately. Where is my brother? I must speak to him right away."

Her heart in her shoes, Carrie tried to intercept the offensive woman. Though she couldn't help her dislike of Dean's aunt she didn't want the woman to barge into the study and trip over her brother's body.

"Miss Sheffield, if you could wait a minute, please. The doctor and Dean are with your brother—"

"What? Get out of my way, young woman. How dare you try to stop—"

To Carrie's intense relief, Justin appeared at his aunt's side and took her arm. "Aunt Bev. Wait. I need to speak to you. Come in here, please."

He led her, protesting loudly, into the room where he had gone with Natalie. Carrie heard his voice though she couldn't make out the words. When Beverley Sheffield screamed, "No! No! Not now!" Carrie shuddered and quickly slipped outside. An ambulance pulled up to the door as she descended the steps. She stood aside as two white-coated men carried a stretcher into the house.

Fortunately, her keys were in the ignition. Just as she turned on the headlights, the gardener came around the side of the house. He stopped abruptly when he saw the ambulance. Carrie was surprised until she remembered that he lived with his mother in a small cottage on the grounds. The blazing lights of the mansion must have attracted his attention.

As she pulled away, she noticed the shock on his face. Well, the sight of an ambulance would do that. She felt shell-shocked herself. How could a person feel numb and, at the same time, be in pain? Weary down to her bones, she had driven home in a daze.

Carrie set the empty cup on the end table and massaged her aching temples. David Sheffield and Alanna's artist were still strangers to her, but John's death seemed to genuinely shock and distress the other members of the family.

Of course it would, if none of them had known about his condition, as Dean claimed. Or was one of them shocked because John rather than Dean had died? Would that matter to the person who wanted Dean dead? She sensed vaguely that the question was important but her tired mind couldn't conceive an answer.

Forcing herself to move, Carrie left the mug in the living room and stumbled back to bed. Just before oblivion claimed her, two questions circled in her mind.

Why had there been three cups on the tray? The appearance of John's desk seemed to indicate that he had been busy with paperwork, much of which had fallen with him to the floor. There was no indication that anyone else had been present.

And what had Beverley wanted to speak so urgently about with her brother?

* * *

Carrie shivered in the fresh spring breeze and pulled the black mohair shawl tighter around her shoulders. She had known a shawl wouldn't be warm enough but she hadn't been able to bring herself to wear a red coat to the burial. The sun had retreated behind dark, pregnant clouds. From the outer edge of the large circle of mourners, she could see the funeral home employees discreetly slipping among the crowd distributing large black umbrellas.

The day before, she had made a brief visit to pay her respects at the funeral home. Many small groups of people stood around, talking quietly. She avoided approaching the family, reasoning that they would be more concerned with friends of long standing. They wouldn't want to bother with someone they'd met only a few days earlier.

Beverley Sheffield looked terrible in an ill-fitting black dress. The dark circles under her eyes indicated sleepless nights. Carrie wondered what it was Dean's aunt had intended to tell John. *Not now*, she had cried. A strange thing to say, under the circumstances. How dreadful for the woman to know she would never be able to confide in her brother again.

Knowing her concern wouldn't be appreciated, Carrie had signed the visitor's book and left.

Now, in the chilly graveyard, she looked for Dean but didn't see him. Perhaps it was just as well. The sight of her might grieve him further, considering everything she'd told him. She hoped he had noticed her signature in the visitors' book at the funeral home.

She couldn't help being disappointed though. There had been no word from him since she'd left him in the study with his father. Of course, he must have been very busy since then. She knew instinctively that all the details of the funeral arrangements would fall to him. He had the strength to shelve his own feelings in order to do what had to be done.

She reminded herself that he might never get in touch with her again. After all, he wouldn't accept her warnings, and experience had taught her that even believers were uncomfortable in her presence. Worse than that, she had sent him home to watch his father die. He might hate her for that. She couldn't blame him if he never wanted to see her again.

Her longing to be with him was sheer foolishness, as were her feelings of loss. How can you lose something—or someone—you never had? He had his uncle and cousins and Aggie. He didn't need her. No, he didn't need Carrie Richards. That truth scraped her heart raw.

She peered past the heads of the mourners until she located him, almost directly opposite, on the other side of the grave. Her heart contracted at the lines of suffering and fatigue newly etched in his face. He seemed to stand alone, despite the family and friends gathered beside him. His face twisted with agony as the coffin slowly descended into the grave. Carrie felt a matching pain in her chest.

He didn't lift his head while the minister delivered a brief prayer. When the mourners murmured a group "Amen," Carrie turned and hurried toward her car. Just as she opened the door, a hand fell on her shoulder. Her heart lurched painfully then she stilled, knowing who it was.

"Carrie."

Tears shimmering in her eyes she turned, one hand lifting to cover his. "I'm so very sorry, Dean. I just wish…. I'm sorry."

"Thank you. Carrie, please come back to the house. I've missed you. And I need to talk to you." His broad torso bent toward her, blocking out everything else.

"The house? But your family won't want—"

"*I* want. Please say you'll come."

Carrie looked up into his pleading eyes. He really did want her to go. How could she refuse him?

"Yes, I'll come." She heard the huskiness in her whisper.

He squeezed her shoulder and straightened, a ghost of a smile on his lips.

"Good. The others are waiting for me. I'll see you at the house." Turning, he strode quickly to the limousine heading the waiting line of cars.

Carrie gazed after him then climbed into her car and waited to fall in at the end of the line. Dean's phrase echoed softly in her mind. "*I've missed you.*"

Despite Dean's personal invitation to attend the wake, Carrie felt like an intruder. After all, she had met the deceased only once. She drifted slowly about the huge drawing room and waited for Dean to approach her. A constantly changing circle of people barricaded him in a far corner of the room. She knew it would be some time before he would be able to disengage himself from the condolence-wishers.

Several matrons, eyes alight with curiosity, cornered her at the buffet table and introduced themselves. As the only unknown mourner present, she found herself the object of their polite but insistent questioning.

"Oh, you say Dean invited you? You're not an old family friend then?"

Carrie explained about her grandmother and her subsequent

acquaintance with Alanna. When she admitted she'd met John just a few days earlier, the women lost interest and moved away. One discontented looking woman lingered, the only one who seemed to notice that, during her highly complimentary comments about the nurse, Carrie had not mentioned how she had met Dean, nor why he would have invited her to his home on this occasion.

"I'm Adele Chambers. I expect you've met my daughter Natalie, Miss—it is Miss, isn't it?—Richards. She was once engaged to Dean, you know. Frankly, I believe he still cares a great deal for her. Perhaps it's as well you are aware of that."

Astounded at the matron's nerve, Carrie was at a loss for a reply. Her daughter was married to another man, yet the woman had the effrontery to warn Carrie off, the implication being that Dean was still taken. Perhaps Adele Chambers was as conscious as Natalie that Dean was the richer catch of the two cousins.

Carrie looked at the woman's barely concealed smirk and felt her temper rise.

"Why yes, Mrs. Chambers, I have met your daughter. She's a beautiful woman. And I'm sure, intelligent enough to know this country's legal system generally allows only one husband per woman, at least only one at a time. I believe Natalie made her choice some time ago. I can't picture Dean standing in line to be second, can you? Now, if you'll excuse me…."

Carrie noted with a surge of guilty satisfaction the woman's outraged gasp and purple-splotched face. Pivoting on her heel she walked squarely into Dean's chest. She clutched the lapels of his suit to keep her balance and groaned inwardly. Had he heard her sarcastic reply to the mother of his ex-fiancé?

She looked up, expecting to see condemnation, perhaps even anger in his eyes. Instead, they held a look of amusement. His sensuous mouth turned up at the corners as he turned his back on the stiff-spined matron and took her hand. As they walked away he leaned down to whisper in her ear.

"My thanks for defending me. That woman has needed a set-down for a long time. Can you imagine having her for a mother-in-law?"

They both glanced back. The woman still stared after them. Deliberately Dean brushed his knuckles over Carrie's cheek and watched with pleasure as Natalie's mother snorted and looked away.

"That wasn't very nice of me, was it? But I enjoyed it immensely. Mrs. Chambers has never forgiven me for refusing to marry Natalie."

"But I bet she'd welcome you back with open arms if—I mean…." Carrie bit her tongue and mentally cringed at the direction her words had taken. Dean would think she was questioning him about his feelings for his cousin's wife.

She needn't have worried. Dean threw her a speculative glance and chuckled in a low voice. "I'm sure she would. For some people, a great deal of money will buy forgiveness for just about anything. I've heard Mrs. Chambers' main interest in life is shopping. Like mother, like daughter. Whoever said 'It's as easy to love a rich man as a poor one' was probably quoting Adele Chambers."

Carrie tsked at the cynical comment but couldn't help smiling. Whatever hopes Natalie and her mother might cherish for eventually ensnaring Dean, they clearly were off the mark. The depth of her relief shocked Carrie. Had she been jealous of Natalie? She shook her head to dislodge the unpleasant thought.

When a warm, muscular arm slid around her waist she jerked in surprise. Looking up she saw Dean staring intently at her, his lips slightly pursed.

"What ideas are running through that intriguing mind of yours now? You appear to be pondering some deep philosophical deliberations."

"Nothing so intellectual, I promise. Dean, I feel quite ... out of place here. I really should go—"

His grip tightened on her waist. "No, please, stay a little longer. It will be over soon. People are already starting to leave. I have something serious to discuss with you as soon as we're alone. Besides, you haven't met my Uncle David yet. And Alanna's artist friend is here too. And my father's lawyer. I think you should meet them all."

Dean met her startled gaze with an expression both earnest and determined.

"Why?"

He hesitated, his lips compressing into a thin line. Then he shrugged slightly. "Can we discuss my reasons later?"

Carrie searched his face and saw that he really wanted her to stay. It didn't really matter why, she couldn't refuse him. "Of course."

Smiling his thanks, Dean led her to the lone figure by the fireplace. Carrie knew immediately that the jowly, thick-bodied man was John's brother. He had the family look, but unlike the other Sheffield males, his face was disfigured by patches of broken capillaries and heavy pouches under his eyes, the lingering signs of his bout with alcoholism. He was quite sober. Carrie couldn't help but admire the man for not reverting to drink under the stress of his brother's death.

He straightened as they approached and took Carrie's hands before Dean could speak.

"You must be Carrie." He beamed at her. "I'm pleased to meet you, though I wish it were under other circumstances. John told me about you and I can see he didn't exaggerate. He always could recognize a good woman."

Carrie thanked him and offered her sympathy. "I would like to have known your brother longer. Some day, maybe you would share some of your memories of him with me."

Some of the sadness left his face as his eyes warmed. He glanced at Dean then back to Carrie.

"I would like that," he said simply. "You have Dean bring you back any time." With a grateful squeeze of her hands, he excused himself and joined a small group by the picture window.

Dean cupped his hand on Carrie's cheek and stroked her skin gently with his thumb.

"Thank you. That was very kind and the perfect thing to say. Uncle David is taking this very hard. John stood by him when his wife left him. He wouldn't allow David's drinking to come between them either. Now David has lost his brother. It will help for him to be able to reminisce about their boyhood and younger years."

Fighting not to press her face into his hand, Carrie nodded. "I was always pestering Greta to tell me about my parents. My own memories are so few, since I was so young when they died. Her stories made me feel closer to them and eased the pain."

She placed a tentative hand on his chest and looked into his face, unaware that unshed tears gave a golden sheen to her coffee-colored eyes. "It does get easier, Dean," she whispered. "You can't believe that now, but I promise you it does."

Their eyes locked. The room around them seemed to disappear, the murmur of voices to fade. Dean's hand tightened on her cheek and his face began to descend. Carrie sucked in a shaky breath, suddenly sure that he meant to kiss her.

A precise, slightly pompous voice shattered the moment. Dean stiffened and dropped his hand.

"There you are, Dean. I think we should discuss this further. Everyone's here right now. It's the perfect opportunity. Just let me—"

"No, Lawrence." Barely controlled impatience underlined Dean's growl. "As I said earlier, I will let you know when and where. There's no reason not to wait a few days. Give people a chance to recover." He put his hand on the small of Carrie's back. "In the meantime, may I introduce Carrie Richards, a friend of mine. Carrie, this is Lawrence Chambers, my father's lawyer."

Dean's aggressive demeanor changed to that of a perfect host. The lawyer was not as successful in hiding his irritation. Carrie did her best to ignore the unsettled atmosphere.

"Chambers? You must be Natalie's father. Your daughter is a very beautiful woman."

The lawyer relaxed fractionally and looked at Carrie for the first time. The three chatted politely for a few minutes but Carrie was glad when Alanna approached with a tall, bearded young man in tow. The lawyer gave the artist a disdainful glance and moved away.

When Alanna introduced her fiancé, he ignored Carrie's outstretched hand and, head cocked to one side, traced a long slender finger down the line of her jaw. Startled by the unexpected gesture, Carrie stepped back. Beside her, Dean tensed and shifted position. Tim blinked and offered an apologetic smile.

"Sorry. I couldn't resist. Would you consider sitting for me, Miss Richards?" He didn't wait for an answer but continued speaking, more to himself than to the others. "Watercolors, I think, to suit your delicate features. Perhaps brocade drapery behind your head? Yes, I think so."

He turned to Dean, pointing with his shoulder to the floor-to-ceiling drapes at the end of the room. "How about it, Dean? Would you let me borrow a panel from that window for awhile?" His open, earnest face gave no sign that his request might in any way be unusual.

"It's up to Carrie, Tim." He moved closer and placed his hand on her shoulder. "As for the drape, it's yours, on one condition. If Carrie's agreeable, then I insist you do the painting on commission. You don't give it away or sell it to anyone but me. Agreed?"

"Agreed. I could sure use the money. What do you say, Carrie?"

Carrie nodded, unable to speak. Her thoughts whirled in confusion. Did Dean really want a painting of her? Or, and she thought it more likely, had he simply seen a way to give the impecunious artist a monetary boost? She knew Dean thought highly of his lovely cousin and maybe he, like herself, was impressed by Tim's laid-back attitude toward the Sheffield riches. The young artist seemed neither embarrassed by his own poverty nor particularly conscious of Alanna's vastly different financial situation. Could anyone truly be that oblivious?

In any case, Carrie couldn't help but wonder where the painting would eventually find a resting place. In the attic, most likely. It was a depressing thought.

By the time the two couples parted, the room had emptied. Empty glasses were abandoned everywhere, the buffet table messy with leftovers. Dean looked around and sighed deeply. Then he pulled himself erect. The sadness in his face lessened as a look of determination tightened his features.

"Would you mind waiting for a moment, Carrie? I need to check something with Aggie, then we'll go somewhere to talk."

Carrie nodded and drifted to the large window as he left the room. She stared out at the manicured stretch of lawn and reflected that death was no less painful for the occupants of a mansion than it was for those who lived in tiny hovels. Agony over the loss of a loved one had nothing to do with bank balances.

About to turn away from the window, she caught sight of a figure at the far side of the lawn, near the edge of the woods that surrounded the estate. For some reason she gained the impression that the figure, a man, had been watching the departing guests.

Her puzzlement disappeared when he picked up a pair of garden shears and walked away, shaking his head. It must be the gardener, Bill Hummell.

She stepped back from the window and looked around for her shawl. She was about to shake it out when a long arm reached past her and took it from her grasp. When Dean draped it over her shoulders Carrie felt the warmth of his breath brush the nape of her neck and his unique scent of soap and man tease her senses. For just a moment she longed to melt against him.

Instead, she forced herself to turn and step away from him. Her feelings were of no consequence and highly inappropriate in light of the situation. The man had just buried his father and she was more aware of her own physical longings than of his grief. Impatient with her selfishness, she pushed aside her yearnings.

"Are you all right, Dean? We can talk another time if you prefer to stay—"

"No!" he barked, then grimaced in apology and lowered his tone. "Sorry. I didn't mean to snap. It's just that I've got to get out of this house for awhile. I know it's crass of me but I can't stand either giving or receiving any more sympathy just now. The others are hurting too, and they seem to expect me to make them feel better. I can't do it any more today."

Carrie wasn't surprised that the others were leaning on Dean. With his strength and new responsibilities as head of the Sheffield chain, they would naturally look to him as their leader and problem-solver. Emotionally as well as economically, Dean was now the family director. Carrie wished with all her heart she could somehow ease the burden that was his to carry from now on.

"Anyway, aside from all that, we have things to talk about," he continued. "In private. How about a coffee shop somewhere?"

"Why not my apartment? Melinda is working the overseas flight, so we won't be interrupted. You can take off your shoes and relax."

"Perfect. To be honest, I'd hoped you'd suggest your place. I can't think of anywhere else I'd rather be right now." He took her arm. "Let's go before someone else corners me."

They didn't speak on the drive. Dean stretched out in the passenger's seat and laid his head back, his eyes closed. Some of the strain in his face smoothed away.

As she drove Carrie repeated his declaration to herself. "*I can't think of anywhere else I'd rather be right now.*" Of course, she knew he only meant somewhere quiet and private, but she allowed herself a tiny surge of delight that he had thought of her home. There were other places he might have suggested.

Traffic was reasonably light and afforded her numerous opportunities to steal glances at the breadth of his linebacker torso, the strong lines of his head and neck, and the half-moon of dark lashes hiding his intelligent eyes. Her fingers twitched on the steering wheel, longing to explore, Braille-like, the sculpted lines of his cheekbones and the thick texture of his rumpled hair.

When his hand suddenly landed on her upper leg she started and barely managed not to swerve into the other lane. She darted a glance at Dean, but his eyes were still closed, his face expressionless. He seemed to be dozing. Loath to wake him, she left his hand where it was, but felt its heat radiate through her entire body, stirring uncomfortable sensations low in her stomach. When they finally reached her underground parking spot she didn't know if she was relieved or disappointed.

* * *

Carrie sipped at her coffee and waited for Dean to speak. When she had discovered he had eaten nothing at the wake, she insisted on making him a western sandwich and was gratified when he wolfed it down. Now she cuddled in her mother's turquoise velvet chair, content to see this bear of a man at ease on her sofa. His long legs sprawled out over the carpet, the impeccably tailored trousers taut over his muscular thighs. He'd removed his shoes with a heartfelt sigh of relief.

She watched his feet, fascinated by the continuous stroking of each foot by the other. The physical mannerism seemed both amusing and sensuous. She just stopped herself from challenging him to try to hold them still for five minutes at a time. Her face must have revealed the frivolous thought because he suddenly raised his feet a few inches from the floor and chuckled.

"I know, I know. I can't help it. But did you know that you wrinkle your nose whenever you're trying not to smile?" At her look of surprise, he grinned, and for the first time in days felt his spirits lift. He gazed with appreciation at the gentle face that had become so dear to him.

"I suspect you're the best thing that's ever happened to me, Carrie. I owe you a great deal, not the least of which is my life. I especially want to thank you for sending me home the other night."

"You don't owe me anything, Dean. I was afraid you might be angry that you had to … witness John's death. That must have been terrible for you."

Dean sat up straight, shaking his head in disagreement. "No, no, sweetheart. You did both of us a great favor. If you hadn't sensed something wrong I wouldn't have had the chance to say good-bye and Dad would have died all alone. What you did was wonderful."

When she realized he meant every word, Carrie sighed with

relief. The thought that he might resent her warning had been tearing her insides to pieces. She blinked back tears of happiness and changed the subject.

"What did you want to talk about?"

He rubbed the nape of his neck, clearly reluctant to begin. Then he leaned forward, his elbows on his knees, his hands clasped together tightly.

"I've been thinking over everything you've said. Even leaving aside this … this apparition business, I have to concede that dismissing my three near-accidents as merely coincidental is pure, pig-headed conceit. In light of the moneys involved, how can I say the Sheffields are exempt from the human emotion of greed? Common sense says it's at least *possible* one of them might be willing to kill for millions. I'd hate for my tombstone to say 'He died of blind stupidity.' So I've decided to be sensible and take steps to protect myself."

Carrie felt light-headed with relief. "What will you do?"

"First, try to discover if anyone has a pressing need for a large sum of money. We share the same home but our personal lives don't overlap all that much. I'm away on business quite a bit, and with the house so large sometimes I don't see some of them for days at a time. Any one of them could have a problem I know nothing about."

"But how will you uncover a hidden problem? No one would admit to it now and risk your connecting the accidents with the secret."

"That's exactly why I've decided to hire a private investigation firm to follow them and try to get a line on their personal finances." His mouth skewed with distaste. "The very idea makes me feel scummy. But I have neither the time nor the expertise to do the job properly myself."

Carrie wondered if this was the time to mention her suspicions. Adverse to discrediting his family, she offered a tentative suggestion. "Maybe we could brainstorm some possibilities, just throw out any … ideas that come to mind, no matter how ridiculous they sound."

"Thank you for the 'we.' I was hoping you'd offer to help me. I know I don't deserve it, after the way I rejected your help before. But you seem to have a feel for people. In fact, I'm sure you have some ideas already. Tell me whatever's come to your mind, sweetheart. Don't hold anything back to spare my feelings."

Thankful for the invitation that freed her from verbal restraint, Carrie collected herself, then suggested possible motives for Tim, Natalie and Natalie's mother.

"The same reasoning could apply to Natalie's father as well, though it's difficult to imagine parents willing to kill in order to assure their daughter's comfortable life be made more comfortable. And of course, Tim's financial problems will be solved when he marries Alanna. It would depend on the degree of greed, I suppose."

She eyed Dean, wondering if he noticed that she hadn't mentioned a blood member of the family.

His crooked smile and knowing eyes told her that he had. "I don't believe Justin would kill me just to benefit himself. But I'm not sure where he would draw the line when it comes to Natalie. Judging from her clothes, jewelry and vacation trips, she's a very expensive wife. I suppose it's possible that keeping her happy may be bankrupting him. The investigating firm should be able to tell us that."

"That's a distinct possibility," Carrie agreed. "I think he loves her very much." She hesitated. "I've only met your aunt and uncle once, so I can only guess at a motive. The one thing that's occurred to me is the possibility that one or the other may be a secret gambler. The stock market, maybe, or betting on horse races?"

Dean nodded, his expression interested. Now that he had overcome his emotional aversion to the idea that someone meant to kill him, his intellect was caught by the challenge of solving the problem. Brainstorming was a device he and John had often employed in their joint effort to expand the Sheffield chain of clothing stores.

"I haven't noticed any hint of that, but it's a valid suggestion. Gambling can become an addiction. It's occurred to me that Aunt Bev is addicted to her charities. She serves on a number of worthy committees and is generous with personal donations. Crazy as it sounds, maybe she plans to rob the rich to give to the poor. It seems an unlikely motive for murder, though."

Carrie shuddered. "Dean, if that's it, she's a very sick woman. There are people who believe any means justifies the end. But murder in the interest of charity? That's pretty hard to credit."

"I know, I'm really reaching. And I don't think that's the answer. Bev is certainly eccentric, even strange, but that's a far cry from insane."

They lapsed into silence. Dean leaned back, his feet instantly resuming their kneading motion. Carrie nibbled on her knuckles. "Blackmail!"

Dean looked up, excitement dawning in his eyes.

"Good thinking. If someone in the family has something to hide, then he or she would need money to pay—"

Her eyes alight, Carrie interrupted. "Dean, maybe it's not a Sheffield. Maybe the blackmailer, on his own, wants his victim to be able to keep paying and figures your death would fatten his takings. His victim may know nothing at all about his murder attempts!"

"God, it would be wonderful to find that no one in the family wants me dead." He ran his fingers through his hair, rumpling it further. "I'll instruct the detective agency to search for some … indiscretion that could lead to blackmail. There'll be fallout when the reason and the blackmailer are known, but then it'll be over."

His jubilant expression faded when Carrie didn't return his smile.

"What's the matter?"

"I don't know exactly." She twined her fingers together in her lap. "That scenario just feels too easy, too convenient. Something tells me the whole thing is much more complicated than that. I agree that of all the possibilities, it's the most attractive. Or rather, the least horrifying."

She forced herself to say the unpalatable. "But I don't think we should assume that the criminal is a stranger. Until we know for sure it would be wise to regard everyone as dangerous."

Dean winced and looked suddenly older. "You're right, of course. My choice of explanation isn't necessarily the correct one. For a man who's been described as practical and clear-sighted, I'm building castles in the air, aren't I?"

He lifted his hands palms out, in a gesture of surrender, and hunched his shoulders in a comically guilty pose. "Of course, I've also been called hard-headed and single-minded on occasion. Can you believe it?"

His eyes invited her to laugh with him. A heartbeat later she did, pleasure thrilling through her at this sign that, despite all that had happened, he hadn't lost his sense of humor, and in spite of his responsibilities, didn't take himself too seriously. She found herself liking him more and more.

When their mirth died away she excused herself to make more coffee. Ten minutes later she found him asleep, his body slumped sideways on the couch.

Knowing how terrible the day had been for him Carrie didn't have the heart to wake him. She wedged a pillow under his head and lifted his legs to the couch. He sighed and shifted but didn't awaken.

His shirt and trousers were pulled taut around him and looked uncomfortable. When he began to snore lightly Carrie decided he was well asleep, and with fingers that suddenly began to tremble, she undid a few shirt buttons, pulled the tail partly free and loosened his belt. Then she draped a lightweight blanket over him and sat down in the opposite chair to enjoy the unexpected opportunity to pretend that the sleeping man belonged exactly where he was. In her home. With her.

Tired from the strain of the wake, she finally dozed off, her head angled awkwardly against the back of the chair.

* * *

A light blue car was climbing the steep road chiseled through the rocky hill. The road was bracketed by a wall of bare rock on one side and by open space overlooking a steep, tree-covered drop on the other. As seven-year-old Carrie watched, an enormous truck crested the top of the hill and began to descend. Then a sharp crack split the air. Suddenly the truck began to weave from side to side, its thundering horn blaring a warning of danger. Brakes squealed as the white-faced driver fought to keep the runaway vehicle on his side of the road. The rear fender clipped the car's front end. Her mother's screams rang in Carrie's ears as the rental car left the road. For an instant it seemed to hang motionless in the sky, then it tipped forward and plunged toward the incline. Through the windshield Carrie saw her father fling his upper body across her mother as the thick treetops rose like spears to greet the plummeting car.

Jolted awake, disorientated, Carrie thrashed and fought against the hands gripping her by the upper arms.

"Carrie, wake up! It's me. It's Dean. It's all right. You're safe."

"Wha—"

Awareness flooded Carrie's mind. She stopped struggling and found Dean kneeling in front of her, his expression full of worry and concern. Dreaming. She'd been dreaming again of her parents' deaths. With a sob, she buried her face in his shoulder and wrapped her arms around his chest. He gathered her close and dropped his chin on her head.

"Shh, shh, it's all right, sweetheart."

Trembling, Carrie clung to his massive frame. As her distress ebbed away, she became aware of the rock hard muscles beneath his shirt and his warmth radiating through to her bones. She felt protected, safe, comforted.

Comforted. Dean was the one in need of comfort. Her sorrow was in the past but Dean had just buried his father that day. Ashamed of her selfishness, she loosened her hold on him and raised her head.

"I'm sorry, Dean. You didn't need another weepy female on your hands. Did I wake you up?"

He shook his head and raised his hands to her shoulders. "No. I woke up and saw tears streaming down your face. When you didn't respond to my voice, I knew you were asleep." His eyes narrowed. "You were dreaming about your parent's deaths, weren't you?"

"How did you know that?" She tried to smile. "Maybe you're a bit psychic yourself."

He returned her smile but his expression sobered as he released her shoulders and stood.

"No, but it isn't hard to figure. You attended a burial and a wake today. It's no wonder you were reminded of your own loss." He grimaced. "I should never have asked you to come back to the house. I'm sorry."

Carrie jumped up. "Cow cakes!"

Dean looked so startled at her reprimand, the one she occasionally used in the classroom to her students' vast delight, Carrie had to swallow a giggle.

"I was glad to be there for you. Besides, I'm used to the

dream and it seldom happens anymore. It's you I'm concerned about. Do you feel any better now?"

"Yeah, I do." His mouth lifted at the corner. "I'd apologize for falling asleep, but I'm not sure I want to hear your reaction."

Carrie nodded. "A wise decision. One needs a very strong stomach to survive my extensive vocabulary." She grinned and leaned close to whisper in his ear. "When I'm *really* incensed, I say 'Oh, ffffffudge!'"

Dean threw back his head and roared with laughter. Pleased that she'd taken his mind from his bereavement, if only for a moment, Carrie laughed with him. Life with this man would be a constant joy. She would bet her paycheck that the woman he married would be the happiest woman in the country.

The thought robbed her of the moment's pleasure. She sighed and fell silent. Dean's laughter trailed away. Sadness returned to his face. He thrust his hands in his pockets. When his gaze focused on his discarded shoes, Carrie sensed he meant to leave. Without conscious thought, she placed her hands on his shoulders.

She kissed him. Or did he kiss her? She didn't know and didn't care. She only knew he needed the comfort she could offer and she could no more withhold that comfort than she could fly.

His mouth felt wonderful against hers. Comfort flowed both ways. Then solace changed to warmth, warmth to heat, and heat to desire.

When Dean's arms circled her and pulled her tightly against his strong body, Carrie sighed and melted against him. Her hands tightened on his shoulders. When she felt the tip of his tongue outline her lips, her mouth fell open.

He thrust his tongue inside. Need exploded in her body. She pressed closer against him and gloried in the evidence of his desire. The realization both amazed and stunned her. She could scarcely believe this magnificent man wanted her.

The kiss seemed to last an eternity.

It ended abruptly.

Dean jerked his head away and dropped his arms. Carrie staggered in surprise. His hand shot out to steady her and then let go, as if the touch had scalded him. Drawing in an audible breath, he stepped back.

"Carrie, I'm sorry. I had no right to do that." He looked away. "I hope you can forgive me."

Carrie swallowed hard. He was sorry he kissed her? Shaking her head and praying her voice didn't reveal the pain in her heart, she managed to answer. "It's been a terrible day for you, Dean. I understand. There's nothing to forgive."

He nodded and, without speaking again, put on his shoes and grabbed his jacket while Carrie phoned for a taxi for him. At the door, he turned to face her. The small smile on his mouth looked forced.

"Thank you. For coming to the funeral. And for … everything." He reached behind him to open the door. "I'll call."

Then he was gone. This time, Carrie didn't go to her balcony to watch him leave the building.

Chapter Eight

Dean gave his address to the taxi driver and leaned back against the seat. His thoughts tumbled over each other like a troupe of acrobats. What was the matter with him? God, he'd practically attacked her. Another minute and he would have ripped off her clothes and buried himself inside her. He'd come so close to losing control. It wasn't like him to treat any woman that way.

And Carrie wasn't just any woman. 'Special' didn't begin to describe her. He groaned at the memory of the sweet taste of her mouth and the feel of her slim body plastered to his.

She didn't try to push him away though. Because she pitied him? As she said, it had been a terrible day. When she thought about it, would she decide he'd used his father's death to take advantage of her? Would she despise him? The thought made him shudder.

"You okay, buddy?"

Dean looked up and met the driver's eyes in the mirror. "Yeah. I'm fine."

"You don't look fine. Woman trouble, I bet. Wanna talk about it? I'm a good listener."

Dean shook his head. The driver shrugged and didn't speak again. When the taxi stopped in front of the mansion, Dean paid the fare. Not questioning the reason, he added a huge tip.

The driver whistled in surprise. "Hey, thanks, buddy. You

take care now. Things will work out. Anyway, no woman's worth the aggravation."

"This one is." Dean turned and entered the dark house. "This one is," he repeated softly.

* * *

"What took you so long?"

"I was asleep. Forget that. I thought we agreed to cool it for awhile. This is dumb. Somebody could see us together. What's so damned important that I had to come out here?"

"When was the last time you read a newspaper?"

"What the hell you talking about? And get me a beer, would ya."

"Get it yourself. And I'll tell you what's so damned important. Things have changed."

"Changed how?"

"The old man died, that's how."

"Hell! What about the will?"

"Don't know. There's something fishy going on. I figured the lawyer would read it today, after the wake. But he didn't."

"Hmmm. Maybe the old guy didn't get it finished before he croaked."

"I don't know if he did or not, but something's not right."

"Hey, these people are rich. They ain't in no hurry. Anyway, you coulda told me all this on the phone."

"That, yes. But not this. I've been thinking and I've decided we've got to get rid of the son right away. He must have inherited the biggest share so we've got to move in case he plans to set up the trust his daddy wanted. Or makes a new will of his own. When he's gone, everybody else will get more."

"I don't like it. The timing's too close. Who'll believe another accident?"

"Nobody will question it. They'll just figure his old man's death made him careless. I'm positive no one knows about the other accidents. Except maybe that woman he's been seeing. And since she's going to go bye-bye with him…."

"Both of them? Christ, why her?"

"Just to be on the safe side. He looks pretty hooked to me. If they decided to elope or something, she'd get his share. I won't let that happen. Remember, the more I get, the more you get."

"Yeah, and don't you forget it. Okay, I'm game. You got a plan to take care of them both?"

* * *

Carrie paid the taxi driver and hurried up the wide wooden steps of the nursing home. Her hand had just grasped the doorknob when she heard her name. Looking around, she saw Greta waving to her from the far end of the wide porch. She wove her way among the other porch occupants, smiling with delight at the sight of her grandmother sunning in a wheelchair, her plaster-clad leg ending in a thick, orange sock.

They exchanged affectionate hugs. Greta, a little pink, introduced Carrie to Ernst Keller, a robust, ruddy-faced man in the chair at her side. His leg was a mirror image of Greta's, complete with cast and matching sock. As the three chatted, Carrie's gaze swung between the two patients, silently noting the man's rather awkward but endearing air of infatuation.

When Greta suggested they explore the grounds, Ernst looked disappointed but gallantly maneuvered his chair to allow them access to the side ramp. Carrie crossed her fingers, hoping Greta's request meant she had news to share. She pushed the chair to a small grove of pines and sat down on the concrete bench. Smiling mischievously, she leaned toward her grandmother.

"Love your sock, darling. Funny, I don't remember seeing it before."

Greta blushed. "Stop your teasing, child. It's keeping my old toes warm."

"Ah, of course, though it looks to me as if the previous owner would like to warm up more than your toes."

Greta threw her a scolding look but couldn't stop a happy smile from spreading across her face. Carrie was delighted. Greta was already a widow when Carrie's parents died and, to her knowledge, had never looked at another man.

She listened attentively as Greta described Ernst's family of three grown daughters, all married with children. His wife had died of cancer three years earlier. He was, as he had confided in Greta, a man who needed a good woman at his side.

"And he thinks he's found that woman in you." Carrie's observation was more statement than question.

In answer, Greta took Carrie's hand and replied, "How would you feel about that, *liebchen*?"

"How would I feel about gaining a grandfather and a parcel of step-relatives? You have to ask?"

The two women exchanged matching grins, their eyes a study in deep, mutual affection.

Then Greta cleared her throat, a somber expression displacing her smile. "Business now. I learned two things, though they may not be important. Alanna's father—his name's David—has been disappearing in the evenings several times a week for the last three months. That's unlike him. According to Alanna he doesn't seem to be upset or worried, but he's often distracted."

"Mmm. And the second thing?"

"Her Aunt Beverley is upset about something. Alanna has no idea what it might be. Evidently the woman has always been a little *wunderlich*—strange—but now, she is happy one day, sad the next. Like a person on a roller coaster. Not sick, just … changeable."

Carrie frowned, remembering her discomfort at Beverley's unpleasant manner when they met. What would cause mood swings in a woman whose lifestyle seemed to consist mainly of charity events and family gatherings? Maybe Bev's life, like her brother David's, encompassed an unsuspected secret.

Carrie shook her head in frustration. "It makes no sense to me. But Dean has hired a private investigator. Hopefully he'll find some answers."

"A private investigator? Does that mean your young man believes in your power? Carrie, that's wonderful." Greta sighed with relief and pleasure. She knew well how difficult it was for her granddaughter to be different. Few men, few people, were comfortable with the unexplainable.

"Greta, my dearest grandmother," Carrie replied sternly, "Dean is not my young man! But yes, he is taking the warnings seriously now. We both feel that the motive must be related to money. There's just so darn much of it."

Greta nodded in agreement. The reasoning felt right, though why someone already wealthy would want more, badly enough to kill for it, she would never be able to understand. But people had been murdered for just that reason in the past, and would be again in the future.

Both women, at the same moment, caught sight of the masculine figure striding toward them.

"Oh, my," Greta breathed.

Carrie blushed as she stood and waited for Dean to reach them. She watched him approach, for a moment observing him through Greta's eyes. Tall. Broad shoulders. A barrel chest. Lean hips. Flat stomach. A man comfortable with his size and virility. A confident man. A powerful man. A man whose kiss had shaken her to her toes.

A trembling started low in her belly, accompanied by a rapid, near-audible thudding against her ribs. Only when she grew lightheaded did she remember to breathe. *Oh, my, indeed.*

If Dean felt any such emotional upheaval, it didn't show. He seemed pleased to see her but no more than that. Pride alone prevented Carrie's welcoming smile from slipping. She prayed he hadn't noticed her physical reaction or recognized it for what it was. Had it not been for the peculiar circumstances involved in their meeting, he would never have pursued their association. What had a vision-prone kindergarten teacher to offer a man like Dean Sheffield?

She was unprepared for his greeting. Before she could say a word, she felt his arm circle her waist and his warm hand settle on her hip. He brushed his lips across her cheek then turned, extending his other hand to Greta. She took it in both of hers, glanced once at Carrie's stunned expression, then bestowed an approving smile on the giant man who was holding her granddaughter so possessively. There was no surprise in her bright eyes.

"So. You are the man whose luck has been so … exceptional."

Dean grinned at the lively eyes staring up at him, not missing the astute double entendre.

"Yes, indeed. I could describe my luck as phenomenal, even … blessed." Their eyes met and held. A question and its answer passed wordlessly between them.

Carrie struggled to comprehend what was happening. She felt much the way she had as a child, when her parents spelled words to each other over her head, words she instinctively knew were important. After the way he'd apologized for kissing her, Dean's arm at her waist confused her. What was in his mind?

When she finally marshaled her wits into something approaching lucidity, she discovered that Dean and Greta had introduced themselves and were launched on a discussion of the occult. She watched Dean closely. Not a flicker of disbelief crossed his face. He asked intelligent questions and listened attentively to Greta's explanations. His interest seemed genuine, his mind open to what must seem inexplicable and unintelligible to a pragmatic businessman. Was he merely being polite? Or was he truly beginning to accept that "there are more things in heaven and earth" than this world dreams of?

Luckily, the two talking so earnestly didn't seem to notice Carrie's lack of contribution to the discussion. She might have felt excluded were it not for the solid feel of Dean's arm at her back. All of her attention centered on the heat that prickled over her body. It took a conscious effort not to caress her cheek, where the imprint of his lips lay like a brand.

Then his arm dropped away and she was able to take a deep breath. Together, they escorted Greta back to the porch. Ernst frowned when Dean leaned down to kiss Greta's cheek.

"Would you mind if I visited again, Mrs. Sonnheim?" Dean's voice held genuine liking.

"I'd love it. But only if you promise to call me Greta." Her smiling face grew serious. "Dean…. Take care of yourself. I mean, take care!"

Dean assured her he would. Ernst relaxed when Dean took Carrie's hand and led her down the walk to his car.

Lines of worry deepened on Greta's face as she watched them leave. The dark cloud surrounding Carrie's companion, that she alone perceived, was spreading to include her granddaughter.

* * *

"The will has disappeared?" Carrie repeated incredulously. When Dean said that he had something to tell her before they reached the house, she hadn't expected anything like this. "But how? When? What does it mean?"

His tone was grim. "It means that at least one person now knows about Dad's plan for the trust fund and house. And doesn't like it. Someone wants the old will to stand, the will that leaves much more to every member of the family."

Carrie's mind buzzed as she tried to sort out the possibilities. Then she saw the flaw in Dean's statement.

"Dean, that person must have known about the new will for some time. And very likely also knew about your father's condition."

Dean's eyes left the road for a minute to gape at her with a look of horror in his face. "Do you mean someone killed my father to prevent the will from becoming final?"

"No, no, Dean, not that!" Carrie put her hand over his and hurried to relieve his pain. "I feel sure John's death was natural. Though that person probably hoped that your death would kill him. Tell me, when did John first tell you about his plans for the trust?"

Dean thought back. "Three weeks ago Monday."

"I thought so. And the first so-called accident happened about ten days later. Don't you see? If someone knew about John's intentions and his state of health, then logic might dictate that you die first, in which case the shock might well kill John. Neither of you would have had time to set up the trust. Then all of John's money, including your share, would go to the family. And, since you don't have any dependents, I assume your own personal wealth would also be shared by the family." She paused. "Am I making any sense?"

"Too much sense." Pain laced his voice. "No investigation

would be needed if one death was clearly an accident and the second the result of the shock of his son's death to a man already dying of heart disease. One accidental death, one natural death. There would be no cause for suspicion, in spite of the size of the estates involved."

A long moment later, he added, "A well-planned scheme. With one major flaw."

Carrie raised her brow. "What's that?"

A wry smile tugged at the corner of his mouth. "Why, my dear murderer didn't take you into account when he set out to decimate my family. He has a formidable foe he knows nothing about."

Suddenly he pulled the car over to the gravel shoulder and switched off the engine. Turning, he leaned toward her and slipped one arm over the back of the passenger seat. His gaze locked on hers.

"I haven't thanked you for everything you've done. I don't know how. Words aren't enough, I know, but for the rest of your life, know that you have my deepest gratitude."

Carrie didn't answer. She couldn't. A drowning person can't speak and she was sinking, drawn deeper and deeper into the turbulent blue waters of his eyes. She gasped as his head lowered and his gaze wandered to her mouth. He looked up again.

"May I?" His husky murmur sent a bolt of heat flaring through her body. He read the answer in her face and slowly, so slowly, brought his mouth to hers.

His lips were soft, tentative, moving over hers like the touch of a feather. His warm, clean breath filled her mouth and the male scent of him swirled in her brain.

Unbidden, her tongue traced the firm line of his lips, exploring their taste and texture. She heard the soft groan in his throat and never knew it was echoed by her own. Slowly he deepened the kiss. His arm dropped to her shoulders and his hand rose to cup her face.

When he finally lifted his head away, Carrie found her arms around his neck, her fingers entwined in his soft, disheveled hair. Her eyes fluttered open. The deep hunger in his face electrified every nerve in her body. Disbelief and joy coursed through her.

Before she could fully assimilate the wonder of it, his arms tightened to pull her against his chest and his lips fastened on the throbbing pulse below her ear. With a small cry of startled delight, she pressed against him, her hands kneading his broad shoulders, her breath uneven and shallow. Carrie forgot the world outside, the swish of passing vehicles, the sunshine pouring through the windows.

A sharp rap on the driver's window shocked them both. Breathless, confused, she fell back against her seat as Dean released her and turned to the window. She was only marginally aware that Dean had shifted to block the intruder's view of her.

"Something wrong, officer?" Dean asked in a level tone.

"Well now, sir, this isn't exactly the time or the place for this kind of thing. Sort of public, you know. How about moving along now. I'm sure you can find a better—" The amused voice stopped in mid-speech when Carrie, recognizing the voice, leaned forward to peer over Dean's shoulder.

"Carrie!" Pure astonishment lifted his voice an octave.

"Hi, Andy." She watched as the color crept up his face, knowing her own cheeks were burning. She quickly introduced the two men.

Andy's gaze darted between the two of them. Then Melinda's fiancé suddenly grinned widely and slapped the roof of the car.

"Wait til I tell Lindy about this. She'll love it. And don't you try to deny it. Hah, I can just picture her face!" Chuckling, he started to turn away, then paused.

"Oh, I almost forgot. I tried to reach you a few hours ago, Carrie. I, er, I looked into that matter Lindy mentioned. Ah, could I speak to you? In private?"

Carrie threw Dean an apologetic glance and climbed out of the car. She followed the young policeman back to the cruiser that neither of them had heard pull off the road. When they were beyond Dean's hearing, Andy stopped.

"That's him? The one you're worried about?" He inclined his head toward Dean,

now sitting still and straight behind the wheel.

Carrie nodded. "Have you been able to find out anything?"

"Nothing startling, probably nothing important. My partner's wife comes from a wealthy family. They're not in the Sheffield's league, but her mother does a lot of charity work and knows Beverley Sheffield. Miss Sheffield has been the subject of gossip for several months now. It seems the lady hardly ever attends their committee meetings anymore and has stepped down from several executive positions. She claims she's not feeling well but no one seems to believe that. As I say, it probably doesn't mean anything. Maybe she's just getting bored with it all."

Carrie nodded, lost in thought. Beverley Sheffield, at sixty-three, could very well be feeling her age. No one's energy level stayed at a youthful high forever. There was nothing suspicious in that.

"Has any one remarked on her behavior, such as a tendency to mood swings?"

"Mood swings?" Andy looked startled. "You think she might be into drugs?"

"No, not really. I've heard she's always been rather eccentric and doesn't mind airing her opinion of people. She can be pretty rude and impatient." She remembered how Beverley had ignored her outstretched hand.

"Maybe so, but not with kids. Evidently, she's one of the favorite volunteers at the children's hospital. The kids love her, they call her Grandma Bev. She hasn't cut back on that work. And she's still on the committee that finds temporary homes for unwed mothers."

Carrie tried to reconcile the conflicting portrait of a woman who loved children as a would-be murderess. It wasn't easy, but she knew people were never all bad. As for rudeness, many people called it honesty. There was some truth in that, though it seemed to her that there was also a place for courteous silence. Frank speech could often be wounding.

"I guess that's not much help." Andy shrugged. "But I'll keep digging. Any suggestions where to look next?"

"Dean hired a private detective. But he won't have a contact so well-placed as your partner's mother-in-law. Try to find out if there's any other interesting gossip going around." She hesitated. "Particularly about Natalie Sheffield." She put a hand on his arm. "Try to be discreet, Andy. And thanks."

"Sure. According to my partner, his mother-in-law loves to talk. It doesn't take much to get her going."

He grinned down at her and patted her hand.

"Sorry I interrupted just now. Next time, better find a quieter road for such amorous pursuits." He threw back his head and laughed at her expression. Then, still chuckling, he walked her back to the car and held the door for her. With a two-fingered salute in Dean's direction, he turned and sauntered back to the unmarked cruiser.

To Carrie's relief, Dean didn't question her. Although he'd hired a private investigator to look into his family's affairs, she wasn't sure he'd appreciate knowing she'd discussed his situation with a stranger.

* * *

Carrie thanked Aggie and slipped into the washroom the older woman had indicated. The room was small, but perfectly appointed. Through an open archway she could see pink and gray marble fixtures that matched the pink walls and thick gray of the carpet in the small anteroom. She sank down on the flowered chintz chair and stared at the woman in the mirror.

It was the same image she saw in her own bathroom mirror. Somehow, she had expected to see something different, some change in her appearance. Some outward sign of the inner turbulence that left her feeling transformed, as more than she had been before, and at the same time, as less. Like da Vinci's *Mona Lisa*, larger than life but incomplete. As she had changed Dean's life, so he had changed hers. She knew whatever happened, or didn't happen, she would never be the same again.

In the mirror, her fingers rose to tremble against her lips. Until the kiss in her apartment and the second by the side of the road, she had thought her heart safe, buttressed behind the certain knowledge that their relationship was temporary. Their worlds had touched, overlapped a bit, but were too different to permit any sort of merging. Oil and water. After all, the fish may love the bird, but where would they live?

A simple kiss, and her heart had burst free from a lifetime of restraint and caution, habits formed over the years to protect herself from a disbelieving world. The irony taunted her. She was in grave danger of falling in love with a man whose nature was radically different than hers. Sooner or later, like Gary, he would walk away. And never know how he had changed her life.

The sight of a single tear trailing down the cheek of her mirrored image startled her. She had never been a crier, never been one to bemoan what couldn't be changed. Scowling into the mirror, she wiped the tear away with the back of her hand and wondered how long she had been sitting there. She splashed cool water on her face and applied a touch of blusher to her pale cheeks.

She would do what she could to help Dean, and when his nightmare was over, she would exit his world. The reason for their meeting hadn't changed. His life was what mattered, not the heartbreak of a foolish kindergarten teacher. Smoothing the pale blue dress over her hips, she lifted her chin, arranged her mouth into a smile and left the room.

Crackling flames in the floor-to-ceiling fireplace created an air of intimacy in the small sitting room. Carrie cradled the wine glass in both hands and listened to the subdued conversations of the Sheffield clan. Now and again someone would speak of John and some past incident, then the topic would veer to a news report, or some business matter. If the attempts on Dean's life had never happened, the ambiance in the room would be exactly as one would expect from a family suffering a recent loss.

No one seemed nervous. No one appeared to pay any more attention to Dean than to the others. If anyone resented her presence at the family gathering, Carrie couldn't detect it. Natalie hesitated briefly when she entered the room and saw her seated beside Dean, but then nodded her head in polite greeting. There was no sign of Beverley's former rudeness. Both women made a point to include Carrie in the conversation and even became somewhat animated when Carrie related some of the more amusing escapades of her young charges.

When Aggie popped her head around the door frame and announced that dinner would be served in five minutes no one stirred for a moment, as if reluctant to summon the energy required to move. Then Dean rose to his feet and extended his hand to Carrie. To her surprise, he released her hand only to drape his arm around her waist and urge her forward. They led the way into the adjacent dining room, the others trailing behind. Dean seated her beside the head chair and took his place. Without being told, Carrie knew the chair had been John's. She ached for the pain the gesture must have caused him.

Conversation ceased abruptly when a loud crash and Aggie's angry shout interrupted the quiet conversations halfway through the meal. Surprise held the diners rigid for a long second. Before Dean could get to his feet, the swinging door to the short hallway that led to the kitchen swung open and crashed against the wall.

Bill Hummell half-fell through the doorway and skidded to a stop. The gardener's wild eyes swept around the table. Incomprehensible gobbling sounds burst from his throat. Then he took a deep, choking breath and cried out hoarsely, "She's dead! She's dead."

He slumped to his knees and buried his face in his hands.

Chapter Nine

The gardener's sobs seemed amplified in the brittle silence that followed his shocking announcement. Then all heads turned when Aggie stepped forward and placed a hand on the distraught man's shoulder.

"Bill, who's dead?"

When he didn't answer Dean stepped behind him, grasped him around the chest and wrestled the shuddering body into a chair. The man immediately slumped forward and buried his head on his arms.

Carrie looked around. Everyone had risen and was milling around, though none seemed willing to approach the moaning man. Then, to her surprise, Beverley Sheffield, her face white and strained, suddenly rushed to the gardener's side and put her arms around his shoulders.

"Hush now, hush. Is it your mother? Where is she, Bill?"

The gardener seemed to calm at her touch. He inhaled deeply and clenched his fists. When he lifted his head a moment later, he had regained his usual, impassive expression. He looked into Beverley's face then shifted to face Dean. Except for a small hitch in his voice his tone was dull, bewildered.

"She's … on the cottage steps. She's been—someone must have—who would want to—" He closed his eyes and bent his head, his teeth clamped on his lower lip.

"I'll go." Dean took charge. "David, help Bill into the sitting room. Alanna, get some brandy for him, please. Justin, you come with me."

Dean started for the door then paused to look over his shoulder at Carrie. She returned his look of inquiry with a helpless shrug, spreading her hands in perplexity. Whether the housekeeper's death was connected to the accidents she couldn't say.

Justin, almost walking into Dean's back, caught the exchange. Curiosity and speculation flitted across his handsome face. Then he followed his cousin through the kitchen and across the lawn to the cottage shared by Irma Hummell and her son.

* * *

While Justin stayed outside with the body, Dean entered the housekeeper's cottage and called the police. He looked around but saw no signs of an intruder. Nothing seemed to be out of place. He recognized the furnishings as belonging to the cottage and was surprised at how little the dead woman had added in the way of personal touches. Irma, with her handyman/gardener husband, had been in residence for about a year. Jonah had died of an aneurysm several months previously. At her request, John Sheffield had hired her son Bill to take over his father's position.

On the dresser in Irma's bedroom, he found a framed wedding picture of a much younger Irma and her husband, and a later picture of Jonah with his arm around the shoulders of a young boy, obviously a pre-teen Bill. Even then his face was unsmiling, expressionless.

Bill's room was completely devoid of any personal touches, other than an afghan similar to several scattered about the house. He knew from Aggie that Irma made them in her spare time. The cottage had an unlived-in air, like an empty motel room waiting for a traveler.

When he returned to the small back porch, Justin looked relieved and said he thought he should join the women back at the main house. His eyes avoided the body sprawled face down on the steps. Dean let him go.

"Don't let anyone leave. I'm sure the police will want to question all of us."

Justin didn't protest the significance of his cousin's observation. The blood-matted wound on the back of the housekeeper's head ruled out natural or accidental death. Someone had bludgeoned the woman repeatedly. Looking ill and muddled, Justin wove unsteadily across the yard. He stopped once to retch, then staggered on.

Feeling exactly the same, Dean swallowed the bile in his throat and forced himself to squat beside the body. Hesitantly he touched her hand. It was quite cold. Though he was no doctor, he knew she had been killed some hours earlier. Why had no one found her sooner? Then he remembered he had asked Bill to scrub down the fountain at the front of the house, a time-consuming job. The back of the cottage would have been out of Bill's sight.

While he waited for the police to arrive, Dean stood and examined the scene. She lay across the steps, her head near the porch and her feet dangling over the lowest step. Four folded sheets lay in a tumbled heap on the middle step, beside the body. It was clear that she had been hit from behind as she began to climb the steps to enter the cottage.

He frowned. How had someone come up behind her without her knowledge? If she had even just begun to turn around, her body would be resting at least partially on one side. But she was on her stomach, her forehead caught on the edge of the step above, so that she faced straight down into the space between one step and the next.

He tried to picture the deed, second by second. The first blow must have been extraordinarily strong, to propel her body forward and down against the stairs. The added blows probably hadn't been needed. Someone wanted to be very sure.

That was a reasonable interpretation of the body's position. But something felt wrong. His gaze roamed over the horrible scene. Then he saw what nagged at his mind. The sheets.

Four clean, folded sheets made a compact bundle. Not terribly heavy but too awkward to be carried in one hand. If she had been clutching them in her arms in front of her when she fell forward, one or more of the sheets should be under her body. None of them were. Instead, they lay in a heap on the steps beside her, partially unfolded, as if she had tossed them aside. That didn't seem likely.

Dean sat down on the steps, bracing his forearms on his thighs. Had the first blow merely stunned her and knocked the sheets from her arms? If so, she surely would have tried to see her assailant. But her position indicated that she hadn't turned at all.

There was no sign of anything that might have served as a weapon. Presumably the killer had carried it away with him.

Some impulse made him grip her shoulder and roll her to her side. Her eyes were open, staring, opaque. Dean shuddered.

"Dear God!"

Her face was twisted in what seemed to him to be horror. Why that, if she didn't see the blow coming? But then, he wasn't familiar with the look of violent death. Though it was too late now, he murmured a prayer that the poor woman had died with no foreknowledge of her fate.

Knowing the police wouldn't appreciate that he had touched the body, he was about to ease it back into the original position when he saw bits of grass on the front of her blouse. Had she fallen on the way to the cottage? He knew that Bill had cut the grass in the area that morning. Gritting his teeth, Dean pulled her further to her side. Both knees of her slacks were covered with cut grass, one torn through. He could see a green smear on the skin of her knee. One elbow and her chin were also stained green and a few bits of grass clung to her lips.

Easing the body back on its stomach, Dean settled on his haunches and ran both hands through his hair. If she had slipped on the grass before she was attacked, she would have continued on to the cottage to change her clothes. He lifted the sheets and examined the folds. Grass cuttings clung to the material.

The explanation made sense. She'd fallen, walked on to the house and tossed the sheets on the steps, intending to change her clothing before taking the soiled sheets back to the big house to replace them with clean. The cottage boasted no laundry facilities.

But surely the fall would have stunned her. She would have sat for a few minutes to get her wind back, then struggled to her feet and retrieved the scattered sheets. Why did she not see her assailant during those few minutes? Or did she? Was her assailant known to her? It was unlikely that she would have turned her back to a stranger.

Dean tried to remember what he knew of the housekeeper but John had done the hiring. With a sense of deep shame, he realized that he had never made an effort to get to know the quiet, withdrawn woman. She did her work well and he really hadn't paid much attention. He didn't even know where Irma Hummell had come from.

"Aggie. Aggie might know."

It occurred to him that Irma's death may have been rooted in the past, and chance alone fated her to die on Sheffield property. Or hers was a random killing by a stranger. There was no reason to believe that this murder and the attempts on his own life were connected. On the other hand, it might be foolish to assume that they weren't.

Baffled and depressed, Dean waited for the police to arrive.

* * *

Lieutenant Mark Balfour made careful notes as Dean described his actions from the time Bill stumbled into the dining room. While they talked, two officers searched the area for evidence and the murder weapon. The body was carefully photographed from every angle. When the overweight, wheezing coroner had examined the body and seemed about to order its removal, Dean eyed the lieutenant then casually mentioned Carrie's presence in the house. Balfour's eyes lit up.

"Would you ask her to join us out here? God, this could mean a real break for us. Maybe she can—" He broke off abruptly and rubbed the side of his nose, his look uncertain. "Uh, do you know…? That is, maybe Miss Richards wouldn't want…." His voice trailed off.

Dean understood and appreciated the man's reluctance to reveal what he knew of Carrie's talent.

"Yes, Lieutenant, I know. She'll want to help if she can. I'll get her."

Lieutenant Balfour, his intelligent eyes hooded in speculation, stared after him as Dean covered the distance to the house. Then he turned and ordered the coroner to wait before moving the body.

Carrie willingly followed Dean back to the cottage although she was uncomfortably aware of the open curiosity in the eyes of the others. She felt her insides shrink with the realization that her secret might be much more difficult to maintain after being publicly singled out by the police. It was not in her, however, to refuse to help.

She greeted Lieutenant Balfour, who had dispatched the junior officers inside the cottage. Balfour, the coroner and Dean stood aside, the latter impressed by the respect in the faces of the other two men. None of them spoke. Three pairs of eyes watched carefully.

Carrie moved closer to the body and stared down at the dead woman, stooping once to press her splayed fingers on the woman's back. Then she backed away and paced a large circle around the area. Finally, she stopped some twenty feet from the body, closed her eyes and began to breathe deeply. Dean watched with curiosity as Balfour moved carefully to position himself behind her. Except for the faint voices of the men in the cottage, the silence was absolute.

Her face grew blank and slack, her arms hung limp at her sides. When her eyes snapped open, Dean drew a sharp breath and felt the hairs on his body stiffen. Her gaze was remote, unfocused, her eyes glassy and huge. Without actually moving, he recoiled from the woman who attracted him so strongly. He knew instinctively that she was unaware of the three men watching so intently.

A moment later, she staggered and dropped her head forward. Balfour, obviously expecting the semi-collapse, grabbed her upper arms and held her upright. Almost immediately she straightened and intelligence returned to her countenance.

Her gaze flew first to Dean, her unspoken plea for acceptance as clear as a shout. Before he could hide his primal gut reaction to the strangeness just witnessed, their eyes met. Pain and sadness flickered across her face, then with unmistakable effort, her expression tightened and she wrenched her eyes away. Dean knew he'd been found wanting and dismissed. The sense of loss nearly overwhelmed him.

"Who moved her?" Carrie's voice was a steady, dispassionate

monotone.

"No one," Balfour said, startled.

Carrie shook her head. "She fell on the lawn."

"Yes, on her way here from the big house. And since she lived here, we assume that she got up and was about to enter the cottage to change her clothes when she was struck from behind."

Incredulity struck Dean like a blow. No one had mentioned the grass stains to Carrie and they could not be seen without turning over the body. How did she know?

"No. I sense that she died on the lawn. There's something wrong about the body. I feel someone's … confusion. Maybe the murder wasn't planned. I can't tell. But why didn't the murderer simply leave her where she fell?"

Balfour pursed his lips as he considered her question. It was clear to Dean that the officer fully accepted Carrie's statement that Irma had been struck down before she reached the cottage. Balfour believed in her. For the first time Dean felt unsure of himself, as if he were less a man than he had thought. True, this was only the second time he had witnessed a demonstration of Carrie's abilities. He'd thought he believed, but realized now that he hadn't accepted. Shame tasted like dust in his mouth. He felt his soul shrivel. Impatiently, fearfully, he shook off the sensation.

"Maybe he meant to hide the body in the cottage? To give himself time to get away before she was found?" Dean hadn't meant to speak but his mind fastened on a possible answer.

Balfour nodded. "You could be right. And either he panicked and ran before he moved her all the way inside or he thought he heard someone coming. Makes sense."

Frowning, Carrie neither agreed nor disagreed. She approached the corpse again and with a quick glance at Balfour for permission, bent and turned the body on its side. The sight of the woman's sheet-white face and empty eyes sickened her. She clenched her lips to contain the scream trapped in her throat and forced herself to examine the clothing. The expected bits of grass and green smears collaborated her assertion that Irma had been struck down before she reached the cottage steps.

Dean knew her next words were addressed to him, though she was looking at the police lieutenant.

"I'm sorry I can't be of more help, Mark. I've no idea if the killer is male or female. I'm sorry."

"You've helped, Carrie," he protested quickly. "I never doubted she was knocked down where she lies."

Carrie shook her head. "You would have. Though any woman, even a normal woman, would likely have seen it first." She glanced at Dean.

He raised his eyebrows questioningly. Carrie's answering smile was feeble but Dean felt his anxiety lessen slightly at the sight of it. He knew he had failed her at the worst possible time.

"Think, Mark. What's the first thing you would do after getting up from a fall on newly-mowed grass?"

Comprehension flooded simultaneously into the men's faces. They exchanged a grimace, discomfited at having missed the obvious.

"Of course! If she had just fallen accidentally she would have brushed off the grass cuttings before continuing toward the cottage. At the very least, she'd have rubbed off the grass clinging to her mouth. Since she didn't, it was because she couldn't." Balfour looked disgusted. "And I didn't see it."

Dean cleared his throat. "So Irma died on the lawn before she reached the cottage and was then moved to the steps." He placed a hesitant hand on Carrie's shoulder. "You were right in every detail."

It was an apology of sorts, but Carrie could still picture his earlier expression. Her unsought ability was as much a part of her as her height and hair color. And it revolted him. Her chest throbbed with a dull ache.

"I haven't proved anything. The evidence speaks for itself." She stepped out from under Dean's hand and regarded the lieutenant and the coroner in turn. "I had no part in this."

They nodded in unison, acknowledging her insistence on silence about her part in any investigation.

"You got it, Miss Richards," the coroner wheezed. "It's a darn shame though."

"No. It's necessary."

The coroner shook her hand then turned back to the corpse. Carrie, Dean and Lieutenant Balfour headed for the mansion.

* * *

Full darkness had fallen by the time the forensic team departed with Irma's body. After Bill described how he had found his mother's body and accounted for his movements that day, the investigating officer allowed Aggie and Beverley to whisk him away. The bereaved man had answered questions readily enough but was unable to offer any reason why someone would wish to kill his mother. Insisting that he should not return to the cottage that night, Aggie and Beverley prepared a room for him in the big house. Flanked by the two women, he climbed the central stairs, his face blank and his steps wooden.

One at a time, Lieutenant Balfour questioned the others. No one could suggest a motive for the crime. No one had noticed a stranger on the grounds that day, although Aggie had seen a man, or rather, a flash of dark red jacket, just inside the woods the week before. She was unable to give any kind of description.

Only David and Beverley, like Dean and Carrie, could offer a checkable account of their whereabouts during the estimated hours when Irma died. David had been at work surrounded by employees who could vouch for his presence. Beverley had also spent the afternoon with others, at a meeting. Natalie and Aggie had opportunity but, it seemed, no motive.

Later, when the lieutenant shared the results of the questioning periods with Dean and Carrie, Carrie was surprised to learn that Justin had spent the afternoon in a downtown theater. He had flushed, evidently embarrassed to admit to playing hooky from work. Unfortunately, he knew of no one who could vouch for his presence.

When the authorities had departed and they were once again alone, Carrie turned to Dean. "Why didn't you tell him about the attempts on your life? You know he isn't seriously considering a member of the family as Irma's killer."

Dean shrugged. "We don't know that there's a connection. I didn't want him digging into family business."

"But that's what your private detective is doing. If there's anything…. Oh, I see. His report will come to you and be private. But Dean, if he discovers a possible motive then—"

"—then I'll tell the police. In the meantime, our dirty laundry isn't police business. Besides, if he knew, his questioning would alert my enemy. This way, my would-be killer can't be sure I've figured out what's going on. It may make him careless."

Carrie knew stubbornness when she heard it.

"All right, I'll keep quiet, too. For now. But I want you to know that if anything else happens, anything at all, Balfour will hear the whole story."

Dean, too, could recognize stubbornness. He wanted to gather her into his arms and assure her he'd be okay, but the wall she had erected between them since he'd witnessed her behavior at the murder scene seemed impenetrable. His own fault, he knew. He deeply regretted his instinctive reaction. It was clear she had been hurt before by similar rejections. She wouldn't trust him easily again.

"Fair enough. The private detective should have a preliminary report for me tomorrow. In the meantime—"

"In the meantime, it's late. Would you mind calling a taxi for me, please?" Her too-polite tone might have been directed at a stranger.

"No!" Dean exclaimed. "I mean, I'll drive you home. Carrie, please, stay a bit longer. Aggie's sure to have a pot of coffee brewing and I think we should have a talk with her. She's the only person in the house who might know something about Irma's background."

Much as she longed to be alone, cocooned in her own home, Carrie could think of no pretext to refuse, except for the one reason she couldn't verbalize. How could she tell him how much it hurt to be with him when she knew that even mild friendship between them was no longer possible? She couldn't. Reluctantly, she assented and followed him down the long hallway to the back of the house.

Aggie had just finished emptying the dishwasher and was storing the clean dinnerware when they entered the kitchen. Her face lit up when she saw them. Pathetically grateful for company, she immediately approached them. Impulsively, Carrie stepped forward and the two women embraced. The unexpected comfort broke Aggie's control. She began to sob. Carrie tightened her hold and signaled to Dean over the cook's shoulder to pour coffee for them all.

When her sobs subsided, the older woman stepped back and wiped her eyes with a corner of her apron. She blew her nose loudly then offered Carrie a watery smile.

"I'm sorry, Miss Carrie, I didn't mean to blubber all over you. The shock…. Poor Irma. I can hardly believe it. I guess nobody's safe these days."

Carrie helped the shaken woman to the table. For a few minutes they sipped at their coffee, not speaking, then Aggie seemed to gather herself together. She touched Dean's hand.

"Mr. Dean, what do the police say? Do they have any idea who did it?" Not waiting for an answer she added, "I'll bet it was one of those killers they let out of prison. Or somebody released from a mental hospital. You know, they keep claiming those people are cured when they're not. Why don't the authorities ever learn?"

"You might be right, Aggie. Right now, I don't think the police have any clues. But they will catch the person responsible, don't worry. Until they do, though, I want you to promise me you won't go outside alone."

The older woman nodded and asked Carrie for her opinion.

"Well, it didn't appear to be a planned murder, so it might have been as you say. Still, someone took a big chance. To attack, in daylight, where anyone might have seen…. Even if the killer is mentally ill, it doesn't mean he's stupid. The trouble is, even a crazy person has to have a motive for what he does, some reason that makes sense to him, even if it doesn't to other people." She glanced quickly at Dean and away.

"I suppose it could have been someone she knew. I mean, someone from before she came here. I imagine the police will be investigating her background, looking for someone who might have had a grudge against her." Having given Dean the opening he needed, Carrie sat back in her chair as a signal to him to take over.

He caught the ball neatly. "Good thinking, Carrie. A definite possibility, I'd say. Unfortunately, I really don't know anything about the woman. You worked with her every day, Aggie. Did she ever confide in you?"

Aggie, relaxed now and looking thoughtful, shook her head. "She isn't—wasn't—a talkative woman. Not unfriendly, mind, but not friendly either. She does—did—her work well. We helped each other out occasionally, you know, at spring cleaning time and when I had a big party to prepare for. The few times we did, mostly we talked about cooking or television programs, things like that. She and her husband were both from down east, I think. Maybe Nova Scotia, I'm not sure. She did say that her husband had been a minor civil servant until he retired. When they moved here they found everything too expensive for his pension. That's why they looked for work. She did say once that the cottage being rent-free made all the difference to them."

"I wonder why they left Nova Scotia after all those years."

Aggie frowned, searching her memory.

"Well, seems to me there was something she said once…. What was it now?" She began to tap her fingers on the tabletop. "Let me think. It wasn't much, though I remember it made me curious at the time. But she didn't explain and I forgot about it."

Carrie and Dean waited silently. Then Aggie snapped her fingers.

"A clean start. That's it. She said something about coming west to make a clean start." The cook's face crumpled. "The poor woman. If she'd stayed home she might still be alive. With her husband dying less than a year after they got here, and now this awful thing."

She heaved a slow sigh. "Trouble seems to find some people no matter where they go. It's a shame. I can't say we were friends, but we got along. She was so quiet, lonely for home maybe, and sad somehow. And of course, the last few months she'd be missing her husband, too."

Shared melancholy descended on the three. Then, moving tiredly, Aggie rose from the table.

"I'm off to my bed now. Turn out the kitchen lights when you go, please." And because she had sensed the new distance between Carrie and Dean, she added, "Don't let this thing bother you too much, mind. At a time like this, everybody needs a special friend." She smiled suddenly. "Don't wait too long or you might have to share the limelight."

Carrie colored and quickly looked away. Aggie didn't know Dean as well as she thought if she imagined the man was seriously interested in a woman who saw visions and apparitions. She felt Dean's gaze on her face then heard him address the cook.

"Limelight? Aggie, don't be mysterious. What are you talking about?"

The cook hesitated then flashed a sly grin at her favorite Sheffield. "I'm not telling any tales out of school, mind, but haven't you wondered what your Uncle David has been doing with his evenings lately?"

Dean gaped at the thin woman. When comprehension dawned his face split in a wide smile. "You mean Uncle David has a girlfriend? That's great!"

"Just remember, you didn't hear it from me. Anyway, I'm just guessing. I've seen that moony look before."

With a knowing glint in her eyes and a small wave, Aggie left the room. Carrie stole a glance at Dean's smiling face.

"You're pleased, aren't you?"

"Yeah. Uncle David has had a rough time of it. It would be wonderful if he's finally found someone special."

"Dean, if Aggie's guessed right, then we can probably eliminate David as a suspect in your accidents. Assuming he was with his girlfriend."

"You're right. That means we're making some progress. Hopefully, the private detective will soon clear the whole family."

Carrie hated to spoil his pleasure at Aggie's news, but she forced herself to point out the truth of his situation. "It has to be someone, Dean. Don't let your guard down."

His face fell. "You're right again, partner. I'll be careful."

Partner? Carrie lifted her cup to her mouth to conceal the

sudden tremble of her lips. Was he saying he still wanted her help? Ever since she'd seen his reaction at the cottage she'd been certain he would want nothing more to do with her. He wasn't the first to be repelled by her strange gift. And she knew he wouldn't be the last. Suddenly, fatigue weighed heavily on her body.

Dean saw her shoulders slump and was reminded of the late hour. Remorseful, he removed the cup from her hands and pulled her to her feet.

The trip to her apartment building was accomplished in silence. Neither had energy enough for further conversation. Neither noticed the light gray car that followed a discreet distance behind.

When he had seen her safely to her door, he left her with a brief "Good night." Then he was gone.

Chapter Ten

The empty school echoed with the remembered clamor of children. As she righted the stacked chairs and arranged them around the low circular tables, Carrie caught herself listening for the footsteps of laughing students in the hall, for the animated voices of her five-year-olds as they barreled through the door. Classes would commence the following week and she wanted the room ready to receive her charges. She never minded the work that sometimes spilled over into weekends and holidays. Catching up on the never-ending paperwork, changing the child-produced room decorations, reorganizing the artists' corner, mending hard-used toys; all tasks impossible to accomplish with children present. The peace and quiet on such halcyon days had always rejuvenated her and reaffirmed her choice of profession. There was no other work she would rather do.

For once, the hushed building failed to work its usual magic. Time and again, her hands fell idle and she found herself staring into space, her heart as empty as the school. Her thoughts flittered from the missing will to the danger she knew still hung over Dean, from the memory of Irma's lifeless body to Dean's abrupt departure from her door. And hanging like a hologram in the air before her eyes, the appalled expression on Dean's face.

He hadn't touched her, hadn't smiled at her, hadn't said he'd call. It was no more than she expected, but it hurt. How it hurt! She could almost hate the power that enabled her to see or know what others could not. Almost, but not quite. Too many people owed their lives and happiness to that power. How could she wish to deny her strange inheritance?

Dean didn't need her help any longer. She had succeeded in alerting him to the danger. Now it was up to Lieutenant Balfour and the private detective to supply the rest of the equation. The riddle of his enemy's identity would be found when the two professionals ferreted out the secret that compelled the culprit to try to solve his problem with murder.

She sighed and glanced around the room, depressed at how little progress she'd made tidying it. Feeling utterly ineffectual and knowing she wouldn't achieve anything more in the classroom that day, Carrie finally slung her purse strap over her shoulder, locked her classroom door, and went in search of the custodian to inform him of her departure.

* * *

Carrie stared unseeing at the concrete wall of the parking lot beneath her building. Totally missing was the sense of eagerness she always felt upon arriving home. Her private space no longer beckoned with its promise of safety and solitude. She slumped over the wheel, resisting the thought of entering the empty apartment. Her stomach growled in protest at its hollow plight, reminding her that she had skipped breakfast. In her fervor to escape her memories of the day before, she had dressed and hurried to the school, hoping to lose herself in work. If she was to avoid a headache she would have to eat something soon.

The hiss of the elevator doors broke her reverie. She didn't look as a short, brawny figure stepped out and moved off to her left. With no conscious awareness of having made a decision she started the car and backed out of her space. Behind her the figure watched as her car ascended the ramp to the street and disappeared. He slapped his hands together as a slow grin crawled across his brutish face.

The inner woman pacified with a substantial lunch at the restaurant near the nursing home, Carrie paused at Greta's door long enough to arrange her expression into what she hoped would pass for relaxed cheerfulness. Greta wasn't fooled.

"What's wrong, *liebchen*?"

"It's good to see you, too," Carrie quipped.

Greta ignored the feeble attempt at humor and hit the button that raised the upper portion of her bed. She folded her arms under her generous breasts and waited.

Resigned, Carrie pulled the visitor's chair close to the bed and sat down. Greta took silent note of her granddaughter's dull eyes and dejected bearing. She waited.

"The housekeeper, Irma Hummell, was murdered yesterday," Carrie said. "I was at the house when her son Bill found her body. She was struck from behind, several times. Her head—" She choked, unable to go on.

Greta sank back against her pillows, the lines in her face deepening. Her mouth quivered. "Oh, *liebchen*." Her whisper shook with dismay.

Their hands met and squeezed as each sought to comfort the other. When she had her breathing under control, Carrie related everything that happened after she and Dean left the nursing home the previous day. Greta listened without interrupting, then zeroed in on what to her was the most important part of the account.

"How did your young man react?"

Carrie shook her head, knowing instantly what her grandmother was asking. She made a valiant though unsuccessful effort to smile and shrugged.

"About what you'd expect. But that's all right," she lied. "He's pretty much convinced that someone is trying to kill him, so I can wash my hands of it now. I've done all I can, and in any case, he doesn't want to see me again. You see," she blinked back tears, "I told you he's not my young man."

"Hmm, he just thinks he doesn't want to see you again," Greta huffed. "Give him time to get used to the idea, *liebchen*. I had the same trouble with your grandfather, stubborn old fool that he was. He came round when I threatened to marry the blacksmith's son."

Greta's satisfied smirk surprised Carrie into a laugh. "And would you? Have married the blacksmith's son, I mean?"

"Of course not! Rolfe was the only man for me. He just needed a jolt to realize that, strange powers or not, I was the only woman for him. Besides," she grinned, "the blacksmith's son had bad breath!"

Carrie threw her arms around Greta, giggling madly and picturing her grandfather's consternation at the ultimatum. He had died when she was fifteen, but she still remembered the tall, lanky man with the thick, drooping mustache and kind, loving eyes.

By the time her giggles subsided, Carrie felt immeasurably better, as her grandmother intended. She wondered if Greta had really told her lover to put up or shut up and guessed she'd never know for certain.

"Now, what's this nonsense about washing your hands? His doppelgänger appeared to you, Carrie, not to me, not to anyone else. To you. Whatever is or isn't between you, he is your responsibility. Until his enemy is found, you must take care of him." Greta's eyes radiated sympathy but her voice was stern.

"Yes, I suppose you're right." Resigned, Carrie nevertheless felt a spark of anticipation flicker into life. One way or another, she would see him again. Her earlier depression dissipated as if it had never been. Frowning in thought, she began to chew on her lower lip.

"I can't get a reading on Irma's death." She glanced at Greta. "There's something wrong about the whole scene, but I don't know what it is."

"Is her death connected with the attempts on Dean's life?"

"I don't know. It may have been a random killing. Or the motive may have originated sometime in her past, before she came to Ontario." Carrie spoke slowly. "The coincidence bothers me though. And the timing. The odds against a random killing, or a grudge killing, occurring in the same household and during the same time period as three murder attempts by a different would-be killer, must be astronomical."

"*Yah*. So maybe, there is only one killer. With your young man, the motive probably involves the money. Not so with this Irma. So why kill her? What would he gain?"

Carrie's brow cleared. Excitement flared in her eyes. "To ensure her silence! She knew something, or heard something or saw something. Or … or noticed something. Whatever it was, the killer didn't dare let her talk about it."

Then the light in her eyes dimmed. "No, that can't be right. If she had some information she would have told Dean. Or someone."

"*Nein*, maybe not, *liebchen*. Remember, she didn't know that someone is trying to kill your Dean. So whatever she saw or noticed probably meant nothing to her. But if Dean died, then she might realize the importance of this something and—"

"—and the killer had to be sure she couldn't give him away." Carrie beamed at her grandmother. "Greta, you're wonderful!"

"*Yah, yah*." The older woman blushed with pleasure. "That's what I used to tell your dear grandfather. He didn't always agree, but what does a man know? Nothing much of anything. That's why the Lord made women. He knew men couldn't survive without us." The twinkle in her eye belied her sardonic tone.

"I heard that and you're absolutely right!"

An empty wheelchair sailed through the door, followed by a smiling Alanna. After a quick glance at her uniform watch, she pushed the chair to Carrie's side and dropped gracefully into it, sighing a little with relief.

"Every man needs a good wife, whether he knows it or not," Alanna said. "Artists, especially. When Tim is painting he loses all track of time. If I didn't bully him he wouldn't eat or sleep. Imagine! It's a good thing we women are such sensible creatures." Her eyes glinted with mischief.

Carrie relaxed at this display of guileless charm. The lovely nurse had obviously not heard their earlier speculation about Irma's death.

"How is Bill coping?"

The questioned sobered Dean's cousin and her smile slipped.

"It's hard to tell. He hides his feelings well. When I left for work this morning he was washing the cars. They didn't really need it but I suppose he's trying to keep busy where he can't see the cottage. I gave him a sedative last night but he insists he's sleeping in the cottage tonight. Poor Bill. He's being very stoic about it all."

"And he has no idea who might have killed his mother?" At Alanna's startled look, Carrie added, "I wondered if something happened in the past. Maybe someone to whom the Hummells owed money. Or, well, someone with a grudge. If the motive lies back east in the past, Bill might have some idea."

Alanna looked intrigued. "I wonder if the police have considered that. They'll look into it, I'm sure. But I doubt if Bill would know about it."

"Why do you say that? Surely, if his parents had serious trouble—"

"But he wasn't living with his parents when they left Nova Scotia," Alanna broke in. "I had a conversation with him shortly after he arrived here. If you could call it a conversation, that is. I wanted to make him feel welcome but he was so close-mouthed that I finally gave up. He did say he hadn't lived in Nova Scotia for about eight years. There were no jobs so he went to Quebec. Montreal, I think."

"Oh." Carrie was disappointed. "Then he only came here to be with his mother after his father died. He must have cared a great deal for Irma to leave his job in Montreal to be with her. That was generous of him."

"I thought so, too." Alanna checked her watch and propelled herself out of the wheelchair. "Well, duty beckons. They want you in therapy, Greta. Your chariot awaits."

Carrie kissed her grandmother's cheek and left.

* * *

Carrie shifted the bag of groceries to her left arm and dug in her purse for her door key. After some fumbling she managed to insert the key in the lock, only to discover the door was unlocked. Startled, she stiffened in alarm. She always locked the door after herself. Always. And she knew Melinda had left the apartment before her, bound for a very early flight to Glasgow.

The possibility of an intruder in her apartment sent a chill shooting down her spine. She backed away from the door and looked around. The hallway was empty and she knew that everyone on her floor would be at work. There was no one to ask for help.

Carrie eased the groceries and her purse to the floor. The intruder, if he was still there, must have heard her groping with the key. When minutes passed in silence, she finally reached for the doorknob and thrust the door open to bang against the inner wall. Nothing happened.

From the hall she could see her small foyer and part of the living room. Everything appeared the same as usual. Could she have forgotten to lock the door? She supposed it was possible. She had slept little the night before and had left in a hurry for school, determined to forget Dean Sheffield by immersing herself in work. It was quite understandable that she might have forgotten.

She forced herself to wait a few more minutes. Finally convinced that the apartment was empty, she left the hall door open and swiftly explored each room, throwing open closet doors, peering under the bed and searching every possible hiding place. Nothing. No one.

Her imagination was working on overtime. Mentally reproaching herself for the unnecessary fright, she returned to the hall to recover the bag of groceries. When the door was locked behind her with both safety chains in place, she stored the groceries away. After checking through the mail and finding nothing but advertisements, she poured a glass of chocolate milk. Finally relaxing, she kicked off her shoes and curled up on the sofa to examine Greta's insistence that she must not abandon Dean.

Her grandmother was right. Her responsibility remained. Whether Dean liked it or not, she could not walk away until his enemy was caught. Or succeeded in his attempt to murder the incredibly wealthy man.

Her mind shied away from the last thought and focused instead on the problem Dean's rejection presented. How could she stay involved when he wanted nothing more to do with her? With John gone, she had no excuse to visit the mansion. The others were mere acquaintances. There would be no invitations from any of them.

Her gaze passed lazily around the room, then was caught and held by the coffee table in front of her. One of the three shallow drawers beneath the tabletop gaped open a good half-inch. Her breath stuck in her throat. No more than two inches deep, the drawers served as catchalls for various odds and ends. More than a month had passed since she last had occasion to open one. A tidy housekeeper, Carrie knew she could not have missed the open drawer for all that time.

Scarcely breathing, she opened the drawers. Nothing seemed to be missing. But then, who would want to steal a few pencils, some elastics, empty envelopes, loose buttons or any of the assortment of worthless miscellany? Slowly, she closed the drawers and lifted her head, her senses suddenly on alert.

Immediately the air felt wrong, smelled wrong, although she could pick up no identifiable odor. Tense, she rose awkwardly from the couch and stood, circling in place and scrutinizing the room. Minuscule differences leaped into prominence. The couch cushions were slightly out of line; a lamp sat off-center on the side table, the framed photograph on the wall behind her mother's chair listed slightly; one book stood upside-down on the lower shelf of the bookcase.

Carrie toured the apartment. The signs of an intruder were many, though so tiny and insignificant they might well have been overlooked had she not noticed the most obvious, the open drawer. One pocket of her winter coat was turned out; a corner of the bedspread was hiked up; the shower curtain was pulled back slightly; the dresser drawer holding her neat piles of undies was open a crack at one side.

Concrete evidence surfaced in the kitchen. She had emptied and bagged the garbage that morning, but a crumpled gum wrapper lay in the bottom

Carrie stared at the wrapper. A sense of violation shuddered through her. Her skin crawled at the thought of some stranger handling her undergarments and examining her belongings. Never before had she felt so helpless, so vulnerable, so defiled.

The sudden rapping on her door made her cry out. She froze and stopped breathing. The rap came again, louder this time, demanding.

"Coming," she called, her voice cracking.

She walked unsteadily into the hall and peered through the peephole. It was Dean. Relief weakened her knees. She fell against the door and fumbled with shaking hands to undo the chains. Her hand clutched the knob tightly for support as she opened the door. Dean's massive form was the most beautiful sight she had ever seen.

"Carrie, I need to—" Dean halted in mid-sentence as he took in her pasty face and anguished eyes. "What the hell—" He stepped inside and reached for her.

With a wild cry Carrie flung herself against him and wrapped her arms tightly around his waist. Her relief was so great she burst into tears, her face buried in his neck. A second later his arm went beneath her knees and before she could move he had pushed the door closed with his hip and carried her into the living room. A part of her wondered at the ease with which he held her, but mostly she was aware only of the warmth of his muscular chest and how good it felt to be in his embrace.

Still holding her tightly, Dean sat down on the couch and pulled her deeper into his arms. His quick glance around the room revealed nothing disturbing. He clamped his lips together to hold back his questions and lowered his head to her hair, muttering meaningless soothing sounds. As her slender body shook with the force of her tears, he became acutely aware of the scent of her skin and the curve of her breasts flattened against his chest. Her hair felt soft as cat's fur against his cheek. Her pant legs had ridden up a few inches to reveal slender, delicate ankles that had a sensual appeal all their own. His abdomen tightened in masculine response.

Gradually Carrie's tears slowed and ceased. Reluctantly, Dean loosened his hold on her, hoping she was too distracted to notice the proof of his arousal pressing against her hip. When she straightened away from his body he fished a handkerchief from his jacket pocket and pressed it into her hands.

"Th-thank you." Carrie buried her face in the hanky. Mortified at having thrown herself at him, and aware that she must look a mess, she couldn't bear to meet his gaze. "I'm s-sorry," she hiccuped. "I've made a mess of—"

"Not to worry. The shirt is drip-dry." Unable to resist, Dean dropped a gentle kiss on her jaw beneath her ear and stood up, swinging around to deposit her on the couch. "One glass of water coming up."

Carrie gave him a tremulous smile and watched as he strode into the kitchen. Beneath the casual, dark brown slacks, the muscles of his thighs and buttocks moved with athletic smoothness. Carrie flushed, caught off guard by the sensual longing that suddenly sped through her veins. Fully dressed, he was magnificent. Naked, he would rival Michelangelo's *David.*

The water banished the hiccups. Carrie sank back against the cushions, exhausted from the emotional storm. Dean sat beside her, though not touching her, his eyes dark with concern. He waited quietly.

"Someone entered the apartment when I was out." Her husky voice contained a note of continuing apprehension.

"What? What was stolen?" Dean glanced around for some sign of disturbance.

"Nothing. That's what's so frightening." Carrie shuddered. "I didn't even realize at first. But then I found signs, small changes, and I knew. Someone has gone through my drawers, the clothes in the closet, the kitchen cupboards. Nothing is missing but everything has been examined."

A look of doubt flashed across Dean's face and was gone. But Carrie saw it. She jumped to her feet and held out her hand to him. "I can prove it."

She led him through the apartment, pointing out the subtle

traces the intruder left behind. The circuit ended in the kitchen.

"I'm a tidy person, Dean. I don't leave drawers partially open and a crooked picture is like the sound of nails on a chalkboard for me. This window was closed when I left this morning. But there's more." She pointed to the gum wrapper in the garbage.

"Neither Melinda nor I chew gum. And I emptied that garbage container before I left the apartment a few hours ago." She heard and hated the pleading note in her voice. If he wouldn't accept her story, if he dismissed it as imagination, she knew she'd cry again. Yet she couldn't blame him. To any eyes but her own, the apartment appeared clean, neat and untouched.

"Do you have a plastic bag?"

Bewildered by the unexpected question, Carrie opened a drawer and withdrew a small sandwich bag. "Will this do?"

"That's perfect." Dean turned the transparent bag inside out and slipped his fingers inside. Then he carefully picked up the wrapper, pulled the bag right side out and sealed it. He held it up in the air.

"The intruder took his time and made a real effort to conceal his presence. I'm betting he wore gloves. He made a mistake though, when he left his used wad of gum behind. The police labs can learn quite a bit about a person from saliva tracings. If he's a secretor, like sixty percent of the population, his blood type can be determined. Then it's a matter of matching with a suspect."

Lightheaded with relief at this indication that he was taking her story seriously, Carrie struggled to recall what little she knew about genetic fingerprinting.

"But a match won't prove that person is the same one who's trying to kill you, would it?"

"No, but the owner of the gum will have a hard time explaining why he or she was in your apartment without your invitation or knowledge."

She stared at him anxiously, knowing he referred to his relatives. "Do you think there's a connection between Irma's death, the attempts on your life, and the gum chewer?" She didn't wait for an answer. "I don't understand. Since nothing was stolen, there are only two possible reasons why someone would break in here."

"Two?" Dean looked at her sharply.

"Well, it seems to me that either the intruder, whoever he was, was some kind of weirdo who gets a thrill from creeping around another person's home, or he was searching for some particular item he thought might be here."

Dean nodded. "Let's assume the latter. More, let's assume there's a connection with my problem. The only item missing, at least as far as we know, is Dad's will."

"But," Carrie protested, "the person who stole the will must be the one who's trying to kill you. The will, the distribution of the money, is the reason he wants you dead. Why would he be searching for something he already has? And why would he search here?"

"Maybe he doesn't have it." Dean rubbed the back of his neck and spoke slowly. "That is, I believe the money is behind it. But suppose my murderous friend knows about the terms set down in the will, but doesn't actually have it in his possession. He would want to find it in order to destroy it. Otherwise he risks the chance it could come to light and demolish his plans."

Carrie pulled out a chair and sat down with a thump. "But that would mean—"

"—two people who know about the terms of the new will. One stole it. The other realizes it's gone and is looking for it. Both greedy, but one merely weak, the other murderous. As for why someone would search here … I suppose he, or she, thought I might have given it to you for safekeeping."

Carrie's heart ached at the look of sorrow and disillusionment on his face and in the slump of his shoulders. Desperate to ease his pain, she changed the subject.

"Why are you here, Dean? I mean, I didn't expect to—"

"I know you didn't." Shame-faced, Dean sat down across from her and sighed heavily. "I can be a stupid bastard sometimes. Will you forgive me?"

Carrie stiffened, his words bringing back a vivid image of his reaction to the scene at the cottage. Dean saw the hurt that leaped into her eyes. He reached out and drew his knuckles down the side of her face.

"What can I say? In spite of everything you told me, I hadn't expected to see something like that. It was a shock. I was afraid for you. I'm so sorry."

He was afraid for me? Carrie met his gaze and saw confirmation in the appeal on his face. The ice encasing her heart disappeared as if it had never been. If he was afraid for her, it had to mean that he cared, at least a little. Her features flowed into a gentle smile.

"The experience is exhausting for me, Dean, but not dangerous. You needn't worry about me. Though it's nice that you did," she added softly.

Relief at her unspoken forgiveness replaced the concern on Dean's face. "The next time, though, I want to be the one standing behind you." His gruff tone didn't quite hide the edge of jealousy beneath it.

As if he had heard it himself, he suddenly stood and held out his hand. "Come on. Pack enough for a few days."

"What?"

"You can't stay here alone. The intruder might decide to 'ask' you where the will is hidden. I want you to stay at the house for a few days, where I can keep an eye on you. You'll be safer there anyway, with more people around."

"But, I don't think…. Maybe a hotel…." Carrie sputtered to

a stop. The rigid line of Dean's jaw told her she had no choice in the matter. If she refused, she knew he would simply carry her there. In her heart of hearts she admitted she was thrilled at this proof that he cared for her safety.

"Yes, sir. Right away, sir. How high, sir?" Teasing, she was pleased to see his taut face relax into an abashed grin.

"Just do it, woman," he growled in mock anger, the pretense spoiled by his twitching lips.

"Bossy, aren't you?" Unaware of the broad smile on her face, Carrie left the kitchen to pack.

Chapter Eleven

"What if the others want to know why I'm staying here?" The question occurred to Carrie for the first time just as they turned to pass through the gates that fronted the Sheffield home. Dean glanced quickly at her and away.

"The house belongs to me now. It's no one's business but mine. I've invited you to be my guest for a time. That's all they need to know."

Carrie nodded, but she knew the family would be very curious. Sooner or later someone, most likely Natalie, would ask her outright. The best answer would have to be no answer. It would be awkward, though. How she longed for the self-confident courage of the socially adept. Carrie dreaded being the center of attention, and she had a feeling that Natalie would not be satisfied with a non-answer.

Correctly interpreting Carrie's suddenly stiff bearing, Dean reached to place his hand over her clenched fingers.

"If anyone is nosy enough to ask, tell them to ask me."

"And how will you answer?"

"Why," he chuckled, "I'll just tell them, politely of course, that it's none of their business."

Carrie laughed and relaxed. What was she worried about? Though his Uncle David was oldest Sheffield, Dean was the head of the family. No one could force him to explain anything. Her thoughts returned to the interview with Lieutenant Balfour.

They had gone straight to the station after leaving her apartment. To her surprise, Dean told Balfour everything about the attempts on his life, the contents of the missing will and Carrie's intruder. The policeman listened without interruption, his frown slowly deepening. It was obvious that he accepted the story as fact, not supposition. Carrie knew it was largely because of her involvement that he did so. George Balfour belonged to the select group who had first-hand proof of her ability. His first comment surprised her.

"You could be in danger, too, Miss Richards. Someone wants that will destroyed bad enough to kill." He turned to Dean, his stare challenging. "What are you going to do about that?"

"Protect her." Dean met Balfour's eyes with a challenge of his own. "You can't do it. She's coming home with me. I won't leave her alone."

Their gazes locked, neither man speaking. Then Balfour gave a satisfied nod.

They discussed the permutations and possibilities of the case for an hour. The policeman agreed it was unlikely Carrie's intruder had left fingerprints behind. They decided not to send an investigating team to dust for fingerprints, on the premise that the intruder could be watching. Hopefully, he would conclude that his presence had not been discovered. His mistaken supposition might make him careless and that could only be to their advantage.

Dean refused to inform his family of the attempts on his life. He explained his reasoning in an emotionless voice.

"My murderous friend might decide it's too dangerous to continue. Then I'll never know which one of them…." He paused and swallowed hard. "I have to know, if only for the sake of the innocent ones. And we can't just forget Irma Hummell. The killer's got to pay for her death."

"But at least tell them you've made a new will," Carrie

begged. "The murderer will know about the trust and that it's too late."

"No." Dean shook his head. "The same reasoning applies."

Lieutenant Balfour looked from one to the other. "I agree with your reasoning, Mr. Sheffield. But there's a flip side to that coin."

"What do you mean?"

"The last attempt on your life was what? Almost a week ago? Before your father's death?" At Dean's sharp nod, he continued.

"No attempt since then. I would guess that your friend decided to lie low for a while, to let some time go by before acting again. But then, for whatever reason, he killed Mrs. Hummell. I feel sure her death wasn't planned or it would never have happened in daylight, on the lawn where someone might have seen."

"So?' Dean asked. "What are you getting at?"

"So that killing must have shaken him. Since you haven't told anyone about your experiences, he may harbor the hope that you haven't realized what's going on. He might decide not to wait any longer, so as not to allow you time to change your will to carry out your father's wishes."

Carrie gasped as Balfour's words sank in. The worn leather chair creaked as the policeman leaned forward, his face earnest.

"As I see it, he can go two ways. He can try another accident. If that's successful, it's not likely to be connected to Mrs. Hummell's death, since, so far as the killer knows, no one knows about the first three attempts. Especially if he can contrive an accident off the estate."

"And the second way?" Dean's voice was grim.

"He could decide to kill you in much the same way as he killed the housekeeper, hoping both deaths will be considered random. That wouldn't be smart, but remember, since the family doesn't know about the trust, all he has to do is claim ignorance like the others. The thing is, the sooner you die, the larger his inheritance."

"He's right, Dean. Your life depends on telling the family everything." Even as she pleaded, Carrie knew Dean wouldn't listen.

"I have to know who he or she is, Carrie. *I have to know.* Even if he gave up on me, who's to say another member of the family won't become a target in the future? And it wouldn't be fair to Bill to let his mother's death get shoved on a shelf, marked down as a random, unsolved killing. No, we carry on as we are and hope we can catch him in the act. With the police investigating Irma's death, he has to be jumpy. Maybe he'll make a mistake."

Carrie gave up but she was well aware that Dean's decision could prove fatal. Briefly, she considered telling the Sheffields the whole story herself. But in her heart she knew she wouldn't betray Dean's trust that way. And he was right. They had to uncover the killer's identity or he might never be safe.

They left Balfour with Dean's promise to get a sample of everyone's fingerprints to match against those found in the cottage. For the police to do so would alert the killer. It was better to hide the fact that the family was under suspicion. Balfour marked the bag containing the wad of gum and put it away. Then he walked them to his office door.

"Be careful, Mr. Sheffield. Be very, very careful."

"I will. We'll be in touch."

Neither Carrie nor Dean saw the somber expression on the policeman's face as he watched them thread their way through the station. As he anticipated, his offer of a bodyguard had been refused. He understood Dean's reasoning; it was essential that the murderer think himself unsuspected. The policeman wondered if the Sheffield heir fully realized just how vulnerable he was.

* * *

The sun had almost set when they arrived at the mansion. The building was starkly beautiful, silhouetted against the reds and oranges burnishing the cotton clouds near the horizon. Even as she admired the stately building, Carrie shivered at the knowledge that it harbored a killer. She turned to the silent man at the wheel.

"I want to visit the cottage tomorrow. To go inside this time. Perhaps I can get a sense of something."

"Okay. It's worth a try. Maybe you can figure out what's bothering you about the scene outside the cottage. It seems pretty clear though, the way it happened."

"I know." Carrie shook her head. "Even when I sense something, my interpretation isn't always right, you know. Maybe it did happen exactly as we thought."

Carrie looked over to the cottage sitting to the side and twenty yards further back of the big house. Light shone through the sheer curtains of the front windows. As she watched, a figure passed between the light and the glass. A second figure, shorter and wider than the gardener, followed the first, his arms waving in broad gestures. Carrie touched Dean's arm and pointed.

"Poor Bill. It must have been hard for him to return to the cottage. At least he has a friend with him. I just realized. I haven't offered him my condolences. I'll do that tomorrow."

Dean parked the car in the garage and escorted her into the house. As they exited the passageway connecting the garage to the house, Aggie darted forward, looking relieved.

"Thank goodness you're here, Mr. Dean."

"What is it, Aggie?"

"It's Mr. Richard. He's sitting on the stairs to the second floor, moaning and rocking. I think he overheard the others talking about Mr. John. I can't get him to budge. Can you go to him?"

"Of course. Carrie, will you excuse me? Aggie will get you some tea or whatever you want." He set Carrie's suitcase against the wall and continued to talk over his shoulder as he hurried down the hall to the main staircase. "Aggie, will you see to a room for Carrie? She's going to visit for a few days."

The cook turned to Carrie, her distraught expression giving way to a welcoming smile.

"Some of the family are in the front room, Miss Carrie. Shall I bring some tea in there or would you rather freshen up in your room first?"

"If I may, Aggie, I'd like to join you in the kitchen for my tea. I need to ask you about something and since I'm going to be here for awhile, I'd like your advice on how to treat Dick. I've never known an Alzheimer's victim before. I would hate to hurt him in any way." She didn't add that the thought of facing the family without Dean by her side scared her to death.

Aggie beamed in approval. With an "Of course, Miss Carrie," she turned and led the way to the kitchen.

Carrie stopped in the doorway and looked around. Her mouth dropped in surprise. The room's size, the vast array of modern appliances, the gleaming cleanliness were only what she expected. What she hadn't anticipated was the sunroom cum greenhouse that extended a good fifteen feet beyond the back wall and was accessible from the kitchen through large sliding glass doors. Without thinking, she rushed into the center of the glass room and pivoted, trying to take in the details all at once.

"How beautiful!"

Two wicker chairs with matching footstools and brightly patterned cushions stood to one side, a small glass-covered wicker table between them. The other side was taken up with a raised bed in which were growing a variety of herbs. Potted cacti of all sizes and shapes lined a raised bench on the far wall. All three glass walls were screened from waist height up, making the room useable in all seasons. A bright blue flagstone floor eliminated any worry about water damage.

"Oh, what a happy room! I'll bet you designed this, Aggie. Am I right?"

The older woman blushed. "Yes, I did. Funny thing, Miss Carrie, you're the first person to guess that. About eight years ago, Mr. John said it was time I had something of my own, besides my bedroom, and he told me to dream up whatever I wanted. Forget about cost, he said, design it any way you want. Oh, he was such a wonderful man. I will always miss him."

She wiped her eyes with the corner of her apron as the two women stood and watched the last minutes of sunset.

"Sometimes, if I wake in the middle of the night, I come out here. With the kitchen lights off, you can see a million stars smiling up there. I like to think of Mr. John and my husband Cyril getting reacquainted and watching over us all. You know, Miss Carrie, a person can be lonely and at peace at the same time. This room has given me a lot of happiness." She sighed, then shook her head and turned to Carrie with a smile.

"You sit down here and I'll fix us some tea."

"May I help?"

"No, no. It'll just take a minute. You relax."

Carrie did as she was told. Twilight was rapidly giving way to full dark. With the kitchen lights on behind her, the glass walls became dark mirrors. Staring at her reflection Carrie thought about John Sheffield. Wealth had not eroded his humanity nor his real concern for those around him. The comfort and happiness of his staff had been as important to him as that of his family. It was almost impossible to believe that someone carrying the same blood in his veins could actually kill for money.

Suddenly, her eyes were caught by a beam of light moving

jerkily along the far edge of the lawn beside the perimeter of the woods. She put her face to the glass and held her hands to the sides of her face to block out the light from the kitchen. Squinting, unsure of what she was seeing, she strained to follow the bobbing light. Just as the light disappeared into the woods she realized what it was.

A flashlight. Before the question fully formed in her mind she remembered Bill's visitor. He must have come visiting on foot. Was there a house on the other side of the woods? Well, of course, there must be. If the man did the same work for another family that Bill did for the Sheffields, then he would be familiar with the paths in the woods.

Feeling silly, and about to sit back in the chair, she was arrested by the sight of a door opening at the far end of the house. She had a glimpse of a narrow set of stairs behind a woman's silhouette before the door closed. Another beam of light cut the darkness. The figure turned to the left, away from the house, then disappeared around a corner in the direction of the cottage.

Carrie sat back. Unless there was another woman in the house, the person headed for Bill's cottage had to be Beverley Sheffield. She smiled. Perhaps the older woman's cantankerous attitude hid a soft heart after all. If Dean's aunt meant to keep the gardener company for the evening, Carrie hoped the rather sullen looking Bill appreciated her kindness.

Or was there a more sinister reason for Beverley Sheffield's rather furtive exit from the house? The woman might not be headed for cottage at all. Was she meeting Dean's would-be killer?

A moment later Aggie paused in the doorway and flipped on a switch with her elbow. A florescent fixture attached to the glass ceiling bathed the sunroom in its own light. Aggie set a tray on the small table and sat down in the other chair. When both women were cuddling a cup of tea she leaned back and smiled sadly at Carrie.

"Poor Mr. Richard. I expect Mr. Dean has got him to bed now. He'll stay with him awhile. This Alzheimer's disease is a terrible thing. Mr. Richard will need a full-time nurse soon, I imagine. I wish you could have known him before. He was a doctor, you know, Head of Surgery at the hospital. The cleverest man, and not a conceited bone in him. His patients loved him. And now," she sighed heavily, "now he's losing it all, poor man, and he knows it."

Carrie was shocked. "I thought Alzheimer's victims didn't know what was happening. It's terrible for their families but I didn't think the victim suffered."

"Miss Alanna explained it all to me. The brain cells start to die. At first the victim just seems forgetful, like anybody else. Someone has to remind him about appointments, or where he left his car keys, or people's names. But as the disease progresses he gets lost, can't remember the way to his office or his room. His personality changes because he knows something's wrong. He becomes aggravated, doesn't trust people anymore because they tell him things he should remember but can't. He thinks people are lying to him."

"That's horrible," Carrie whispered.

Aggie nodded in agreement. "Eventually he will even forget the names of things, what season it is and how to use a knife and fork, how to tend to his body needs, things like that. He'll be as helpless as a baby and will need just as much supervision."

"Dick hasn't reached that stage, though?"

"No, and it may be a long time before he does. Some people deteriorate faster than others. The worst part for Mr. Richard now is that he forgets that Mr. John died. He keeps searching for him and every time he learns about the death he goes through the trauma of hearing about it as if it were for the first time. And that could go on for months, maybe years."

Carrie shuddered and tried to blink back the tears that flooded her eyes. Aggie patted her hand. "We all try our best to avoid telling him. But when he gets angry—paranoid, Miss Alanna calls it—then we have to tell him."

"Is there anything I can do?" Carrie's voice was thick with tears.

"Just try to be natural with him. Don't let on you know anything's wrong. He probably won't remember you. Try to pretend you're meeting for the first time, so he won't realize he's forgotten you. It's all any of us can do."

"I'll certainly do my best."

"Do your best about what?"

The slow, tired voice startled both women. Neither had heard Dean enter the kitchen. Now he carried a kitchen chair into the sunroom and sat facing them. Aggie told him of their conversation while Carrie wiped her eyes and blew her nose. For the first time she wondered if a heart could literally break. Dick's suffering made her want to curl up into a ball on the floor and howl in rage. Her parents' deaths were merciful in their swiftness.

Declaring she wanted to watch a particular television program, Aggie left before Carrie remembered she had a question for the cook. She poured a cup of tea for Dean, happy to see that he seemed content to remain where they were for the time being. She sensed he wasn't ready after the emotional incident with Dick, to face the others just yet. Hoping the quiet ambiance of the room would soothe him, she sipped her tea in silence.

When he finally spoke she knew he'd recovered.

"You're a very restful person to be with, Carrie. I think I could sit here forever with you."

Pleased beyond speech, Carrie reddened and looked away,

missing the tender, half-smile that lifted the corners of his mouth. Not knowing how to answer such a statement she blurted out the first thing that came to mind. "I meant to ask Aggie about the cups."

"The cups?"

"You remember, Aggie came to the door when John … when you were with your father. She dropped the tray." She glanced at Dean, sorry she had reminded him of that painful scene. His lips had tightened but he nodded for her to continue.

"Well, there were three cups on the tray. I wondered who had been with him and why they left without waiting for refreshments. Their departure must have been just minutes before he … before he…."

"Before he died. It's okay, love. Don't fret. I can talk about it. It would hurt far more to have people pretend he never existed."

Relieved, Carrie went on. "I wondered if those people saw the will. Or if John put it away while they were there. Or if he talked about it. Or whatever. Maybe Aggie knows who was there, since John asked her to serve coffee."

"It was Lawrence Chambers, John's lawyer, and his secretary. When I called to tell him of John's death, he said he had brought the new will and the copies for John to sign. His secretary was there to witness their signatures."

"Was the will signed?" At Dean's nod, she added, "Then surely Mr. Chambers has a copy."

"No. Unfortunately, his secretary got a call that her oldest son had been in an accident. They rushed out. Lawrence drove her to the hospital. He said the three copies were left on John's desk, in a filing folder. He hadn't even remembered the will until I called him with the news about John. The heart attack must have happened shortly after they left."

"Then, between the time they left and we got there, someone came in and took the will. Dean, either John allowed that person to take the will or he left the room for a few minutes or—"

"—or someone walked off with it, leaving John lying on the floor." Pain shone bleakly in his eyes as he hunched forward. "Since we don't know exactly what happened, I tell myself he probably went to the bathroom and the will was taken while the room was empty. If I ever find out differently...." His fists opened and closed in a white-knuckled promise.

Her heart aching for him, Carrie found herself kneeling in front of him, her hands cupping his face.

"Don't torture yourself, Dean. I'm sure the room was empty or the person wouldn't have dared, in case John lived long enough to tell what he had done. Please don't think the worst. Don't do this to yourself."

Dean's eyes met hers and his expression slowly changed. He searched her face as if to memorize every feature. Suddenly his hands shot out to grip her waist. He rose to his feet, taking her with him, and then his arms wrapped around her and crushed her to his chest.

At first Carrie was too surprised to struggle. Then she didn't want to. She lifted her arms and curled them around his neck. Her fingers stroked the silky, jet black hair at the nape of his neck. She rejoiced to be where she'd wanted since the first time she'd seen him. Her arms tightened around him.

His lips descended to ravish her mouth, his feverish tongue pushed past the barrier of her teeth and explored the honey softness within. One large hand lifted to hold her head as he sucked the juices from her mouth and swept his tongue savagely across her lips. A low primal growl burst from his throat as he opened his thighs and pulled her hips against his groin. Carrie pressed against him, all her woman's sensuality bursting into life.

Astonished at the instant, raging fire that scorched her

insides and the instinctive recognition of the masculine hardness pressed against her abdomen, Carrie couldn't move, couldn't think, could hardly breath. Her awareness encompassed the taste of his mouth, the scent of his skin, the sound of his ragged breathing, the heat radiating from his body and the pleasure-pain of her rigid nipples and aching womb. Nothing else existed.

Just as she thought she would faint, he suddenly tore his mouth from hers and pushed her away. She staggered and would have fallen but for his quick hands grabbing her upper arms with a grip she knew would bruise. Gasping for breath Carrie opened her eyes and cringed at the look of shame on his face. It was the last thing she expected to see.

What had she done wrong? Humiliation drained the color from her face. From somewhere she found the strength to twist out of his hands and step back. With a sob, she turned her back to him and wrapped her arms around her quivering stomach.

Dean stared at her bowed head and bit back the stream of curses that filled his mouth. What in hell was the matter with him? He had never treated a woman like that before, never even come close. He had nothing but contempt for men who used their strength against women. Yet he had almost lost control and dragged her to the floor. He had behaved like a rutting animal, had almost assaulted the woman who saved his life three times. Black shame rose up like bile. Shame and fear.

He couldn't blame her if she wanted nothing more to do with him, but the thought of never seeing her again drove a dagger into his heart. He had never felt real fear before, not even of his faceless enemy. Now he almost gagged against the bitter taste.

"Carrie, I'm so sorry. I didn't mean to…. I wasn't thinking. Please don't be afraid. It won't happen again, I promise. I … I don't know how to explain…."

When she didn't move, he laid his hands on her shoulders and winced when she jumped. With soft strength he turned her around and lifted her head until she was forced to meet his gaze.

"That wasn't me, Carrie. I mean, I'm not that kind of man. I don't know what happened, but I apologize. I just.... Please don't hate me."

The pleading tone in his voice gradually penetrated Carrie's misery. With an overwhelming sense of relief, she realized that his disgust had been directed at himself. She placed a trembling hand against the leaping pulse under his jaw and whispered,

"I don't hate you, Dean. I could never hate you."

As he searched her eyes, the tension slowly left his tight muscles. God, he didn't deserve a woman like this. "What can I do to make it up to you?"

"Two things." Carrie spoke lightly, wanting to reassure him and to get past the emotional scene before he guessed that she'd wanted him as much as he wanted her. "Lead me to the powder room, then buy me a drink."

"As good as done, my lady," Dean replied, his pleased voice thanking her wordlessly for the change in atmosphere. "I'll show you to your room. It has a connecting washroom. Take all the time you want."

* * *

To disguise the effects of her recent encounter, she splashed cold water on her face and applied more make-up than usual. Except for her kiss-swollen lips, her appearance should pass inspection. Not knowing if the family changed for the evening and afraid to look ridiculous if she overdressed, she opted to change her casual pullover for a full-sleeved peach silk shirt. A braided rawhide belt and a slim, wrap-around tan skirt completed the outfit. It would have to do.

Thirty minutes later Carrie descended the wide, curving staircase to the ground floor. She would have liked to call it a night, to crawl into the queen-sized bed and remember the moments in Dean's arms. But it was early yet, just past nine, and Dean was waiting for her. Besides, it would be a mistake to dwell on the electrifying experience in the sunroom. Especially since there would be no repeat performance.

Her outfit did very well, if the look in Dean's eyes could be believed. He stood at the base of the staircase, watching her descent. Though she thought she had regained her composure, suddenly it was hard to breathe. She was relieved when he took her arm without comment and led her into a room she hadn't seen before.

A huge stone fireplace took up the end wall. Around it clustered three overstuffed sofas and two slightly shabby-looking leather chairs. One wall was covered with family photographs of various sizes, some obviously the work of amateurs, others studio portraits. Nubby beige drapes were closed to shut out the night. The room looked comfortable and lived-in. A room for people to share with those they cared for.

Not all of the occupants were as welcoming as the room. Alanna interrupted her conversation with Natalie to call out a cheerful hello. Natalie's face, when she turned to see who merited such a friendly greeting, went still. She glanced quickly at her husband then, unable to do otherwise, offered Carrie a stilted smile. Justin and Tim displayed genuine pleasure upon seeing Carrie. In a few minutes she found herself seated by the fire, chatting happily with Alanna about Greta's progress.

Deliberately, Carrie kept her eyes from Justin and was rewarded when Natalie finally relaxed and joined in the conversation. Dean poured a glass of wine for her and a cognac for himself. He smiled encouragingly at Carrie and joined the men's on-going debate on the merits of their favored baseball teams.

When Beverley Sheffield walked in a half-hour later, Carrie had slipped off her shoes and curled her legs under her, listening attentively to Dean's cousins discuss the newest spring arrivals at their favorite boutiques. The fact that the shops' prices were far beyond anything she could afford didn't prevent her from enjoying the conversation. Carrie loved pretty clothes, though her closet held mostly serviceable garments chosen with the dusty rigors of a classroom in mind.

"Hi, Aunt Beverley. Back from another committee meeting?"

Beverley inclined her head at her smiling niece. "Where else? I don't know why I bother. Every meeting seems to drag on longer than the one before. Would you believe it took over an hour for that flock of biddies to decide how to allocate the money the bazaar netted? I was bored out of my mind." She plumped herself down in one of the leather chairs and heaved a long sigh.

Carrie shrank into the sofa, struggling to compose her face before Beverley noticed her stunned expression. Why had the older woman lied? What reason could she possibly have for concealing her visit with Bill Hummell, if that was where the woman had spent the last hour? No one would disapprove of such a charitable act. Suspicion crept down Carrie's spine and settled in her stomach.

When Dean caught her trying to smother a yawn a little later, he reached for her hand and helped her from the sofa. She held on to him for support as she fumbled her feet into her shoes.

"Oh, must you leave so soon?" Alanna sounded disappointed.

"Carrie's had a long day," Dean replied nonchalantly. "I'll see her to her room."

The silence that greeted his comment revealed the group's

surprise. As Dean predicted, no one questioned the arrangement. Carrie smiled to herself. At the doorway she turned, feeling surprisingly poised and at ease, to wish five curious faces goodnight.

As they climbed the stairs she slanted a glance at Dean. He caught her eye and began to smirk. He looked like a little boy who had just outsmarted the adults. "Did you ever see such fishy faces? I wish I'd had a camera."

Carrie laughed softly and leaned against his shoulder. "I had the most awful urge to stick out my tongue and waggle my fingers behind my ears. I guess there's a bit of naughty little girl in me still."

"Don't ever change then, Carrie. I like you just the way you are. Brave, beautiful and bewitching." He spoke lightly, but Carrie heard the approval in his voice and felt a melting warmth curl around her heart. Maybe she wasn't the social coward she'd always imagined.

When they reached her door he informed her they were to meet with the private detective at eleven the following morning. To her disappointment, he touched a finger to her lips, warned her to lock her door, bade her a good sleep and left her immediately to enter the room next to hers.

Fortunately, she fell deeply asleep the moment her head touched the pillow.

She awoke to find the house in an uproar.

Chapter Twelve

Carrie lay still for a long moment, distracted by the unfamiliar bed and the weight of early morning sunshine invading the room. As she remembered where she was, she became conscious of raised voices, slamming doors and hurried footsteps coming from the hall. Alarmed, she swung her legs off the bed and reached for her dressing gown. She padded barefoot to the door and opened it. The hall was empty, the voices now rising faintly from the floor below.

What was happening? Deciding she should dress and see if she could help, she stepped back into the room and closed the door. Just as she reached into the closet, the sound of the shower running in her bathroom penetrated her consciousness. She froze in surprise. The shower stopped. Turning her head slowly to stare at the closed door she heard the shower curtain swish back. The sound of masculine mumbling accompanied the faint squeal of the cabinet door opening.

It had to be Dick! Dismay washed over her. Somehow Dick must have mistaken her door for his own. What should she do? An anguished cry from the bathroom decided her. He mustn't see her. If Dean went to him first, Dick might never realize he had barged into a guest's room—a female guest, at that. She shivered at the thought of the man's distress.

A hand fumbled at the bathroom door. Galvanized, Carrie sped barefoot across the room and into the hall. She closed the door softly behind her and headed at a run for the stairs. When she was halfway down, Dean ran across the foyer below. He didn't see her.

"Dean!"

It took several more steps to break his momentum. He looked up. Worry creased his forehead and drew his mouth into a tight line.

"I can't talk to you now. Dick's missing and—"

"He's here! In my room. Showering."

Dean's face cleared as he bounded up the stairs two at a time. He took both her hands in his, then frowned at a sudden thought. "He didn't hurt you?"

"Oh, no. I was asleep. I don't think he even knew I was there. I left before he saw me and realized he's in the wrong room. You go to him. I'll find the others and tell them he's okay. I…. What is it?"

Carrie's heart began to pound at the intent look that settled on his face. Slowly he lifted her hands and drew them apart. Seemingly against his will his eyes lowered in slow motion down to her feet and back up, to pause at the neckline of her pale blue shorty nightgown. His glazed eyes were smoky, burning. Suddenly Carrie realized the knee-length gown hung open, revealing the upper swell of her breasts and her legs from ankle to thigh.

"Oh!"

Her soft exclamation brought his eyes up to her rounded mouth. He swayed toward her then abruptly shook his head and let her go. Her hands trembling violently, she pulled the sides of the dressing gown together and tied the sash.

"I'll tell the others. You're not exactly dressed for it. Come on."

He took her hand and pulled her up the stairs. She didn't argue. He was right. She couldn't go racing around the house dressed as she was. She could just imagine Natalie's reaction if Justin saw her in this state.

Footsteps sounded in the foyer below. Dean leaned over the railing. When Aggie came into view he called to her to tell the others they could stop searching.

"Thank God!" The heartfelt exclamation drifted up the stairs.

Carrie, still dazed by what she had seen in Dean's eyes, climbed the stairs beside him. Her mind cleared when Dick exited her room and looked belligerently up and down the hall. He strode towards them, his plaid dressing gown flapping around his legs, his bearing stiff. He stopped dead in front of Dean.

"I want to know what's going on! Someone has stolen my razor and taken all my clothes away. I won't have it, I tell you! Who's doing this to me? I'm going to call the police. They'll catch—" The furious tirade stopped abruptly when his gaze fell on Carrie, who was standing behind Dean's shoulder. Incredibly, his thunderous expression instantly smoothed into a pleasant smile.

"Well, hello. You must be a friend of Dean's." He put out his hand. Carrie immediately stepped forward and shook it.

"And you must be Dick. I'm so pleased to meet you at last. My name is Carrie Richards. I'm visiting here for a few days." She offered him her sunniest smile.

"Oh?" He turned to Dean. "About time you brought a woman home. John will be delighted." He grinned slyly. "He's been wanting grandchildren for a long time."

Dean laughed and draped an arm over Dick's shoulder. He darted a quick glance at Carrie then casually guided Dick down the hall. "Guess we'd better get dressed. Aggie will have break-fast ready soon."

Carrie waited until Dean steered Dick into his room and

closed the door. She didn't want Dick to see her enter the room he had just left, though the whole incident seemed to have left his mind. She understood now why Alzheimer's victims became paranoid. It must seem that people around them conspired against them by making changes without their knowledge. Her heart ached with sympathy.

She showered, and remembering their appointment with the private detective, put on a lightweight, pink knit dress. The sound of voices led her to a small breakfast room near the back of the house. As she drew closer, she heard references to Dick's condition. She stepped through the doorway.

David, Justin and Alanna were grouped around the table. Beverley and Natalie were absent. Carrie wondered about that until she remembered that they had no need to rise early for work.

David, who had arrived home late the night before, after everyone had retired, looked surprised to see her. The look changed to one of knowing amusement when Dean entered and hurried to pull out Carrie's chair. Dick, dressed, shaved and quietly polite, took the seat beside her, forcing Dean to sit between his cousins.

Desultory conversation centered mostly on the Sheffield stores and the weather. When the others finished eating and excused themselves, leaving only Dick and Dean, Carrie found herself recounting humorous tales of her students' antics. Dick, whose long-term memory was still largely intact, countered with tales of the youthful exploits of the Sheffield cousins.

Finally, after commenting that he hoped John would soon be back from his business trip, he wandered into the kitchen looking for Aggie. Carrie forced herself to meet and hold Dean's eyes for the first time since the unnerving incident on the stairs.

"He doesn't remember being in my room, does he?"

"No." Dean grimaced. "I was hoping to get the nursing

home in operation before hiring a full-time nurse/companion for him. The idea was that he wouldn't realize, for a time at least, that he is one of the patients. But I'm afraid we no longer have the luxury of waiting. The deterioration of his short-term memory seems to be accelerating. He needs someone right now."

Carrie wished with all her heart that she could ease the heavy burden Dean carried. True, he had the shoulders of an Atlas, but responsibility could be a heavier load than even a colossus could bear for long. She released an involuntary sigh. Dean heard. Her compassion for Dick pleased him enormously. He checked his watch.

"We'd better get moving if we're going to be on time for that appointment."

"What appoint—? Oh, yes. I'll get my purse and jacket and meet you at the front door." Behind her, Carrie heard Dean call to Aggie that they were leaving.

Beverley, wearing an out-of-date but obviously expensive skirt and sweater set, was in the hall when Carrie left her room. The older woman stopped in front of her, an uncertain expression on her face.

"Good morning, Miss Sheffield. Er, were you looking for me?" With a face as innocent as she could make it, Carrie gave the woman a friendly smile. She hoped her eyes didn't give away her knowledge of the older woman's lie the night before.

"No. Yes. I mean…." Bev's answering smile was forced. "Aggie mentioned how much you liked her sunroom. You must see it in the daytime to fully appreciate it."

Carrie heard the question and the anxiety underlying the statement. Beverley seemed afraid that she had seen her night-time excursion to the cottage. Or was it merely embarrassment because of her lie about the committee meeting?

"Oh, I hope to visit with Aggie again," Carrie said artlessly. "But if you'll excuse me, Miss Sheffield, Dean is waiting for me."

"Of course." The woman moved aside reluctantly. Carrie could feel eyes studying her back as she walked to the stairs. It was a relief to leave the house.

* * *

"Want to share?"

"What?" Startled, Carrie turned her head to see Dean raise one eyebrow.

"Your thoughts. You looked miles away."

"Oh. No. Yes. Dean, this will sound strange, though it probably doesn't mean anything." Carrie shifted uncomfortably. If it weren't for the situation she wouldn't dream of revealing Beverley's trivial lie.

"I think Beverley visited Bill in his cottage last night," she said slowly.

"That's not strange. Beverley's heart is softer than one would guess from her crusty exterior." Dean glanced away from the road and frowned when Carrie continued to look concerned.

"Dean, she lied. Remember she mentioned how long and tedious the meeting was? Well, she wasn't at a meeting. She was at Bill's. Or at least I saw her leave the house with a flashlight when I was in the sunroom. I can't be certain where she went, though."

"You're sure?"

"Yes. And just now, before we left the house, I ran into her. She knew I was in the sunroom last night. I didn't want to embarrass her so I let on I saw her. Why in the world would she lie about a thing like that?"

Dean looked puzzled. "I don't know. She's a bit eccentric but I've never known her to lie. I wonder if she met Bill's guest."

"No, she didn't. I saw him leave several minutes before she

left the house. He went through the woods."

"Through the woods? At night?"

"I saw his flashlight. Though now that I think of it, I just assumed it was the person we saw through Bill's window. The light came from the direction of the cottage."

They were silent for the rest of the trip.

* * *

"So, that's it. I can keep digging if you like. Do you want me to continue surveillance on the subjects?"

Owen Rogers, the owner of Confidential, Inc., leaned back in his black leather chair and put his arms behind his neck. He waited, his gaze swinging from the massive man seated in front of his desk, to the delicate beauty beside him. He didn't know why Dean Sheffield was investigating his relatives' movements and he didn't care, except that his job would be easier if he'd known more details.

Dean finally broke his silence. "And you're certain one of them didn't fly anywhere in the last two weeks?"

"The only thing certain is that none of the ticket sellers can remember seeing any of the people whose pictures you gave me. But they see hundreds of people every week. If one of the subjects left town by plane, he or she paid in cash and used a false name. Or a disguise."

Carrie looked at Dean as he skimmed the typed report provided by the short, slight detective whose bland, forgettable face was an asset for surveillance work. He had given them very little to go on. Too much time had passed to uncover much information about the movements and activities of the Sheffield individuals the week of the accidents.

"Have any of them met with anyone unusual?"

Rogers turned intelligent eyes to Carrie.

"Unusual?"

Carrie bit her lip, uncertain how to explain. "I mean … someone unlikely, someone who didn't seem to be the type you would expect them to know. Oh, say someone disreputable or rough looking."

Owen Rogers shot Carrie a knowing glance. "Ah, a person from another social stratum. Someone hired to do a specific job, possibly something illegal? In other words, an accomplice."

Carrie flushed. For all his ordinary appearance, Owen Rogers was quick. She nodded helplessly at the detective.

"No, nothing like that. But I'll tell my agents to keep an eye out for such an encounter. That is, unless you wish to terminate the case, Mr. Sheffield."

Dean looked up, considering. When he spoke, his tone was brisk, businesslike. "Continue the surveillance, Mr. Rogers. On everyone. And add this Grace Taylor Uncle David's been seeing to the list. Call me at any time if anything new comes up. Otherwise, I'll be in touch with you in a day or two." He stood up and offered his hand. "I should tell you that I intend to share the contents of your report with a police friend of Miss Richards. Do you have any objection?"

Owen Rogers smiled. "Not at all. The police and I get on very well. They have facilities and methods not available to me and vice versa. I hope you will inform me of anything relevant or helpful you might learn through official channels."

Dean readily agreed. He took Carrie's arm and a few minutes later they exited the parking lot beside Rogers' building.

Dean smiled at Carrie. "Are you as hungry as I am?"

"Hungrier."

"Good. Let's try that new Swedish restaurant. Aunt Bev says they set out an excellent smorgasbord at lunchtime. Then we'll drop in on Lieutenant Balfour."

"No!" Carrie exclaimed abruptly, then reddened at Dean's

questioning gaze. "I think we should call from the restaurant and ask him to meet us there. Or anywhere away from the station."

"Are you sensing something?" Dean looked baffled and a little apprehensive.

Carrie stifled a soft sigh at his reaction. "No. But I've been thinking. The would-be killer must have followed you, waiting for the opportunity to stage the accidents. He would have to keep track of your movements and could be following you—us—even now."

Comprehension dawned on Dean's face. "I should have thought of that. It would be a stupid mistake to let him see us entering a police station. Damn, I'm not thinking very straight."

Carrie laid a comforting hand on his arm. "I wouldn't be thinking straight either if I knew someone was trying to kill me."

Dean nodded his thanks for her understanding and lifted one hand from the steering wheel to cover hers. He squeezed lightly. Carrie withdrew her hand, twined her fingers in her lap and concentrated on not noticing the hot prickling sensation that seemed to burn the skin on the back of her hand.

Dean maneuvered the car down the gravel lane to the parking lot behind the restaurant. The deep, narrow lot was almost filled but they found an empty space near the boundary fence. Before they left the car, he used the car phone to leave a message for the policeman to join them. Retrieving a paper sack from the trunk of the car, he ushered Carrie into the restaurant.

Carrie sipped at her glass of white wine as they waited for Mark Balfour. Dean's face was impassive, unreadable, but his fingers tapped restlessly on the tabletop. She sensed he had retreated into himself and had almost forgotten her presence. She couldn't blame him. To be forced to have one's family investigated would disturb anyone. No, she couldn't blame him, but she felt shut out. It hurt. She broke the silence that had fallen over them.

"Do you think David's friend might be involved in what's going on?" Owen Rogers had discovered that Grace Taylor, a widow with three grown children, operated a freelance accountancy business from her home. She and Dean's Uncle David were frequent companions.

Dean blinked and returned to the present.

"We can't rule her out. David is comfortable financially but she might be eager for more. When her husband died during that convenience store robbery, she was left with three small children and not much insurance. Marrying into the Sheffield money must be an appealing prospect."

"I suppose it is. But how would she know about John's will?" There was only one answer to that, but Carrie hoped to keep Dean from brooding. "If she knows, then David told her. At the very least, it would mean he took the will, hoping to betray his brother's final wishes. It … I can't believe it of him!" Dean shook his head, but not before Carrie saw the pain in his eyes. She wanted desperately to wrap her arms around him and offer words of comfort. What words, she didn't know.

Balfour arrived and dropped heavily into the chair beside Carrie. He signaled for a coffee and leaned back with a sigh.

Agreeing to eat before discussing the case, they trooped to the smorgasbord table. Balfour perked up at the sight of the vast array of toppings on offer, and heaped his plate to overflowing. Dean and Carrie ate enough to appease their hunger but the policeman devoured the open sandwiches with relish.

"Mmm, best lunch I've had in months," he finally declared after the waitress had cleared their table and refilled their cups. "Usually it's a stale sandwich or a greasy burger, when I have time to eat at all. Well, on to business. Did you get those fingerprints, Mr. Sheffield?"

"Make it Dean, Lieutenant." Indicating the large paper bag on the seat beside him, Dean nodded. "They're all here. I've marked each glass with the user's name. Mine and Carrie's as well. I assumed you'd need ours for elimination purposes."

"Good. And I'm just Balfour." He leaned his forearms on the table and lowered his voice. "We found three sets of prints and a partial thumbprint that doesn't match the others. Two sets must belong to Mrs. Hummell and her son. They were all over the cottage. The third set was mainly in the living room, with a few in the kitchen. Probably a visitor."

"Where did you find the extra thumbprint?"

"Now that's rather interesting. It was on an empty can of beer in the trash. Three other cans yielded the same prints we found in Bill's bedroom."

Carrie held up her hand and curled her fingers around an imaginary can of beer. "How could anyone hold a can with just a thumb?"

"It can't be done. There's only one explanation. Whoever drank that beer wiped the can off before putting it in the trash. A rather odd thing to do, wouldn't you say? Luckily, he or she wasn't quite thorough enough, but unfortunately, a partial print can't help us."

Carrie and Dean exchanged glances.

"What?" Balfour asked alertly.

"Bill had a male visitor last night," Dean answered. "He may be the person who left that thumbprint. And we think he left on foot through the woods. It might be a good idea to see if we can discover the path he took."

The policeman looked interested. "Usually when someone doesn't want to be identified, it's because he has something to hide. I wonder if Bill Hummell is privy to his visitor's secret."

"Maybe this man had something to do with Irma's death. Suppose she discovered him, or someone, in the cottage when it should have been empty."

"That's it!" Carrie straightened in her chair. "That's what's been bothering me about the scene. We thought she was just about to enter the cottage when she was attacked. We had it backwards. She was *leaving* the cottage when she was attacked. She must have heard someone in the cottage—or overheard a conversation—probably just as she opened the cottage door. Whatever the case, she turned and ran for safety. Whoever it was heard her and followed."

Dean grimaced. "I think you're right. That would explain the look on her face. She knew she was in danger. But she wouldn't have run from her son's friend. It seems more likely that she surprised a stranger in the cottage." He rubbed the back of his neck. "But why bother to disguise the fact that she was leaving, rather than entering, the cottage? Taking time to move the body was a risky thing to do."

"People do weird things when they panic," Balfour interposed. "He probably knew Bill was working at the far side of the house. He didn't expect to be interrupted. Irma caught him off guard. All of which makes it likely that her assailant was a stranger."

"And not connected with my problem," Dean added, "although the coincidence still bothers me."

"Is there any way at all that Bill Hummell could have known the contents of your father's will? About the trust?"

Dean pondered Balfour's question. At last, he nodded reluctantly. "Someone knew at least a week before my father died, probably earlier than that. I suppose Dad may have forgotten to cover up his rough notes when he left the room for a minute. Someone could have entered the study. If Irma went in to clean and spotted his notes, she might have told her son. For that matter, Bill does small repair jobs around the house. He may have come across the notes himself." Shrugging, he added, "But then, any member of the family could have done the same. And the fact remains, neither Irma nor Bill could hope to profit from my death."

Carrie turned to Balfour and recounted the information gathered by Owen Rogers. The policeman took careful notes while she spoke. When she finished, he returned his notepad to his pocket.

"I'll look into this Grace Taylor's finances. But if she's after David's money, I don't think she's seen any of it yet. Your uncle's accounts show no more withdrawals than can be accounted for by an active social life. I can't say the same for your cousin's wife."

"What about her?" Dean asked.

"In the last six months, Natalie has charged five flights, two to Toronto and the others to three different American cities."

"Not to resorts or holiday spots?"

"No. The flights to Toronto were same day returns. She stayed overnight in Boston and Detroit and two nights in New York City. You don't know anything about these trips?"

Dean shook his head.

"How about her husband? Does he pay her credit card bills?"

"I doubt it. He gives her a generous monthly allowance and she has quite a few credit cards in her own name. I know she visits friends out of town on a fairly regular basis. That may account for the trips."

"Could be. Still, it wouldn't hurt to know the exact destinations. Can you get me a copy of their phone bill? I can get the information, but it would take awhile. That might give us a lead."

"I'll do that. Is there anything else?"

"Two more items. First, it's possible Justin Sheffield has a problem. He recently cashed a five thousand dollar bond. We haven't been able to discover why he needed such an amount in cash. According to his bank records, he's a long way from insolvent. It may not mean anything but I have to wonder why he didn't write a check. Unfortunately, I can think of a number of possible reasons."

Carrie saw the surprise in Dean's eyes before he shuttered them. When he didn't comment the officer continued.

"Your aunt's total withdrawals have remained about the same as they have for the last few years. The dollar value hasn't changed by much but the method of withdrawal has."

"What does that mean?"

"She's made several large withdrawals over the last three months or so. Again, in cash. Maybe the money is meant for some charity or charities. She certainly is generous with her money." Admiration colored the officer's voice. "But until recently, her donations have always been made by check. It's a little odd, but it may not mean anything." Balfour spread his hands. "That's about it. No unusual activity in Alanna Sheffield's account, or in Mrs. Scully's."

"Did you check into Lawrence Chambers finances?"

Both men looked at Carrie. Balfour spoke first. "Who's Lawrence Chambers?"

"Dad's lawyer. And mine. I never even thought about him. He's not family." Dean glanced speculatively at Carrie then turned back to Balfour. "At least, only family by marriage. Natalie is his daughter."

The officer's eyebrows rose. Dean continued speaking. Carrie and Balfour could almost hear him mentally ticking off each statement.

"I don't know anything about his personal finances. But his wife Adele makes an art of spending money. His daughter would be considerably wealthier if Justin inherited a share of my estate as well as John's. And," he added in sudden realization, "I only have Lawrence's word for it that he left John's will behind when he and his secretary rushed out. Maybe the will wasn't even ready for signatures then, and the meeting was about something altogether different."

Carrie laid a hand on Dean's arm. "What was Mr. Chambers annoyed about back at the house, the day of the funeral?"

Dean frowned. "He wanted to read the will, since everyone mentioned in it was present. I know the timing's not that unusual, but at that point, I didn't want to admit the will was missing. And I wasn't in the mood to think about inheritances anyway."

"Would your father have informed his lawyer that you knew the contents of the will?"

"Yes. Dad told me some days earlier that he would let Lawrence know that I was the only family member who knew the stipulations in the new will."

Their waitress approached with the coffee pot but all three shook their heads. When she was out of hearing, Mark Balfour took up the issue again.

"Could Lawrence have been acting? I mean, pretending he wanted to read the will so you wouldn't think he knew it was missing? Maybe he wanted to delay the setting up of the trust fund to give himself time to cover up some unsavory activities of his own."

"Like using Sheffield money for his own purposes?"

"Something like that," Balfour agreed.

They discussed the possibilities a few minutes longer, then the officer rose to leave.

"I'll see what I can find out about Chambers' financial status. Wouldn't hurt to confirm the secretary's son's accident, as well. And it might be interesting to look into Grace Taylor's reputation."

He gathered up the fingerprint samples Dean had collected and left, assuring them he'd be in touch the moment he learned anything new.

* * *

They were on the freeway headed back to Dean's house when he broke the silence.

"What are you thinking?"

Carrie had sensed Dean's eagerness to believe the lawyer was involved with the attempts on his life. He made a far more appealing villain than a blood relative. She hated to stamp out his hope. "You won't like it."

"So what else is new these days?" Dean threw her a lopsided smile. "Might as well tell me. But I think I can guess. You don't think Lawrence is involved, do you?"

"No, I don't think he is, though I've been wrong before. I can't explain. It isn't that I *know* he's not involved. It's rather that I know a family member *is*. I'm sorry, Dean."

"Don't be sorry. I guess I know it, too. God, what a mess!"

The traffic had thinned as they approached the city limits. Housing developments gave way to rolling, wooded hills. Dean increased his speed, suddenly anxious to reach his home, though it no longer seemed the safe haven it once had. A nondescript gray car moved into the inner lane to pass. His thoughts on the information gained that morning, Dean paid little attention. The gray car pulled abreast, then ahead.

Suddenly the driver flashed his right direction signal and began to pull over in front of Dean's car. Only a few feet separated the two vehicles. Dean realized immediately that a collision was inevitable.

He hit the horn, yanked the car to the right and slammed on the brakes at the same time. The pedal shot to the floor. Carrie screamed as the car careened towards the shallow ditch beside the road and the trees beyond. The memory of her parents' deaths flashed through her mind.

They didn't reach the trees. The speeding car plunged into the ditch and rolled over onto the passenger side, plowing fifty feet along the bottom before slowing to a stop. The gray car accelerated and disappeared around a curve.

Chapter Thirteen

Windmills humming in the breeze. Boys on bicycles coasting downhill, wheels thrumming on the asphalt. Wet clothes swishing in the washer. Heartbeat thumping in her head.

Cramped, uncomfortable, unable to shift position in the metal-hard bed, Carrie forced the dreams away and struggle to awaken. Her eyes fluttered open, then closed again, wondering at the dream that turned her room into an arched enclosure of gravel and green grass and blue sky. Her cheek slid a few inches across the hard, smooth pillow and arrested her downward drop into darkness.

A frantic male voice rang like knuckles on tin in her ear. Carrie muttered thickly and turned her head. Irritation forced her eyes open. Her vision blurred, cleared, and blurred again. Something sticky trickled through her hair and followed the curve behind her ear. Her left shoulder hurt where cruel fingers dug into her flesh. She whimpered in protest.

"Wake up, Carrie! Are you hurt?"

The panic edging Dean's voice pierced her confusion. Groggily, she stared into the face inches from hers and saw fear blazing in the smoky blue eyes. At the same moment, she became aware of the car door pressing against her side and the seatbelt cutting into her hips.

"Dean?"

"Thank God!" His breath gusted out in a warm blast across

her cheek. "We've had an accident but it's okay. The car is lying on its side. Just hold on, I'll have you out in a minute."

Carrie closed her eyes and listened to Dean's grunting efforts to unfasten his seatbelt and open the driver's door. The smell of gas irritated her nose. A draft curled around her knees and the sound of turning wheels slowed and stopped. In some small, detached part of her mind she realized that only a minute or two had passed since the car overturned. Her fingers searched automatically for the belt release and collided with Dean's.

"I've got it. Hang on."

Painfully, she lifted her head as a siren sounded in the distance, its volume increasing rapidly. She opened her mouth to speak. The pressure binding her hips disappeared. Agony shot through her as her head smacked the window again. Then merciful blackness descended.

* * *

A needle of pain lanced through her eye. Carrie twisted her head away and heard a satisfied voice murmur something over her head. Blinking furiously, she lifted a hand to her throbbing skull. Two large trembling hands imprisoned hers and squeezed with gentle force. Cautiously, fearful of increasing the pounding in her head, Carrie opened her eyes and squinted at the unfamiliar white ceiling, white walls, and the figure in white leaning over her.

"Here you are then, safe and sound. Nothing broken at all. A few bruises and a goose egg worthy of Ripley's." The throaty, soothing voice came from a matronly woman holding a pencil flashlight and smiling widely. "And a very lucky child you are, too."

Carrie slanted her gaze sideways and saw a disheveled Dean holding her hand, his face a study in misery. She tightened her fingers in his.

"You're not hurt?" When he shook his head she shivered in relief.

The nurse beamed at them both, then informed Dean in a no-nonsense voice that he had five minutes before she kicked him out.

"You may come back later, but this child needs to sleep. Five minutes, mind, not a second more." She shook a warning finger at Dean and left, closing the door behind her.

"I…. What happened, Dean?"

"You don't remember?"

Carrie started to shake her head, then stopped to wait for the dizziness to pass. "No, nothing."

"We were pushed off the road by a careless driver. Or a drunk driver." He hesitated. "Or a murderous one."

Carrie's eyes widened.

"I'm inclined to think the latter." Deep anger underlined his grim tone. "The driver didn't stop and he must have seen what happened. A little too coincidental for my book."

"I guess we were pretty lucky." Carrie gave him a shaky smile. "But," she frowned, "how did the police get there so quickly?"

Dean looked uncomfortable. "They were already on their way. With an ambulance."

It took a moment for that to sink in. "You mean before the accident actually happened? But how … Greta!"

Dean cleared his throat as a dull red crept up his face. "Yes. A woman called to report an accident. A Mrs. Greta Sonnheim. The dispatcher assumed she'd actually seen it happen. But the call was logged almost ten minutes before our lethal friend made his move." His grip on her hand tightened as he shook his head, unable to meet her eyes. "Not that I'm not grateful, but I'm still having a hard time with all this … this…."

"Yes," Carrie sighed. "I can tell."

When Dean glanced at her sharply, she managed a ghost of a smile. "And no, I can't read minds. Like everyone else, I just interpret tone of voice, body language and facial expressions, all the *normal* methods of communication. That's all."

She hadn't meant to be sarcastic but her head was pounding. Between pain and disappointment that he couldn't see past her ability to the woman she really was, her store of energy was too depleted to allow for politeness. What right had he to be disturbed by her talent when he owed his life to it?

He wasn't being reasonable and she resented it. Every time it seemed he'd accepted her for the way she was, he'd proved her wrong. She didn't want gratitude or admiration, just acceptance. Was it so much to ask?

Dean gritted his teeth and stared at his shoes. He could think of nothing to say. He couldn't protest that she misjudged his attitude. Any denial would be dishonest as well as futile. She could read him too well. He had hurt her and, judging by the bitterness in her voice, he wasn't the first to do so. Three times she had saved his life and in spite of the danger, had dedicated herself to his safety.

And how had he repaid her? With skepticism and aversion and suspicion.

He had never considered himself an intolerant man before. Suddenly he saw himself for what he was: ignorant, narrow-minded, and arrogant. The hot flame of shame cleansed his soul. Of a sudden, her strange talent didn't matter. He lifted his head, prepared to apologize and beg her forgiveness. He was too late.

"Time to go, young man. You may come back this evening." The nurse planted herself at the foot of the bed, making it very clear that Dean's time was up.

He nodded in surrender and brushed his lips on Carrie's

cheek. "I'll be back."

"Wait, Dean. Would you call Greta? She'll be worried—"

"I did, love, as soon as we got to the hospital. She knows you're all right, but I'll call her again when I get home. You rest now." He loosened her hand and left the room, dragging his feet in frustration. He ached to share his acceptance with her but he needed privacy for the telling.

Carrie swallowed the pain tablets the nurse offered and promised not to sleep until the prospect of concussion had past.

* * *

Carrie ate the last spoonful of pudding and pushed the tray away. The meal had been unappetizing, but the kindly bullying nurse insisted she eat every bite. It was easier to obey. The pounding in her head had lessened but various aches and bruises clamored for their share of attention. She yearned for a long soak in a hot bath, but that would have to wait until after Dean's visit. A visit she both dreaded and desired.

His continuing aversion ate at her, like rodent teeth nibbling at her heart. Still, some masochistic part of her yearned to see him. He had some feeling for her, she was certain. But not enough to overcome his distaste for her abilities. The future promised to be as colorless and unappealing as the bland hospital meal.

A knock on the door wiped the gloomy thoughts from her mind. Dean! The door swung open to reveal Beverley and David Sheffield. Carrie swallowed her disappointment and forced a welcoming smile on her face. Dean must have told the family about the crash but she hadn't anticipated visitors.

Five minutes later Carrie found herself relaxing, something she hadn't thought she could do in Beverley's presence. Surprisingly, the woman seemed as friendly and as sincerely concerned as her brother. There was no sign of the rude eccentricity she had displayed on their first meeting.

They discussed the problem of drunk drivers, the weather, Dick's unwitting intrusion in her room that morning, Carrie's work and Dean's plans for the expansion of the clothing chain. Talk of the travel involved led to a sharing of their vacation trips. Carrie described in glowing terms the motor trip she and Greta had taken a few years before, to the Atlantic provinces.

"I've never been east, but you were, weren't you Bev?" David turned to his sister.

"Yes, I visited a college friend in down east once. A long time ago. I had a lovely time but I haven't seen her since then. We wrote for a few years but eventually lost touch."

A knock on the door brought three heads around. Dean entered, carrying a flower arrangement and a gift wrapped package. He looked larger than life and incredibly handsome. A stranger would never guess he had been in a car crash a few hours earlier. Carrie knew she looked pale and unattractive in the genderless hospital gown. Not that it mattered.

Stifling his irritation at the sight of Carrie's visitors, Dean approached the bed. He ignored their audience and bent to brush his lips over her cheek. When her eyes widened he winked, then set the flowers and package on the windowsill.

"I can't believe how lucky you two were." Beverley shook her head. "Maybe there's something to this guardian angel business after all."

Carrie and Dean exchanged glances.

"Have the police been able to trace the driver?" David queried his nephew.

Dean shook his head. "I doubt they'll ever discover his identity. It all happened so fast. I didn't see the plate number or the driver. I think it was a gray sedan but I couldn't even swear to the color."

"Did you see anything, Carrie?" David persisted.

"Nothing. One minute we were on the highway, the next minute I was here. Even if they caught the right person I wouldn't be able to testify."

"Terrible thing," David scowled. "The driver was probably drunk." He looked at Dean. "And you say there was no collision? In a way, that's too bad. I've read that the police can sometimes trace a car from paint chips. Looks like whoever it was is going to get away with it."

After a few more minutes dissecting the accident Beverley and David rose to leave. Both Sheffields encouraged Carrie to return to their home. To Carrie's surprise, Beverley was especially insistent.

"I understand your grandmother's unable to stay with you. You come back to the house. We'll all take care of you. You can never be sure about head injuries, so you really shouldn't be alone for a few days." With a final smile, she followed her brother out the door. Dean closed it behind them and took the chair closest to the bed.

Immediately self-conscious, Carrie clasped her hands together to keep them still. "It wasn't a drunk driver, was it?"

"No, it wasn't." His tone was grim. "The brake line was cut. It held just long enough for us to leave the city limits and reach the highway."

"Where the speed limit is higher."

Dean nodded. "Our so-called drunk driver wanted to ensure that we went off the road at the fastest speed possible. He probably expected the car to overshoot the shallow ditch and plow into the trees. If I ever get my hands on him—"

Carrie recoiled from the furious glint in his eyes. He didn't notice her sudden movement.

"Lieutenant Balfour did a quick check on the family. It appears that none of them could have been driving the car. It's remotely possible that it was a coincidence."

"But you don't think so, do you?"

"No. I think this was the fourth attempt. This time he meant to make doubly sure. Sabotage the brakes and force us off the road at top speed. The bastard! He didn't care that you could have died too! Believe me, he's going to pay dearly!"

A chill crept down Carrie's spine at the violence in his voice. She had seen him angry before, but not like this. The chill turned into warmth when she realized that his rage was triggered by fear for her. Would he feel the same if some other woman had been with him? If it had been Natalie in the car? She wasn't sure she wanted to know.

"Does the lieutenant have any idea when the brake line was sabotaged?"

The glitter faded from Dean's eyes, as Carrie intended. He shrugged and rubbed the back of his neck.

"We figure it was done when we were in the restaurant, or the brakes would have failed earlier. The buildings backing on that parking lot were windowless. The brush at the fence line would easily conceal someone if another diner appeared to retrieve his car. You were right, he must have been following us. We gave him the perfect opportunity to mess with the brakes. But thanks to you, we didn't lead him to the police station."

Carrie nodded. "Your aunt and uncle seemed to accept the story of a drunk driver. They'll tell the others. So we do have one thing going for us. The murderer still can't be sure we're on to him. Hopefully, he'll convince himself that you're not suspicious. But Dean, I think you should…."

"What?"

Knowing it was a waste of breath, Carrie still had to try. "I think you should go away for awhile, take a vacation somewhere safe. Don't tell anyone where you're going. The killer has to be getting frustrated. He—"

Dean immediately shook his head. "It wouldn't help. He'd simply wait for me to return. Besides, he could follow me again and I'd never know it. No, we can only hope that frustration will make him careless."

Carrie was forced to agree. Running away would solve nothing. At least he was still saying "we." She knew, even if he didn't, that their lives were irrevocably entwined until this was over. Greta was correct when she insisted that Carrie was responsible for this man's well-being. But, oh, she was so afraid for him.

She dropped her head and stared at her hands. He misunderstood.

"Don't be angry, sweetheart. Can't you see? I have to know who's doing this. For Irma's sake, if nothing else. Besides," he coaxed, his voice softening, "he can't hurt me. I have my very own guardian angel watching over me." He cupped her chin and turned her head to face him. His head lowered slowly, his eyes never leaving hers.

Carrie forgot to breath. Her lips parted, her mouth suddenly dry. His warm breath danced on her skin as her eyes closed. Then she felt the feather-touch of his mouth on hers, electrifying her body to her toes. She heard a tiny sob and realized that it came from her own throat.

The door swung open.

"Whoops! Sorry, folks, visiting time is over."

Sitting up abruptly, Dean threw the nurse a look that usually made strong men back away. It had no effect.

"I know, I know. My timing's not the greatest. None the less, you handsome devil, this poor child needs a good night's sleep." She grinned cheerfully. "The doctor says she'll be discharged in the morning. You may take up where you left off then." She looked from one to the other. Her smile widened. "I'm sure you'll both remember where you were. Now, say goodnight, that's a good lad."

Dean accepted defeat. His lips curled up in a reluctant smile, he brushed his knuckles along Carrie's jaw and left, promising to return for her the next morning.

The moment the door swung closed behind him, Carrie's bruises clamored for attention. Gratefully she swallowed the sleeping pill the nurse offered and sank into the bed. Dean's voice followed her into sleep. *My very own guardian angel.*

* * *

Dean dismissed the taxi and accompanied Carrie to the private investigator's waiting room, stepping aside to allow Carrie to enter first. They had just left the hospital and, although he was anxious to get her home, he wanted to tell the investigator about their near fatal accident the day before. The receptionist, Owen's plump, pretty niece, waved them to chairs, explaining that her boss was with a client but should be free in a few minutes.

Carrie leafed through a magazine and ignored the young woman's curious glances at the bandage on her forehead. The pounding in her head had shrunk to the tolerable burden of a normal headache. The doctor assured her that her aches and pains would disappear within a few days. Considering what could have happened to her, she wouldn't complain.

Beside her, Dean sat silently contemplating his shoes. Sleep had been slow in coming the night before. He still found it almost impossible to accept that a member of his own family would kill him. But even without Carrie's revelations he knew it had to be true. There could be no other explanation for four near fatal accidents in the space of two weeks. The damaged brake line was the first piece of physical evidence.

He had finally dozed off near dawn but woke with a hoarse cry, his heart pounding with fear, his body damp with sweat. In his dream, the car had rolled end over end to smash into the thick grove of trees. Not so much as a scratch for himself, but Carrie's body was twisted and broken, her neck bent in an impossible angle. He had leaped from the bed and spent the rest of the night sprawled on the chair on his balcony, afraid to sleep again.

The realization had crept up on him as the sun rose over the horizon. He was in love with her. Her psychic ability was no more a liability than a superb singing voice or a talent for mathematics or a photographic memory. It was part of what made her special, unique. But only a part. He loved the whole woman; her kind heart, her love of children, her intelligence, her lovely face and body, her generous soul. Together they made up the woman he wanted to spend the rest of his life with. But he knew he had hurt her badly.

He shifted restlessly in the chair. Now more than ever, he wanted this mystery solved. Until the danger was past and he was assured a future, he could not ask her to share that future.

Ignoring the interested, sidelong glances from the young receptionist, he started to reach for Carrie's hand. The opening of the inner office door arrested the motion. Through the partially opened door they heard Owen offer regrets to his unseen visitor.

"I'm afraid you must find another investigator, Mr. Sheffield. My caseload is simply too full at the moment. I can't take on another client for the time being. Good day, sir."

Shocked, Dean's gaze flew to Carrie. Her eyes reflected his astonishment. Before either could speak, the door opened wider and Justin Sheffield strode through. The disappointment on his face changed to consternation, then to something like guilt, as he caught sight of his cousin. He stopped dead in his tracks, his mouth working soundlessly.

The two men gaped at each other, then Justin muttered a

greeting and rushed from the room, almost running. Owen stepped into the doorway, his eyes going first to his niece. He too faltered in surprise when he recognized the other occupants of the room. A moment later, amusement shone in his face.

"Looks like I'm going to have to revise my theory of the nonexistence of coincidence. Judging by your expressions, neither of you knew Mr. Sheffield was here."

He gestured for Dean and Carrie to enter his office. After shutting the door, he took his seat and laid his hands, palms down, on the desk. His smile slowly died as he looked at his two silent clients and then swiveled his chair to face the window. They waited for him to speak. Finally, he seemed to make up his mind and turned back to them.

"I can't remember the last time I was faced with a problem like this. Your cousin walked in off the street. Unfortunately, he told me why he wanted to hire me before he gave me his name. Had I known who he was, I wouldn't have allowed him to explain his need for my services. It would have been a clear case of conflict of interest and, sadly, my ethics won't allow me to accept payment twice for the same work." A wry smile twisted his lips. "Not that the money wouldn't be welcome. However, although there's no contract between us, Mr. Sheffield has the right to expect that his confidence will not be broken. I cannot, in good conscience, tell you the reason he wished to hire me."

Dean sighed, trying not to let his disappointment show. He respected Owen's position, indeed, he would have been disturbed if the investigator had betrayed his cousin's confidence. "I understand," he said.

Owen appreciated his client's restraint and was pleased that Dean hadn't tried to persuade him to reveal the purpose of his cousin's visit. For that reason, he decided that total secrecy wasn't necessary.

He spoke slowly, searching for suitable words. "You must

realize I would not have told you your cousin came here, had you not seen it for yourself. Since it's not possible for me to 'unhear' his story, I must treat it as private information. But I believe I can say two things without breaking his confidence."

Carrie and Dean unconsciously leaned forward.

"One, the task he wanted me to undertake has nothing to do with your problem, so far as I can see. It's a strictly personal matter. And two, he was prepared to pay me five thousand dollars, cash, as a retainer."

Owen sat back in his chair and watched the changing expressions on his client's face. Relief, pleasure, gratitude, puzzlement; the same emotions were eloquently mirrored on Carrie Richards' intelligent face. The significance of the retainer struck them at the same moment.

"Not payment of a gambling debt or blackmail," Carrie breathed. Of course, the existence of a personal problem didn't exclude an involvement in a murder plot. Justin Sheffield could be the guilty party.

Her attention returned to the conversation.

A deep frown creased Owen Rogers' face as he listened to Dean's account of the car crash. His worried eyes never left his client's face.

"Your lethal friend is getting careless. Or desperate. He took quite a chance this time. He couldn't be sure the crash would kill you and, for all he knew, you might have seen his face or noted the license plate. At the very least, unless he believes you're incredibly naive, he must be afraid that you have figured out what's going on. Which means time is running out for him."

"I've thought of that," Dean replied. "His next attempt will likely be soon. And much more direct. Four accidents have been failures. Since it seems pretty certain there must be two in on the plot, the person who hired him must be losing faith in his accomplice."

"Speaking of time passing," Carrie interjected, "has anyone mentioned the reading of John's will?"

Dean's eyes were bleak as he answered. "Both Natalie and Beverley mentioned the omission at breakfast this morning. Casually, but I had the impression they had discussed the subject before I joined them."

"Who brought up the topic first?"

"Natalie. But I think she was asking for both of them."

Carrie pondered this news. True, it was customary for a will to be read shortly after the deceased's funeral. But in this case, John's heirs should have no pressing need for the immediate distribution of his wealth. Except greed and impatience. Then she realized what she'd missed.

"Isn't it rather unusual for Beverley and Natalie to breakfast so early?"

Dean caught her meaning instantly. "Thanks for reminding me." Turning to the investigator he explained. "I meant to tell you right away but seeing Justin here drove it out of my mind. Natalie mentioned that she would be flying to Montreal today to visit a friend and expects to be back late tonight. When I teased Aunt Bev about her early rising, she said something about an appointment at her bank. Both were quite vague and changed the subject. I didn't think I should press them further."

"Not to worry, they're both being followed." Owen looked enthused. "This may be a lucky break for us. It's our first opportunity to discover what your cousin's wife is up to. Of course, her mysterious trips may be exactly what she claims, merely innocent visits with friends. My operative will call the moment he has something to report. I'll get in touch with you immediately."

With nothing more to discuss, they took their leave, first requesting that Owen's receptionist call for a taxi. As they waited at the front door of the building, Dean seemed to read

Carrie's mind. His first words alluded to the breakfast conversation.

"I can't quite picture Natalie and Beverley conspiring together in a murder plot. But then, neither can I picture one or the other plotting alone. Until recently, I thought Beverley and I were close."

And Natalie? Do you still feel close to her? Carrie didn't have the nerve to ask. The answer might be more than she could bear.

"It may have been simple curiosity that prompted them to mention the will, Dean."

"Or simple greed."

He sounded so sad and disillusioned, Carrie yearned to put her arms around him and comfort him. There was nothing to say, because he could be right. Money was so often the root cause of crimes. Nor was the desire for riches a characteristic only of the poor. For some people, regardless of their present wealth, the desire for more becomes an overriding obsession—incomprehensible to Carrie, but confirmed by crime statistics everywhere.

The arrival of the taxi interrupted her cheerless musings.

* * *

The restaurant was small, but bright and spotlessly clean. Somehow it didn't seem to be the sort of place that would attract a man as accustomed to expensive elegance as Dean must be. Carrie tried to hide her surprise when they entered but Dean intercepted her expression and merely murmured, "You'll see," in her ear.

He took her arm and steered her to the only empty table. They were hardly seated when the swinging door to the kitchen opened and a short, slight man stepped into the room, bearing a crowded tray that should have been too heavy for him. He plunked the plates down unceremoniously in front of four eager looking customers, then turned back to the kitchen.

His face split into a wide grin when he spotted Dean. In seconds, he was beside the table, enthusiastically pumping Dean's hand.

"My good friend! Hey, it's great to see you again. Where the hell you been lately? Ruby will be hoppin' mad she missed you. Wait 'til I tell her. She's taken the day off. Parents day at the school, you know. I tell her not to bother the teachers. The kids, they do all A's and B's. I think she goes to hear good things so she can brag to the neighbors."

As the delighted man chattered on about his wife and children, Carrie thought of David and Goliath. The disparity between the sizes of the two men was arresting. Dean's immense bulk hovered over the slight form of the restaurant owner but their smiles were identical.

Her amusement faded when he mentioned his youngest son. The name brought back memories. Disconcerted, Carrie tried to shrink into her chair. Surely he wouldn't recognize her? It had been a year, no, closer to two, since she'd been involved with his family and he had seen her for only a few seconds.

"Eddie," Dean said when he finally managed to get a word in, "I'd like you to meet my friend, Carrie Richards."

"Pleased to meet— Hot damn, it's you!" Eddie's eyebrows rose as his eyes widened in excitement. He scooted around the table to sit in the empty chair beside her. Grabbing her hand, he stared into her face, his own assuming a look that bordered on adoration.

"I never got a chance to thank you for saving Joey. The lieutenant wouldn't tell us who you were. Ruby and me, we've been watching for your face for two years, hopin' to get the chance to tell you how much we appreciate what you did. But don't worry none, we'll never tell nobody about you. Holy heaven, wait 'til

I tell Ruby. Bet she don't believe me. I wish she was here to meet you, Miss Richards."

"Call me Carrie." There was no point in claiming the small man was mistaken. "But please, Eddie, ask Ruby to keep it to herself."

"Gotcha, Miss Richards. I mean, Carrie." Without loosening her hand he shot a glance at Dean. "This man mountain you're with, does he know what you done?"

Carrie saw the avid curiosity in Dean's eyes. She shrugged, embarrassed by the situation. But she knew he wouldn't let it go, so Eddie might as well have the pleasure. "I did very little, Eddie, but go ahead."

A customer called Eddie's name and raised his empty cup. With a careless gesture Eddie signaled to the man to go behind the counter and help himself. Then he leaned toward Dean and lowered his voice.

"A few years ago some young punks tried to make me pay protection money. Of course I told them what they could do with their protection, but they snatched Joey. Ruby made me go to the police. I didn't want to, but she wouldn't listen to me, bless her stubborn hide. Lieutenant Balfour borrowed some of Joey's clothes for Miss Richards here to hold, and she figured out where they'd stashed him." He shook his head in remembered amazement. "I weren't supposed to see her, but I did. Never believed in that kind of funny stuff before, but I sure as heck do now."

"I take it the police found Joey?" Dean was fascinated by the story, though he was uncomfortably aware that Eddie hadn't let go of Carrie's hand. Was he actually jealous? Yes, he was.

"Yup. Right where Miss Richards said to look. The punk guarding him got drunk and fell asleep. They caught him, easy as pie. He ratted on his pals and all of them are coolin' their miserable souls in prison.

"Joey was a trooper," Eddie added proudly. "Claimed he was fine, just mad cuz they wouldn't bring him cheeseburgers. He had a few bad dreams but it only took a couple of weeks 'til he was his old self again. Some kinda kid, eh! And," he smiled at Carrie, "some kind of woman!"

Carrie blushed scarlet. Grinning, the little man stood, bowed with gallant charm and released her hand.

"Fair's fair, I always say. So Miss Richards—Carrie—you ask this overgrown bear how he single-handedly saved my family's business. Now, I'm going to cook you the best omelet you've ever tasted." He winked at Dean. "If you don't tell her, I will." With that, he disappeared into the kitchen, returned almost instantly with two mugs of coffee, then vanished again with a muttered "Tell her" in Dean's ear.

"So, you heard him, tell me," Carrie demanded, curious and very grateful for the chance to shift the spotlight. She crossed her arms over her chest and sent him an imperious look.

Dean lifted his shoulder in a casual shrug. Then he explained that Ruby once worked for the Sheffields as a housekeeper until one day he happened to notice the exhaustion in her face. Some discreet questioning revealed that the woman worked another six hours in the family restaurant after her day at the mansion. With three small children and little collateral, the couple were unable to obtain a bank loan, which would have enabled them to hire a waitress, arrange for a baby-sitter to care for the children in the evenings and upgrade the restaurant kitchen.

Dean had promptly fired Ruby, driven her to the restaurant and given the couple a check to cover their needs.

"No big deal," he said now to Carrie. "Don't look at me like that. There was no hardship involved on my part. And Eddie paid back every cent." In fact, he loved the admiration shining in her eyes, but he wanted her approval for himself, Dean Sheffield the man, not for one simple act that hadn't even dented his bank account.

They were both relieved when Eddie returned with the lightest, fluffiest looking omelets Carrie had ever seen.

"Enjoy, my friends." He hurried away to take orders from a group of new arrivals.

With her first bite Carrie understood why Dean had not asked her preference. The omelet was superb. By unspoken agreement the subject uppermost in their minds was ignored. They ate without exchanging a single word, the atmosphere both comfortable and relaxed.

Later, over a second cup of coffee, Dean broke the contented silence.

"What do you make of Justin's behavior?"

Sighing inwardly at the abrupt but inevitable ending of the brief recess, Carrie set her cup on the table and met Dean's eyes.

"Only one thing comes to mind. Baldly put, I'd guess that Justin wanted to hire Owen to have Natalie followed. Presumably, he suspects her of having taken a lover."

Dean winced but nodded in agreement. "That's what I've been thinking, too." His anguished look vanished, to be replaced by fierce anger.

"How could she do that to him? She has to know he loves her. How could she hurt him that way?"

Carrie covered his white-knuckled fist with a gentle hand. Natalie had cheated on Dean. And maybe now the woman was cheating again, cheating on her husband. Was Dean still suffering because of her betrayal?

"We could be wrong, Dean," she said softly, "and if not, Justin's suspicions may be unfounded. The obvious answer isn't necessarily the correct answer."

"You're right, of course. Still, I'm afraid—"

Carrie gaped in astonishment at the change that spread over Dean's face. The anger was gone, replaced in an instant with a large smile directed past her shoulder. When he lifted his hand in a wave, she twisted around in her chair.

Chapter Fourteen

Dean's Uncle David appeared at Carrie's side, his hand clasping that of a pillow-plump woman at least five inches shorter than his own five foot ten. Her dark auburn hair, liberally threaded with gray, coiled in a thick braid that hung over one shoulder. Her generous mouth seemed made for smiling. It was a strong face, not pretty, but saved from homeliness by elongated, vivid green eyes that sparkled with a cautious eagerness.

Dean stood as David introduced Grace Taylor, then invited the couple to join them. The quartet chatted in the willing-to-be-friendly but slightly stilted manner of people alert for personality clues. Within a very few minutes it was clear that Grace Taylor was a cheerful, witty, unpretentious woman. More, her affections were as centered on David as his were on her. His obvious pride in his companion warmed Carrie's heart.

When the couple's meals arrived Dean pushed back his chair, explaining that he and Carrie were on their way to visit Carrie's grandmother so she could see for herself that Carrie survived the car crash.

David put up a restraining hand. "I'm glad we ran into each other, Dean. I've a favor to ask. You could help me—Grace and me—if you'd agree to buy my shares in the stores. I'll explain when we have more time, but think about it, won't you, and we can discuss it later."

Dean was shocked but managed to contain the avalanche of

questions that tumbled into his mind. It was the last thing he would have expected to hear from a Sheffield.

"Ah, yes, certainly, I'll think about it." He laughed suddenly. "This is a joke, isn't it? You had me going there for a minute."

His uncle grinned ruefully. "No joke. Give it some serious thought, Dean. You'll understand later. In fact, I think you'll even approve."

Dean's eyes narrowed as he searched his uncle's face. When David winked at Grace and took her hand, Dean's expression grew thoughtful. "All right, I'll give it some thought. Are congratulations in order here?"

"Well-l-l," David drawled, "as a matter of fact, yes. It was a job of work, I can tell you. But I finally convinced this lovely lady to be my wife. We'll be telling the others at dinner tonight."

Dean and Carrie offered the blushing couple their best wishes. Grace seemed relieved as well as pleased at Dean's enthusiastic acceptance.

Finally, they left the happy couple to enjoy their lunch. Dean said little in the taxi ride to the nursing home and Carrie wondered what he really thought about his uncle's engagement and unusual request. As far as they knew, David could afford to marry without relinquishing his shares in the family business. Was Grace demanding more than a new name?

They cut short their visit with Greta when the older woman began to yawn. Her eyes twinkled when she admitted that she and Ernst had sat up late, talking in the patients' lounge.

By the time the taxi deposited them at the mansion, Carrie was longing for a hot shower and a nap. Her muscles were stiff, and the aches and pains caused by the car crash hinted only too vividly at the physical discomfort of old age.

Correctly interpreting the strain in her face, Dean insisted she rest for the afternoon. Carrie agreed thankfully. She hesitated at the door of the study when the phone rang. An apologetic

Owen Rogers reported that his agent had lost Natalie when an anti-abortion protest march had filled the streets and hidden her from his view. They exchanged despairing grimaces. As she slowly climbed the stairs, Carrie reflected that they were no closer to discovering Dean's enemy now than they were at the beginning. If only she *did* have a crystal ball.

* * *

Carrie pulled the sash of her dressing gown tighter and cracked open the door. Her heart thudded to the beat of the phrase "This is crazy, crazy, crazy" that looped through her mind in a continuous refrain.

The hall was empty. She listened. Nothing. Finally she opened her door and scurried down the hall to the suite of rooms belonging to Justin and Natalie. With Natalie in Montreal and Justin at the store, she would never have a better opportunity to snoop. A part of her hoped the door would be locked. A larger part prayed she would be able to enter and search for something—anything—that might explain Natalie's mysterious trips.

The knob turned in her hand. Carrie slipped inside, closed the door gently, then slumped against it. When her trembling ceased she straightened and scanned the suite.

The sitting room surprised her. There were potted plants at the balcony doors, ferns hanging from the ceiling, a huge green and cream Schefflera in the corner. Given Natalie's sleek elegance, she had been expecting stark, modern furniture, perhaps a brilliant abstract painting. Instead, the textured cream walls, numerous bookcases and maple cottage furniture exuded an air of homey warmth. Perhaps Natalie was more of a homemaker than her appearance suggested.

A small maple desk in the corner caught her eye. Quickly,

Carrie sifted through the contents of the single drawer, but found nothing of special interest. Reluctantly she headed for the bedroom, distaste for the self-assigned task unpleasant in her mouth. She felt like a Peeping Tom.

A king-sized waterbed dominated the room. Two maple bureaus stood side by side on the far wall. She skirted the bed and opened the top drawer of what was obviously Natalie's dresser. Carrie searched each drawer, disturbing the contents as little as possible. Her face ached with tension.

Under a pile of sweaters in the bottom drawer lay a bundle of business-sized envelopes secured with an elastic. She riffled through the envelopes, checking the postmarks. They matched the destinations of Natalie's mysterious trips. All of the envelopes were typed.

Excitement coursed through her. At long last, some progress! If the letters revealed that Natalie had a lover, the police could investigate his background. The man, with or without Natalie's knowledge, could prove to be the author of Dean's accidents. Carrie found herself hoping that Dean's ex-fiancée wasn't aware of her lover's murderous activities.

She hesitated. Should she take the letters back to her room? If they proved to implicate her in a murder plot, Natalie wouldn't dare announce their disappearance. But if the letters were innocent and Natalie missed them, Carrie could find herself accused of theft.

Inhaling deeply, she clenched her jaw and removed the top envelope from the bundle. Someone knocked on the door. Panic locked her muscles. She stood rigid, scarcely breathing, sure her chattering teeth could be heard through the walls.

The knock came again. A door opened. She stuffed the envelopes in the pocket of her gown and looked around frantically for a place to hide. How could she possibly explain her presence here? Instinct send her diving to her stomach at the far side of the bed. She moaned softly and tried to sink into the carpet.

Two voices, one angry, reached her ears. She strained to hear, but the words were unintelligible, barely audible. Then understanding penetrated the buzz of dismay in her mind. The speakers were in the hall. No one had knocked at the door of the Natalie's suite. No one had entered. A false alarm. Carrie melted into a relieved puddle, and wondered if her bones would ever hold her upright again.

Barely breathing, she waited. After an eternity of minutes, she heard a door close and footsteps move slowly down the hall. She lay still, waiting for her pulse to return to normal.

Finally, clutching the bed for support, she struggled to her feet. She had to get out. If Natalie or Justin were behind the murder attempts and found her here— She shuddered and forced herself to creep to the door. No sound disturbed the stillness. She summoned all her courage and slipped out of the room.

Moments later her bed squealed in protest as she flung herself down. She yearned to climb under the covers and pull them over her head. She'd make a lousy criminal! The thought suddenly seemed absurdly funny. When hysterical laughter burst from her throat she buried her face in the pillow.

When the seizure finally passed, Carrie checked the time. She gasped in dismay. Dean had suggested she join him and the others in the front parlor for a drink before dinner. As a guest in the house and because of her own reserved nature, the thought of upsetting the family's routines by tardiness disturbed her.

She stared at the bundle of letters. Maybe she…. No, Natalie's letters would have to wait a few minutes. She'd shower and dress for dinner first and then read one letter.

Just as she drew the first letter from its envelope a knock sounded on the door and Dean asked if she was ready. Carrie gasped and clutched the letters to her chest.

"I'm coming," she called back. Guilt for her snooping washed over her. She thrust the letters under her pillow. Three minutes later she and Dean strolled into the sitting room. Carrie hoped she looked more tranquil than she felt.

* * *

After a delicious dinner of fresh salmon with mushroom and chestnut sauce, Dean and his Uncle David excused themselves and disappeared into the study. Carrie felt certain they would be discussing David's proposal to sell his shares in the family business.

The three women moved to the cozy sitting room. When Aggie entered carrying a coffee tray, Carrie was pleasantly surprised to hear Beverley invite Aggie to join them.

"You're one of the family, Aggie, and Grace soon will be. We need to get acquainted, to become friends. It's important for families to be friends, not to leave anyone out."

Smiling broadly, Aggie chose a chair by the fire and turned eagerly to Grace. "I'm so happy Mr. David has you to help him over this sad time, his brother's death and all. Tell us about your children, Grace. Are you a grandmother yet?"

Grace Taylor was more than willing to talk about her family. The other women enjoyed her tales of the disasters and triumphs of her offsprings' growing years. Finally she cried off, insisting she wanted to examine the rogue's gallery on the wall. Beverley and Aggie took turns identifying the figures in the pictures that covered almost a century of Sheffields.

Carrie was as intrigued as Grace with this look into the past. Dean greatly resembled his father when John was the same age as Dean was now. She wished she had had the chance to know his mother Lucy, whose arms were draped around her husband

and son in almost every picture. It was hard to believe that the sweet-faced, tiny woman had given birth to a baby who had grown to tower over her.

The pictures of Beverley fascinated Carrie. As a child her animated, laughing face had been almost pretty. The hair styles of the time flattered her teenage face. One particular pose revealed a voluptuous figure that was undoubtedly a source of envy to her friends. Carrie wondered why the attractive young girl had changed into the severe woman who now ignored fashion and so frequently scorned social courtesies.

Still, this evening Beverley was making every effort to put Grace Taylor at ease. Carrie could only assume that she cared a great deal for her brother and approved of Grace, if only because the woman made David happy. Dean's aunt revealed more sensitivity and generosity than Carrie would have foreseen.

Two of the group pictures portrayed Natalie clinging to Justin's arm and looking beautiful. In each, Carrie noted with relief, Dean stood some distance from his ex-fiancé.

Centered among the others was a large sepia-toned picture of a somber looking couple, the woman standing stiffly behind the seated man. The couple's old-fashioned clothing suggested a wedding portrait of the kind taken decades earlier. Carrie wasn't surprised when Beverley identified them as her parents. In spite of the age of the picture, she could see Dean's resemblance to his grandfather Peter, the founder of the first Sheffield Men's Wear.

The wall of photographs chronicled the lives of three generations of the family. Carrie wondered if Grace would be invited to add a picture of her children and grandchildren to the collection.

When David and Dean joined them Grace glanced quickly at her fiancé. Carrie saw her sudden tension fade when both men threw her matching smiles. Had Dean agreed to buy his uncle's shares? Surely David, if he knew nothing of the new will, would be expecting to receive a large portion of his brother's estate. What did he want so badly that he would sell his shares in the family business? What did Grace want? Or was the sale of his shares a ruse, designed to portray him as a man who looked for money honestly?

An hour later Aggie and then Beverley excused themselves and retired. David and Grace left soon after.

Carrie stared into her snifter of brandy. She ached to ask for the details of David's reason for selling his shares, but she kept a tight rein on her tongue. It was, after all, family business. If it had nothing to do with the murder attempts, or even if it did, Dean had every right to keep the information to himself. Would he trust her with David's confidential concerns? Unaware she was frowning, Carrie almost didn't hear his quiet voice.

"Are you feeling any better?"

"What? Oh, yes, I'm fine." She wasn't feeling fine at all. She wanted him to talk to her. About anything. But his question heightened the physical aches she'd managed to ignore all evening.

"Liar," he said softly. "I can see you're hurting. You should soak in a hot bath before you sleep again."

"You're right. I'll do that now." She set the barely-touched brandy on the side table and prepared to stand. He wasn't going to confide in her. She avoided his gaze to hide her disappointment.

"David knows about Dad's plan for the trust."

Carrie threw him a startled glance. "You told him?"

"He already knew. No, that's not quite right. He wasn't surprised. Evidently he and Dad had discussed, in vague terms, what could be done for Dick. David hadn't known about Dad's health, but he claims he once saw some brochures and pamphlets on Dad's desk regarding setting up a trust. He didn't know my father meant to turn the mansion into a home for people with mental diseases, but he guessed that little or none of John's fortune would be left to the family. The prospect didn't seem to bother him."

Carrie hesitated. "Do you believe him?"

"I guess I do." He sighed unhappily. "I might have doubted it if we hadn't discussed his shares first. He wants to establish his own independent men's wear store, but specialize in clothing for tall and large men. Grace will work with him as his accountant. If I buy his shares he can operate in the black right from the beginning. Dad's death has made him conscious of his age—he's fifty-nine—and he's determined that if Grace is widowed a second time, she won't suffer financially the way she did after the death of her first husband."

"So you told him about the will and confirmed his assumption that most of John's estate is to be tied up in the trust." Carrie frowned in thought. "Does he know the will is missing?"

"He doesn't seem to and I didn't tell him."

Carrie didn't reply.

"What are you thinking?"

She sighed unhappily, loath to feed his doubts. She spoke slowly, unwillingly. "The business about his shares could be a clever attempt at misdirection." She met Dean's pained gaze but forced herself to continue.

"If David is the one trying to kill you, then he probably took the will—the new will—himself. Under the old will he stands to inherit much more and so do you. We figured from the beginning that the murderer wants the old will to stand and for you to die before you can comply with your father's wishes."

"What are you getting at? What have the shares to do with any of it?"

"They don't really, except as a way to divert suspicion from himself and allow him more time to accomplish your death. I'm assuming a business transaction of that nature takes time. In the meantime, just in case you've realized what's going on, he's placed himself at the bottom of the list of suspects by readily acknowledging that he knows, or suspects, that he won't be inheriting from his brother. And isn't bothered by that. Then, if you die in the immediate future he'll still have his shares plus a part of your fortune. Of course, he may be exactly as he seems, a man concerned with providing for the woman he loves and wanting no more than what's already his due."

Dean groaned and leaned back, scrubbing his face with his hands. "God, what a mess!" He threw Carrie a look of pleading. "Are you absolutely certain that it's a member of the family who's trying to kill me?"

"Yes. I'm sorry."

At her woebegone look he smiled wryly. "You've nothing to be sorry for, love. I'm the one who's sorry. You could have died in that crash yesterday and that would have been my fault."

"That's nonsense. I didn't have to be with you, and in any case, the fault lies with the person who caused the crash. Don't you dare feel guilty about anything."

His smile widened at her admonishing tone. "Yes, ma'am. I mean, no, ma'am. May I ask you a question, ma'am?"

Carrie felt a tingle of pleasure at the spark of mischief in his eyes. Delighted that his mood had lightened, she nodded and smiled back at him. If he only knew it, she couldn't imagine denying him anything, let alone an answer to a question. Then his smile disappeared.

"Why are you still with me, Carrie? You've accomplished what you set out to do—warn me of the danger I'm in. After yesterday, I could certainly understand if you decided that your part in this was over."

Flustered by the unexpected query, Carrie reached for her snifter in an attempt to gain time. It was a troublesome question. She had done her job. Dean believed her warning. He hadn't asked for her help in the first place. Why was she still involved?

But she knew why, and for the first time admitted it. Against all her good sense, she had fallen in love with him. *Fool!* she thought angrily.

"Carrie?"

She glanced at him and away, praying he would read nothing in the heat she felt burning in her cheeks. "I … I feel a responsibility. And … curiosity. I want to know this person's identity. And … and besides, if I'd walked away and not done everything I could, and something happened to you, I'd feel guilty for the rest of my life."

"Oh."

Was that disappointment in his voice? What did he want her to say? She shook her head, denying the bubble of hope that popped into her mind. She cast around for a way to divert his attention. And her own.

"The pictures. They're intriguing. Your mother was a lovely looking woman. It must have been terribly hard for you and John to lose her."

The ploy succeeded in shifting Dean's gaze from her face to the collection on the wall.

"I still miss her," he admitted. "Her death hit all of us hard. Dick almost as much as my father."

"Dick?"

"He never married, and not for any lack of willing women. Dad told me once that many tried to catch his interest. He dated sporadically up till about ten years ago. But Dad always suspected that Dick was in love with my mother. If he was, he never mentioned it. Dick knew my mother was in love with my father. The three of them were very close friends for years."

"Oh, Dean, that's so sad. Poor Dick." Carrie blinked back her tears and searched for a happier topic. "That picture of

Justin and Alanna having the water fight is delightful. Does the family have a summer cottage?"

"Yes, near Georgian Bay. It's hardly more than a large shack, but it's been in the family for years. As kids, we could hardly wait for school to finish. Dad said he and Beverley and David felt the same when they were kids, though there was no indoor plumbing then."

"That must be Georgian Bay behind Beverley then. The picture on the far end."

Dean got up and moved closer to the wall. He peered at the picture, then shook his head. "I don't think so. At the cottage there was a long, narrow sand bar covered with low scrub about a hundred yards out from shore. This picture appears to have been taken somewhere else. Look at her. She couldn't have been any more than seventeen or eighteen. She was very attractive, wasn't she?"

Carrie nodded. "Yes. But this is the one I like best." She pointed to a picture of a teenaged Dean standing between his parents and towering over them. All three wore broad smiles.

Dean smiled. "I like that one, too." He sobered. "That was taken shortly before Mom get sick."

He turned away from the pictures and put an arm over Carrie's shoulders. "You're looking tired again. I've kept you up too late. Come on, I'll walk you back to your room."

At her nod, Dean guided Carrie toward the door, very aware that she had not objected to his proprietary gesture. If he was very lucky, she might one day forgive him for the hurt he had caused her. If he was very, very lucky, she might even come to love him as much as he loved her.

Preoccupied with his thoughts and with the pleasure of her closeness, he didn't immediately notice her sudden stiffening. Only when she gasped and stopped dead in her tracks did he realize something was wrong.

"Carrie, what is it?"

She didn't answer, but slowly turned back to face the room. One look at her slack face and wide, stunned eyes reminded him forcefully of the incident by the cottage. Instantly, he stepped behind her as Lieutenant Balfour had done and grasped her upper arms. He waited, his heart thudding painfully.

A moment later her head dropped as she sagged like a puppet with its strings cut. Dean scooped her up in his arms and carried her back into the room. He deposited her on the sofa and tucked an embroidered pillow under her head. Then he knelt beside the sofa and clasped her hands in his. He gazed anxiously at her milk-white face.

Carrie became aware first of the familiar exhaustion that always followed such episodes. She knew instantly what had happened, though she had no memory of collapsing. She never did.

Gradually her senses cleared to anchor her in space. She inhaled deeply. Dean's clean male scent told her he was near. Once again, he had witnessed the psychic phenomenon. Despair arrowed through her chest. She'd made a spectacle of herself again. It just wasn't fair!

Flinching, Carrie opened her eyes, expecting to see distaste, perhaps even revulsion. She couldn't immediately decipher his expression. When she identified only anxiety and concern, she felt her body slump deeper against the cushions in surprised relief.

"Carrie?"

She summoned a shaky smile and reassured him with a husky whisper, "I'm fine." She swung her feet to the floor and put her hands on his shoulders to pull herself up to a sitting position. "Really, I'm fine."

Dean pushed himself up and dropped down onto the sofa beside her. With gentle fingers, he turned her head and searched her face. At last, satisfied that she had come to no harm, he gave her a bashful grin.

"That's … kind of scary. There's no danger of it happening when you're driving, is there?"

Carrie glowed. Scary was fine, she could live with that. "No, it never has. Greta says the survival instinct protects a psychic from personal danger at those times. Dean, doesn't it bother you anymore?" She held her breath, almost dizzy with hope.

"No, love. Not in the way you mean. I…. Carrie, I want to apologize. My reaction—"

"No apology necessary. I tend to forget how shocking it must be for someone not familiar with the sight. But Dean, I'm really not a freak, or abnormal—"

"No. Just special." Sudden heat flared in his eyes. His voice thickened. "Very special."

He lowered his face. Carrie felt his warm breath caressing her cheek. He drew closer, his lips all but touching hers. Then he hesitated, as if to give her time to pull away. Mesmerized by the hunger in his face, Carrie stilled, unaware that her lips had parted.

With a strangled groan, his mouth descended to cover hers as he wrapped his arms around her and pulled her to his chest. Carrie leaned into his body and twined her arms around his neck. At her response, he deepened the kiss, his tongue frantically exploring the silken cavity of her mouth. Sensual delight flooded her body, her aches and bruises forgotten. When her tongue demanded the same privilege, his hands slid down her back to her sides, brushing the fullness of her breasts. She gasped, overwhelmed by the desire that spread like liquid fire through her body.

At the sound, he tore his mouth away and dropped his hands. "I forgot. Your bruises." Regret and need threaded his voice.

"What bruises?" Carrie smoothed her palms down his broad chest, marveling at the rock hard muscles of his body.

Dean's mouth twitched up at the corners, but having remembered the punishment she had suffered, he ignored his body's clamoring protest and called a halt. He could wait. If it killed him, he could wait.

When he leaned back, placing a few inches between them, Carrie wasn't sure if she was disappointed or relieved. It was a kiss, just a kiss, but no kiss had made her feel like that before. Hot. Needy. Almost out of control. Though she had little experience, she knew where such feelings could lead. And that would be a terrible mistake. If they made love, even just once, she would never be able to forget him. But he would forget her.

Thrilled as she was that he desired her, she knew she didn't measure up to the kind of women he was accustomed to dating. A year from now, maybe sooner, he wouldn't be able to recall her face. When this was over—

"Oh, heavens! I didn't tell you."

Dean caught her meaning instantly. Eagerness filled his face. "What?"

"The pictures. The answer is on that wall." Her face fell. "But that's all I got. Nothing specific, no name. Just that the answer, at least a clue, is there, right in front of our faces."

As one, they stood and approached the collection of pictures. Earlier, Dean's aunt had explained the arrangement. From left to right, the photos depicted the passage of years. Peter and Martha Sheffield, first as a couple, then with their three children, Beverley, the eldest, then John and finally David. Each succeeding picture showed them at ever older stages, then as young adults.

The second row began with John's and David's formal wedding pictures. Following those were pictures of the three cousins, Dean, Justin and Alanna, as children, arranged in chronological order. Many of these also included their parents and Dick.

The third row was incomplete. Pictures of the cousins as adults were followed by Natalie and Justin's wedding picture. There were no small children in the third row. Carrie guessed the next picture would be Alanna and Tim's wedding portrait.

Finally, Dean turned to her, his look questioning. Carrie shook her head. The collection seemed to be no more than what it was, a pictorial history of three generations of a family. No one picture beckoned. Yet she was certain the solution was there.

She backed away as far as she could to see the collection as a whole. There was something … . For just a second she thought she knew. Before the knowledge could coalesce in her mind, it slipped away beyond her grasp. Her shoulders slumped.

Dean forgot his own disappointment when he saw Carrie's frustrated expression. He crossed the space between them and gathered her in his arms. She closed her eyes and listened to the slow, steady thud of his heart.

"Well, isn't this cozy?"

Carrie jumped and tried to step back, but Dean's arms merely tightened around her.

"Hello, Natalie. I didn't hear you drive up." No embarrassment tinged his voice.

"Obviously." The word splashed like a brick into water and sank.

Carrie didn't know what to say. A quick, upward glance at Dean's closed face told her he had no intention of speaking further. The silence stretched until Natalie's face colored. She started to turn away, then swung around.

"I'm sorry. I almost forgot." Her apologetic tone seemed sincere. "I'm glad you weren't seriously hurt in the crash, Carrie."

Carrie nodded her thanks. With an awkward little wave of her hand and a quick "Good night" flung over her shoulder,

Natalie disappeared.

When her footsteps had faded, Dean dropped his arms, took Carrie's hand and drew her toward the stairs. She didn't resist. Fatigue dragged at her footsteps. Neither spoke until they reached her door.

"Sleep in as long as you want in the morning. I have to spend a few hours at the main store. We'll meet for lunch here."

Carrie looked up anxiously. "You will be careful, Dean?"

"Of course. Good night, sweetheart. Don't forget to lock your door." He bent and kissed her forehead. "I'm just going to check on Dick before I go to bed. See you tomorrow."

Carrie watched him until he disappeared around a corner, then slipped into her room and closed the door behind her. Kicking off her shoes, she flicked on the light switch, then crossed the room to close the draperies. When she finished in the bathroom and pulled a nightgown over her head, she crawled wearily into bed, craving the oblivion of sleep.

The lump under her pillow brought her lurching upright in shock. Natalie's letters! How could she have forgotten them? She scrabbled beneath the pillow and drew out the elastic-held bundle. Rigid with mortification, Carrie stared at them and moaned aloud.

It was too late to return them to Natalie's suite now. Whether or not the contents pointed to Justin's wife as the culprit, it seemed best that she not have warning that her secret had been uncovered. Now their return to their hiding place would have to wait on another opportunity. Had Natalie already missed them? Carrie cringed. As the only stranger in the house, she would be immediately suspect. What would she do if Natalie accused her of stealing?

She rocked in misery, her arms locked around her knees, the hated bundle resting innocently, mockingly on the bed beside her. Finally, her mind cleared. She forced herself to think rationally.

Natalie knew the contents of the letters. There was no particular reason to suppose she would look at them tonight. It was late, she was undoubtedly tired. Carrie would surely get a chance to sneak them back in the drawer tomorrow. And if the letters incriminated Natalie in some deadly scheme, she wouldn't dare mention them at all.

Carrie's tense muscles gradually relaxed. She picked up the bundle and discarded the elastic. The letters were arranged by date, the most recent on the top. Drawing in a deep breath, Carrie opened the first letter and began to read.

Chapter Fifteen

Ten minutes later Carrie replaced the last letter in its envelope and leaned back against the pillow. She stared unseeing at the opposite wall, reflecting on the irony that, contrary to popular belief, wealth alone didn't guarantee happiness. Sympathy for Justin's wife surged through her.

Natalie Sheffield was a beautiful woman married to a handsome man, a man she loved, according to Dean. Wealth, position and a lovely home were hers; a lifestyle many would envy. And yet, she lacked the one thing that many less financially-fortunate women enjoyed. Natalie Sheffield wanted a baby.

The envelopes in Carrie's hand contained reports from specialists Natalie had visited. Her out-of-town visits to friends were, in reality, appointments with various gynecologists in different cities. The results didn't vary. None of the intrusive tests and examinations she had endured had uncovered a reason for her failure to conceive.

That she had not confided in her husband about the appointments, Carrie was sure. Why else would she lie about her destination? Clearly, it hadn't occurred to Natalie that Justin might misinterpret her absences. Carrie shook her head in exasperation. Why in the world didn't they talk to each other? For the first time in her life, Carrie was tempted to meddle. If Justin were to somehow discover the contents of the letters....

No, she couldn't do that. Not only would she be unmasked

as a snoop, it was none of her business. Besides, if Justin hired a private detective to follow his wife, he would find out for himself. She could only hope he would confront Natalie with his knowledge. If ever a couple needed to communicate, it was Natalie and Justin Sheffield.

Yawning widely, Carrie slipped the bundle of letters in the drawer of the bedside table, turned out the light and snuggled down under the covers. In minutes, she was deeply asleep.

* * *

To her disappointment, the breakfast room was empty when Carrie entered it in mid-morning. Knowing the three Sheffield males were out of the house, she had hoped to find Beverley and Natalie present and to discover Natalie's plans for the day. In her mind, the pilfered letters were burning a hole in her table drawer. Carrie knew she wouldn't relax until they were safely, and secretly, back where they belonged.

The door to the kitchen opened. Aggie entered the room and beamed at Carrie. "Good morning, Miss Carrie. I hope you slept well. You're looking much better today."

"Thank you, Aggie. I do feel better. Here, let me help you with that."

Carrie unloaded the tray Aggie held and was relieved to see three cups with the pot of coffee. Beverley and Natalie were expected, then. Somehow, she had to find out if Natalie would be leaving the house so she could replace the letters without fear of being discovered.

After assuring the gently scolding cook that she wanted only toast and jam, Carrie sat down at the table. As she sipped at the coffee and waited for the others, Carrie's thoughts wandered to the dream that had awakened her. White-coated men with stethoscopes swinging from their necks pushed lawn mowers in a circle around the body of the housekeeper, which lay on a mound of grass cuttings on the floor of the small sitting room. On the wall, the people in the framed photographs seemed to be speaking, though she couldn't make out the words. The open mouths seemed to be moving in unison, as if they were trying to communicate the same message.

She shuddered. There had been a distinct air of menace about the dream, but the meaning, if there was one, eluded her.

Footsteps in the hall chased the dream from her mind. Carrie straightened in her chair. Feeling like one of her students, she crossed her fingers and held her breath.

Beverley Sheffield entered first, the previous evening's friendliness replaced by an air of anxiety. She nodded at Carrie and took a seat without speaking. Carrie's gaze flew to Natalie's perfectly made-up face. She, too, merely nodded and sat down. Beneath the make-up she looked tired and depressed. To Carrie's vast relief, there was no sign that she had discovered the theft of the letters.

At first, Carrie thought the doctors' failure to find a reason for Natalie's barren state would be regarded as good news. Further reflection changed her mind. If a cause could be found, so might a cure. She wondered if the fault lay with Justin. She suspected that Natalie had not asked her husband to see a doctor. Or perhaps she had and Justin refused.

Had they considered adoption? Carrie could think of no way to bring up the topic of babies without revealing her ill-gotten knowledge of Natalie's problem. As if reading her thoughts, Beverley suddenly addressed the two women.

"One of the girls at the home for unwed mothers is going to deliver her baby today. Josie's had a hard pregnancy and she's already ten days overdue. The doctor is going to induce delivery if labor doesn't start this morning. She's so tiny and she's scared to death." The middle-aged woman frowned into the distance.

"I'm worried about her. Her health is poor to start with."

"Will she keep the baby? Or put it up for adoption?" Carrie carefully avoided looking in Natalie's direction.

"She wants to keep it, but I don't see how she can. She's only fifteen. Her parents kicked her out when they found out she was pregnant. Since then, they've relented a little. She can go home after the birth if she wants, but they refuse to accept the baby. To be fair, they both work and there's very little money. And they have three other children. Josie should go back to school, but of course the baby can't be left alone."

"That's very sad," Carrie said. "Under the circumstances, I suppose she has no choice but to give the baby up for adoption."

Beverley's mouth thinned into a straight line. "She's not alone in that. Many unwed mothers are in the same position. But Josie's so unhappy."

Natalie spoke for the first time. "At least if the baby's adopted, she'll know it will have a good home. That should make her feel better."

"Maybe," Beverley muttered. "Well," she stood up abruptly, "I must get going to the hospital to be with Josie. I'm her coach. Would you tell Aggie I may not be back for dinner?"

"Yes, of course." Natalie smiled at her aunt. "It'll all work out. Let us know if Josie has a boy or a girl."

After Beverley left, Natalie lapsed into silence, a small smile on her bemused face. When Aggie popped in to replace the cooling coffee with a fresh pot, Natalie blinked and seemed to come back to the present.

"Aunt Beverley is such a fraud." She threw Carrie a surprisingly shy smile. "She likes to pretend she's a Grinch, but her heart is big enough for two. She really cares about those poor girls."

Ridiculously pleased by Natalie's companionable tone and suspecting the woman wanted to make up for her rudeness the night before, Carrie returned the smile. Since reading Natalie's letters, she felt drawn to the woman who didn't have everything after all.

"She would have made a wonderful mother. Dean told me how great she was when he and his cousins were children."

When the mention of Dean's name brought no reaction from Natalie, Carrie decided to take a chance. "Do you plan on having a family yourself?"

The pain that blossomed in the other woman's face made Carrie instantly regret her boldness.

"I'm sorry. I shouldn't have spoken. It's none of my business." She pushed back her chair.

Natalie's hand lifted in a gesture of appeal. "No, don't go. I know you didn't mean to hurt me. It's just...." She paused and searched Carrie's face. "Could I talk to you for a few minutes?"

"Of course." Carrie eased back into her chair and waited.

Natalie chewed on her lower lip for a minute, then turned candid eyes on Carrie. "I do want a baby. I know I don't appear to be the mother type, but I really want to give Justin a family. I've been to several specialists the last few months, but none of them can tell me why I haven't conceived. I don't know what to do next."

"Have you considered adoption?"

"Yes, but I don't know what Justin would say to that. I'm afraid he's not interested in being a father. He hasn't mentioned children for several years."

"Have you talked about them?"

Natalie shook her head. "Since there doesn't seem to be anything wrong with me, I hate to suggest that he's the one who's … inadequate. Justin's a very virile man. I don't want to hurt him."

"May I make an observation?" Carrie asked, a bud of excitement growing in her mind. At Natalie's encouraging gesture, she went on. "Suppose Justin hasn't mentioned children because you haven't. Maybe he thinks that you don't want to be a mother. He does love you, you know. It may be that he's given up the idea of having a family because he thinks you don't want one."

Hope dawning in her eyes, Natalie stared open-mouthed at Carrie. Then her mouth snapped closed and immediately stretched into a wide smile. She slapped her forehead in a comic gesture. "How totally dumb can a woman be? I never thought of that. You may be right. Carrie, you're wonderful!" Natalie bounced out of her chair. "I'm going to change into my sexiest dress and take my husband out for lunch. Maybe I can talk him into taking the afternoon off."

She circled the table and stooped to give Carrie a hug. "Thank you, thank you, thank you," she whispered feverishly in Carrie's ear.

"Natalie, I could be all wrong, you know. It was just a guess." Carrie cautioned. "But even if I am," she added, "it's something that should be discussed between you."

She had to laugh at the elegant Natalie Sheffield dancing around the table like a little girl. "Good luck!" she called after her.

As Natalie's footsteps faded down the hall, Carrie reached for her coffee cup. She could feel the sappy smile on her face and recognized the feeling of satisfaction that was the reward for helping another.

She finished her coffee and began to pile the dirty dishes on the tray Aggie had left on the buffet, then took them to the kitchen. With the cook's thanks ringing in her ears, she made her way to the small sitting room at the front of the house. From there, she would be able to see Natalie's departure and know when it was safe to sneak the letters back to their hiding place.

The wall of photographs seemed to beckon. Once again, she examined each picture. Nothing in particular caught her attention. The display was an attractive but unremarkable visual account of the family. Was she mistaken in believing the pictures of the past held a clue to the present?

When Natalie left the house with a jaunty step, Carrie replaced the letters then returned to the sitting room to wait for Dean to join her for lunch. Again she examined the pictures, this time moving from the most recent back to the earliest, the wedding portrait of Dean's grandparents. Again she found nothing unusual.

When Dean stepped into the room, she was tracing each member of the family, individually, from childhood to adulthood. The similarity between Dean and his father, viewed at comparable ages, was astonishing. She didn't doubt that the son would be as attractive in his middle years as the father.

"Hi."

Engrossed in the pictures of Dean, Carrie hadn't heard him enter. She jumped and spun around, then blushed hotly at the yearning that rushed through her body. The perfect fit of his dark blue suit seemed to accentuate the breadth of his shoulders. Her fingers itched to comb through his tousled hair. The admiring smile in his eyes made her glad she had dressed in her favorite pink wool slacks and matching cowl neck sweater.

"Sorry. I didn't mean to startle you." He walked to her side and scanned the wall of pictures. "Would it help to examine the family albums? These pictures are just a sampling."

"I don't think so." Carrie's fingers curled up in frustration. "The answer, or part of it, is here. I know it." Her shoulders slumped. "But I can't see it."

Dean draped his arm on her shoulders and gave her a brief hug. "It'll come to you. But come and sit down. I have some news."

Carrie sat on the edge of a chair and waited impatiently while Dean closed the door and took a seat opposite her.

"I called the lieutenant from the store this morning. He was just about to call me. The fingerprints in the cottage have been identified. Most of them were Bill's and Irma's. A few in the living room belong to Aunt Beverley. And remember the thumbprint found on one of the empty beer cans in the trash?"

"Whose print was it?" Carrie's voice trembled with excitement. They had a break at last.

"A man named Walter Trent. He has a long record of arrests for breaking and entering, but only one conviction, three years ago, in Quebec. Some minor convictions for brawling. He likes to use his fists. Balfour is going to send a messenger here with a copy of his picture."

"Then he must be the man who killed Irma. It fits, Dean. He must have broken into the cottage to steal and Irma walked in on him. He panicked and killed her."

Dean frowned. "That's what I thought at first, too. But it doesn't feel right."

"Why not? He already had a record and it would go harder for him for a second offense. You said he's been violent in the past."

"The can of beer bothers me. He must be a pretty cool customer, to break into a place in daylight, not knowing when someone might appear. Yet he took the time to have a beer. Bill said nothing is missing and there was no evidence that the place had been tossed."

"I see what you mean," Carrie said. "Someone that arrogant, that sure of himself, shouldn't have panicked. He could have escaped through the woods before Irma raised the alarm. So why did he kill her? Unless…."

"Unless what?"

"Unless she knew him and could give the police a positive identification." Then she shook her head, rejecting her own conjecture. "It's not enough to explain murder. All he actually did was enter a house and drink a can of beer. The law would charge him with mischief and give him a slap on the hand."

"You're right. Besides, Irma lived in Nova Scotia all her life until she came here. This Walter grew up in Quebec, in a small village near Montreal. When would they meet? And unless they find the murder weapon with his fingerprints on it, there's no proof he was the killer. He could claim he was there earlier, or even the day before."

"But why would he go in, have a beer and leave without taking anything? Come to think of it, why would he hope to find anything worth stealing in the cottage? The mansion is a far richer target."

Dean gave her a look of admiration. "A good point. I suppose he could have been hiding in the woods to scout out the territory with an eye to finding the best way in. Maybe he entered the cottage simply because he was thirsty. He would have heard the mower at the other side of the house and figured no one would see him."

"So he may have had nothing to do with Irma's death at all." Carrie grimaced. "We're right back where we started."

They brooded in silence for a few minutes. Dean scrubbed his face with his hands. His dejection was a palpable presence in the room. Then he lifted his head.

"I talked with the private investigator, too. Rogers had nothing new to report. None of the family has done anything out of the ordinary. No one has met with a questionable character. If Natalie has a lover, she hasn't been with him here in town."

Carrie took a deep breath. She'd been dreading the moment when she told Dean about Natalie's trips out of town. Shame had been eating at her ever since she returned the letters. She deeply regretted her behavior, an act completely out of character. And, as it turned out, unnecessary. What would this do to Dean's opinion of her?

"Natalie doesn't have a lover." The words burst from her throat.

Dean looked startled. "You had another revelation?"

"No." Carrie forced herself to meet his eyes. "She's been trying to find out why she hasn't become pregnant. The out-of-town trips were appointments with different specialists. She wants to give Justin a child."

A slow smile spread over Dean's face. "That's great news. Justin has talked to me a few times. He wants a family, but he says Natalie doesn't. I know it bothers him." He shook his head. "If only those two would sit down and talk about it."

"That's what I said to Natalie."

"She talked to you about it?" He didn't hide his surprise.

Carrie nodded. "This morning, at breakfast. Beverley told us about a teenage unwed mother she knows who's having her baby today. We were talking about adoption and how this Josie will likely have to give up her baby. After Beverley left, Natalie told me about the doctors' reports. Physically, there doesn't seem to be any reason why she can't conceive. But she thinks that Justin doesn't want children."

"Do you think she'll take your advice?"

Carrie smiled, her face alight. "I think so. She practically ran out of here to take Justin to lunch. I doubt he'll return to the store today."

When Dean chuckled, Carrie suddenly realized what she had implied. Scarlet stained her cheeks. Then she caught Dean's eye. When Aggie poked her head around the door to announce that lunch was ready, she found them laughing companionably.

* * *

"The accomplice! Maybe Walter Trent is the accomplice."
Carrie stopped dead beside an empty flower bed and turned to

Dean. They had been walking slowly over the grounds after lunch, as they once again talked over the little information they had about the private lives of Dean's family. Now excitement suddenly bubbled inside her.

When he didn't reply, Carrie continued. "Don't you see? If Trent was there to meet the person who hired him, it would explain why he didn't steal anything and why he felt relaxed enough to help himself to a beer. It wasn't a break-in, it was an appointment, a conference."

"And Irma walked in on them," Dean added slowly. "She probably heard enough to understand what they were talking about."

"Exactly!" Carrie exclaimed. "They couldn't let her tell what she'd overheard! That's why her body was moved, to hide the fact that she was leaving the cottage."

"The only other prints in the cottage were Aunt Beverley's." Dean's words seemed forced from deep within him.

To her dismay, Dean's face darkened with pain as he turned away from her. Why wasn't he pleased that— She gasped as the implication hit her. If Irma's death hadn't been a random killing, then a member of Dean's family was already a murderer.

Without thinking, she wrapped her arms around him and began to rub his back, as he had done for her. His body shook as if buffeted by a hurricane force. Carrie felt anger growing inside her for the person who had caused him such pain.

Carrie thought of the woman who had been so concerned about Josie, who'd been so kind to Bill Hummell. Could that same woman be capable of murdering someone she'd known for a year? Unless Walter Trent had killed Irma before Beverley had a chance to stop him. But that still made her an accomplice to murder. And a conspirator in a plan to murder her nephew.

They stood in the middle of the yard until his trembling ceased.

"Beverley might have been visiting Irma," Carrie offered tentatively. "We don't know she was meeting Walter."

"True." Dean sounded incredibly weary. "But I never saw any evidence that she and Irma were friends."

"You're away at work every day, Dean. You wouldn't necessarily know."

He nodded. They fell silent then. Carrie threaded her fingers with his and they began to walk again. They still had nothing concrete, she realized. If one of the family had a specific, urgent need for a large sum of money, they had yet to discover it. And if the motive for murder was just plain greed, how were they to determine which Sheffield harbored that deadly passion?

Then Dean broke the silence.

"Let's find Aggie. Maybe she can tell us if Beverley and Irma were friends. She may have seen something from her sunroom."

As they stepped into the house, the front door slammed shut. The sound of clattering steps, half-running, half-stumbling, pulled them to the foyer. They stopped in amazement at the sight of Beverley Sheffield lurching blindly for the stairs. Tears streamed down her anguished face as hoarse sobs burst from her throat.

"Aunt Bev!"

The distraught woman paused at the sound of her name and swung around so violently she stumbled and would have fallen, had Dean not reached her in time to grab her by the upper arms. Her legs buckled as she fell against him. Carrie hurried to wrap her arm around the woman's waist and together they half-carried the bitterly sobbing woman into the small sitting room.

She dropped heavily into the sofa and immediately doubled over, her arms wrapped tightly across her stomach. Dean and Carrie sat down on either side of her and put an arm around her heaving back.

When a flour-coated Aggie dashed into the room, Carrie

asked her to find some brandy. Nodding, the cook disappeared, an anxious frown on her face.

Carrie caught Dean's eye over Beverley's bowed back and mouthed "Josie." For an instant he looked at her blankly, then comprehension flooded his face. His mouth tightened with pity as he tenderly patted his aunt's shoulder.

When Beverley's violent sobs diminished, Carrie offered her a handful of tissues. She sat up stiffly and blew her nose, then eagerly gulped down a huge mouthful of the brandy Dean thrust at her. Shuddering with the shock of the drink, she leaned heavily against Dean's shoulder and clutched Carrie's hand tightly.

"They're dead," she moaned. "They're both dead. Josie and her baby. They died in the delivery room."

Shocked, Carrie could only stare. Both of them? Because Beverley had mentioned earlier that Josie was in poor health, she had anticipated the news of Josie's death the moment she saw Beverley's distress. But the baby, too? And as her coach, the middle-aged woman would have been holding Josie's hand when they died. Carrie felt her heart break for the fifteen-year-old and her child, and for the devastated woman beside her.

Then Beverley suddenly stood up and began to pace the floor. She stared from Dean to Carrie, her red-rimmed eyes glaring in anger, her hands clenched into wildly waving fists.

"It's so unfair! She made one mistake and her parents threw her out. For *one* mistake! If they had loved her more, had taken care of her, she might still…. She was only fifteen! How could her parents do that to their own daughter? How could they not want their grandchild? Josie wanted that baby. They were going to make her give it away."

She stopped abruptly and stared into the distance, her arms falling limply to her sides. "Maybe it's better this way." Her voice dulled to an emotionless monotone. "At least Josie won't spend the rest of her life feeling guilty, missing her baby, wondering if he was happy, if he was loved. If he had forgiven her for giving him away. Maybe it's better this way."

Before Carrie or Dean could move, she turned and left the room. They looked helplessly at one another as Beverley slowly climbed the stairs.

"She couldn't kill anyone," Dean finally said.

Carrie started to nod in agreement. Then she paused. What if Beverley's concern for the abandoned, unwed mothers had somehow persuaded her that she could do so much more to help if she were richer? Was she capable of planning Dean's death in order to get her hands on his money? Anything was possible.

Carrie didn't voice the dismal thought.

* * *

Sighing heavily, Carrie shifted position for the hundredth time. Her tired brain stubbornly resisted sleep. Her thoughts returned to the elegant nightclub where she and Dean tried to forget, for a time, the threat hanging over his head and Aunt Beverley's pain. Success eluded them both. She hadn't been able to suppress her fears for his safety. Dean's frequent lapses into silence told her he, too, was preoccupied with unpleasant thoughts.

The time-out an unqualified failure, they returned to the house early. Although she knew the effort was futile, she tried once again to convince Dean to gather the family together and inform them of the murder attempts.

"When the murderer knows you're on to him, he'll give up," Carrie pleaded. "You'll be safe then."

"No." Dean shook his head in denial. "If he's responsible for Irma's death, he's already a murderer. A successful one, since the murder weapon probably won't be found after all this time. He has nothing to lose and much to gain if he kills me."

"Then go away for awhile. If you're out of his reach he may become impatient and make a mistake."

"I can't do that, Carrie. He's tried four times and failed. I agree, he must be getting desperate. When he tries again, we'll have him."

"You don't know that. What if he succeeds this time? Even if he's caught, that won't help you."

Dean heard the fear in her voice and squeezed her hand, but his face lost none of its determination. "As long as I have you for a guardian angel, he can't kill me." His expression softened as he smiled into her fearful eyes.

"Oh, Dean," she whispered in despair, "we don't know that either."

"Yes, we do."

A few minutes later she excused herself and climbed the stairs to her room. Now, in spite of her fatigue, sleep refused to claim her. The school semester would begin in less than a week. How could she watch over him then?

A knock on her door startled her upright. Dean called her name. Carrie jumped from the bed and slid into her dressing gown and slippers, then she hurried to unlock her door.

"What's wrong?"

"I'm sorry to disturb you, but Dick's missing from his room again. I hope you'll forgive me for waking you, but the more people looking for him, the better."

"I wasn't asleep." She patted his arm to offer a touch of comfort. "Where do you want me to start looking?"

"If you'll wake Aggie and start on the ground floor, I'll wake up the others. I'd rather not disturb Beverley, but I don't know how many of the others are home."

"We'll find him, Dean. Try not to worry," Carrie called over her shoulder as she headed for the stairs.

Turning on the lights as she went, Carrie made her way to the back of the house, through the kitchen and down a short hallway to Aggie's bedroom. A soft moan stopped her hand in mid-knock. Whirling around, she held her breath, straining to hear. Only silence greeted her.

Finally deciding she had imagined the faint sound, she was about to turn back to Aggie's door when she heard a muffled sob. Two doors, both closed, lined the short hall. Carrie hesitated, then slowly opened the nearest door to find a collection of mops, brooms, pails and other cleaning equipment. She closed the door and moved to the next, on the other side of the hallway.

The hall light illuminated the first few stairs leading down to a dark cavity. An agonized whimper floated up from the black depths. Certain she had found Dick, Carrie fumbled for a light switch. A bare bulb in the ceiling above the bottom step revealed a pajama-clad Dick seated on the bottom step, his legs sprawled straight out before him, his hands clasping the sides of his bowed head.

A cry burst from his lips as his head swung up. He twisted around to face the stairs, his narrowed eyes blinking rapidly against the light. Tear tracks on his face and red swollen eyelids testified to his terror. Before Carrie could move he scrambled around and started up the stairs, using his hands and feet like a child.

Realizing he was physically unhurt, she retreated through the kitchen and down the hall. Dean met her at the foot of the foyer stairs.

"No one is here except Beverley. I didn't wake—"

"I found him. Hurry!" Carrie pulled on his hand. "He's very frightened but I don't think he's hurt."

When they reached the kitchen they found Dick pressed tightly against the wall. His eyes were wild with fright and confusion. He threw up his hands and tried to back away as they approached, but when Dean spoke his name and clasped his arm, his face cleared.

He smiled widely at Dean and Carrie, his ordeal seemingly forgotten in an instant. Carrie snapped off the light and closed the basement door.

"Would you like a snack, Dick? I could bring it up to your room." Perhaps he had come downstairs looking for something to eat.

Dick's face brightened. He nodded happily.

Dean threw a grateful smile at Carrie over his shoulder and began to lead the shuffling man back to his room. By the time Carrie joined them with a tray of toast and cheese slices, Dean had managed to change Dick's dirt-streaked nightwear for clean pajamas and help him into bed.

Propped up against the pillows, Dick invited them to share his snack. They pulled up chairs to either side of the bed. The basement wasn't mentioned. When the older man began to yawn, Dean and Carrie exchanged looks.

"I'll take the tray back to the kitchen in a few minutes, Carrie. You go ahead."

Carrie wished the two men goodnight and started to leave. A lovely antique bureau beside the door caught her attention. She paused a moment to admire it and spotted the corner of a light beige folder wedged between the bureau and the wall.

Her heart turned over. Although the folder could be anything, she instinctively, instantly, knew what it was. She looked back. Neither man was looking her way. Quickly, she bent and pulled the file folder from its hiding place, then slipped through the door. A few feet down the hallway, she stopped.

Should she look in the folder? Yes. No. She clutched the folder to her chest and made herself wait for Dean.

When he had called a final goodnight to Dick and closed the

door, she held out the folder. His somber expression slowly changed as he stared at it. When he finally lifted his gaze to hers, his eyes were full of hope.

"Is it—?"

"I think so. I haven't checked."

His hand trembled as he took it from her. He took a deep breath and opened the folder. Carrie watched his face and knew she was right when a wide smile spread over his features. Suddenly his arms were around her.

"What have I ever done to deserve you? It's Dad's will. Dick must have picked it up and then forgotten about it. And to think it's been in his room all this time." His arms tightened around her.

"I'm so glad," she murmured, unconsciously pressing closer.

"I'll call Lawrence first thing in the morning and have him arrange for the reading of the will in the afternoon. Do you know what this means, Carrie? Once John's will is read, there's no longer any reason for someone to kill me. Except for finding Irma's killer, it's all over."

Carrie stiffened in his arms, then leaned back from the waist and looked anxiously into his face. "You've made your own will then? An official will, witnessed and registered?"

"Well, no, not yet. I mean, Lawrence is working on it, but it's not ready for my signature. But when everyone knows what Dad wanted—"

Carrie's fingers dug into the muscles of his back. "You're not safe until it's finished!" she said urgently. "Don't you see? The bulk of John's fortune is yours now, isn't it? If you die before your will is finalized, then everything that's yours will be divided among the family, none of it going to start the trust. Dean, the danger isn't over."

His face fell as he sagged in her arms. "Damn!"

Carrie pressed her face to his chest, trying to blink back frustrated tears. They stood quietly for a moment, then dropped their arms as one and turned to walk to her room.

"One thing must be done right away." Dean sighed heavily. "Tomorrow I'll see about hiring someone to stay with Dick day and night. The disease seems to be accelerating and it will take some months to renovate the house and turn it into a nursing home. But I'm afraid Dick can't wait. Oh hell, Carrie, it sickens me to see his fine mind disintegrating like this!"

Carrie tried to comfort him. "At least now you can go ahead with John's plans."

"That's true."

Something in his voice made her look up. Her breath caught in her throat when she saw his expression. A glow deep in his eyes started a bud of heat in her stomach unfolding and growing. All thought of wills and Dick and murder fled from her mind. But even as her heart leaped in response, Carrie reminded herself that what Dean felt was gratitude. Heartfelt gratitude, yes, but no more than that. Still, she couldn't look away.

Then the front door slammed. Startled, she stepped back. The moment was lost. Laughing voices floated up the staircase, making her suddenly aware of her night attire. She pulled the neck of her dressing gown more tightly across her throat and, with a whispered goodnight, hurried to her bedroom.

Dean stood still, watching her gently rounded bottom recede down the hall. When her door snicked closed, he drew a deep breath and walked unsteadily to his own room, the file folder in his hand momentarily forgotten.

CHAPTER SIXTEEN

"Tilt your chin slightly to the left. No, no, the left. That's better. Now bring up your knees and wrap your arms around them. Wait, edge your skirt back to expose your feet. That's better. No, that's perfect."

Carrie did as she was told and wondered why she had agreed to pose for Alanna's fiancé. She felt just as self-conscious and as uncomfortable as she'd known she would. Her suggestion that Tim take a photograph and paint from that had been met with a disbelieving stare.

"I work with live models only, Carrie," he'd said, rejecting her idea with a dismissive gesture and a slightly aggrieved tone. "No camera can do your face justice."

Privately, she assumed he meant to enhance her looks. No camera could do that. Resigning herself, she wondered how long the portrait would take to complete. And how the family was reacting to the contents of John's will.

No sound penetrated the door of the small sitting room across the hall, where the Sheffields had gathered a few minutes before with Lawrence Chambers. She knew Dean would be positioned to watch for any revealing expression. It was doubtful he would learn anything. The person who had prior knowledge of the will would certainly be prepared to mimic the reaction of the others.

"You're frowning, Carrie. And your chin's drooping again.

Wait a minute." Looking vexed, Tim jammed his brush between his teeth and strode across the tarpaulin-protected carpet to reposition her head. Muttering under his breath, he returned to his easel.

Carrie plastered a smile on her face and gazed out the bare window. Tim had opted to use the large room where the wake had been held. The drapery he'd requested lay arranged in artful folds over the high-backed sofa where she posed.

Bored, Carrie gazed out the window at the lush green sweep of lawn leading down to the road. A thick line of poplars hid the passing cars, except at the opening for the lane leading to the house. She watched as Bill Hummell walked across the yard a few feet from the house. He was carrying a pair of pruning shears. A large canvas sack swung from his shoulder. A twinge of guilt reminded Carrie that she had yet to offer her condolences for his mother's death.

"That's enough for today, the light's changing. Same time tomorrow, Carrie." It was more of an order than a request.

Carrie nodded and rose stiffly to her feet, surprised to discover almost two hours had passed. She stretched her protesting muscles and cast a look of entreaty at the artist.

"Not a chance," Tim said, correctly interpreting her expression. "I told you, no one sees my work until it's finished." He grinned at her.

"Tyrant!" she exclaimed. "Ah well, I think I need a cup of tea after that. I had no idea posing is such hard work. Want to meet me in the breakfast room for a cup?"

"Sure. I'll clean up here and be with you in a few minutes."

A fist propped under her chin, Carrie listened in fascination to Tim's tales of summers spent in various artists' colonies across Canada and the United States. She sighed in envy when he described a six-month stay on the Left Bank in Paris. It would take at least another four years before her special Paris savings account grew large enough to permit her to realize her dream trip.

Finally, footsteps in the hall signaled the end of the family meeting. Dean entered the room first. Carrie's eyes flew to him but his impassive expression told her nothing. David, Beverley and Alanna followed, wearing identical expressions. David's arm was draped over his sister's shoulders. The will had brought with it the reminder that one of their number was gone. Sadness hung in the air.

Tim jumped up and folded Alanna in his arms. She leaned against him and dropped her head on his shoulder. Carrie wished she had the right to offer Dean the same comfort.

Beverley refused a cup of tea, but the others sat down. Carrie poured them each a cup, then, hoping she wasn't overstepping the bounds of a guest, excused herself and made her way to the kitchen in search of biscuits. There was comfort to be found in food.

Aggie stood in her sunroom, her head bowed and her arms wound tightly around her middle. She glanced at Carrie and quickly looked away to hide her wet eyes. Sensing the older woman needed comfort as much as the others, Carrie approached her and gently eased the thin woman into her arms. A brief second of resistance, then Aggie burst into tears and clung to Carrie.

Blinking back her own tears, Carrie patted the woman's shoulder and gazed unseeing into the backyard. A movement caught her eye. She turned her head and saw Beverley leave the house by the same door as before. Intrigued, she watched Dean's aunt walk along the back of the house and wave to someone out of sight around the corner.

Bill Hummell? It was true that Beverley had been there for Bill when the gardener needed comforting. Still, surely she would look to a member of her own family when she herself was in need. But people reacted to grief in different ways. Maybe Beverley merely wanted to relay instructions to an employee. Her tears for Josie and her child might have bankrupted her emotionally.

When Aggie exhausted her fund of tears, she drew back with a grateful smile. Together, she and Carrie prepared three plates of assorted biscuits and carried them into the breakfast room. They joined the others at the table.

"Are you okay, Aggie?" David asked, his voice sympathetic.

"I'm fine now, Mr. David. I can't get over Mr. John's kindness. I never dreamed he would leave me such a large sum of money."

"He loved you, Aggie," Dean said simply. "Will you stay on and help me run this place as a nursing home? We'll be hiring a lot of extra kitchen help and naturally you'll be in charge. But of course, if you'd rather retire—"

"Never say the 'r' word, Mr. Dean! Of course I'll stay."

"Thanks, Aggie. In the meantime, start thinking how you want to enlarge the kitchen. Alanna," Dean turned to his cousin, "do you think the manager at the nursing home would mind if Aggie toured the kitchen? It would help to give her an idea about extra appliances and space that she'll need."

Alanna assured them that wouldn't be a problem and, rather shyly, asked if Dean would consider hiring her when the home was operational. Dean readily agreed, then turned to Carrie and suggested they walk around the grounds.

* * *

As they strolled the perimeter of the back lawn, Dean admitted ruefully that no one had showed any anger, or even disappointment, upon learning that the bulk of his father's money had not been left to family. "On the contrary, they all seemed pleased that the mansion will become a home for people like Dick. I could swear they were sincere."

"You've told them that you're changing your will in order to carry out John's wishes, in case something happened to you." It wasn't a question. Carrie shivered and decided to make one more try.

"Dean, please be sensible. Go away for awhile, just until your will is ready. Once everyone knows it's finalized and signed, there'll be no reason to—"

"I can't do that." He shook his head firmly. "The only way we're going to find out who killed Irma and tried to kill me is for me to be ... available."

"An available target, you mean. Dean, the killer knows that time is running out. He won't try another accident. What if he decides to use a gun?"

"None of the family has ever owned a gun."

"You can't be sure of that, and anyway, this Walter Trent may have one. If he's the accomplice, he could shoot you anywhere, anytime."

Her own words suddenly made Carrie realize how exposed they were. Someone could be hiding even now in the woods that edged the yard. With a rifle aimed at Dean's heart.

She pulled her arm free and began to search the line of trees. Her psychic ability had offered no advance warning of the sabotaged car. She couldn't count on the doppelgänger to alert them to the next attempt on Dean's life. That the murderer would try again, she had no doubt at all.

She was about to suggest they return to the safety of the house when Dick and a tall, broad-shouldered man emerged from the woods. Jack Sawyer, whom she'd met that morning, had been hired to watch over John's friend. Although built like a wrestler, capable of handling any emergency, he was a highly recommended nurse. His casual clothing and amiable, laid-back manner concealed that fact from Dick. Carrie and Dean waved to the pair.

As they drew nearer, something in Dick's hand glinted in the sunlight. Dick thrust it out when he came to a stop in front of them. The object was coated with dirt and dead leaves. Dick brushed at it and exposed more of the satin pewter finish.

"Look at this," he exclaimed. "Someone lost this thing. I tripped over it and almost fell. Why would anyone bury something like this?"

Behind him, Jack gave Dean a knowing look. Dick hadn't been told of Irma's death, but Jack had been informed. If her killing had been a random act, Dean wanted Jack to be on guard.

"It's a bowling pin, a trophy," Carrie said in surprise. "How extraordinary." Then she drew in her breath sharply. Could this be the blunt instrument that killed Irma?

Dean had the same thought. Using his handkerchief to avoid smudging any fingerprints, he commandeered the trophy, knowing Dick would forget about finding it. Dick and his companion wandered off while Dean and Carrie returned to the house to call Lieutenant Balfour.

They waited for him in the small sitting room. Carrie fought against the hope that quickened her heartbeat. If the bowling trophy proved to be the murder weapon, if Walter Trent's fingerprints were on it, and if he could be found, chances were good he would name his accomplice rather than go to prison alone. If, if, if!

When Balfour finally arrived, his eyes lit up at the sight of the trophy. "The lab will tell us for sure, but I'm willing to bet this is it. Pray God we can lift some fingerprints from it."

"I wonder why Bill didn't mention it was missing?" Dean looked puzzled.

"It's Bill Hummell's? Are you sure?"

"I think so. Well, I don't actually know that this particular trophy is his. But the theory is that Irma was killed because of the conversation she overheard. Whoever did it must have grabbed something close at hand and chased after her. Didn't you notice the display of bowling and baseball mementos on the shelves by the living room door?"

"Yes, I did. I guess I forgot them, since Hummell said nothing was missing."

Carrie spoke for the first time since the lieutenant entered the room. "I can understand why Bill wasn't thinking clearly. After all, he'd just found his mother's body and been told someone murdered her."

With a shrug of agreement, Balfour handed them an large brown envelope.

"These are pictures of Walter Trent. Have either of you seen him before?"

Carrie and Dean examined the head-and-shoulders pictures. The number held against his chest made it clear they came from police files. Neither could remember ever seeing the man.

Balfour invited Dean to accompany him to locate Bill and ask if he recognized the trophy. Dean agreed and turned to Carrie.

"I'm going to ride back into town with the lieutenant. Owen Rogers should have copies of these pictures for his operatives. The more eyes on the lookout, the better. And I want to tell him the will has been found." He bent and pressed a kiss on her forehead. "I'll be back by eight at the latest. We'll go out for dinner. Tell Aggie, would you?"

Carrie nodded and watched the men leave. When she was alone again, she leaned back in the chair and thought about Dean's kiss on her forehead. And the other kisses. Knowing it was a mistake, still she allowed herself to daydream what her life would be like if Dean were around to kiss her every day. To do more than kiss her. Her eyes fluttered closed. She watched Dean make love to her on the screen of her imagination. The daydream changed to dream as she dozed.

The murmur of voices startled her awake. She sat up abruptly, then yelped as a sharp pain shot down her neck to her shoulder. Her head had twisted to one side when she fell asleep. As she massaged the sore muscles she silently acknowledged she had no one to blame but herself. A fitting punishment for daring to imagine her and Dean as a couple. What man would willingly spend time with a woman who might slump into a slack-jawed trance at any moment? No man would risk that humiliation in front of his family or his peers. Nor could she blame him.

Remembering the voices, she stood and approached the door, embarrassed to think that a member of the family might have wished to use the room, only to be turned away by her slumbering form. The hallway was deserted and absolutely still. Perhaps she'd dreamed the voices.

A stealthy rustling sounded in the room behind her. Carrie whirled around. No one was there. Yet she sensed a presence and an urgency in the air. Her eyes circled the room and came to rest on the wall of photographs. She felt the hairs stiffen all over her body. One hesitant step at a time, she approached the middle of the room and stopped, facing the pictures.

Gradually, the sense of something missing seeped into her mind. Had someone removed one of the pictures? The wall looked unchanged. To be sure, she lifted one frame from its nail, revealing the discolored wall behind it. The absence of a picture would be immediately noticeable.

She started to turn away then swung back again. Had one picture been exchanged for another? But why would anyone do that? Carefully, certain the display held a clue if only she could see it, Carrie examined each picture again.

Fifteen minutes later she shook her head in defeat. Every picture was familiar. The Sheffield family had been smiling for the camera for years.

Faint sounds drifted in from the kitchen. Belatedly, Carrie remembered the message from Dean. She hurried to the kitchen and informed the cook that she and Dean would be dining out.

Still conscious of her aching neck, Carrie went to her room. She had time for a long soak in the tub before dressing for dinner. While the tub was filling, she peered into the closet. It would have to be the little black dress. She spread it out on the bed and kicked off her shoes.

Then she paused. Now would be a good time to run over to the cottage with a word of sympathy for Bill. If the bowling trophy did belong to him, he would be terribly upset to think that it might be the weapon used to kill his mother. It would only take a few minutes.

She wiggled her feet back into her shoes and turned off the taps. The water wouldn't have time to cool. Quietly, she left her room and descended the stairs. The front door was closest. She walked along the front of the house, then veered across the side lawn to the cottage. As she knocked, then entered at Bill's invitation, a car pulled off the road into a small clearing on the far side of the woods. The driver removed a gun from the glove compartment and shoved it into the pocket of his dark red jacket.

Then he set out along the familiar path through the trees, twenty minutes earlier than he was expected.

CHAPTER SEVENTEEN

Dean paid the taxi driver, added a generous tip, then bounded up the front steps of his home. Hired transportation seemed an elementary and sensible precaution, at least for the time being. But he missed his own car.

He crossed the foyer with long strides. He had spent more time with Owen Rogers than he had intended. His careful perusal of Rogers' reports on the movements of the members of his family had yielded nothing of interest. Now he wanted only to forget the whole mess for a few hours. An evening out with Carrie would be a welcome break.

Eager to see her again, he took the stairs two at a time. At her door he paused, then knocked softly. When no answer came, he told himself she might be napping, and if so, he should remind her of their dinner date. He grinned to himself, knowing the excuse was no more than that. He missed her every moment they were apart. He craved the sight of her. It was that simple.

He opened the door and peered in. His heart plummeted at the sight of the empty bed. Then he spotted the dress already laid out and the closed bathroom door. She must be getting ready.

He closed the door softly and continued down the hall to his room, a vision of her wet, naked body vivid in his imagination. Stripping away his clothing, he plunged ruthlessly under a cold spray. Soon. He would see her soon.

* * *

Carrie finished the coffee Bill insisted she accept and set the mug down on the table beside the couch. Her eyes strayed to the row of trophies displayed on the shelves by the door. Bill's gaze followed hers. His face expressionless, he admitted that the pewter bowling pin found in the woods was his. Neither speculated on the reason why it had gone missing nor the probable use to which it had been put.

Thanking him for the coffee, Carrie rose to her feet. Bill stood at the same time and stepped close to her, his eyes intent on her face.

"Thanks for coming over." He paused, a speculative look in his eye, then suddenly blurted, "You look like a smart lady. Smart enough, I bet, to get a rich man to the altar. Is that the plan?"

Carrie stepped back, her eyes wide with surprise, as much at his sudden change in manner as at his words. Telling herself to make allowances for his grief, she struggled to keep her voice light.

"There is no plan, Bill. Dean and I are just friends, that's all."

He laughed in derision. "From the way he looks at you, I'd say you're very *good* friends. I gotta tell you, you're wasting your time with him. Now, you and me could have a great time together. Think about it."

Carrie gaped at the man. His leering expression was as crude as his words. She whirled and headed through the kitchen for the back door. Behind her, the gardener snickered.

The door opened just as she reached for the knob. Startled, she stopped abruptly and found herself face to face with the man whose picture she had seen a few hours earlier. The man who'd left his thumbprint on an empty beer can. The man who might have killed Irma Hummell and tried to kill Dean.

"You!"

Instantly realizing her mistake she tried to push past him. She didn't make it. Walter Trent saw the recognition in her face and shoved her back into the room. He stepped in and closed the door behind him.

"Well, well, it's the snooty girlfriend. Looks like we're going to have a two-for-one day, Bill. I told you things would work out."

A chill swept down Carrie's spine. Trent's face wore a smirking mask of cruelty. She shuddered when his tongue darted out to lick his thin lips and his marble-hard eyes made a leisurely sweep down her body. She opened her mouth. He pulled a gun from his pocket and aimed it at her heart. The scream died in her throat.

"Don't be dumb," he grated. "I got no reason not to kill you."

Carrie turned to stone. For a moment, fear drove the air from her lungs. She couldn't think, couldn't move, couldn't speak. Would he really shoot her? His twisted grin told her he would.

Then the meaning of his words penetrated the buzzing in her head. He knew Bill, had called him by name. Comprehension dawned. Walter Trent was Bill Hummell's accomplice. But why? What had Bill to gain from Dean's death?

Ignoring the gun, she turned to the man behind her. The gardener was leaning against the door frame, his feet crossed at the ankles, his arms folded over his chest. He watched her, a faint smile on his lips, one eyebrow lifted in a mocking gesture.

There was something about his face, something....

Then she knew. Not everyone can lift only one eyebrow at a

time. But Dean could. And Justin. So could Uncle David. Her sight sharpened. His blue eyes were slightly darker than Dean's, but the same shape. Like Justin's, his dark hair fell over his left brow. She watched him toss it aside with the same head movement she had seen Justin make several times. Why hadn't she seen the resemblance before?

Before she could prevent it, her arm lifted to point. "You're a Sheffield." Her voice sounded strangled.

He looked surprised, then frowned and straightened. "You're crazy," he growled.

"No, I'm not. You're a Sheffield. And you're the one who's been trying to kill Dean!" Anger rose hot and burned away her fear. "And for what? For money! How could you?"

"You don't know anything about it." Sullen resentment darkened his face. "They have everything and I have nothing. Nothing! I deserve my share."

A part of her mind noted that he hadn't denied her accusation. Suddenly, the full extent of her danger slammed into her. This man killed his own mother. Or at least, became an accomplice after the fact. No, Irma must have been his adoptive mother. But she had brought him up, cared for him, loved him. Carrie struggled to keep her voice steady.

"Why didn't you tell the family who you are? None of them would have begrudged you your share."

"Like hell they wouldn't! Rich people don't give away money. My own mother won't admit she got knocked up and then gave me away. Now she thinks a few thousand will keep me quiet. And I'm supposed to sit by and let all that money go to take care of old goats like that crazy old Dick. Not likely!"

Complete understanding rocked her on her feet. The strange sensation in the sitting room, the feeling that something was missing. Not some*thing*, but some*one*. One Sheffield had been omitted from the family gallery.

Bill had to be Beverley's child. Illegitimate child. It was the only explanation. The months spent at the east coast, far away from any family acquaintance, hadn't been simply a trip. No wonder she seldom smiled for the camera. No wonder Josie's parents' refusal to keep their grandchild had upset her so much. Beverley saw herself in Josie.

"Beverley hated having to give you up, Bill. Forty years ago, a single woman had no choice. She was young, too young to fight her parents. I don't think she's had a happy moment since then."

If she had hoped to soften his attitude toward his birth mother, she hoped in vain. His laugh carried no humor in it.

"Tell me another one, sugar. With a rich family like hers, how unhappy could she be? She won't even tell me who my old man is. Why didn't she marry him, tell me that!"

"I don't know. Maybe her parents wouldn't let her. Maybe he wouldn't marry her. Or couldn't marry her."

"Yeah, well, it doesn't matter now, sugar. I've come for what's mine. As soon as my old lady has her share of dear cousin Dean's money, she's going to have an accident herself. She's already changed her will in my favor. Then I'll have everything that's hers."

"Half of what's hers, you mean, old buddy. You wouldn't want to forget that I get the other half. I sure as hell worked hard enough for it."

Carrie jumped at the cutting voice at her elbow. For a few minutes she had forgotten Walter Trent and his gun. A two-for-one day, he'd said? With horror she realized they meant to kill Dean that very day. Time was running out for him, since they obviously knew about the plan to create a trust to finance the nursing home. How could she warn Dean? She tensed, her eyes darting around the room.

"Forget it, sweetie." Trent seemed to read her mind. "You're not going anywhere. Park yourself on that chair and keep your mouth shut." He gestured with the gun.

"What … what are you going to do?" she whispered, her mouth too dry to swallow. Gingerly, she sank into a chair.

"Well now, Bill and I will have to talk about that. You're a complication, missy. How in hell did you figure it out, anyway? No one else realized Bill was one of them."

Carrie shrugged, pretending an insouciance she didn't feel. "I suppose because I'm an outsider. The others have no idea there's another Sheffield. And," she turned to Bill, "you don't look that much like them. I don't understand how you can kill your own family. You said Beverley's been giving you money. Isn't that enough?"

Bill's face purpled. "No! All I wanted at first was for my mother to admit who I am. What would it matter today, forty years later? Why shouldn't I live in the mansion and share the wealth? But no, she refused to tell the others. Some loving mother, eh?"

Carrie wondered if it had been pride or shame that kept Beverley silent. It occurred to her that the trauma of Josie's death might change her mind and cause her to claim her son. On the heels of that thought, she realized it was too late. Far too late. Murder had been committed.

"That was when," Bill continued, "I got in touch with Walt, here. If I can't have the Sheffield name, I'll sure as hell have the Sheffield money." The color had receded from his face, leaving him looking hard and utterly ruthless.

"I take it you have undeniable proof of your identity. Why didn't you go to John or David yourself? Either one of them would have helped—"

"Don't be ridiculous! They would have run me out of town."

"You're wrong."

"Forget it." He waved his hand dismissively. "I'm taking care of myself, just as I've always done."

Trent had sat down on the couch facing Carrie. The gun never wavered in his hand. Now he spoke to Bill without taking his eyes from Carrie.

"Grab us some beers. We need a new plan. Sweetie here will have to go, too. We got to figure the best way to do it."

Lightheaded with dread, Carrie struggled to keep her face impassive. She wouldn't give Trent the satisfaction of seeing her fear. She sat still, willing her knees not to knock. Why hadn't she told someone where she was going?

* * *

Dean paced the foyer. What was keeping Carrie? She hadn't struck him as a woman who deliberately kept a man waiting. He glanced at his watch, then smiled in self-derision. She wasn't late. His eagerness to see her made the time seem to drag.

He wandered into the small sitting room and scanned the wall of photos. What had Carrie sensed? Nothing looked out-of-the-way, nothing had changed. The last photo had been taken three years earlier at the surprise birthday party for John. He stepped closer and peered at the picture of his father. He stood between his brother and sister, his arms over their shoulders and a happy grin on his face. Dean swallowed hard. In spite of the ache in his chest, a small smile lifted the corners of his mouth. John had been a wonderful father and Dean would never forget him.

Justin and Natalie's wedding picture caught his eye. He thought of Carrie's revelation. Perhaps it wouldn't be long before another generation of Sheffields graced the wall. He caught his breath at the sudden vision of Justin's children playing with his own. His and Carrie's?

Dean closed his eyes and knew with absolute certainty that

he wanted Carrie to be his wife. If only he could be sure she felt the same. If only he lived long enough to marry her and give her his children. If only....

* * *

The two men made no attempt to lower their voices. As Carrie had guessed, their plan was for Trent to shoot Dean the next time he left the house to walk the grounds. As soon as they spotted him, that day or the next, Bill would make an excuse to speak with someone in the house, ensuring himself of an airtight alibi. Trent would fade away through the woods and be gone before the family reacted. Dean's death, like Irma's, would be recorded as a random killing. It was risky, but four attempts at staging an accidental death had failed. Now they were running out of time and, as Trent boasted with a wolfish grin, a bullet through the heart can't fail.

Carrie listened with horror. She didn't dare look at her watch but she knew it must soon be time for their dinner date. How long would Dean wait until he began to look for her? When he couldn't find her in the house, he would search the grounds, unknowingly becoming a target. Would they kill her before or after Dean? If they were both to die, she hoped she would be first.

From her position, Carrie could see through the kitchen to the back door. Should she make a dash for it? She knew she'd never make it but maybe the sound of the gunshot would alert Dean. With despair, she realized no one would hear the shot unless they were close to the cottage. And with no window on the mansion side of the cottage, she had no way of knowing when someone was on the grounds.

She needed to do something before Dean came within range of Bill's gun. Taking a deep breath, she leaned forward. Instantly, the two men stopped talking and tensed.

"You don't look stupid, Mr. Trent." Her heart seemed to stop beating as he scowled. She forced herself to go on.

"You surely don't think Bill will just hand over half the take, do you? When he has an alibi for the time of the shootings? When the family can testify he was right here on the grounds when Dean's so-called accidents happened?"

Trent glanced sideways at Bill. "He wouldn't dare cheat me. And besides, the family doesn't know about the accidents."

"That's true," Carrie said. "But the police do. And so does the private detective who checked out everyone's whereabouts, including Bill's, on the days of the accidents."

"Police!"

"Of course." Carrie heard the steady tone in her voice with relief. "You underestimate your cousin badly," she threw at Bill, "if you think he hasn't figured out what's going on."

The two men exchanged glances. The slight uncertainty in Trent's face gave her the courage to continue.

"How do you think I recognized you? The police know someone's trying to kill Dean and they showed us your picture. You left your fingerprints in the house the day you killed Irma. On the can of beer you drank. I'm sure they'll find more on the bowling trophy."

Suddenly Trent's gun was pointing at Bill. "You didn't tell me they found the bowling pin. You were going to let me take the fall!"

Bill flung up his hands.

"No, no. I was going to tell you today, only she got here first. It doesn't matter anyway. We're going to kill Dean today, then you'll disappear like we planned. In a few months, when things have died down and I've got the money, I'll meet you to give you your share. It can still work."

"You're *both* stupid," Carrie goaded, "if you think the police will give up when a man as wealthy as Dean is shot to death. Three deaths in less than three weeks, all here on the estate—they're bound to suspect Bill. Beverley knows who you are. You can't kill us all. The police will find out you're a Sheffield and then they've got their motive."

Bill paled. "They won't be able to prove it," he blustered.

"Maybe not, but you'll be watched. If you try to connect with Trent, they'll have you both. So you'll be here with the money and Trent will be on the run for the rest of his life. With no money."

She turned to Walter Trent.

"If you're smart, you'll cut your losses right now and leave the country. Maybe your pal Bill will send you some money in a year or two. Or maybe not."

Trent stared at her with hate-filled eyes but his expression betrayed his acceptance of her reasoning. He turned his head to stare at Bill.

"Don't listen to her, Walt. You can see what she's trying to do. We're buddies, of course you'll get your share."

"Will I?"

"Yeah, I give you my word. Listen, you can't bail out on me now. She'll tell everything she knows. How far do you'll think you'll get with no money? And if I'm in prison there won't *be* any money. We have to kill her. And my cousin. There's no point stopping halfway to the end. It'll just mean I won't be able to get the money to you as quick as we thought."

Carrie felt her heart slide into her shoes. Bill was right. They'd gone too far to stop now. She couldn't save Dean. Something tore apart inside her chest.

A knock at the back door jerked her head up. Dick stood on the narrow porch, looking over his shoulder in the direction of the big house. Carrie raised her hand, palm out, to the men who jumped to their feet. "Wait. It's Dick. Don't hurt him. He doesn't know anything."

To her relief Bill relaxed and shook his head at Trent. "It's just the crazy old guy. I'll get rid of him. In a few minutes he won't even remember he was here. Stay out of sight."

Trent remained standing, but backed another step away from the open door to the living room. "Make it quick."

Carrie ignored the gun trained on her chest and strained to hear the conversation. She caught the words "towels" and "Irma," and remembered that Dick had not been told about Irma's death. He hadn't known her long or well and the family felt that he would soon forget her entirely. There was no point in distressing him with the knowledge of her death.

She heard Bill tell him that Irma was away on holiday. He accepted the news and left. Had Dick seen her through the screen door? The small hope died as she realized it didn't matter if he had. He would likely forget within a few minutes.

Bill returned to the living room.

"The old crock's gone. He's not a problem. But she is." He slanted his head toward Carrie.

Trent walked over to Carrie and placed the gun against her head. She froze and inhaled sharply. Bracing herself, she closed her eyes and thought of Dean and of what might have been.

Nothing happened. An eternity passed. Finally she opened her eyes. Walter Trent smirked at her.

"Not this way, sweetie. No bullet for you. Unless you try to move or scream." He chuckled and darted a glance at the gardener.

"I got a better idea. We need another accident. With no bullet holes the police can't know for sure that it was murder. We'll use her for bait to get Dean in here. Sooner or later he'll come looking for her."

Suddenly, pain cannoned through Carrie's head. Blackness swallowed her instantly. She didn't feel her body slam to the floor.

* * *

Dean checked his watch. Carrie was ten minutes late. A sense of foreboding crept into his mind. The feeling that something was wrong grew until he could wait no longer. He climbed the stairs and tore down the hall with a ground-eating stride.

With no thought for propriety, he burst through her door. The dress lay on the bed exactly as before. Then he gasped at the thought that she may have fallen and hit her head on the tub. He crossed the room and paused at the bathroom door. If she was all right, she wouldn't appreciate him violating her privacy.

He rapped sharply on the door and called her name. When she didn't answer, he thrust open the door, half convinced he would see her lifeless body submerged in the water. The relief that surged through him when he realized the room was empty turned his legs to jelly. He clung to the door and leaned his forehead against it.

When his heartbeat slowed, he straightened. The tub held three or four inches of clear water. What had changed her mind about a bath? He dipped his hand in the water and found it cool. Could she have forgotten their dinner date? The waiting dress on the bed said she hadn't.

His apprehension deepened. Whoever sabotaged his brakes in town, had known Carrie was with him. And hadn't cared. A chill as cold as death swept over his body.

Then he shook his head. He was a practical, rational man, not given to premonitions. His imagination was reacting to the whole situation. Carrie had simply lost track of time. Perhaps she was walking over the grounds or visiting with Aggie and forgot the time.

He left the room and returned to the ground floor. The phone on the foyer table rang as he walked past it on his way to the kitchen. He scooped it up, impatient with the delay.

"Dean Sheffield here."

"It's Greta." The fear in her voice electrified him. "Something's wrong with Carrie. I can't sense her. Find her, Dean. She needs you."

"Can you tell where she is?" It didn't occur to Dean to question Greta's remarkable statement or to wonder at his own immediate acceptance.

"Only that she's not far from you. But be careful, Dean. Danger waits for you."

Dean dropped the receiver and raced to the kitchen. Aggie's sunroom protruded beyond the walls of the house and gave the best view of the grounds at the rear. No one was in sight.

In the woods then? His head swung from right to left in an agony of indecision. Dusk would arrive in half an hour. If he chose the wrong direction, it would be full dark before he could search on the other side of the house.

When Dick and Jack Sawyer strolled around the corner Dean waved urgently. They met at the back door.

"Have you seen Carrie anywhere?"

Dick started to shake his head but the nurse touched his shoulder gently. "Seems to me you said Carrie was visiting Bill. No, I guess not. I must have been thinking of something else at the time." Neither by his words nor by his tone did Jack suggest that Dick had suffered a lapse in memory.

Dick grinned and punched Jack lightly in the arm. "Dean, this fella's the worst listener I ever met. Don't pay any attention to him. He never knows what he's talking about."

Dean forced himself to laugh with the other two men. Chuckling boyishly, Dick reached for the door but Dean kept his eyes on Jack. The moment the older man looked away, Jack tilted his head in the direction of the cottage, then nodded vigorously.

"Ten minutes ago," he mouthed soundlessly.

Relief and apprehension warred in Dean's mind as he nodded his thanks and strode along the back of the house. He remembered Carrie's intention of visiting the gardener to offer condolences. Surely Bill Hummell posed no threat to her. The observation failed to dispel his foreboding; Greta's fear and his own inexplicable uneasiness doubled with every step. He rounded the corner.

The cottage stood silent and unremarkable. The absence of lights gave the small building an air of abandonment. Dean hesitated. Jack had not said that he had seen Carrie, only that Dick claimed to have done so. And whenever they met, Dick had been unable to remember Carrie's name. How could he…. But there was no tracking the broken paths through the older man's mind.

Dean climbed the back steps and knocked on the screen door. There was no response. He knocked again and called Carrie's name, then Bill's. A slight sound, as insubstantial as the slide of a slipper on a carpet, teased his ear. Dean pressed his face to the screen and cupped his hands at the sides of his face. The interior of the cottage was dim, featureless.

When his eyes adjusted to the gloom, a mound of pink became visible as a blurry contrast to the dark carpet. A cry of horror tore from his throat.

Dean yanked the screen door open. A moment later, he dropped to his knees beside Carrie. Deaf and blind to all but his burgeoning fear, he didn't sense the approaching blow. He was unconscious before his body sprawled across Carrie's still form.

* * *

Pain hammered in her skull. A great weight pressed her spine into a hard surface and immobilized her ribs. Her tortured lungs labored to draw in the life-giving air.

A terrible sense of danger swam into Carrie's groggy mind. She resisted the longing to sink back into the darkness of oblivion, and tried to move. Her legs scrabbled feebly but the weight on her upper body held her fast. Air, hot and harsh, burned her nostrils and forced her tearing eyes to open.

She frowned up at the unfamiliar ceiling and could make no sense of the gray, fog-like scarves swirling overhead. Her burning eyes dropped, then focused on the bulky weight pinning her to the floor.

Almost idly her gaze traced the line of the heavy object. White collar. Rumpled black hair, a narrow ribbon of red slowly dribbling downward. A wax-white face pressed to the floor, trapping her right arm under the heavy neck.

Dean! Memory awoke with her cry of alarm. Bill Hummell. Walter Trent. The gun. Her sudden descent into darkness. She struggled to sit up, but her strength was no match for Dean's weight.

Had they killed Dean? No, it couldn't be! Fear bent her elbow until her hand found his head. Her fingers plunged into his hair and tangled themselves in the thick mass. Her wrist protested as she half-lifted, half-pushed his head closer to her shoulder. She screamed his name in his ear. There was no response.

Her wrist gave way. His head dropped to her shoulder. Tears poured from her eyes. He was dead. The only man she had ever loved was dead. Sobbing, she twisted her head and kissed his forehead.

Then she stiffened. Warm breath touched the skin of her neck. He was alive! She called his name over and over. Still, he didn't respond. But he was alive! The weakness of relief drained her meager strength. She lowered her head, her body limp with gratitude. Her eyes closed as she slipped back into darkness.

* * *

Aggie served Bill, Dick and Jack their coffee, then poured a cup for herself. No one spoke as the group watched the last fiery rays of the sun sink below the horizon. No one noticed the frequent glances Bill threw to one side of the property. No one noticed his jiggling foot or the tight set of his shoulders.

Jack turned to Aggie. "It's so quiet tonight. Is everyone out?"

Bill tensed as he waited for her reply.

"Far as I know." She smiled. "Mr. David's with Miss Grace and Mr. Dean and Miss Carrie went out to dinner. Miss Alanna's working the night shift."

The gardener relaxed. The corners of his mouth turned up.

"Oh?" Jack replied. "Dean found her then?"

Bill's smile disappeared.

"Found who?" Dick's voice was utterly innocent.

"Carrie. I think she was late for their dinner date." Jack turned to Bill. "She's a nice lady, isn't she? They make a striking couple."

Bill hesitated, then nodded. "Sure do."

Aggie chuckled. "Might be having a wedding around here before long. Maybe two."

No one replied. When Jack said nothing about Carrie visiting the cottage, Bill's face gradually regained the color that had drained away at the first mention of the woman's name. He knew the nurse hadn't seen her in the cottage. Evidently Dick hadn't mentioned it to him. Bill hissed softly in relief.

Aggie rose and switched on the radio. The soothing notes of a sixties ballad filled the room. She refilled their cups and sat down again. Jack began to hum softly to the music.

* * *

Flickering red light danced on Carrie's eyelids. She stirred and gradually became aware of a crackling sound and thick, hot air scorching her lungs. She coughed, then coughed again, her chest protesting violently.

Only half aware, she opened her eyes. Thick acrid smoke poured from the wine-colored couch and rose to deepen the layer swirling against the ceiling. Fingers of fire scrabbled at the wallpaper. Foot-high flames chewed at the edges of the carpet, steadily closing in on the prone couple.

Carrie screamed Dean's name and bucked, arching her back as high as she could. Dean moaned, but his limp body was too heavy for her. With the strength of fear, Carrie rolled out from under him. She crouched beside him and shook his shoulders. His head flopped loosely. A gargling in his throat turned to harsh coughing but he didn't waken.

Carrie looked around in despair. Fire surrounded them. The air burned her throat with a chemical caress. She gripped Dean's arms and tried to pull him. It was no use, he wouldn't budge. Even if she managed to drag his heavy weight, it would mean towing him face down through the flames.

Carrie sobbed and bent to cradle his head in her arms. "Damn it, wake up! Dean!"

He moaned again and moved his head, but didn't open his eyes.

From the corner of her eye, she caught sight of the edge of a bathtub through a doorway on her left. Water! She set his head gently back on the carpet and headed in a crouch for the bathroom, keeping her head down below the worst of the smoke. The ring of fire at the edge of the carpet measured at least a foot in width. The door frame in front of her had begun to smolder. Heat reached toward her and for a moment her body refused to move forward any further.

Dean moaned again. The sound catapulted her across the

fiery barrier. Nothing was burning in the bathroom, but the acrid haze of smoke reached down from the ceiling to the basin. Carrie fumbled with the taps of the tub. When water gushed down, she snatched at the towels and threw them under the deluge. A pail sat on the floor under the leaking pipes of the basin. She thrust it under the tap and waited until it was half full, then dropped the soggy towels into the pail.

Leaving the tap running, she climbed into the tub and thrust her head under the wonderfully cool liquid, then cupped her hands and scooped the water over herself until she was as sodden as the towels. Grunting with effort, she heaved the pail from the tub and turned back to the living room.

The painted door frame had begun to blister and release fumes that burned like hot needles in her eyes. In the few minutes since she'd been in the bathroom, the ring of fire had crept closer to the center of the rug. Dean lay as before, but even unconscious he had pulled his legs up to his body to escape the heat of the encroaching flames.

Carrie hugged the pail to her chest and straightened. She leaped across the barrier, shrieking as fire licked at her ankles. Sobbing her terror, she poured water over his head. He *had* to wake up. Or he would die.

* * *

Aggie sat up and sniffed. She sniffed again and got to her feet.

"I smell smoke. Where's it coming from?"

"So do I." Jack jumped to his feet and peered out into the night. "I don't see anything."

Bill stood and pretended to sniff the air.

"It's coming from that side." Aggie pointed. "A bonfire? No, it must be the cottage!"

"I'll call the fire department." Bill started back into the kitchen.

"No, you come with me." Jack grabbed him by the arm. "Aggie, you call the fire department. Dick, you stay here with Aggie." He pulled Bill through the door that led to Aggie's garden. "The place is empty, isn't it? Carrie couldn't still be there, could she?"

Bill gasped in shock. "N-no," he stammered. "She left before I came into the house. Aggie said she's out with Dean." Suddenly realizing how strange his dragging heels might appear, Bill thrust Jack aside and raced toward the side of the house.

They stopped abruptly at the sight of angry flames devouring the roof. Black smoke poured through the screen door and billowed into the air. Jack started for the back steps.

"You can't go in there," Bill screamed. "It's too late to save anything."

Jack crouched at the bottom of the door and peered into the house. All he could see were flames and smoke gyrating in a wild dance of destruction to the music of the roaring, crackling inferno. Coughing harshly, he backed away and joined Bill, thankful for the lack of breeze. The mansion was safe, but he didn't think the firefighters would be able to save the cottage.

With deep sympathy, he dropped his hand on Bill's shaking shoulders. In the space of a week, the man had lost his mother to an unknown killer and now his possessions were being destroyed.

The two men stood side by side, silently waiting for the fire trucks. A moment later, Dick and Aggie joined them.

* * *

Dean's eyes flew open. His hands flew up to clutch his head as his gasp of pain drew smoke deep into his lungs. He doubled over, wracked with painful coughs.

"Dean, Dean. You must get up." Carrie dug her nails into his shoulders. "We have to get out of here." She leaned over and shouted in his ear. "Dean!"

He groaned, then suddenly grew alert. For a split-second he stared around, then pushed himself to all fours. Carrie emptied the rest of the water over his body and draped a dripping towel over his head. She pulled the other over her own head and tried to rise. Her thigh muscles strained. A coughing seizure knocked her off balance. She fell heavily on her side.

Large hands closed over her hips and hauled her to her knees. Bracing her hands on the floor, she bucked and jerked with the force of her chest spasms.

"Which way?" Dean yelled.

Carrie lifted her head. Beyond the wall of flames she could just see the black and white tiles of the kitchen. Unable to speak, she pointed.

A second later, she felt Dean sling her over his shoulder. He staggered, crouching as low as he dared, in the direction she'd indicated.

Cool air flowed over her as he smashed through the screen door and leaped down the steps. Shouts rang in her ears. The sensation of falling stopped abruptly as hands seized her and lowered her to the cool grass. The towel was yanked from her head.

She levered herself up on her elbows. Beside her Dean lay prone on the lawn. The lower legs of his trousers were burning, but before she could move, Jack began to beat at the flames with the wet towel. She rolled over to be closer to Dean and saw Bill Hummell backing away from the group. She pointed.

"Stop him! He did this!" Her voice was only a croak, but Jack heard her.

He looked over his shoulder and saw the glittering fear in the gardener's eyes. Cursing, he scrambled to his feet and took off after Bill. The gardener's eyes widened. He whirled around and began to run along the side of the house.

Just as he reached the corner, Beverley appeared in his path, her eyes frantic and her face red with exertion. Bill thrust out an arm and knocked her violently out of his way, just as the nurse threw himself forward in a perfect tackle. Beverley and the nurse went down in a tangle. The collision left them winded and momentarily helpless. Beverley's expression betrayed shock and a heartrending entreaty as she lifted her head to gaze after her fleeing son. By the time two fire trucks, a police car and an ambulance roared up the drive, Bill had disappeared into the woods.

A moment later an oxygen mask descended over Carrie's face and she felt herself lifted onto a stretcher. She thrashed in protest until she saw Dean being slid into the ambulance beside her. He turned his head toward her. She thought he smiled behind the mask. She smiled back, then closed her burning eyes. It was all over.

* * *

It was all over. Carrie sat on the edge of her bed and stared out at the intensely blue sky. Her mixed feelings appalled her. Dean was alive. There would be no further attempts on his life. But tempering her joy in that thought was the realization that he didn't need her any more. In a few days she would return to her life as Miss Richards, kindergarten teacher and psychic. He would—had already—returned to his world of business and wealth. They weren't likely to meet again.

"All over," she whispered. Feeling the tears gather in her eyes, she shook her head, determined not to give in again to the over-whelming desire to cry. It wasn't as if there had ever been any chance for them. Their worlds, their backgrounds were too different. She was too different. Dean understood that as well as she did. The fact that she hadn't seen him since the fire made that very clear—even though the nurse said he'd phoned several times to inquire about her.

She had seen Lieutenant Balfour. The police officer visited her in the hospital the day after the fire. The doctors had insisted she remain overnight, to monitor her recovery from the smoke inhalation and to watch for signs of concussion. From a sympathetic nurse, she learned that Dean had refused hospitalization and left after submitting to treatment in the emergency ward.

His ankles and calves received third degree burns, but because his head had been at floor level and his breathing shallow during unconsciousness, he had escaped serious damage from the acrid smoke.

Walter Trent and Bill Hummell were dead. Lieutenant Balfour outlined the police reconstruction of the accident that killed them. Evidently Trent had waited in his car in the woods just off the road, presumably hoping to discover if the fire did its intended job. Bill must have joined him and revealed their failure. With their victims alive, both men had become fugitives. The car pulled out of the small clearing onto the road so recklessly that an elderly man on a bicycle narrowly missed disaster.

There would be no Sheffield money for either of them. Balfour figured that in his rage, Trent tried to shoot Bill, who must have struggled for the weapon. One bullet had splintered the windshield. Trent lost control of the car, which left the road and crashed into a tree, very near the spot where he had forced Dean's car from the road. Both men died instantly.

By the time Carrie haltingly explained the events in the cottage, her throat was too sore to ask the policeman if Beverley had been privy to her son's murderous intentions. Balfour left then and she had leaned back to wait for some word from Dean.

No word arrived. When the nurse returned with discharge papers, she accepted the woman's offer to phone for a taxi. She arrived home to an empty apartment.

The quiet apartment no longer seemed the haven it once had. Fatigue finally overcame her restlessness. She was in bed by eight. The phone remained silent all night.

Now Carrie chastised herself for her lingering lethargy and forced herself off the bed. Greta would be waiting. Balfour had assured her that her grandmother knew she was safe, but she knew Greta would need to see for herself. And, Carrie admitted, she needed to be with Greta. She needed to be with the one person who loved her.

CHAPTER EIGHTEEN

The moment Greta saw Carrie standing in her doorway, she held out her arms. Carrie rushed across the room, sat on the edge of the bed and threw herself into her grandmother's arms. To her dismay, she burst into tears. Greta pulled Carrie's head into her shoulder and rocked her, just as she had done when her beloved granddaughter suffered the usual scrapes and bruises of childhood.

Finally, Carrie sat up and wiped her face with the backs of her hands. When Greta silently handed her a box of tissues, she smiled her thanks and blew her nose vigorously.

"That was just … reaction. I'm all right now."

"I know, *liebchen*. Dean said the danger is over for both of you."

"He was here?" Carrie felt a flash of hurt that he had visited Greta but not her. Then she was ashamed. It was kind of Dean to take the time to reassure her grandmother.

"Yesterday morning. He told me the whole story. It's not a nice thing to say, but I can't be sorry those men are gone. A sad, sad thing for Dean's poor aunt, though."

"Then Beverley wasn't a part of their scheme?"

Greta looked surprised. "Dean hasn't told you?"

Avoiding Greta's eyes, Carrie answered in what she hoped was an indifferent tone.

"No. Actually, I haven't seen him since the fire." She

shrugged, pretending indifference. "I expect it'll be in the papers. With the trust to set up, and the problem of the cottage, he must be very busy. His business will need his attention again, too. School reopens in a few days, so life will soon be back to normal for me as well. Which reminds me," she took Greta's hand, "when they toss you out of here, I'd like you to come to live with me."

"Oh no, I can't—"

"Your house has too many stairs," Carrie interrupted. "And you don't need all those rooms. If you sold it, together we could afford to rent a larger apartment, preferably one with no stairs. I worry about you alone—"

"There's no need to worry, *liebchen*. I won't be alone and Ernst and I will need all those rooms when his family visits." Greta's eyes twinkled.

Nonplused, Carrie simply stared. With everything that had happened since she'd been here last, she'd forgotten about Greta's admirer.

"You're getting married! That's wonderful!" She kissed her grandmother's cheek.

"You approve then?" The gruff voice came from the doorway.

Carrie turned to the shyly smiling man in the wheelchair. Today a green-and-white striped sock rode jauntily at the end of his cast, the mate for the one on Greta's foot.

"I approve." Carrie solemnly shook his hand, then laughed and leaned down to embrace her soon-to-be step-grandfather. "This is wonderful. When can I meet your children and grand-children? I can't believe I'm going to be part of a large family! Maybe I could baby-sit once in a while? May I call you Ernst? When will the wedding be?" She grabbed Greta's hand. "You must let me be a bridesmaid."

When Ernst and Greta started to laugh, Carrie realized she

was babbling. Blushing, she looked from one to the other, then grinned sheepishly.

"Is this a private party or may anyone join in?"

Carrie's head snapped around at the sound of the deep voice. Her breath caught in her throat at the sight of the large man in the doorway. Dressed in a charcoal, raw silk suit, cream shirt and blue and cream tie, Dean looked too good to be true, the living embodiment of every woman's fantasy.

"What are you doing here?" She hadn't intended to sound rude but his unexpected appearance had scrambled her wits. Dean didn't seem to notice.

"I was looking for you."

"Oh."

The other occupants of the room and the room itself faded as their gazes met and held. Carrie saw a warm glow deep in his eyes and felt an answering heat rise like a tide through her body. Neither spoke nor moved. Time stretched like an elastic band until Greta loudly cleared her throat. Carrie blinked and glanced back at her grandmother. The older couple exchanged amused smiles.

"You run along with Dean, *liebchen*. Come and visit me again before school starts."

Carrie nodded and kissed her grandmother's cheek. When she hesitated, Ernst tilted his head and smilingly tapped his own cheek. She laughed and loudly kissed her grandfather-to-be. As she walked toward him, Dean held out his hand.

His fingers curled around hers. His grip was warm and firm. Tentatively she threaded her fingers through his and swallowed when he smiled broadly. As they walked down the empty corridor she knew her feet were treading on air.

Carrie took two extra paces before she felt the tug on her arm and realized Dean had stopped. She turned back to see why and sucked in her breath at the look on his face.

"I can't wait."

He pulled her into his arms and lowered his head until their lips met. With a sigh, Carrie melted against him.

At first the kiss was uncertain, tentative, questioning. When Carrie moaned and wound her arms around his neck, a growl of satisfaction rumbled in his chest. He deepened the kiss, his tongue caressing her lips, seeking entry. Carrie opened her mouth in welcome. His arms tightened around her until she could feel every inch of his body pressing against her. She felt her breasts swell and an ache begin to throb in her abdomen.

"A-hem! Cough, cough."

They broke apart and found two elderly men gripping walkers regarding them with interest. Carrie blushed scarlet and sidled close to the wall to let them pass. One man chuckled and elbowed his companion.

"A pretty sight, eh, Sid. Very entertaining. Makes me wish we could turn the clock back a few years." He smiled at Dean. "We hate to disturb you, young man, but we're supposed to keep moving. 'Sides, in my day, we looked for a spot more private than a public corridor." He offered a knowing wink.

Dean laughed. "You're absolutely right, sir. We'll get out of your way right now."

He took Carrie's hand and led her down the hall. Behind them, they heard Sid's rusty voice begin to describe a long past incident. "I 'member one time, there was this yeller-haired gal working in a tavern. I surely did fancy her. Then one day the circus came to town and…."

Dean didn't let go of her hand until she was settled comfortably in the passenger seat of a brand-new minivan. Why hadn't he bought another sleek sports car? She watched him round the front of the car to the driver's side. He climbed behind the wheel, then leaned over to drop a quick kiss on her nose.

"Lunch?"

Carrie nodded. She could think of nothing to say. Dean stopped at a take-out restaurant and returned a moment later with two soft drinks and two hamburgers. Five minutes later, they sauntered through a small public park and claimed a brightly-painted bench, half-hidden in a grove of lilac bushes.

"Are you all right, Dean? Your burns—"

"I'm fine," he interrupted. "Carrie ... I was so worried about you, even though the doctor said you'd have a complete recovery. Are you sure you should be up and about so soon?"

She nodded. He'd been worried? Before that thought could grow in her mind, she hurried to change the subject. "Tell me about your aunt. How did she react when she found out that Bill tried to kill you?"

Dean sighed. "She doesn't know. And hopefully, she'll never know. Since both Trent and Bill are dead, there's no one to prosecute. Lieutenant Balfour agreed to keep Bill's part in it quiet, since it was Trent who actually killed Irma."

"His fingerprints were on the bowling pin?"

"Yes, and the police lab proved it was the murder weapon. We figure Trent was the one who staged all the accidents, although Bill probably helped to undermine the boulder that gave way under me. They had to ensure that Bill always had an alibi or he wouldn't have been able to collect his inheritance."

Carrie shuddered. "But what explanation did you give Beverley to account for Bill's being in the car when it crashed?"

"Balfour suggested that Bill may have panicked and run because he thought he'd be accused of causing the fire through carelessness, even though Aggie and Jack assured her he was in the sunroom with them when the fire broke out. The papers will report that Trent took Bill as a hostage when he realized that we survived the fire and could identify him."

"So she'll never know that her son was an accomplice to

murder."

"Not unless you tell her."

Carrie stiffened. "You can't think I'd do that! She's suffered from guilt all these years because she gave him up for adoption. Now he's dead, just a few months after she found him again. She doesn't deserve more pain. Dean, I would never tell her the truth about him!"

Dean took her hand and squeezed it gently. "Hush, sweetheart, I know that. Beverley has told the family that Bill was her son. They've rallied around her wonderfully. She's going to be all right."

"I'm glad she told them," Carrie sighed. "Guilty secrets eat away at the soul. She'll find some peace now. Maybe she'll be smiling in future family photographs."

Dean stretched his arm on the top of the bench behind her head and dropped his hand on her shoulder. A squirrel approached and stopped a few feet away. It sat up on its hind legs, regarding them with bright eyes. When neither human paid any attention, it chattered in disgust and moved away, its tail held high in indignation.

"How did you know Bill was a Sheffield when the rest of us couldn't see it?"

She touched his eyebrow, which immediately lifted in a question. "It all came together when I saw him lift one eyebrow, just like you Sheffields do. Then I finally understood what I'd sensed in the sitting room, that someone was missing from the family gallery. I only wish I'd realized sooner."

Dean pulled her close to his side and burrowed his fingers into her hair. Carrie slipped an arm around his waist and laid her cheek on his massive chest. Her heart skipped erratically as his other hand brushed the underside of her breast and came to rest on her side. She closed her eyes and inhaled his spicy male scent. Long, slow minutes passed in silence.

"Carrie?"

"Yes?"

"Look at me," he whispered.

She tilted her head back and looked up.

"I can't wait."

She stared at him blankly then comprehension dawned. "Who said you had to wait?"

Hunger flared in Dean's eyes. His mouth descended to hers and all thoughts of the past days disappeared. An eternity later he lifted his head a fraction. His breath gently caressed her lips.

"You will, won't you?" he murmured.

"Mmmm? Will what?" Carrie nibbled at his chin.

"Marry me? I know I've acted like a louse, but I love you so much, Carrie."

Joy flooded through her and overflowed in happy tears. Then she hesitated. "But what about my psychic ability? Can you live with that? Won't it bother you?" She held her breath.

"It's part of who you are. And the only thing that bothers me is that you haven't said yes. I want you to be my wife, Carrie. I need you. Will you at least consider it?"

Carrie cupped her hands around his face and adopted as stern a voice as she could manage. "Will you give me children?"

A smile replaced the uncertainty in his face. "As many as you want. A classroom full of Sheffields."

Carrie laughed. "That's a few more than I had in mind!" Then a sudden thought struck her. "So that's why you bought a minivan instead of another sports car."

He looked suddenly anxious. "Are you angry? I didn't mean to take you for granted. It just seemed—"

"—the practical car to buy. I'm not angry. I'm thrilled."

"You are? Does that mean you love me? That you'll marry me?"

"Yes and yes! I love you. I'll marry you. I'll have your children."

Suddenly she was on his lap, his strong arms wrapped around her, his heart beating wildly against hers. Dimly she heard the scolding chatter of a squirrel, the only witness to their embrace. Laughing softly, she pulled Dean's mouth to hers.

Desire ignited deep inside her. She wanted this man. Now.

Wrenching her mouth away from his, she slipped from his grasp and stood. Dean looked up, uncertainty and longing flowing over his face. "What? What's wrong?"

Carrie held out her hand. "Nothing's wrong. Let's go to my apartment."

At his look of confusion, she smiled and echoed his own words, "I can't wait."

Dean leaped to his feet and took her hand. He swept her into his arms and kissed her with all the love in his heart. Then they headed, almost running, for the parking lot.

Somewhere in her head she sensed her grandmother's smiling approval.

Retired teacher JANE ANN TUN, a book-a-day reader, lives on a farm near Ottawa, Canada, with her husband and 2 cats. Her time is spent reading, writing, gardening, and of course, concocting adventures for the characters that live in her head.

Jane is also the author of *Time Lapse.*